THE COWBOY'S AUTUMN FALL

by

SHANNA HATFIELD

The Cowboy's Autumn Fall
Copyright 2012
by Shanna Hatfield

ISBN-13: 978-1480107649
ISBN-10: 1480107646

All rights reserved.

Shanna Hatfield
shanna@shannahatfield.com
shannahatfield.com

This is a work of fiction. Names, characters, businesses,
places, events and incidents are either the products of the
author's imagination or used in a fictitious manner. Any
resemblance to actual persons, living or dead, or actual
events is purely coincidental.

To those brave enough to fall...
may there always be
loving arms to catch you.

Books by Shanna Hatfield

FICTION

The Coffee Girl

Learnin' the Ropes

QR Code Killer

Grass Valley Cowboys Series
The Cowboy's Christmas Plan
The Cowboy's Spring Romance
The Cowboy's Summer Love
The Cowboy's Autumn Fall

The Women of Tenacity Series
The Women of Tenacity - A Prelude
Heart of Clay
Country Boy vs. City Girl
Not His Type

NON-FICTION

Savvy Holiday Entertaining
Savvy Spring Entertaining
Savvy Summer Entertaining
Savvy Autumn Entertaining

Chapter One

"He who would not be idle, let him fall in love."

Ovid

"Disgusting. Absolutely disgusting," Brice Morgan muttered to himself as he made his way through the crowd gathered for Trent and Lindsay Thompson's wedding reception.

If he had to watch one more couple gazing dreamily at each other, Brice thought he might be sick. Enduring all the romance he could handle for one evening, he sat down next to his sister, Tess, at a large table beneath one of the white canopies. Leaning back in his chair, he shook his head in irritation and sighed.

"Maybe you need to work some moves like that into your routine, man," Travis Thompson said, leaning around Tess and thumping Brice on the shoulder. Travis and Brice, just days apart in age, had been best friends since they were old enough to push each other down.

Following the direction of Tess' pointing finger, Brice watched Travis' adopted six-year-old niece, Cass, dance with the wild abandon of a happy child next to her uncle and his new bride. Arms flailing, red curls bouncing, the little girl spun around and around, giggling with giddy excitement.

5

"That would definitely get you some attention," Tess teased, offering Brice a sassy grin. "I'm sure all the girls would be lining up to dance with you."

"Definitely," Travis said, nodding his head in agreement. "Anyone under the age of ten or over the age of seventy would be putty in your hands."

Before Brice could form a snappy comeback, Travis leaned over and whispered in Tess' ear, making her blush.

Rolling his eyes, he realized sitting next to Travis and Tess, basking in their newly declared love for one another, wasn't the best choice if he was trying to get away from the love fest this wedding was turning out to be.

Travis' older brother Trent was goofy in love with his bride of a few hours. If that wasn't bad enough, Travis' oldest brother Trey and his wife Cady were sitting across the table from him whispering sweet nothings to each other and looking more in love than a couple wed eight months had a right to.

Brice sighed again and swiped a hand over his face. All this talk of love and romance was ridiculous. It was the stuff that kept school girls twittering and old ladies and love-starved women buying romance novels. In his opinion, it was a bunch of mush perpetuated by florists, candy companies, and sappy-minded idiots.

"You okay, BB?" Tess asked, using the nickname she'd given him when she first learned to talk. Less than a year apart in age, Tess couldn't quite say "baby" so her brother was stuck bearing her version of the term.

"Just great," Brice said, trying to hide his annoyance as Trey stood and took Cady's hand in his, kissing her fingers.

"Cady, darlin', will you please dance with me?" Trey turned on his charm. He gave his wife a pleading look, one that everyone knew inspired Cady to do whatever Trey wanted. "I know you're pooped and you shucked off your shoes half an hour ago, so you can waltz out there barefoot for all I care, but come dance with me. Please?"

"I'd be honored, boss-man," Cady said, getting up from the table and stuffing her tired feet back into her high heels, letting Trey pull her toward the dance-floor.

Swallowing down another sigh, Brice supposed he should be used to the Thompson brothers and their romantic tendencies by now. It was practically legendary in their small community of Grass Valley, Oregon.

Growing up nearby, Brice, Tess, and their brother Ben spent as much time here at the Triple T Ranch with the three Thompson boys as they did at home on the Running M Ranch. That was before Trey, Trent, and Travis were all love struck.

Sitting back in his chair and looking around, he had never seen the Triple T look quite so nice, especially in mid-August. From the fresh coats of paint on the outbuildings to the flowers blooming profusely in every available corner, the ranch looked like it could be featured in a home and garden magazine.

The big yard was set up like a fairyland with billowing tents, enough white lights to line the landing strips at PDX, and a portable dance floor where he could see Trey drop Cady into a dip while Trent twirled Lindsay in his arms.

The only reason Tess and Travis weren't out on the dance floor was due to the pair of torn hamstrings Travis received the previous month when he rescued a little boy windsurfing. Only able to walk for short stretches without crutches, dancing wasn't on Travis' current list of activities approved by his physical therapist, who also happened to be Tess.

"I hate for you to miss all the dancing, honeybee," Travis said, rubbing his hand across Tess' shoulders. "Why don't the two of you go show them how it's done?"

Tess kissed Travis' cheek and gently patted his leg. "The only guy I want to dance with is you, Trav. I'm fine sitting on the sidelines tonight."

"Give me a break," Brice muttered under his breath, again rolling his eyes. If those two kept this up, he might even regret the extensive efforts he made all summer to get them together.

"I heard that," Tess said, leaning closer to Brice and smacking his arm. "What's gotten into you tonight, grumpy britches? You're usually the life of the party."

Brice shrugged. His sister was right. Usually the first one on the dance floor and the last one to leave, Brice loved to have fun, be the center of attention, and keep everyone entertained. Tonight, he just wasn't interested. Maybe it was because he was here all alone. After spending weeks getting rid of the last little twit who'd sunk her claws into him, Brice was tired of playing games, tired of the meaningless relationships, tired of looking for someone special.

"Excuse me," a soft voice said next to Brice and he turned to look into the face of a lovely girl. Petite with golden-blond curls cascading down her back and sparkling blue eyes, a dimple popped out in her cheek when she smiled at him. "Would you like to dance?"

"Absolutely," Brice said, getting to his feet and taking her hand as she walked toward the dance floor.

"You must be related to Travis' girlfriend," the girl said as they settled into the rhythm of a moderately fast dance. "You look a lot alike."

"Tess is my sister," Brice said, smiling at his dance partner, admiring her well-shaped form and beautiful face. "How do you know Travis?"

"He's my cousin," the girl said, bringing her dimple back out of hiding with a big smile. "I'm Sierra Bishop. My mom and Denni Thompson are sisters."

"Nice to meet you. I'm Brice Morgan and I've known the whole Thompson clan since I was born," Brice said, admiring the way Sierra moved on the dance floor while casting teasing glances his direction. She was not only a very good dancer, but also an accomplished flirt. He had met a few of the Thompson boys' cousins, but obviously they'd been holding out on him with this branch of the family tree.

Deciding the evening had just gotten a lot more interesting, Brice asked Sierra for the next dance and they both grinned when Travis limped onto the dance floor, pulling Tess behind him.

The band played Blake Shelton's *Honey Bee*, thanks to Trent and Trey's prompting, drawing the interest of all the guests. Most everyone knew the song was the inspiration behind Travis' nickname for Tess. As the crowd clapped and cheered, Tess' cheeks turned bright red, but she buried her face against Travis' chest and kept on dancing.

"Do you think there'll be another wedding soon?" Sierra asked, eying the couple as they became much more involved in sharing loving glances than dancing.

"Probably," Brice commented, glad to see both Tess and Travis so deliriously happy, even if it was a little nauseating.

As the song ended, Brice walked Sierra over to the refreshment table and handed her a glass of sweet tea. They were standing there talking when a young woman came up beside Sierra and whispered something to her before pouring herself a cup of punch.

Studying the two of them, Brice could see a resemblance although the girls didn't seem to share much in common. Where Sierra was short and bubbly, the other girl was older and taller with an aura of self-confidence. Her rich honey-gold hair fell in short curls above her shoulders and Brice would have guessed her to be about five eight or so if she'd kick off her incredibly high heels.

Turning to look at him with eyes the same brilliant turquoise shade of blue as Trey Thompson's, Brice thought he'd been struck by lightning when an electrifying jolt shook him from the top of his head right down to the toes of his polished cowboy boots.

Half expecting smoke to billow around him, Brice forced himself to stand still.

"Brice Morgan, this is my sister, Bailey," Sierra said, putting a hand on the arm of the woman Brice decided in the last dozen seconds he was going to one day marry.

Brice leaned forward and offered his hand which Bailey took in hers. Ignoring the snap of heat that shot up her arm at his touch, Bailey studied the tall, muscled man before her and liked what she saw.

"A pleasure to meet you Mr. Morgan," Bailey said in a smooth voice that made Brice think of something silky and rich. Her hand in his felt soft and so right, he hated to let it go.

"The pleasure is all mine, Miss Bishop," Brice said, reaching to doff a hat he forgot he wasn't wearing. Quickly recovering, he gave her his most charming smile. "May I ask you for a dance?"

"You may," she said, handing her cup of punch to Sierra and placing her hand back in Brice's as he led her to the dance floor. Bailey glanced over her shoulder and caught the look of surprise on her sister's pretty face. This was the first time any member of the male species chose Bailey over the perfectly perky Sierra.

Looking into the bottomless depths of her eyes, Brice realized he had never, in his twenty-five years of living, felt this way about another person. While his heart pounded wildly, the rest of the world suddenly disappeared, leaving him with his attention completely focused on Bailey.

Trying to maintain his composure, Brice was glad the dance was a slow one. It gave him time to start a conversation with the woman in his arms.

"Welcome to Grass Valley, Miss Bishop," Brice said, maintaining the formal tone of their introduction.

"Thank you, Mr. Morgan. We've been here a few times over the years, but it's always fun to visit," Bailey said, glancing up at Brice. Even with her heels on, she had to tip her head back slightly to study his face. Lush brown hair was cut short and styled with a spiky wave in the front. Eyes the color of root beer held a spark of mischief and his teeth gleamed white when he smiled. Deciding he was definitely handsome, she smiled back at him. "Please, call me Bailey."

"Bailey," Brice repeated, liking the sound of her name on his lips. What he'd like even more was the taste of her lips on his. He supposed that was pushing things a bit since they'd just met a few minutes ago.

Carrying on a conversation about generalities, they were oblivious that the tempo changed as they continued to dance the next three dances in each other's arms. Finally, Brice asked Bailey if she'd like something to drink and escorted her back to the refreshment tent. Sierra was long gone, so Brice poured Bailey another cup of punch and fished a bottle of water out of an ice-filled tub for himself.

Bailey finished her punch in a few swallows and refilled it while Brice was looking around for an empty table where they could sit and chat.

Taking her elbow, he walked her to a table where her aunt sat visiting with his parents.

"Bailey, honey, I see you met our Brice," Denni Thompson said when Bailey sat down beside her. "This is Mike and Michele Morgan, Brice's parents."

"How lovely to meet you both," Bailey said, suddenly feeling a little light headed. She probably needed to eat something, since she'd missed eating her dinner, distracted by some work details she'd received. Sierra told her to put away her phone and enjoy the reception, so she of course ignored her sister and responded to three text messages. By that time, her plate had disappeared and she was left watching Sierra work her charm on the single male population attending the wedding.

Denni put her arm around Bailey and gave her a hug as they all visited for a while. Bailey felt oddly detached from herself, being chatty and carefree. Normally quiet and reserved, Bailey much preferred to sit back and analyze the conversations going on around her than actively participate. She assumed her behavior was due to the fact they had flown in from Denver that afternoon and she was a little punchy from the excitement of the wedding.

"Brice, why don't you get us all some cake," Michele said, looking at her son as he gazed adoringly at Denni's niece.

"Sure, Mom," Brice said, getting to his feet, hoping Denni wouldn't let Bailey escape before he got back. "Coming right up."

Brice soon returned trying to balance five pieces of cake on flimsy paper plates and managed to get them all on the table without dropping one. Seeing Bailey's empty cup of punch, he went to get her a refill and poured himself a glass of tea.

Finishing their cake, Bailey seemed interested in spending more time with him, so Brice asked her to dance again. He nearly bore a hole through his brother with a cold glare when he cut in. Knowing he riled his brother, Ben returned Bailey to Brice's keeping at the end of the dance with a wiggle of his eyebrows.

"Your brother seems nice," Bailey said, watching Ben walk away, surprised at how much the two brothers looked alike. In fact, if there wasn't a definite age difference between the two, it would have been easy to think they were twins.

"He has his moments," Brice said, pulling Bailey a little closer into his arms. When she didn't offer any resistance, he ran his hands up and down her back, fighting the urge to kiss her.

Observing her as they danced, he realized she wasn't the most beautiful woman he'd ever seen. Her nose was a little too wide and a gap between her two front teeth would keep her from being considered magazine cover quality, but she had a heart-shaped face and skin that looked like smooth porcelain.

Although her mouth was small, her lips were moist and inviting. She had long legs, a nice curved figure, and apparently worked out by the toned muscles visible in her sleeveless dress. The most important thing Brice noticed was how absolutely perfect she felt in his arms.

"I enjoyed meeting your parents," Bailey said, glancing around like she was looking for someone. "Mom and Dad are around here somewhere. I'll introduce you if I can find them."

"I'd like that," Brice said, knowing it was hard to find anyone in the crowd of hundreds of guests filling the Triple T Ranch yard. Since it was getting late, some of the guests were starting to leave. It wouldn't be long before Trent and Lindsay tossed the bouquet and said their goodbyes, then the cleanup process would begin.

Brice promised to help tear down the tents after the crowd cleared out, so he hoped to spend the next few hours with Bailey. He suddenly wondered if she was staying at the ranch or elsewhere. "Where are you staying?"

"Here at the ranch," Bailey said, enjoying the feel of Brice's arms around her. It had been a while since she had allowed herself the pleasure of being close to a man. This particular man was doing funny things to her ability to reason as his warm, leathery scent kept teasing her nose and his engaging smiles kept drawing hers out in return. "I have some business to attend to Monday and then I'll head back to Denver with the family on Thursday. We all want to make sure we have time to visit with Nana."

Brice smiled as he thought about Ester Nordon, grandmother to the rowdy Thompson brothers. She had the same brilliant blue eyes as Trey and Bailey and was known for her gentle yet formidable spirit.

"You definitely don't want to miss that opportunity. I've had my ears boxed by your Nana more than once," Brice said with a grin.

"I'm sure you did nothing to deserve it," Bailey said, smiling at Brice and finding herself wanting to kiss the mole that rested at the edge of his bottom lip. Shaking her head to rid herself of the notion made her dizzy, so she leaned forward and pressed her cheek against Brice's firm jaw. She felt his arms tighten slightly around her and let out a contented sigh.

Usually one to take things slow, Brice felt like he'd been hurtling headlong down an unchartered course since his eyes connected with Bailey's. He had never before been so enraptured with a woman.

"Bailey, I know this sounds crazy…" Brice started to say, but was cut off by cheers and clapping when it was announced that Lindsay was ready to toss the bouquet. Turning with his arm around Bailey's waist so they could watch the fun, Brice cheered when Trent shot the garter in a high arc and Travis captured it by sticking one of his crutches up in the air.

The crowd went wild with applause when Lindsay tossed the bouquet straight to Tess. Someone hollered "two down, one to go," causing Tess' face to turn a bright shade of red. It seemed to be a fact of general agreement that there would be another Thompson family wedding in the near future.

"That is perfectly splendid," Bailey said, leaning closer to Brice. "I didn't realize Travis was that serious about your sister."

"He didn't either until a few weeks ago," Brice said, taking Bailey's hand and leading her along with the crowd as they followed Trent and Lindsay out to where a carriage waited to whisk them away. Given the lateness of the hour, Trent and Lindsay were going to spend the night at their cute little cottage down the road then leave in the morning for a week on the Oregon coast. The carriage would drive them the few miles from the Triple T to their house.

Waving as the carriage rolled down the long driveway, the guests began saying their goodbyes. It didn't take long for the crowd to depart and the remaining family and friends to dive into the monumental task of tearing down the decorations and picking up the debris left from the celebration.

Brice and Bailey helped clear off tables, fold linens and carry gifts into the house where Trent and Lindsay would open them upon their return. Bailey was uncommonly thirsty and drank three more cups of punch while she helped move the gifts inside.

Noticing that plenty of help was making short work of the mess, Brice caught Bailey's hand and tugged her away from the chatter of the others down to the pond where Lindsay and Trent exchanged vows earlier in the evening.

Hundreds of white lights illuminated the area, hanging in the trees and draped over shrubs. It was beyond lovely and Bailey stopped at the bottom of the hill where the trail ended to take it all in.

Brice watched Bailey and smiled, wondering if she enjoyed evenings like this in Denver. Frogs and crickets created a soft serenade and a slight breeze cooled the warm summer air. In addition to the shimmering white lights around them, a canopy of stars twinkled overhead.

"Wow," Bailey said, tipping her head back to stare at the night sky. She wasn't sure if she moved or Brice did, but she found her head resting against his shoulder and his arm around her waist as they gazed at the stars. It was one of the most romantic moments Bailey had ever experienced.

Feeling completely unlike herself, she spun around, throwing her arms around Brice's neck and putting her lips to his.

Brice's surprise rapidly gave way to acceptance as his arms went around her and he pulled her closer, deepening the kiss.

Sure her lips were on fire, Bailey was torn between wanting the kiss to end immediately and go on forever. Tremors rocked through her and her heart felt like it might take flight from her chest in its frenzied beating.

"Brice, I…"

Lips moving insistently against hers kept her from saying more. It was probably a good thing since she couldn't remember what it was she was going to say. Brice worked his way from her lips down her neck and back up to her ear. Moaning, she buried her hands in his thick hair. Tipping her head back to give him better access to her neck, he pulled her flush against him.

Suddenly he released his hold and took a step back as reality crashed down on him. What was he doing? This was Travis' cousin and from all appearances, she wasn't the kind of girl to get embroiled in a passionate encounter upon first meeting someone.

"I'm sorry, Bailey," Brice said, trying to catch his breath and recapture some small degree of sense.

"Don't apologize, Brice," Bailey said, leaning against him, even though she knew she shouldn't. She should be offended, annoyed and angry.

Only she wasn't.

She was, however, lightheaded, emboldened, and more interested in the good-looking cowboy standing in front of her than she thought she'd ever be about a man.

Brice took a series of deep breaths, started to say something and stopped. Swiping a hand over his face, he took another deep breath. It would be way too easy to take advantage of the situation and he wasn't going to let it happen.

Finally, Brice turned toward the path leading back to the house, urging Bailey up the trail. "I think we better get back. We both seem to be under some sort of spell."

"Spells can be magical," Bailey said, casting him a look that filled him with renewed longing. The heat in her vivid blue eyes made Brice trip. He had to take a few hurried steps to catch himself, causing Bailey to giggle.

"Bewitched is more like it," Brice muttered under his breath. He was doing some fast thinking as they walked back up the hill. If Bailey left Thursday that only gave him about ninety-six hours to convince her she was the woman for him and to stay in Grass Valley permanently.

"You can't be bewitched. I can't wriggle my nose," Bailey said in a breathy voice, turning her face to Brice. "See?"

"Yes, I do see," he said, trying not to kiss her again with her face so close to his. Actually, he was finding it difficult to see anything except the alluring woman who was standing next to him, warm and willing for his attentions. Gently pushing her forward, they continued walking.

Cresting the hill, it looked like the work was done and those left behind were either going to the bunkhouse, the ranch house, or getting in their cars to go home. He watched Travis limp beside Tess as she walked to her car and whisper something in her ear that made her smile. Brice knew he'd have a few minutes before he needed to

SHANNA HATFIELD

leave since Tess was his ride home and she obviously wasn't quite ready to tell Travis good night.

Leading Bailey around the corner of the ranch house where it was dark and quiet, he put his arms around her and let her warmth seep into him. He never imagined holding a woman would make him feel like he was finally complete, but that's exactly how he felt with Bailey.

"Can I see you tomorrow?" Brice asked as Bailey pressed against his chest, melting into him while obliterating his restraint.

"Umm, hmm," she said, eyes closed and face upturned to his. Feeling weightless and wonderful, she grinned. "But you better kiss me good night first."

"Yes, ma'am," Brice said, dropping his head to her mouth, giving her a kiss that made bright lights explode behind his eyes and his gut clench with heat.

Bailey wrapped her arms around his neck and leaned so far into him, he was all but holding her up.

"Oh, Brice, I think I just love you," she said with a giggle followed by a hiccup. She toyed with the wave of his hair that fell across his forehead and purred in his ear. "You're so sweet and sexy."

Pulling back, Brice studied her, trying to determine if she was sincere in what she was saying. Bailey had been somewhat reserved and quiet when they first met. As the evening progressed she became more and more relaxed and now she was quite... uninhibited. If he didn't know better, he'd think she was drunk, but all he'd seen her drink was punch.

Narrowing his eyes, Brice realized the punch must have been spiked. Thinking back, he remembered seeing the rotten Bradshaw boys hanging around the punch bowl when no one else was around. They were famous for their ability to spike just about anything in liquid form.

"Punch, Bailey. How much punch did you have, sugar?" Brice asked, gently untangling her arms from around his neck and helping her walk around the corner of the house.

"I don't know. Five or nine or eleventy-three cups," Bailey said, knowing she sounded stupid, but unable to keep her mouth shut. Feeling flushed and dizzy, she was having the most difficult time simultaneously holding open her eyes and moving her feet forward. Despite that she felt completely light and without care. She giggled again and leaned against Brice's arm. "It was yummy."

"I'm sure it was," Brice said dryly, trying to keep her walking upright in her high heels.

The third time she stumbled, Brice sighed and picked her up in his arms. Hurrying up the back steps, through the mud room and into the kitchen, he wasn't surprised to see a few people milling around. Sierra was there talking to an older woman who looked enough like her, he assumed she was her mother.

"My gracious, is she hurt?" the woman asked as Brice tried to set Bailey down and she refused to let go of his neck.

"No, but she's probably going to have a humdinger of a headache tomorrow," Brice said, bending his head and sliding it out of Bailey's grasp. He set her down on her feet, but her legs were wobbly and she tilted dangerously to the right.

"I hate to ask, but would you mind? I'm her mother, Mary Bishop" the woman said, pointing toward the great room. She tried to hide a smirk behind her hand. "I can't believe she's snockered."

"No problem. Just point me in the right direction. South or North Wing?" Brice said, happy to help as he picked up Bailey, enjoying the feel of her body close to his, even if she was drunk.

"South," Mary said leading the way. Knowing the house well, Brice followed Mary and Sierra through the kitchen and dining area, past the great room and down the hall to the south wing of the house. "I'm Brice Morgan, a good friend of Travis."

"Thank you, Brice. I hate to meet you under this embarrassing circumstance, but it's our pleasure. My apologies for Bailey," Mary said, sounding more amused than distraught over Bailey's drunken state. "I can honestly say she's never been drunk before. I don't know what inspired her to do so this evening."

Brice laughed and both Sierra and Mary turned to look at him. "It's not her fault. I think the punch was spiked. I mistakenly thought she found me handsome and clever. Guess it's just the punch."

Sierra smiled, glad to see her sister show some spark of interest in a man regardless of how drunk she may have been.

"Oh, she liked you, Brice, or she would never have danced with you in the first place. She's not much of a socializer," Sierra said, sharing a knowing look with her mother.

Brice carried Bailey into a guest room and gently placed her on the bed. When she reached up looking like she would kiss him again, he turned his face so all she got was his cheek. It wasn't that he didn't want about a thousand more kisses from her, he just preferred she be sober without her mom and sister watching.

"Well, isn't that something?" her mother said, observing the way Bailey was clinging to Brice.

"I told you, Mom," Sierra whispered, having already informed her mother about the cowboy who swept Bailey off her feet. "Now do you believe me?"

"Yes, I do," Mary said, watching as Brice kissed Bailey on the forehead and told her good night.

He turned and gave them both a grin before walking toward the door. Mary put a hand on his arm, smiling warmly before he stepped into the hall.

"Thank you, Brice. I hope we'll see you again before we leave the ranch."

"I'd like that," Brice said, tipping his head to both Sierra and Mary. "I look forward to seeing the lovely Bishop ladies soon."

Rather than retracing his steps through the house, Brice walked to the end of the wing and went out the door, hurrying around to the side yard where Tess was parked. Seeing Travis with his hands buried in Tess' hair, Brice grinned.

"I think you two have done more than enough of that for one evening. Come on, Tessie, let's head home," Brice teased as he walked up to the car.

Tess jerked away from Travis, giving her brother a stern glare that only made him laugh.

"Thanks, dude," Travis said, shaking his head at his friend. "Don't think we didn't notice you saying goodnight to Bailey a minute ago."

Brice stopped the snappy retort he was going to give Travis and instead climbed into Tess' car.

Watching his sister blow a kiss to Travis, he felt compelled to blow one as well and bat his eyelashes dramatically, earning an elbow in his side from Tess.

Heading down the driveway, Tess was quiet while she seemed to pull her thoughts away from Travis. When Brice glanced at her again, she offered him a teasing smile. He was going to have to be careful or Tess would give him a hard time about his attraction to Bailey.

"You like Bailey, don't you?" she asked, already knowing the answer.

"Maybe," Brice said trying to sound uninterested.

"She's quite pretty with all that honey-colored hair and those intense blue eyes. I wonder how come she and Trey are the only ones to inherit Nana's eye color."

"Don't know. Just the way genes work I suppose."

"I happened to notice you two getting pretty friendly out back a little while ago. Don't you think that is kind of pushing the limit considering you just met her?" Tess asked with a raised eyebrow.

"I would say yes, except I figured out she was drunk."

"Drunk! How'd she get...oh, the punch," Tess said, turning off the road into their driveway.

"So it was the punch," Brice said, slapping his leg. "Let me guess, the Bradshaw boys?"

"I assumed so," Tess said, parking the car and turning off the lights. "Travis said they asked a couple of their hands to keep an eye on the punch bowl, but there were a few minutes when it went unguarded. I guess we should have thrown it out, but Travis didn't think the boys had time to dump anything into the bowl."

"Well, apparently they did," Brice said, keeping a hand on Tess' elbow to steady her as they walked through the gravel to the back sidewalk. "I thought Bailey was completely taken with my undeniable charm and dashing good looks. Instead it was just the punch talking."

Tess laughed as they went in the back door.

"Maybe, but I hope it at least had something good to say."

Brice grinned. It definitely had something to say. Something along the lines that love at first sight wasn't such a far-fetched crazy notion after all.

Chapter Two

*"Falling in love consists merely in uncorking
the imagination and bottling the common sense."*
Helen Rowland

The sultry scent of woods on a warm, crisp autumn afternoon blended with well-worn leather invaded Bailey's dreams. She could feel strong, muscled arms around her and kept envisioning sparkling brown eyes, filled with heat and mischief.

Turning on her side in bed, she breathed deeply, inhaling the delicious scent that made her think of cowboys, harvest moons, and love.

Love?

That was completely ridiculous. Frowning she opened one eye to see Sierra pulling back the drapes and letting the bright summer sunshine fill the room.

Pain shot through Bailey's head and she thought she might be violently ill. Rolling onto her back, she moaned and placed a pillow over her head. The entire room was spinning, her throat was dry, and she wanted to cry.

With startling clarity, everything that happened the previous evening came rushing back to her and she wished more than anything that a cavernous hole would open up and swallow her, bed and all, into its dark depths.

What had she done?

"Oh," she whispered, clutching the sheet tightly in her hand in hopes it would help stop the spinning. She heard

Sierra close the drapes then felt her weight dip the mattress near her head.

"Hey, sleepyhead. We're all ready to leave for church," Sierra said, lifting the pillow from Bailey's face. "Mom thought you might want to go. Brice will be there."

"No," Bailey groaned, not able to bear seeing him again. She had no idea what caused her to behave so outrageously last night, but she was mortified. "I can't see him."

"Why not?" Sierra asked, tugging Bailey's clenched fist from the sheet and patting her hand. "I got the idea he really likes you."

Bailey pried one eye open and squinted at Sierra, who sat wearing a broad grin.

"I behaved like... like an inebriated trollop!" Bailey said, closing her eye.

"Yep, you sure did. It was awesome. I've never seen you quite like that before. I'm not sure Brice knew what to make of you either," Sierra said, bouncing on the bed causing Bailey to grab her head with both hands and hold on in hopes it wouldn't explode. "Did you know you were drunk?"

"I was what?" Bailey asked with a startled cry, replaying the evening in her head. She did not imbibe in alcoholic beverages. She didn't have time for such nonsense. All she'd had to drink was fruity punch. Many, many cups of fruity spiked punch.

"Drunk. According to Mom, you were 'three sheets to the wind.' Dad couldn't stop laughing and Trey and Cady were livid that someone spiked the punch," Sierra said, toying with one of her long curls, relishing the opportunity to torment her sister. Bailey rarely did anything that would cause a raised eyebrow, always the epitome of a professional career woman. "Apparently you're the only one who drank too much of it. Way to go!"

"I'd most certainly appreciate it if you'd stop talking now," Bailey said, wishing Sierra would leave her alone. It was bad enough to recall what she'd said and done, but Sierra was enjoying her suffering entirely too much.

Four years younger than Bailey, Sierra was the one who was always doing something silly or off the wall. She took after her fun-loving mother that way. Bailey, on the other hand, was more like their father with an analytical way of thinking and, when it came to her career, a one-track mind.

Sierra stood and looked down at Bailey with a sense of compassion. "Do you really feel awful?"

"Remember the time you got sick in Mexico?" Bailey asked, glad Sierra had stopped wiggling the bed. "When you begged Dad to shoot you and end your misery?"

"Gosh, you don't feel that bad, do you?" Sierra asked, recalling the days of horrid illness that made her want to die.

"No. I feel worse," Bailey whispered.

"I'm sorry, sis," Sierra said, sounding genuinely remorseful over Bailey's state. Especially since she didn't knowingly get drunk. "I've got to go, but I brought you a glass of water and one of orange juice as well as some toast. Dad said the best cure is water and sleep."

"Thanks," Bailey said, fluttering a weak hand Sierra's direction as she left the room.

Moving at the pace of a snail, she worked herself into a sitting position and reached for the water, draining the glass before setting it down. She waited to see if the water settled in her stomach before nibbling the toast and drinking the juice.

Sliding back down in the bed, she noticed the room wasn't spinning quite so violently and let out a sigh. Thinking back over the previous evening, she remembered Sierra introducing her to the very good-looking cowboy named Brice. He was tall and charming with broad shoulders that tapered down to a narrow waist.

She couldn't recall ever having a man be so attentive to her. The evening started fine as they danced and talked. The amount of punch she consumed seemed to be aligned to the loosening effect the alcohol had on both her lips and her inhibitions. At one point, she recalled throwing her arms around Brice and kissing him like he was the last available man in the universe.

A vision of her head tipped back, his lips on her neck, her leg wrapped around his flew through her mind. Had she really…? "Oh, my," she groaned.

Heat flushed her cheeks and she knew, without a doubt, she had to leave the ranch before she chanced running into Brice. Bailey was humiliated to think how she'd behaved, hanging all over him, flirting with him.

Remembering an enthusiastic declaration of love, she sat bolt upright in bed and held both her head and stomach. The more she remembered the more panicked she became. Had she really called him sexy? She had not, in her entire life, uttered that word to anyone, let alone a man she'd met a few hours earlier.

Attempting to get out of bed made the room spin again so Bailey eased her way back down against the pillows. There wasn't a whole lot she could do today to apologize for what she'd done so Bailey finally relaxed and fell back asleep.

In her dreams, Bailey's imagination went wild with tempting possibilities regarding Brice while shoving common sense into the far corners of her thoughts. Dreaming of the feel of his lips on hers, she awoke later with a smile. Brice's tantalizing scent that brought a warm fall afternoon to mind filled her nose and she breathed deeply.

"Hey, sugar," a deep male voice whispered close to her face. With a start, Bailey opened both eyes to find two sparkling brown eyes looking back at her.

Blinking rapidly, she decided she was hallucinating. Her mind must have conjured Brice from her dreams.

Forcing her eyes to stay open, Bailey took in the fact that Brice appeared to be very real as he sat on the edge of her bed, smiling at her, looking just as deliciously handsome as he had last night.

"Remember me, Bailey?" Brice asked, gently picking up her hand and holding it in his calloused one. She didn't know why, but Bailey noticed how clean and well-tended his nails looked, especially for a hard-working cowboy.

Unable to meet his gaze, she continued staring at his hands and slowly nodded her head.

He squeezed her hand and released a breath. "Good," Brice said, as tension flowed away from him and he seemed to relax. "That's good."

Her plans to run away before she was forced to face Brice flew right out the window. Bailey shook her head, trying to find the words to adequately express her deep sense of shame and regret. Not one given to displays of emotion, Bailey was irritated to feel a tear slide down her cheek.

"What's wrong?" Brice asked, wiping it away, his fingers gentle on her creamy, smooth skin.

He could barely sleep last night, thinking about Bailey. Ignoring Tess and Ben's teasing as he hustled them all to get ready for church, he wanted to be there early to make sure he saved a place beside him for Bailey. Brice was thoroughly disappointed when Sierra sat down, whispering that her sister was quite ill.

Unable to contain his antsy need to see her, both Tess and his mother scowled at him when he couldn't keep his foot from jiggling through the pastor's sermon. As soon as the service was over, he practically ran out the door in his haste to get to the Triple T. Arriving at the house, he knew the door would be open, so he let himself in, walked to her room and stood watching Bailey sleep for a few moments before the temptation to kiss her smiling lips got the best of him.

Stealing a kiss, Brice stepped back, knowing she was waking up. As soon as Bailey opened her eyes, he could see the regret and despair filling them. He didn't know why she was so worked up. It wasn't her fault she'd imbibed in the spiked punch. None of them knew what the Bradshaw boys had done. After Brice, Trey and Travis, along with the boys' parents lectured them this morning, he hoped they'd think twice about doctoring up drinks again. At twenty-two, they should have long outgrown such childish pranks.

Brice felt a little piece of his heart break at the lone tear sliding down Bailey's cheek. "Don't cry, Bailey. Everything's just fine."

"No, it is not," she said, slowly scooting back against the headboard until she was sitting up with the sheet clutched under her chin. "My most sincere apologies, Brice, for my reprehensible and completely disgraceful behavior of last night. I deeply regret my inexcusable actions and hope you'll be able to forgive both my inebriated state and inconceivably deplorable conduct."

Brice sat looking at her like she was speaking a foreign language.

"What she said is she thinks she acted like a strumpet, she didn't mean to, and she's sorry," Sierra said as she flounced into the room followed by Mary and Ross Bishop.

"Sierra, don't tease your sister so," Mary said, unable to hide her smile. She reached out a warm hand to Brice, who stood and shook hers. "Brice, nice to see you again. Sierra said you wanted to check to make sure Bailey had survived her encounter with the Bradshaw boys special punch recipe. By the way, this is my husband Ross. I didn't get a chance to introduce him at church."

"Pleasure to meet you, sir," Brice said, realizing it probably wasn't the most socially acceptable thing for him to be in Bailey's room while she was still in bed, considering they just met last night.

"It's nice to meet you, Brice. Sierra and Mary told me all about your coming to Bailey's rescue," Ross said with a grin, entertained by his unflappable daughter's current state of dishevelment. "Thank you."

"I'm sorry I didn't figure out sooner that the punch was throwing her for a loop," Brice said, looking over to see Bailey staring at them all with a narrowed glare. Her hand clasped something small around her neck and she seemed to be rubbing it back and forth with nervous fingers. He wondered if it was the strange little necklace he'd noticed her wearing last night.

"We appreciate you getting her safely in the house," Mary said, taking Brice by the arm. "You'll be joining us for lunch, won't you?"

"I wouldn't miss it," Brice said, sending Bailey another glance while Mary and Ross escorted him out of the room and back toward the kitchen.

Sierra waited until they were out of earshot to sit on the bed and flop back next to Bailey.

"If you don't get out of that bed, take a shower and act like a normal human, I'm not going to be able to keep from throwing myself at your boyfriend. He's one smokin' hot babe," Sierra said with her usual dramatic flair.

Bailey glared at her. "In no sense of the term is he my boyfriend."

Sierra sat up and gave Bailey a critical once-over. Her sister looked like she'd been dragged backward through a knothole, as Nana liked to say, but a shower and a little makeup would do wonders.

"Bailey," Sierra said, in her best no nonsense tone, yanking away the sheet and tugging on her sister's hands. "You will get up, get clean and get over yourself. Any woman with even an ounce of common sense would be snatching up every second she could spend with that very cute man who, for reasons I can't understand, seems to be quite taken with you. Now quit pouting and move it."

Knowing from past experience Sierra would not leave her alone until she got what she wanted, Bailey put her feet on the floor and stood, clutching the edge of the night stand while she waited for the room to stop spinning.

Sierra propped herself under her shoulder and helped her stumble into the bathroom. Bailey was chagrined to see she still wore the dress she had on last night. Huffing at the effort, Sierra breathed deeply and grinned.

"Man alive, is that his scent on your dress? That is to die for, Bailey. I think I could eat him with a spoon," Sierra said, propping Bailey against the bathroom vanity. Sierra unfastened the hook at the top of Bailey's dress and slid down the zipper before leaving her sister alone in the bathroom.

Glancing in the mirror, Bailey was shocked by her appearance. Dark smudges ringed both eyes, her hair looked like it had never seen a comb and her lips had absolutely no color to them at all.

Turning on the shower, she waited for the water to heat then stepped in and enjoyed the warm spray for a few minutes before washing her hair. She flipped the faucet over to cold and forced herself to stand in the freezing water until she was completely chilled. By then, she was no longer dizzy and was beginning to feel more like herself.

Blow drying her hair, she applied mascara and some lip gloss, then slipped on a white and turquoise flowered sundress.

"Eat him with a spoon, indeed," Bailey muttered to herself as she shoved her feet into a pair of white wedge sandals. Spritzing on a quick spray of perfume, she squared her shoulders and, in a vain move completely unlike herself, pinched her cheeks before opening the bedroom door and walking down the hall.

The family was eating outside on the patio between the two wings of the house, so Bailey watched them for a moment from the great room before going outside to join them.

Stepping across the patio, she forced herself not to smile when Brice jumped up from the table where he was sitting and stood waiting for her approach. Her common sense told her to go sit at the table where Nana, her mother and Aunt Denni were visiting with Cass.

Squelching that thought, she strode toward the table holding the food, barely acknowledging Brice with a curt nod of her head as he walked up behind her.

"You look like you're feeling better," he said quietly as she filled her plate. She was feeling better. Ravenous, in fact. Now that her dizziness had fled, Bailey looked forward to sampling many of the tasty looking choices available for lunch. She turned to see Brice pour her a glass of iced tea, which he continued to carry as they made their way back to where he was sitting by Tess, Travis and Sierra.

"Hey, Bailey, nice to see you out and about," Travis said, leaning around Tess. "I'm sorry about the punch last night."

"Had you known, I'm sure you would have immediately remedied the problem before it escalated into anything disastrous," Bailey said, smiling at her cousin. "No need to apologize. Since the only one suffering adverse effects from the experience seems to be me, I would think that is sufficient reason to not give it another thought and consider the matter dismissed."

"What she said is that it's no big deal since she's the only one who got drunk and to just forget about it," Sierra said from across the table, ignoring the cool glare from her sister.

"You would better earn my gratitude by not paraphrasing my communications," Bailey said, giving Sierra a pointed look.

Shrugging her shoulders, Sierra went back to talking to Ben, who had joined their gathering and sat down beside her.

"What do you do for a living, Bailey?" Tess asked as she sat holding Travis' hand. Brice was interested in the answer to that question as well, because he couldn't recall Bailey talking about her job last night. He hoped it was something she could do somewhere within an hour or two of Grass Valley because he was determined she was going to fall in love with him before she returned to Denver. "I thought someone mentioned archaeology?"

"Close," Bailey said, sitting with a perfect posture as she wiped her mouth on a napkin and returned it to her lap. "I'm a paleontologist."

"What's that?" Ben asked, from across the table, interested in finding out more about the girl who had turned Brice's head. His brother was never in short supply of girls to date, but Ben had never seen him so taken with a girl, particularly one who seemed to be so serious and scholarly.

"I study fossils and attempt to use them to reconstruct the history of Earth and the life that once lived on it," Bailey said, in a matter-of-fact tone as she buttered a roll so soft she could imagine it melting in her mouth.

"How's that different than anthropology?" Brice asked, curious about the different types of research work.

"Here we go," Sierra said under her breath, leaning back in her chair. "This will take a while."

Bailey sent her sister an annoyed stare before taking a bite of her roll and deciding to give a very brief answer to the question.

"Anthropologists study humans. Archaeologists study human artifacts. Paleontologists study fossils, which are any trace of a past life form," Bailey explained then offered Sierra a raised eyebrow.

Sierra grinned and sipped her iced tea.

"Do you go out on digs?" Brice asked, excited by the news of her occupation since there happened to be a fossil site with active work a couple of hours from Grass Valley.

"I most certainly do. The work in the field is invigorating and fascinating," Bailey said, with a light shining in her bright turquoise eyes. "It's one of the things I enjoy most about my career."

"She really digs digging in the dirt," Sierra said, making everyone chuckle.

"Did you know there's a fossil site just a few hours from here?" Tess asked, wondering if Bailey had plans to go to the John Day Fossil Beds while she was visiting.

"Yes. I have an appointment tomorrow morning to meet with the director of the project to discuss their most recent findings," Bailey said, although she didn't change her facial expression, the tone of her voice betrayed her excitement.

"That's awesome," Brice said, thrilled at this tidbit of news. Before he could make any further comment, Bailey asked what Brice and Ben both did. Ben explained his job working for a barge company out of Portland and Brice talked about his work for a construction company in The Dalles. He was happy their current project was just up the road in Moro, building a house and barn for someone moving into the area. It saved him the hour-long commute into The Dalles every day although he did miss carpooling with Tess, who also worked in The Dalles in the hospital's physical therapy department.

After lunch, everyone seemed to wander off their own direction and Brice asked Bailey if she'd like to go for a walk. He figured he was safe from too many prying eyes because Sierra was playing with Cass and some of the younger kids, Tess insisted Travis spend some time with his legs elevated so they went inside to watch a movie and Ben headed back to Portland.

Bailey hesitated only a moment before agreeing to go and they strolled down the hill toward the pond again. Still embarrassed over her previous evening's behavior, Bailey made sure to keep a respectable distance away from Brice as they walked.

Even without the white lights twinkling and a blanket of stars overhead, the setting was still quite lovely. Spying a bench beneath a willow tree, Bailey wandered that direction and sat down.

The fluttering in her stomach, the tingling in her toes and the fuzzy feeling in her head were sensations completely foreign to her. Deciding to blame it on her hangover, she ignored the charge of electricity that shot through her when Brice sat beside her and took her hand in his.

"So, Bailey, do you recall coming down here last night?" Brice asked, leaning back against the bench and stretching out his legs.

"There is some degree of recollection of walking down here and studying fixed luminary points in the night sky," Bailey said, sitting primly on the bench. She remembered far more than stargazing. There was hugging and kissing and the overwhelming desire for Brice to hold her as close as humanly possible.

With his scent permeating her senses and his warmth against her side, the unreasonable longing to repeat the experience swept over her with full force. As much as she hated to admit it, she wanted him to kiss her again, to see if the feel of his lips against hers was as magical as she remembered or if it was just a lingering part of her dreams.

"Do you always talk like that?" Brice asked, with a teasing grin, assuming her formal, scientific way of speaking came from her profession. According to Sierra, Bailey was all work and no play.

Brice had plans to change that.

"Like what?" Bailey asked, knowing she sounded like a stodgy professor most of the time, but it served her well in her career. People took you seriously when you could talk academic circles around them. A tall, fit young woman with honey-gold curls, striking blue eyes, and a penchant for fashion had a hard time getting people to take her seriously unless she could intimidate them a little.

"Like you're giving a lecture at Harvard."

"I've only done that once," she said, distracted by the way Brice's muscles rippled beneath the cotton fabric of his shirt every time he moved his arms.

"Seriously?" Brice asked, somewhat in awe. He'd managed to get a two-year degree in construction management before he left school for good and began working construction full time. He spent evenings and weekends working on the family ranch and if he had any spare time, he liked to make handcrafted furniture and carve wood.

"Why would I say something that wasn't true?"

"I didn't mean...never mind," Brice said, so enraptured with Bailey he forgot to be frustrated by her literal take on his comments. Settling more comfortably on the seat the Thompson brothers referred to as the kissing bench, he placed one arm behind Bailey while the other kept her hand captive in his. "I want to know all about you. Tell me everything there is to know about Bailey Bishop."

"There isn't much to tell," Bailey said, staring at her hand clasped in Brice's larger one. She noticed scars and callouses on his fingers along with an undeniable strength, yet he cradled her hand so tenderly, like it was something he was afraid of breaking. She herself had big hands for a woman with long capable fingers. Her nails were usually chipped and her cuticles were ragged enough to give any good manicurist nightmares for a week. Such was the price of digging in the dirt and rocks for a living.

"Sure there is. Let's start with your full name. How tall are you? How old are you? What kind of food do you like? Those kinds of questions," Brice prompted.

"Bailey Lorinda Bishop. I was born twenty-seven years and fourteen days ago. I stand five feet, seven point nine-three inches tall," Bailey said, rattling off information with scientific precision. "Like any female, I refuse to share my weight. I like a wide variety of foods, but I have a particular fondness for anything with pumpkin. Fall is my favorite season and I enjoy reading books about ancient history. I am hopeless at idle chit-chat, I dislike disorganization and someday I hope my work will be remembered for making a breakthrough contribution to civilization."

For a guy who was the life of the party, considered the sports page and comic strip in-depth reading, and liked to live in the spur of the moment, he could see a few potential issues to overcome if he wanted to have a relationship with Bailey. Not one to give up easily, Brice was ready to rise to the challenge. This was, after all, the girl he planned to marry.

Watching the sun highlight streaks of pure gold in her hair, Brice decided the summer dress Bailey wore was a perfect complement to her golden skin and amazing blue eyes. Just gazing into their depths made him think of a tropical beach.

Taking a deep breath, he realized Bailey smelled like the funny green tea his mom was always drinking with a hint of something sweet thrown in just to further ensnare his senses. He'd never before found anything enticing about the scent of tea, but Bailey's unique fragrance was definitely making him rethink his opinion.

Itching with the desire to bury his hands in her hair and taste the sweetness of her kisses again, Brice tried to keep his thoughts from getting too far off track. He wasn't sure how many of the kisses they'd shared last night had been because Bailey genuinely liked him or because she was drunk. Brice gave himself a mental scolding for not figuring out her drunken state sooner.

"What do you do for fun?" Brice asked Bailey, pulling his gaze from hers as he looked out at the pond and the cattle grazing in the distance. Although many people thought Grass Valley was somewhere near the end of the earth, Brice loved the peaceful openness of the community where he grew up.

"Fun?" Bailey asked, repeating the word like she hadn't heard it before. It took her a moment to think of what she did do for fun.

When she wasn't working at a dig site, writing a paper or in a lab studying fossils, she read papers written by her peers, traveled to new fossil sites, lectured about her discoveries, and studied past American civilizations. She rarely spent time with her family, had no real friends and other than occasionally sitting down to embroider or crochet as a way to be productive while still letting her mind wander over fossils and facts, she didn't have a hobby.

The one thing that kept her from being a complete geek was her love of clothes. Despite her work, despite her scientific approach to life, the one thing Bailey did enjoy that she considered frivolous was shopping for cute clothes. She had a weakness for anything that resembled fashions from the forties and fifties, especially shoes, but she sure wasn't admitting that to Brice. She barely knew the man, even if she'd thrown herself at him the previous evening.

That thought made her face flush red as she sat upright, adjusting the skirt of her dress.

"Whatever you do for fun, it sure makes the roses bloom in those pretty cheeks of yours," Brice teased, watching color flame in her face. "Want to let me in on the secret?"

"I most certainly do not," Bailey said, feeling defensive. Brice somehow managed to throw her off kilter. No one else did that and Bailey didn't like it one bit. She liked order and organization and predictability. Brice was about the most unpredictable person she'd ever encountered. According to information Sierra gleaned from Travis, he and Brice did crazy things like race cars, ride bulls and windsurf.

"Aw, come on, sugar, there must be something that made you blush like that. Something that you enjoy doing," Brice said, giving her a smile so full of white teeth and charm, she felt lightheaded.

"I assure you beyond some occasional embroidery work and a rare shopping trip, I am completely and utterly devoted to my career," Bailey said, sounding too matter-of-fact even to her own ears. What really sounded like fun, what she would die before acknowledging out loud, was kissing Brice. Repeatedly.

"Then I guess I'll just have to wonder what naughty things you're stitching because you've surely got a red face, sugar."

Jumping to her feet, Bailey put her hands on her hips and gave Brice a sharp look. "Mr. Morgan, I'll have you know just because of one evening of inebriated shenanigans, you have no right to assume that I do anything as questionable as embroider items of a wicked nature. I thank you for your care last evening, for your consideration today, and will now bid you goodbye."

Bailey turned to march back up the hill but before she'd taken three steps, she felt herself swept off her feet and into Brice's arms.

Caught completely off guard, Bailey gasped and wrapped her arms around Brice's neck, her face just inches from his.

"You're just about the cutest thing I've ever seen when you're all riled up," Brice said, sitting on the bench with her across his lap. "If the sparks shooting from your eyes could cause bodily harm, I reckon I'd be plenty scorched."

"Indeed, Mr. Morgan," Bailey said breathlessly. She was surprised she could even form words with the way her traitorous body and emotions were betraying her. Her heart was galloping wildly, her stomach felt weightless and she wanted, more than anything in the world for Brice to kiss her.

Common sense demanded she slap Brice's handsome face, march up the hill and catch the first plane back to Denver. Much to Bailey's dismay, her common sense had, during the course of the last twenty-four hour time period, completely disappeared only to be replaced with thoughts and longings absolutely alien to her.

Attempting to hold herself stiffly away from Brice, it was impossible when her limbs felt languid from his nearness and she was melting against his solid chest.

"I may be totally wrong, and I'm sure you'll set me straight in a hurry, but I think you want to kiss me every bit as much as I want to kiss you. Don't you?" Brice asked, slowing bringing his lips toward hers until only a fraction of space separated them.

Bailey was in agony. So close, yet not close enough.

"You have some of the most…imaginative ideas, Mr. Morgan," Bailey said, leaning back as her eyes locked on Brice's lips. She noticed the corners of his mouth turn up in a grin and she wanted, so very badly, to feel his lips pressed to hers.

"I'm just getting started," Brice said, his voice husky and deep as he took Bailey's lips captive in a tempting kiss. Electricity shot between them and ignited the fire that had been smoldering since he first said hello to her at the wedding.

Her lips beneath his were every bit as luscious as he remembered from last night. Except now it was Bailey, not the alcohol, returning his passion.

"Brice," Bailey whispered, losing herself in his arms and his kiss. Pressing closer to him, she felt his hands sliding across her back. Raising his head, she pulled him back for another searing kiss, hearing him whisper her name as he trailed his hand along her leg.

Where things would have gone from there, neither one would know because Cass chose that precise moment to run down the hill and interrupt their afternoon interlude.

"Brice? Where are you?" Cass called looking around and not immediately seeing the couple on the bench beneath the willow tree.

Startled from their passionate encounter by the sound of the little girl's voice, Brice nearly dumped Bailey on the grass but managed to grab her before she tumbled off his lap. Staring intently at each other, they were desperately trying to catch their breath along with their ability to think rationally.

"Brice! Whatcha doing?" Cass asked, running over to the bench with her red curls flying every direction. She leaned against Bailey's knees, which rested on Brice's thigh from her position across his lap. Placing a little hand on Brice's shoulder, Cass gave him a pat. "Uncle Travis said you spent enough time spooning and you should come back to the house."

"He did?" Brice said, making a mental note to be sure and thank Travis later for being so helpful this afternoon.

He'd remember to make sure Cass interrupted Travis the next time he wanted to be alone with Tess.

"Yep. What's spooning?" Cass asked, looking at Bailey. "Why are you on Brice's lap? How come your face is all red? Did you get sunburned? My mama has some gel stuff she put on me when I got sunburned. Want me to get you some?"

"Thank you, Cass," Bailey said, getting off Brice's lap and taking Cass's hand, starting back toward the house. "I don't have a sunburn, although I'm feeling a bit warm, but thank you for your kind offer to help. I think you should ask Brice all about spooning. I'm sure he'd love to explain it to you."

Bailey sent a saucy smile over her shoulder at Brice.

Brice grinned back at her, loving the playful look on her face. He decided to walk a few steps behind the girls, the better to watch Bailey. So far, he wasn't disappointed with the view.

Cass turned to look at him and started in with more questions. "What's spooning, Brice? Huh? Do you have spoons? Is it a game? Can I play? Will you teach me? Can my friend Ashley come play, too? Do you have fancy spoons? I've got pink tea party spoons with fairies on them. Will that work? Huh, Brice?"

Swiping his hand over his face, he rolled his eyes and caught up with Bailey and Cass. Taking the little girl's hand in his, Bailey held Cass' other hand as she took a few running steps and swung between them with a giggle. Leave it to Travis to give Cass an old-fashioned term for kissing, then expect someone else to tell her what it meant.

"I really think you should ask Uncle Travis to explain that game to you, kiddo."

Chapter Three

"'Tis one thing to be tempted, another thing to fall."
William Shakespeare

"What do you mean gone? She can't be gone!" Brice said, looking over Travis' shoulder expecting Bailey to suddenly appear. "She promised to go out to dinner with me tonight. She said she wasn't leaving until Thursday."

Blindsided by Bailey's abrupt departure, the air whooshed out of Brice's lungs and his legs felt wobbly.

Pushing Brice down onto a barstool at the kitchen counter, Travis poured him a glass of iced tea and slid it across the counter. Cady was outside grilling chicken, Cass was playing in the barn with the dogs and no one else was in the ranch house at the moment.

"What happened?" Brice finally asked, tossing his Stetson on the counter and rubbing his hand across his face. "I thought she had an appointment at the fossil beds today?"

"She did. Bailey borrowed Cady's car and left early this morning. She rolled back in here just after noon and said she had to leave today. Aunt Mary and Sierra both tried to talk her into staying, but she didn't seem to hear a word they said. When Sierra reminded her about your date tonight, she got a funny look on her face, but went on with her packing," Travis said, sitting down at the table and leaning his crutches against the chair next to him. "Uncle Ross went off with the hands this morning to help with wheat harvest, otherwise he may have been able to talk to her."

"Dude, she just can't be gone," Brice said, refusing to accept the information his best friend was offering. "She... I..."

"Look, Brice, I've never seen you like this over a girl before. Bailey's a little... intense when it comes to her work. According to Aunt Mary and Sierra, she has never had a relationship that lasted more than three dates because she keeps her focus entirely on her career. She's a great girl, but I'm not so sure she's the right girl for you. Whatever happened at the fossil beds today got her stirred up enough about her job, she felt the need to rush off without even telling you goodbye. Doesn't that say something to you right there?"

"Yeah, it does," Brice said, sliding off the stool and pacing the floor next to Travis. "She's in love. She just doesn't want to admit it."

Travis couldn't help the snort of laughter that escaped. "Are you crazy, man? You just met her Saturday, today is Monday. You're talking about a girl who'd rather spend time with a ten thousand year old bug encased in rock than she would with a real live breathing human. She doesn't do people or relationships and you think she's in love? With you?"

Brice glared at Travis and paced a few more steps before sitting on the bar stool again.

"You're my best friend, man, and I don't want you to get hurt," Travis said, leaning forward with his elbows on his knees hoping Brice would be reasonable. "Trying to create something between you and Bailey is insane. You're mister life-of-the-party. She's a perpetual party-pooper. It would never work. Did you listen to the way she talks? She sounds like a walking encyclopedia. I know she's cute, but think about it, dude. She's just not the right girl for you."

"I know it sounds crazy, Trav, but something happened between us."

"What exactly did happen between you?" Travis was feeling suddenly protective of his inexperienced cousin, even if she was older than him.

"Nothing except a few kisses."

Travis raised an eyebrow at Brice.

"Okay. More than a few and they were the most amazing thing I've ever experienced. Come on, Trav, you and Tess are in love. You know what I'm talking about. That electrified jolt that hits whenever you touch her."

"Yeah, I do," Travis said, his face softening just thinking about Tess. "But if you think Bailey's going to wake up one day and decide she's in love with you and come rushing back to Grass Valley, you better think again. You only met her two days ago, bro. Just let this go."

"Would you let it go if it was Tess?" Brice asked already knowing the answer. "Something happened between us, something I can't even explain. I felt it, she felt it, and I think she's using her job as an excuse to run away from the feelings she doesn't know how to handle. I think what we shared scared her. Heck, it scared me."

"And when did you get your degree in psychology, Dr. Morgan?" Travis asked, teasing Brice. His laughter was cut short when Brice surged to his feet with a red face and clenched fists.

"Laugh all you want, but I'm telling you, I'm going to marry that girl or die trying," Brice said, snatching his hat from the counter, storming out of the house and slamming the door behind him.

He was stomping toward his pickup when Sierra and Mary pulled up in Cady's PT Cruiser.

Jumping out of the car, Sierra waved at him and he stopped.

"Brice, I'm so sorry," Sierra said, grabbing his hand and looking at him with sympathy in her eyes. "Mom and I talked until we were blue in the face trying to get her to stay, but once Bailey makes up her mind, you might as well give up."

"Did she say why she had to leave in such an all-fired hurry?" Brice asked, trying to curb his anger.

"She said something about an urgent need to return to her current dig site. She's been in Las Vegas for the past several months," Mary said, walking up to stand beside Sierra. "Don't take it personally, Brice. This is what Bailey does. She gets all excited about a site, works on a dig for a while then moves on to the next one. She's worked all over the country."

Brice didn't know that. He just assumed she worked in Denver, near her family. Evidently it was just a place for her to go when she was between projects.

"Would she talk to me if I called her?" Brice asked, not sure he really wanted to know the answer.

"Maybe," Sierra said with a hopeful lift of her eyebrow.

"Look, Brice, you're a wonderful young man and I appreciate you offering Bailey your friendship while she was here, but the fact of the matter is she's just not good with people. As much as I love my daughter, relationships are definitely not her thing," Mary said, giving Brice's arm a pat. "You can certainly try giving her a call. I'll give you her phone number, email address, you can even send her a note in care of our house, but just don't get your hopes up."

Unable to speak, Brice nodded his head.

"Brice, are you staying for dinner?" Cady called with a wave from the back step. "Tess will be here soon to give Travis his therapy. Why don't you join us?"

"Sure," Brice said, following Mary and Sierra back in the house.

Mary dug a business card out of her purse and wrote something on the back before handing it to Brice. It was a card for Bailey. Plain and simple - stating her name, with a title of paleontologist, a phone number and an email address, along with a web address. On the back Mary included their home address in Denver.

"She didn't give me many details, but I did get the impression she would be back in Denver in a few weeks. From there, goodness only knows what she has planned. She wouldn't say whether her appointment today went well or not. With that girl, it's so hard to tell if she's excited because something good is happening or because she's miffed about something not going like she planned."

"Thanks for this, Mary. I appreciate it," Brice said, feeling his confidence in easily winning over Bailey slowly deflate.

"You're welcome," Mary said, suddenly wishing Brice had taken an interest in Sierra instead of Bailey. The two of them were a lot alike with their fun, outgoing personalities, and he seemed like a genuinely nice young man.

Mary hoped someday Bailey would meet a man who would capture her heart and shift her focus to family and home instead of always being so intent about her career. Her desire for grandchildren was strong and with the direction her oldest daughter was going, the responsibility for providing the grandkids was going to rest solely on Sierra's slight shoulders.

><><

Glancing out the plane window from her seat, Bailey let out a sigh. Fully admitting her reason for leaving today had nothing to do with her job and everything to do with Brice, she used her work as a convenient excuse to escape the tumultuous feelings he stirred inside her. Feelings that could be dangerous to keeping the focus on her career.

Bailey knew before she ever graduated from high school she was going to spend her days married to her career. She had to be. Her work took intense focus and the ability to pack up and move at a moment's notice. What kind of family life could she have when she was off on some new dig for months at a time? It wasn't fair to expect a spouse to go with her or to wait for her while she was gone. Children were out of the question. In addition, Bailey didn't want the distractions of a family.

Her sites were set on being one of the top ten paleontologists of her time and the only way to make that happen was to block out everything else except her work.

Paleontology was her life.

At least that's what she wanted to believe, even though every time Bailey closed her eyes she saw a pair of root-beer brown eyes staring back at her. She could hear Brice's laugh, and see his warm smile with that incredibly enticing mole at the bottom of his lip. Thinking about his mole brought to mind the heated kisses they'd shared and caused her mouth to water with the desire to feel his lips moving on hers again.

Yesterday, when they'd shared the passionate encounter beneath the willow tree, Bailey was hoping it would prove her fascination with Brice was a lingering effect from her inebriation. But it wasn't.

He was even more handsome, more charming, more…everything than her dreams. If Bailey would allow herself to fall in love, the one guy who had a remote chance of winning her heart was Brice. He was the only man she had ever let close enough to kiss her like he had. The only man she'd wanted to kiss in return. He tasted like the most delectable delicacy she'd ever eaten and smelled even better.

Breathing deep, she could almost smell his scent and it made her heart ache.

Straightening in her seat, Bailey also straightened her resolve. She had no business getting involved in a relationship with any man and, in particular, that handsome fun-loving cowboy.

Brice could derail her career plans faster than anyone else she'd ever met and she wasn't about to let that happen. She'd worked too long and too hard to get where she was and she wasn't going to let a silly little thing like love get in the way.

"Love?" Bailey said, whipping up her head and startling the man sitting next to her. He gave her a disgruntled look and returned to reading a magazine.

Love? Where had that thought come from? There was no reasonable explanation for the emotions bringing threatening tears to her eyes or the ache to her stomach. What Bailey failed to take into account was that love has a way of being completely unreasonable.

Trying to analyze her feelings and thoughts, Bailey acknowledged she was attracted to Brice. Extremely attracted. He was everything she wasn't - outgoing, charming, spontaneous, fun, exciting. It also didn't hurt that his eyes sparkled with life and mischief, or his teeth gleamed white against his tan face. She tried to block out the vision of his hard, tight muscles and strong chin. Brice was tall, virile, and hands-down, the most delicious smelling male she'd ever encountered.

Letting thoughts roll around in her mind, Bailey came to the conclusion that her feelings were the culmination of too much stimulus from the weekend. Between the fairy-tale wedding, accidentally getting drunk, and the atmosphere of the ranch that seemed to ooze with romance, she allowed herself to get caught up in the moment.

It had nothing to do with being swept into Brice's strong arms. Nothing at all.

Leaning back against the seat and relaxing, Bailey decided if she continually reminded herself it was the circumstances and not the man causing her to have romantic notions maybe she'd be able to convince herself it was true.

Reflecting over her day, Bailey arose that morning determined to get away from Brice as fast as possible. After their kisses by the pond yesterday afternoon, she knew the more time she spent with the man, the harder it was going to be to push him away.

Borrowing Cady's car, she drove to her meeting with the director of the John Day Fossil Beds. The appointment went very well. So well, in fact, Bailey was offered the opportunity to come join the team.

Looking over the samples they collected, touring through their museum and lab, as well as visiting a few of the areas where they were working, Bailey knew she wanted to take the position.

Forcing herself not to clap her hands with excitement, she was giddy thinking about the work she could accomplish in Oregon. Comprised of three separate units, there were more than 700 fossil localities in the John Day Fossil Beds. Work was ongoing with the plant and animal fossils as well as the ancient soil and rock samples.

Bailey knew researchers from around the world worked with the paleontology staff there because the fossil plant resources of eastern Oregon were some of the most abundant and diverse to be found anywhere.

This was an opportunity her career couldn't afford to miss. She'd just have to figure out a way to stay far away from Brice.

Telling herself again that her feelings for the engaging man were a temporary loss of common sense, she knew by the time she returned to Grass Valley in a month he'd have long forgotten about her. That would make it much easier for her to avoid falling into the temptation that was Brice Morgan.

Instead of going home with her family to Denver Thursday then heading back to Las Vegas to work next week, Bailey switched her ticket to fly directly into Las Vegas that afternoon.

As the plane landed, Bailey had everything planned out. Taking a taxi to the room she was renting, she changed her clothes, gathered her work gear, and drove north to the fossil site where she'd spent the past several months working. The last thing she needed was to spend time alone with her thoughts, so she jumped back into work full force.

She spoke with the project director and let him know she planned to leave in two weeks. Bailey would drive to Denver, spend time with her family before Sierra went back to school to finish her master's degree, then drive on to Oregon.

What Bailey failed to take into account as she completed her work in Las Vegas was Brice's persistent pursuit of her. It was bad enough she couldn't get him out of her thoughts during the day, but at night she was in misery. She could smell his scent and hear his voice, longing for his presence.

The first week she returned to Las Vegas he left her a voice message every single day. He also sent her multiple texts and emails, none of which she returned.

Her resistance began to wane during the second week and by the time she arrived in Denver, she was desperate to see him. Pulling up at her parent's home in a secluded neighborhood, she parked her Jeep around back and snuck in the patio door. The house was cool and welcoming and smelled like pumpkin pie, her favorite.

Following the sound of voices in the kitchen, she walked in and surprised both her mom and Sierra.

"Hey, did you bake that for me?" Bailey asked, draping her arm around her mother's shoulders.

"Bailey, honey!" Mary said, hugging her daughter to her flour-coated apron.

Sierra gave her an exuberant hug and grin. "We figured you'd show up at some point today and Mom wanted to make sure you knew we were glad to have you home."

"Thanks, I can't wait to have a piece," Bailey said, inhaling the scent of pumpkin as she leaned over the pie cooling on the counter. Going to the refrigerator, she poured herself a glass of juice and sat down at the table in the breakfast nook where a pile of open catalogs with marked pages alluded to the fact her mom and sister had been discussing fashion, hairstyles and all things feminine. Bailey enjoyed those conversations on occasion. Smiling, she picked up a catalog and was surprised by the number of things that caught her eye.

"We knew you'd like that one," Sierra said, flipping ahead a few pages and pointing to a dress that Bailey knew she had to have.

"I love it," Bailey said, devouring the rest of the catalog then starting at the cover again.

"I think we've lost her, Sie," Mary said, shaking her head although she was smiling at both her girls.

Bailey looked up and grinned, noticing not for the first time how much her mom and sister looked alike. She sometimes thought they seemed much more like sisters than mother and daughter. They were petite, vivacious and fun. Although Mary wore her hair in a very short style, she and Sierra shared the same shade of blue eyes, the same little dimple in their cheek when they smiled, the same ability to charm anyone.

Tall and strong, Bailey took after her dad, a professor at the University of Denver in the mathematics department. She knew her analytical way of looking at life came directly from him. Right now, she was calculating how long it would be before Sierra wanted to go out shopping, her mother offered to take her for a manicure, or they started questioning the last time she went on a date.

"Something came for you," Sierra said, handing Bailey a small box. Sierra barely restrained herself from tearing it open, wanting to know what was in the box she was sure Brice sent to Bailey.

Reading a Grass Valley postmark, Bailey assumed it was from one of the Thompson cousins. She didn't know why they'd mail her something when she'd be seeing them in another week. Trey and Cady, along with Travis, invited her to stay with them at the ranch house for as long as she wanted. Since the area where she'd be starting her work with the fossil beds was less than an hour from their house, she liked the idea.

Rather than trying to find somewhere to rent or staying in a tent, she'd have a lovely room and private bath all to herself. Bailey also liked the idea of getting to know her Grass Valley family better.

Pulling a knife from her pocket, making Sierra roll her eyes, she cut the tape on the box edges and opened it to find a narrow box about four inches long. Opening the lid, she took out a beautifully carved needle case. Acorns adorned both ends while the center was smooth and tapered. Unscrewing an acorn, she opened the case to find a piece of paper tucked inside. Tipping it up, she finally caught the edge of the paper and tugged it out.

Unrolling the small sheet on the table, she was surprised to see the words were brief:

Bailey,
Thought this would give you some place to keep the needles you use for your wicked stitchery. Miss you.
Your friend,
Brice

Bailey felt heat flame into her cheeks and she quickly folded the note, shoving it in her pocket.

"Who's it from?" her mother asked, picking up an acorn and examining the fine craftsmanship and detail.

"Brice," Bailey said, picking up the needle case and admiring the work. Turning it around and around in her hand, she noticed a tiny "BM" that could only mean Brice made it. She had no idea he could work with wood, let alone create something so delicately perfect. If this was an example of his work, he was an extremely talented artist.

Feeling guilty for not returning any of his messages and ignoring him the last few weeks, she assumed he'd given up because she hadn't received a single text, email or call for the last three days.

Loathe to admit it, she looked forward to his texts, which usually were witty one-liners, and his emails that shared a line or two about his day and asked about hers. What she liked the most were the voice mails he left. She could sit and listen to his voice all day and never get tired of hearing it. As much as she knew she shouldn't, she saved every one of his calls and listened to them over and over again.

"When did this come?" Bailey finally asked, holding the needle case reverently in her hand with a look on her face that had both her mom and sister sending each other knowing glances.

"Today," Sierra said, wondering how Brice knew Bailey's one seemingly normal activity was needlework. She embroidered beautiful pillow cases, table cloths and curtains that left Mary and Sierra wondering how a girl who dug in rocks and dirt for a living could create such delicate, dainty stitches. One year for Christmas, she'd made them both embroidered duvets with matching shams. If Bailey's head wasn't buried in a book about people who'd died thousands of years ago, she could often be found stitching on some project.

"Today?" Bailey asked, her voice high pitched and wavering. Unless it had been lost in the mail, Brice must have just sent it. Grabbing the box, she checked the postmark. Three days. He mailed it three days ago. Maybe he hadn't given up on her yet. "Does he know I'm going to be in Grass Valley?"

"Not that I'm aware of," Mary said, frowning at Bailey. "You yourself begged Trey and Travis to keep it a secret. I don't know why you think that's necessary. He'll find out you're there soon enough. Good gracious, between his sister dating Travis and his friendship with your cousins, he's at the house a good deal of the time. Why is it you're so set on avoiding him?"

"I'm not trying to avoid him," Bailey said, refusing to make eye contact with her mom. "Brice creates an unnecessary divergence from the diligent attention that is essential in furthering my paleontology endeavors."

"So you can't keep your mind on your work with the cute cowboy in your thoughts. Is it his smile, that luscious scent or the way he looks in Wranglers that has you so distracted?" Sierra teased with a sassy tilt of her head. Turning to her mother, she grinned. "Told you, Mom."

"Told Mom what?" Bailey asked, clearly annoyed with her sister.

"That you have a thing for Brice," Sierra said in a sing song voice as she jumped away from Bailey's swatting hand.

"That's positively ludicrous."

"Positively," Sierra grinned, sitting back down at the table. "Why don't you just admit you're as attracted to him as he apparently is to you. There could be worse things in the world than having a really nice, unbelievably good-looking guy want to spend time with you."

"Yes, there is," Bailey said, indignant at the direction the conversation had taken. "You could be unemployed because you let a man and your infatuation with him thwart your career."

"Why can't you have both, honey?" Mary asked as she started gathering up the pile of catalogs, handing Bailey the one she liked. "Why does it have to be a career or love? Why can't you have both?"

"Because I can't, that's why," Bailey said, getting up from the table and gathering the box, her needle case, and the catalog. "I'm married to my career, in love with my chosen profession and passionate about my work. That should be sufficient for anyone. Love and romance are for those without aspirations of importance."

"You mean delusions of grandeur," Sierra said quietly under her breath. Just not quiet enough that her sister didn't hear.

"I refuse to…"

"That's enough, both of you. Sometimes the two of you act like you're still in grade school," Mary said, flustered. Bailey got the most ridiculous ideas and once they were in her head, it was nearly impossible to get her to change her mind. Maybe Ross could talk some sense into her about balancing a career and a relationship. "Now both of you go change into something pretty. When your father gets home, we're going out to eat. No arguments. Move it."

Watching her two girls walk down the hallway, bantering with each other, Mary smiled. Poor Brice had a long battle ahead if he thought he could win Bailey's heart. She hoped he was up to the challenge.

Chapter Four

"Who bravely dares must sometimes risk a fall."
Tobias G. Smollett

"Do you think she said yes?" Brice asked Trent as they sat in the front yard of the Triple T Ranch, drinking iced tea and enjoying the warm September evening.

Tomorrow they planned to finish up the last of the haying at the Running M Ranch, but for tonight, Brice and Ben were hanging out with the Thompsons at the Triple T waiting to find out if Tess accepted Travis' marriage proposal.

"Do you think he worked up the nerve to ask?" Trent asked instead of answering Brice's question. "From recent experience, I can honestly say I'd rather go to the dentist and get six root canals without deadener than go through that again."

A slap on his arm from his wife made Trent cringe with feigned pain. "You don't have to beat me to death, princess."

"You just hush up, cowboy, and keep your opinions to yourself," Lindsay said, sitting back in her chair.

Travis was a basket case of nerves most of the day. Cady made an elaborate chocolate dessert with ribbons of chocolate on top where Travis hid the engagement ring. Lindsay helped arrange flowers and ironed a tablecloth while Cass gathered up every candle she could find.

With the help of a couple of the ranch hands, Travis hauled the cake, china and glassware as well as the candles and flowers down to the fort where the Thompson and Morgan kids used to play. It was there that Travis first kissed Tess when he was six and fell in love with the sweet girl, so he decided it was the perfect place to propose.

Glancing at his watch in the fading light, Brice looked at Ben who shrugged his shoulders and laughed at something Trey said.

Trent got up and walked to the edge of the yard, looking in the direction of the fort. "Maybe one of us should go see if they're okay. Trav still isn't back at a hundred percent with those legs of his. What if he rolled the four-wheeler or something?"

"If he had, Tess would have called on her cell or come back to the house to get us. Sit down and stop your worrying," Lindsay said, shaking her head at Trent. Her husband was the peacemaker of the family, which meant he was also the one who worried about the health and well-being of everyone.

Abandoning plans to be a vet, Trent returned to the ranch along with Trey, who had aspirations of being a history professor, when their father suddenly passed away of a heart attack more than seven years ago. The ranch had thrived and prospered under their joint efforts and now that Travis was home after six years in the service, the three brothers purchased the adjoining ranch with ambitious plans for expansion.

It seemed they were expanding their family as well as their acreage since Trey and Trent both took brides in the last eight months and Travis had plans to wed Tess as soon as she would agree to marry him.

They sat visiting for another twenty minutes before Trent took out his phone and called Travis. "Did she say yes?"

Apparently the answer was affirmative because Trent pumped his fist in the air. "Okay, see you in a bit."

All conversation ceased as they waited for the report.

"It looks like there's going to be another wedding," Trent said with a broad grin.

"Awesome. I always knew those two would wind up together," Brice said, getting up to shake Trent's hand, then Trey's. "We grew up like brothers and now it's going to be official."

"Did he give you any details?" Cady asked, wanting to know when the lovebirds planned to get married. She and Trey took an entire week from the time he proposed to the time they exchanged vows while Trent and Lindsay spent the summer planning their wedding.

"Nope, but he said they'll be back soon," Trent said, pulling Lindsay out of her chair and swinging her around.

"Trent, you're going to make me dizzy," Lindsay said, clutching his arms as she laughed. "Let me go."

"Never, but I will put you down," Trent teased, returning Lindsay to her chair.

The headlights of a four wheeler soon illuminated the yard and everyone jumped up to hug both Tess and Travis. After Tess spent the last two months at the house every day helping Travis with his physical therapy, everyone felt like she already belonged there.

Cady and Lindsay were admiring Tess' ring and the guys were slapping each other on the back good naturedly when they noticed headlights coming down their long drive.

Trey and Cady gave each other a knowing look before glancing at Brice.

A Jeep none of them recognized pulled up by the mud room door and in the dim light it was hard to make out any details. As the person stepped around the corner of the house into the front yard, Brice, who had been hugging

Tess, slowly dropped his hands from his sister and felt his legs tremble.

Bailey.

She'd come back.

"Hey, everyone," Bailey said, taking in the group collectively, but quickly noticing Brice. He stood gaping at her with wide eyes, like he was seeing a ghost. Choosing to ignore the voice in her head that demanded she rush over and fall into his arms, she instead tried to sound casual. "I'm sensing an overwhelming amount of excitement in the air. What's going on?"

"Tess and Travis just got engaged," Cady said, stepping forward and giving Bailey a hug. While they were close she whispered in her ear. "No one told Brice, just like you asked, but this is quite a shock to him."

"I see that," Bailey whispered, not realizing how hurtful her actions would be to Brice. First she completely ignored his attempts to reach out to her. Then she failed to acknowledge the wonderful gift he sent. To add insult to injury, she refused to let anyone tell him she was coming back to Grass Valley for an extended stay. It was obvious to anyone looking that Brice felt betrayed and angry.

Knowing now was not the time or place to apologize to Brice, she turned to give Travis and Tess affectionate hugs and offer her congratulations.

"When will you two be exchanging nuptials?" Bailey asked as she made the appropriate comments over Tess' lovely ring.

"The second Saturday in October," Tess said with a warm smile brightening eyes that were a darker shade of brown than Brice's.

"What?" Cady and Lindsay asked in unison. That was just a month away.

"We don't want to wait long," Travis said, kissing Tess on the cheek as he squeezed her hand. They shared a private look that said a month was going to seem like forever. "We'd like to get married at the fort with just family and then have a reception at the Running M. Tess thought the barn would be an ideal place for a big party. Does that sound okay?"

"That sounds great, Trav," Trey said, thumping his youngest brother on the back. Tess had been an unofficial sister since they all played together as rowdy youngsters. Trey was thrilled she would finally be part of their family, especially when she was so good for Travis. If not for her gentle love and encouragement, he didn't know what would have happened to Travis when he refused assistance in dealing with his post-traumatic stress disorder. Because of her, Travis finally decided he needed help and had been making remarkable strides in his recovery. "Do you plan to live here at the ranch or do we need to see about fixing up the Drexel house?"

"If none of you object, we'd like to live at the Drexel house. I think one set of honeymooners per house is plenty and Trey and Cady had first dibs on the ranch house. It makes sense for the two of you to stay here, especially since Cady feeds us all," Travis said, making Cady blush and Trey grin. "I thought we could go over tomorrow and see what we can do between now and the wedding."

The three Thompson brothers purchased the neighboring Drexel ranch right before Trent's wedding. It increased their property to the south and also gave them the opportunity to present Lindsay with the house she'd rented from Mr. Drexel for the past three years as a wedding gift. She and Trent loved the little cottage home located just a few miles down the road. Mr. Drexel had used it as houing for his ranch foreman before turning it into a rental.

Another half-mile past their house was a long driveway that wound up to the Drexel farmhouse. Talking excitedly, the Thompsons all agreed to meet there early the next morning.

In a matter of minutes, Brice found himself standing alone in the yard with Bailey. Dressed in cargo pants and a T-shirt with well-worn hiking boots, she looked gorgeous to him. A profusion of her hair fell in finger-tempting waves and curls around her face, making Brice shove his hands in pockets to keep from reaching out to feel the silky strands between his rough fingers.

In the past month, he replayed every moment they spent together, recalled every taste of her lips, and hungered to hold her in his arms again. At night, she haunted his dreams wearing the turquoise sun dress she had on the last time he saw her. The dress made her eyes an even more brilliant shade of ocean blue while accenting her lovely assets.

He fantasized about running his fingers through all her thick honey-gold curls and kissing every inch of her heart-shaped face. On more than one occasion, he found himself sniffing his mother's tea, just to bring to mind Bailey's unique fragrance.

Finding a website where she regularly contributed blog posts, he stared at the photo of her dressed in khaki shorts, a white tank top and hiking boots with a ridiculously ugly hat hiding her beautiful curls. He read every single thing she'd written even though most of it was a bunch of technical lingo that meant nothing to him. It somehow made him feel closer to her.

When she didn't return his calls, texts and emails, he wasn't overly concerned. He spent his free time hand-carving the needle case and shipped it to Denver where Mary assured him Bailey would eventually stop by.

Hoping the gift would be an incentive for her to at least send him a word of thanks, he wasn't surprised when he heard nothing from her. After all, he wasn't sure when she'd be in Denver again.

To see her standing in the yard at the Triple T, acting like she'd never left, never ignored him, never pretended what happened between them was nothing, he was angry. And hurt. Not only had she kept her return from him, she'd obviously asked the Thompson clan to keep him in the dark as well.

Part of him wanted to walk off and never see the infuriating woman again. The other part - the spontaneous, caring, loving part of Brice - wanted to hold her close and never let her go.

"Brice, I..." Bailey said, taking a step toward him, wary of the cold look in his usually warm brown eyes. Unable to convince herself Brice meant nothing to her when she hadn't seen or talked to him for weeks, it was impossible to do so when he stood an arms-length away, strong and handsome, smelling so good. As hard as she'd tried, she couldn't forget the way he filled out his jeans and shirts to perfection, the way his hair begged for her fingers to run through it, the way the sound of his voice made warmth pool in her middle.

Knowing what she needed to do, Bailey squared her shoulders and took a deep breath. "I owe you an apology."

"You do?" Brice asked sarcastically, his jaw rigid as he tried to fight down his anger. "What would that be for, Miss Bishop? Maybe for ignoring my text messages, phone calls or emails. Or did you not receive any of those?"

Bailey had the grace to blush with embarrassment.

"Maybe it was for the gift I sent. I understand if you didn't care for it, but most people would at least say thank you or return it," Brice said, glaring at her through narrowed eyes. He hadn't moved since she approached him, but every muscle was tight and tense as he stared her down. "Or maybe you feel the need to apologize for asking my closest friends to keep your impending arrival a secret. It certainly couldn't be the way you took the friendship I offered, ground it under your heel and threw it in my face."

Brice sighed and swiped his hand over his face. "I guess I'm the one who should apologize. I'm sorry for bothering you, for thinking you might like me enough to treat me with even the most basic amount of decency. You've made your feelings toward me clear, so I'm done, Bailey. Goodbye."

Brice turned and stalked off toward his pickup. Bailey watched him go, knowing she should let him walk away, let him walk out of her life, but something in her wouldn't let her do it. Before he reached the corner of the house, she was beside him, her hand on his arm, looking into his face with regret and a little fear.

"Brice, I'm sorry. It was unforgivably rude of me to ignore your efforts at friendship and I realized as soon as I got here how wrong it was not to tell you I was coming," Bailey said, trying to keep her thoughts in order while fire zipped through her fingers where her hand made contact with Brice's skin. She'd tried to forget the electrical charge that snapped between them any time they got near each other. It was back in full force. "It was selfish and cruel and I'm sincerely sorry."

Brice continued to glare at her but he didn't make any effort to leave. She took that as a positive sign.

Opening a pocket on the side of her pants, she drew something out and placed it in Brice's hand. He glanced down to see the needle case he'd sent her. Raising his head, he gave her a quizzical look.

"I love the case, Brice. Not only is it a thing of beauty, but one of purpose," Bailey said, growing breathless. Since she opened the box and discovered the case from Brice, she'd kept it with her, either in a pocket or her purse, and took it out often to feel the smooth wood in her hand, envisioning Brice's calloused fingers carving it. "You are a very talented artist."

"It was nothing," Brice said, extremely pleased she liked the gift, but still curious why she hadn't said anything. She certainly knew how to get in touch with him if she'd wanted to.

"It is something, Brice. Something lovely and thoughtful and very much appreciated," Bailey said, taking the case from his hand and returning it to her pocket. "It was wrong of me not to thank you sooner, but I'm saying it now. Thank you for a wonderful gift."

With Bailey's fingers searing through his skin, her fragrance enveloping him, and the glow of her eyes drawing him in, Brice was finding it difficult to hang on to his anger.

"I don't think that quite cuts it," Brice said, trying to appear disappointed and mad. It was hard to do when he was lost in her eyes, drunk on her perfume, entranced by the sound of her voice. Reaching up he brushed a lock of her side swept bangs from her eyes before lightly tracing the contour of her cheek.

Bailey looked at him confused, so he took a step closer, leaving just a breath of space between them. "I'm going to need a more elaborate gesture of gratitude before I accept either your apology or your thanks."

"What do you have in mind? I can cook a little. Do you want some cookies? I could crochet you a potholder or embroidery something for you," Bailey said running down her mental list of things she could do for Brice to show her gratitude. "I've got a fossil or two I might be willing to part with."

"That won't be necessary," he said, putting first one work-worn hand then the other around her waist, pulling her to his chest. "A kiss would be sufficient."

"Oh," Bailey said, realization dawning that Brice was teasing her. The conclusion that one kiss couldn't hurt, combined with her desperation to feel his lips on hers, forced her to quickly agree. "Just one, though."

Brice lowered his head to hers. His lips moved against hers softly at first, then rapidly changed to demanding and soon Bailey was lost in his arms, in the kiss, in the heat sucking her into a place where only she and Brice existed.

When he finally lifted his head, Bailey put her hands around his neck, drawing him back toward her wanting mouth, but he resisted.

Brice cocked one eyebrow and gave her a look she couldn't interpret, but his eyes no longer looked quite so angry. "You said just one."

Trying to find her mental footing as her breathing returned to normal, Bailey admitted to herself she needed many more kisses from Brice. One would never do. She'd been kidding herself for the past month if she thought the wedding and her inadvertent inebriation had been the cause of her attraction to Brice.

The man himself was the attraction, there was no denying it.

Brice released her and turned back toward his truck, walking away from her. Bailey felt bereft and abandoned as she stared at his retreating form, registering exactly how good he looked wearing his boots, Wranglers, and a cotton shirt.

Hating the tears that stung the backs of her eyes, she realized Brice was going to get in his truck, drive away, and there was nothing she could do about it.

"Brice, please don't leave," she said, frozen in place by her fear of rejection. It was a new and disturbing feeling for her. Not getting what she wanted was something completely foreign to Bailey. She had always been able to decide what she wanted, determine the best way to get it, and make it happen. With Brice, though, her careful reasoning and cool approach were not going to work. In fact, it seemed to have the opposite effect. "Please, don't go."

As he continued walking toward his truck, Bailey resigned herself to living the rest of her life with the memory of that last sizzling kiss. Turning toward the house, she was nearly to the door of the mud room when Brice swept her into his arms, raining kisses on her cheeks and down her neck.

"I missed you so much, sugar," Brice said in a raspy voice near her ear, making shivers work their way from her toes to her head. "Don't run away from me again. I don't think I can take it. At least give me a proper goodbye."

Bailey nodded her head in agreement and pulled Brice's lips to hers for another kiss.

"Forgive me?" she asked, kissing his chin, then the mole beneath his bottom lip. She'd dreamed of kissing it dozens of times in the last month.

"Yes, but I'm still plenty mad at you," Brice said, setting her back on her feet. "You might have to put a little effort into absolving your transgressions."

Bailey didn't have a lot of practice at acting repentant and making up with people when her behavior caused problems. Her mom and Sierra were easily appeased with a shopping trip or a visit to the nail salon. She and her dad had an unspoken understanding and could apologize without uttering a word. Other than Nana and her father's mother, she had very few people she cared enough about to keep appeased.

Until now. Until Brice.

"I'm truly and deeply sorry, Brice," Bailey said sincerely, without any idea on how to make things right. She decided to be honest with the man who still had his arms around her, holding her close. "I'm terrible at relationships. I don't know the first thing about doing this right with you and I tend to be distracted by my work. You may have noticed, but I'm really good at ignoring people when I feel they may interfere with my concentration and I'm not very good at being wrong or sorry."

"I'll help you work on that," Brice said, nuzzling her ear. Bailey knew for a fact she'd never experienced such an exciting tingling sensation. She thought her toes might actually curl in her boots.

"I might like that," Bailey whispered, leaning into Brice and raising her lips to his again. He met her passion head on and they were once again lost in their kiss.

"Get a room, bro," Ben teased as he slapped Brice on the back and wiggled an eyebrow at his brother.

Bailey blushed and took a quick step away from Brice, who stood glaring at his brother and shaking his head.

"We need to head home, lover boy. We've got all that hay that needs baled and stacked tomorrow, you know," Ben said, walking to Brice's pickup. Brice forgot Ben was even at the ranch once Bailey arrived. Ben was lucky Brice hadn't given in to his initial impulse to drive off mad. Tess was around somewhere with Travis and could have given Ben a ride home. Eventually.

Still blushing, Bailey turned to go up the steps into the mud room, but Brice caught her hand. "Bailey, can I see you tomorrow? It'll be late, but maybe we can go for a drive or something after dinner."

"That would be satisfactory," Bailey said, returning to her formal manner of speech. When she was in Brice's arms, she forgot about being an uptight professional in the science community. She was just a woman being held by a man she liked more than any she'd ever met.

Brice grinned and kissed the back of her hand, in an old-fashioned yet endearing gesture.

"Tomorrow, then."

Ben started the pickup and turned on the lights, so Brice ran across the yard and jumped in the truck, waving at Bailey through the open window.

Watching the tail lights go down the drive, Bailey rolled her lips together. She knew she should have let

Brice stay angry with her and continued ignoring him, but one look at his handsome face, at the hurt in his eyes, and she couldn't do it. As much as her head was telling her to run, her heart was telling her to stay and enjoy every minute of being with Brice.

Chapter Five

"It is never too late to fall in love."
Sandy Wilson

Two pickups drove up the long graveled driveway of the former Drexel ranch and parked in front of the big farm house.

Tess arrived early at the Triple T that morning and joined the family for breakfast. So excited about the engagement and the house, she had barely slept and no one seemed surprised when she gave a perfunctory knock on the kitchen door at half-past six, anxious to go see what would soon be her home.

As soon as the dishes were done, they piled into Trey's pickup and drove to the house, meeting Trent and Lindsay there. One of the ranch hands was keeping tabs on Cass, deciding they could get a better idea of what needed done without the lively child under foot.

Travis helped Tess out of the pickup while Trey assisted Cady, then offered his hand to Bailey.

Although Bailey had no intention of going with them this morning to explore the Drexel house, they all insisted she come. Tess, who shared Bailey's love of 1940s fashions and styles, thought Bailey would have fun seeing the farmhouse which Trey said was built in 1943.

Standing in the yard looking at the house, it appeared to be in great shape. A new roof and paint job had been completed in the past year, giving the house a fresh, clean look.

Tess grasped Travis' hand and squeezed as they gazed at the light gray two-story house with crisp white trim. Wide steps led up to an angled porch with doors to both the right and left. Fishing a key from his jeans pocket, Travis unlocked the door on the left and they all walked into a light and airy living room with two banks of big windows. A brick fireplace filled one corner, but it was the antique furniture that caught Bailey's eye. A chair in need of upholstery appeared to be in good shape, along with two occasional tables and a vintage lamp.

"Did Mr. Drexel leave a lot of furniture?" Bailey asked, running her hand across the smooth wood of the fireplace mantel.

"Some, it appears," Travis said, looking around the room. "I don't think any of us have been in the house since he moved out. We've been a little busy with other things."

"Oh, like what?" Trey asked, thumping Travis on the back as they turned a corner into the dining room where a huge table with eight chairs sat in the early morning light. A door there led back out to the porch. "A wedding, harvest, school starting, someone needing physical therapy for two months. Is that what you mean?"

"Oh, hush, boss-man, and quit teasing," Cady said, taking Trey's hand in hers. He wrapped his arm around her waist and kissed her cheek, making Lindsay and Tess smile.

From the dining room they wandered into a spacious kitchen that had been recently updated with tile floors, granite countertops and new appliances. A small island offered a well thought-out design of additional cupboard and counter space while bar stools were tucked under one side, offering a place for two to sit and eat.

To the right of the kitchen was a room that would be perfect for an office with a built in set of cupboards all along one wall and a small closet. It also had an outside entry onto the porch where it ended on the side of the house.

Going back down a short hallway, they found a large coat closet across from the stairs and a small guest bathroom. A few steps more down the hall was a utility room. Mr. Drexel must have needed the washer and dryer because the room sat empty.

"His new place must not have included all appliances," Travis said, looking across the hall into what appeared to be a mud room. There was plenty of space to plug in a freezer next to a large closet boasting both rods and shelves. A rack with hooks and pegs graced the wall by the door that opened into a two car garage.

"I won't have to park outside in the rain or snow. No more scraping windows," Tess said, excited at the thought or parking in the garage.

"I'd scrape them for you, honeybee, should the need arise," Travis said, running his hand across her shoulder.

Bailey ignored the look of love and adoration that passed between Travis and his bride-to-be. Public displays of affection made her uncomfortable and unsettled. People should be able to show restraint around others.

On the heels of that thought, Bailey recalled the way she'd behaved with Brice, on more than one occasion, out in the open at the Triple T where anyone could watch. Feeling her neck heat as she recalled their ardent kisses, Bailey quickly changed her focus to the group sauntering down the hall in front of her.

They entered the master suite which was an addition to the original house. It was roomy and the women all let out a gasp of surprise to see a beautiful antique bed set, including a king-sized four-poster bed with finely carved posts, a large dresser with an ornate mirror and a chest of drawers. The mattress was missing from the bed, but they would have purchased a new one for it anyway.

"Oh, wow!" Tess said, gently touching the warm cherry wood of the headboard. "I can't believe he left this behind."

"We can get something new, honeybee, if you'd rather," Travis said, knowing his fiancé would want to keep every stick of furniture in the house because she preferred the antiques to modern styles.

While the guys checked out the access from the room to the porch, the girls oohed and aahed over the large walk-in closet and the spa-like bathroom with a garden tub and huge shower.

"Are you sure neither one of you wants this house?" Tess asked, looping her arms with Cady and Lindsay as they walked down the hallway toward the stairs.

"Nope, it's all yours," Lindsay said with a smile. She loved her little cottage home, especially now that she shared it with Trent..

"I'm perfectly happy where I am," Cady said, sending Trey a private look as he came back in the door, which earned her a wink.

"Let's check out the upstairs, then," Tess said, leading the way up the steps to the second floor where they found three more bedrooms, two bathrooms and a large room that Travis said was definitely going to be his man cave. A fireplace occupied one corner and a door led out to a small balcony.

"None of that girlie stuff in here," Travis said, already envisioning a big screen television with overstuffed chairs.

"Whatever you want, Tee," Tess said, giving him a warm smile as she used her nickname for him. She knew Travis would let her decorate the house however she wanted, so she was more than happy to have one room be his domain.

"You, mostly," Travis whispered in her ear as they walked out of the room. He gave her a swat on the bottom as the girls decided to investigate the attic and the guys went to check the foundation and locate the well so they could have the water tested.

While the men clattered down the stairs and went outside, Tess located the string to pull down the attic stairs in the closet of one of the bedrooms.

The stairs creaked and groaned as they unfolded, but looked sturdy enough. The girls climbed up the steps chatting and laughing. Stepping into the room, they didn't have time to look around or even get their bearings as feathered beasts squawked and flapped their wings around their heads.

Surprised, the girls all screamed and ducked.

Bailey was thoroughly impressed with the speed her three cousins generated tearing back into the house and up two flights of stairs to rescue their women.

"What's wrong, princess?" Trent asked, the first of the men to come up the stairs, with Trey and Travis right behind him.

The winged terrors turned out to be starlings that had taken over the attic with nests. As terrified as the women had been, their screams turned to hysterical fits of laughter when the birds escaped through a hole in the window. Only Bailey had regained enough sense to speak as the men looked around the attic, expecting to find blood and destruction.

"My summation of the situation is that the birds discovered entry into the space through that hole in the window and set about to create an indoor living environment," Bailey said, pointing to a corner where evidence of the birds' activities was hard to miss. "Protective of their nests, it seems they took us for a threat and proceeded to flog us."

The three men, hands on their knees trying to catch their breath and calm their racing hearts, turned to see Tess, Cady and Lindsay hold each other up as tears of laughter streaked down their faces.

Glad the girls were fine, Trey and Travis took longer to find the humor in the situation than good-natured Trent.

Bailey ignored them all and looked around the space, taking in the pieces of furniture that were in excellent condition, old paintings, pieces of pottery from the Art Deco period, boxes of old books, and steamer trunks.

Going to a trunk, she unlatched the leather straps and opened the lid to reveal a cache of clothes.

"Tess, come look at this," Bailey called, knowing Tess would go wild for the vintage fashions.

"Oh, gracious," Tess said, sinking down by Bailey as they pulled out dresses from the forties and fifties along with hats, gloves and even a few handbags.

"She'll be here all day playing with those clothes," Travis grumbled, but couldn't hide the grin on his face, pleased that Tess had treasures to sort through. "I'm going to go call someone about fixing that window, then we better head over to the Running M."

While Travis made the phone call, Trent and Trey found a piece of cardboard to cover the window and tacked it into place then removed the bird nests.

Meeting back outside, Travis, Trent and Trey climbed into Trent's truck, along with Tess, to go to the Morgan ranch while Cady, Lindsay and Bailey returned to the Triple T.

"Won't Tess need her car?" Bailey asked as they headed opposite directions once they reached the highway.

"One of us will take it over later," Cady said, driving Trey's big pickup back to the ranch house. She'd come a long way in the year since she'd moved to Grass Valley from her job as an assistant to a big-shot Seattle attorney where she'd never seen a cowboy, driven anything with a stick-shift or even owned a pet before. "Michele called this morning and invited us all for a barbecue tonight so we'll make some food to take over. You'll go with us, won't you, Bailey?"

"Certainly," Bailey said, looking forward to seeing Brice. She wondered if the Running M Ranch looked like the Triple T, with lots of outbuildings and a big ranch house. "May I be of assistance in the preparation of the food?"

"Sure," Cady said, grinning at Lindsay who found Bailey's formal mode of speech entertaining. Lindsay was a school teacher who spent her days talking to kids who were five and six.

"What are you planning?" Bailey asked as they walked into the kitchen.

"I thought we could..." Cady was interrupted by Cass flying in the back door followed by her dog, Buddy.

"Mama, guess what?" Cass said, launching her active little body toward Cady.

"Cassidy Marie! You get that dog out of here right now. You know the rules," Cady said, pushing Cass toward the door and pointing at the dog. Buddy barked and followed Cass outside.

"No pets in the house?" Bailey asked and Lindsay nodded, trying to hide her smile. Given the opportunity, Cass would sleep with the gangly dog Trent found at Lindsay's house and rehabilitated from a homeless thief to a loyal family dog. Cass loved playing with the dog even more than her fairy dolls or riding her pony, Smokey. The other two ranch dogs, Bob and Bonnie, were also good playmates just not quite as well-loved by Cass as Buddy.

Never that interested in having a pet, although Sierra had several through the years, Bailey didn't want the responsibility of caring for one. She didn't dislike animals and sometimes enjoyed playing with them, she just didn't want to be the primary caregiver of a living thing. Seeing Cass' adoration of the dog stirred something soft and tender in Bailey's heart.

Looking out the door, she saw Cass pat Buddy on the head and talk to him before running back in the mud room and kicking off her shoes. Hooks for chore coats, bins of gloves, pegs for hats and shelves for boots and shoes lined the entry wall of the mud room. Bailey realized Cady kept the house so clean because the guys weren't allowed to wear their boots inside.

"Mama, I forgotted about Buddy, but I took off my shoes," Cass said as she flew back into the kitchen, hugging Cady around the waist. "Tommy took me for a ride on his horse and we chased a cow and saw a hawk and I found another pretty rock."

"My goodness, you were busy while we were gone, weren't you?" Cady said, kissing Cass on the forehead and holding out her hand to admire the rock the little girl pulled from her pocket. The stone was shaped like a tear drop. "You'll have to put this in your treasure box."

"See, Aunt Lindsay," Cass said, taking the rock from Cady and handing it to Lindsay. "Isn't it pretty. Like a big lady's tear."

"It's very pretty, Cass," Lindsay said, passing the rock to Bailey to admire.

Bailey held it up to the light and made a show of examining the rock before bending down and giving it to the little redheaded girl who was bouncing off one foot to the other. In the short time she'd spent with the family, Bailey had noted Cass' inability to be still. She was a bouncing, jiggling, wiggling little ball of fire that chattered nonstop. From what Travis said, she even talked in her sleep.

Cass, who was orphaned just after Thanksgiving, would have become a foster child or left to an aunt that was even worse than her deadbeat alcoholic mother if the Thompsons hadn't stepped in. Trey and Cady, who was his housekeeper and cook at the time, decided they wanted to keep her and filed for joint custody. They not only got custody of the child, but wed soon after and proceeded to adopt her.

"Indeed, Cass, this is a very special rock. You should do like your mama said and put it with your collection," Bailey said with a serious expression on her face, positioning herself so she could talk to Cass eye to eye.

"Okay," Cass said, impulsively hugging Bailey before racing off to her room.

Unfamiliar with childish hugs, Bailey took a moment to savor the feel of tiny arms around her neck and the warm, sunshiny scent of a child. She discovered she rather enjoyed the moment.

"She's a lively child, isn't she?" Bailey said, turning her attention back to Lindsay and Cady.

"That's putting it nicely," Cady said with a grin. "She's a live wire who keeps us on our toes, but we love her."

Love seemed to be something that filled the Triple T ranch house right up to the rafter, Bailey mused as she washed her hands and helped Cady and Lindsay prepare food for lunch as well as the barbecue that evening. Love and a whole lot of laughter.

><><

Coming in for lunch hot and hungry, Brice washed up and sat down at the table with his parents, Ben, Tess, the three Thompson brothers, and the hired hands.

"I invited the girls and your hands for dinner," Michele said, directing her comment to Trey.

He looked up and smiled. "That's great. We'll make this last day of haying into a regular party."

"We deserve some kind of celebration after all this backbreaking work," Ben said, taking another serving of the chicken casserole Tess made for lunch.

"Going soft on us, city boy," Mike teased his oldest child, who spent most of his time in Portland where he worked for a barge company. Ben had been there long enough he'd worked his way up to a management position, coming home to help on the ranch when he had a spare weekend.

"Nope," Ben said, flexing his bicep and earning a raised eyebrow from his mother. "Just saying we have more than earned some fun at the end of this long grueling day of working for a slave-driver, old man."

Mike narrowed his gaze at Ben and Brice hid a chuckle, enjoying the family banter. He watched Travis wink at Tess and saw her cheeks pink at the attention. It was a good thing the two of them settled on a wedding date sooner rather than later. Knowing his best friend like he did, Brice was feeling the need to keep an eye on Travis until a ring was placed on Tess' finger.

Thinking about weddings and romance made his thoughts wander to Bailey. Looking at the three Thompson brothers across the table, he realized Bailey looked a little like her cousins. She definitely shared Trey's unusual turquoise blue eye color and thick, honey-gold hair. Although seeing those same traits on her created a whole different reaction for Brice.

Planning ahead for the evening, he smiled to himself wondering if he could get her alone out in the barn for a few minutes of stolen kisses. Only he hoped they'd be freely given.

"Whatever you're thinking about, you probably shouldn't be," Tess whispered, leaning near Brice. He felt his ears grow hot as he looked at his sister and she gave him a knowing grin. "Caught you daydreaming, didn't I?"

"I'm not admitting anything," Brice said, giving her a playful poke to her ribs, making her jump in her chair.

"Are you two ever going to grow up and act like adults?" Michele asked, watching her youngest offspring.

"Not if we can help it," Brice said, nudging Tess with his shoulder, making everyone laugh.

Heading back out to the hay fields after lunch, Trey called Cady, asking her to send over their crew so they could get the haying done before dinner time.

Finishing up with a few minutes to spare before Michele said the barbecue would begin, Brice hurried to the house to get a shower, shave and put on clean clothes. He slapped aftershave on his cheeks, ran a little gel through his hair and finger-combed in a wave then shook his head at his efforts to impress Bailey. Popping a breath strip in his mouth, he grinned at his reflection and ran out the door.

Going to the back yard where everyone would gather, Brice noticed Bailey with Cady, Lindsay and Cass. She wore a simple cotton dress in a deep shade of wine with ballet flats while her hair framed her face in soft curls.

Brice thought she was beautiful and took a moment to watch her interact with his family and hers. Although she was somewhat reserved, she wasn't shy, and laughed at something Cass said. Bending down, she let the little girl finger the stone on her necklace and answered her questions before patting Cass on the head and looking around.

Her eyes connected with Brice's and he felt himself pulled into the deep ocean of blue. Covering the expanse of yard between them with a few quick steps, he took her hand in his and kissed her cheek, making her blush.

"Hi," she said, looking at him with warmth in her gaze and her smile. Brice inhaled her unique scent and itched to run his fingers along her the column of her slender neck. Her lips were the same deep wine shade as her dress and he wondered if they'd taste sweet, like a ripe berry. He planned to find out before the evening was through.

"You look gorgeous," Brice whispered, leaning down so his lips were close to her ear. Although she tried to suppress it, a shiver of pleasure slid up her spine and she straightened, stiffening her posture until Brice placed a hand on her shoulder and gave it a gentle squeeze. "Did you enjoy your day?"

"Yes, I did," Bailey said, telling him about spending the day cooking with Cady and Lindsay. Lindsay mostly cut up vegetables and kept Cass out of the way, but Bailey learned a lot of tricks and tips from working with Cady. The woman was a wonder in the kitchen. "Did you know Cady thought about being a chef at one point in her career?"

"Yeah, I heard that. She would have been a great one, but I'm glad she moved here and married Trey instead. That way we all get to enjoy her cooking," Brice looked at the heavily laden table covered with tempting creations. "Did you make anything, sugar?"

"I did," Bailey said, glad that she was a good cook, when she wanted to be. It wasn't because of any particular desire or talent on her part. She followed recipes to the letter, and they always turned out because of it. It was a matter of measures and practical applications, after all.

"Well, what do I need to sample and then rave about?" Brice asked with a teasing smile, looking down at her with teeth flashing white against his tan. Bailey loved the way his forehead wrinkled when he smiled, like his entire face was genuinely pleased.

"Perhaps I'll let it be a mystery for you to unravel," Bailey said, folding her hands at her waist and swishing her skirt back and forth. It brushed against Brice's leg and made him think all kinds of crazy thoughts.

"I bet you I can figure it out," Brice said, giving Bailey a look of challenge, shoving his hands in his pockets to keep from running his fingers up the sides of her dress.

"I don't wager money," Bailey said, raising an eyebrow at Brice. Was he one of those people who gambled and did all sorts of addictive things? Somehow she knew he didn't.

"No money, sugar," Brice said, taking a step closer to her, sporting a cocky grin. "Something far more valuable."

"Like what?"

"Kisses," Brice said in such a deep, husky voice it made heat climb up Bailey's neck.

"Kisses, indeed, Mr. Morgan," Bailey said, smiling at his teasing, despite her efforts to look stern.

"I'm not kidding around, Ms. Bishop," Brice said, giving in to his desire to run his finger along her neck. The contact of his skin to hers made something pulse between them. "Kisses are serious business."

Unable to concentrate with Brice touching her neck more softly than she'd have thought possible with those big, calloused hands, Bailey nodded her head.

"So you agree?" Brice asked, his eyes intently fixed on hers.

"Yes," she said, thinking she'd agree to just about anything Brice said at that moment as his scent swept over her and she felt caressed by the warmth of his presence.

"Good," Brice said, breaking her gaze to look over the food table. "If I figure out what you brought, you have to give me three kisses."

"Three? That seems a bit excessive," Bailey said, keeping her voice steady, although she had to work hard to do it. If Brice had asked for a dozen, she'd have dropped enough hints he would figure out what she made and then happily delivered all twelve kisses.

"Come on," Brice said, grabbing her forearms and pulling her closer to him.

She placed her hands on his chest to both steady herself and keep a little distance between them. The feel of his muscles beneath her fingers did anything but steady her as her head swirled with ideas that had nothing to do with keeping away from Brice.

"Live a little. You can exact your own payment if I guess incorrectly."

"That puts a different perspective on this," Bailey said thoughtfully. "If I win you have to do whatever I ask of you for the rest of the evening."

"Deal," Brice said, lifting an eyebrow at her, pondering what she might ask. "Maybe I'll lose on purpose."

"You might not like what I ask of you. What if I ask you to keep Cass entertained or serenade everyone with old campfire songs? You could get garbage duty or be forced to clean up all the dishes by yourself."

"Not happening," Brice said, determined to win their bet. "Are you in?"

"I suppose so," Bailey said with resignation. "Otherwise you'll badger me until I agree."

"I don't badger anyone," Brice said, insulted and indignant.

"Since when?" Tess asked as she stepped beside them, giving Bailey a hug. "I love your dress, Bailey. Is it one from that website you told me about it?"

"Thank you, Tess. Yes it is," Bailey said, casting Brice a glance over her shoulder as Tess led her off talking about retro fashions.

His dad banged a knife on the galvanized tub filled with ice and bottled beverages, getting the attention of everyone there. He asked a blessing on the meal and thanked everyone for their help that day. While Brice had taken time to clean up, the rest of the men were still hot, sweaty and dirty, a fact that was noted by Bailey as she filled her plate, studying Brice from the corner of her eye.

He stood talking to Travis and Trent, laughing at something Travis said. He wore jeans and a black T-shirt, but he somehow made even the simplest attire look quite appealing. His hair had that little wave in the front that made her long to run her fingers through it and he smelled like every wonderful thing she loved about fall.

As though he could read her thoughts, he looked over and caught her eye, raising his eyebrow at her suggestively. She narrowed her gaze with a disapproving glare then walked over to sit by Cady and Cass.

Brice studied the selections on the table as he filled his plate and knew he was in trouble. Pausing with a spoon midair, he had no idea how he'd figure out what dish Bailey made.

"What's wrong, dude? You're holding up the line," Travis said, nudging him with his elbow.

"I bet Bailey I could figure out what she brought and I've got no clue," Brice admitted quietly to his friend.

Travis snorted and slapped him on the back. "And the payout on that bet is something, no doubt, you don't want to lose. I can't help you with this, because it wouldn't be fair. Having spent the better part of the last two months stuck in the house around the girls, though, I can tell you to pay attention to the details."

"What's that mean?" Brice asked, continuing to dish food on his plate as he moved down the table.

"It means what I said. Pay attention to the details, like dishes and things," Travis said cryptically before wandering off to sit with Tess.

Trying to decipher what Travis was telling him, Brice turned to sit by Bailey, irritated to find she planted herself in the middle of a full table with no room left for him.

As he walked by to find an empty seat at another table, she offered him a saucy grin. Annoyed, he decided if Bailey wanted to play games with him, he would play to win.

Shoveling food into his mouth, Brice was about half-way through his plate full of food when he figured out what Travis was saying. Dishes and things. He knew what serving pieces his mom owned, thanks to years of being forced to help with the dishes, so he could automatically eliminate those. Lindsay generally didn't cook, so that left the dishes from the Triple T. How to figure out what was made by Bailey and Cady? They were both people who strived for perfection, but Cady had mellowed quite a bit in the last year going with speed and necessity over frills and fancy due to the nature of being a busy ranch wife.

Brice hurriedly finished what was on his plate and returned to the food table, critically surveying each dish, each serving piece. There, among the desserts, was a perfect cake. It was perfectly smooth, perfectly flat on top, perfectly positioned on the cake stand. It looked like something Bailey would create.

"Do you need something, honey?"

Brice glanced across the table to see his mom looking at him with a knife in her hand.

"Yeah, Mom. Can you cut me a slice of that cake?" Brice said pointing to the cake he was sure Bailey baked.

"Sure," Michele said, cutting Brice a big slice and setting it on his plate. "That looks yummy. I haven't had carrot cake for a long while. Take a bite and let me know if it's good."

Brice forked a bite and instead of tasting it, held it for his mom.

She closed her eyes as she chewed. "Yep, that's good. I bet Cady made it."

"Maybe," Brice said, watching Bailey watch him. He pointed to the cake and gave her a victorious smile. She nodded her head with a look of defeat.

Walking past her on the way back to his seat, he bent down long enough to drop something in her hand and whisper "you'll need this for later."

Bailey felt heat fill her cheeks when she opened her hand to find Brice's tube of lip balm.

"Is my brother harassing you?" Ben asked from across the table, entertained by what was going on between Brice and Bailey.

"Not exactly," Bailey said, putting the lip balm in the pocket of her dress and trying to return her attention to the conversation going on around her. She had no idea how Brice figured out what she baked, but she'd have to pay up on that bet. Instead of dreading the moment Brice would demand payment, Bailey was greatly looking forward to it.

After everyone ate their fill, the Triple T hands headed back to the ranch to finish up the evening chores. The Thompsons and Morgans, along with Bailey, walked out to the barn where Tess and Travis wanted to have their wedding reception. Unlike the barn at the Triple T that was full of stalls, storage and tack rooms, the barn at the Running M had a huge open floor with stalls against a back wall. A loft overhead had stairs that ran up to it, rather than a ladder. A large sink with a work counter sat in one corner next to a small bathroom.

Tess shared her vision for the reception with the group and the women enthusiastically embraced her ideas while the men braced themselves for some hurried work in the next few weeks.

When anyone asked for his opinion, Travis would smile and say "whatever honeybee wants." In truth, he didn't care what was planned, how elaborate or simple. Travis was much more interested in the honeymoon. Tess left the planning of that detail up to him and he was determined to make it memorable.

The group wandered outside to discuss parking, set up, and a myriad of wedding details. As Bailey followed along, Brice caught her wrist and tugged her back in the barn, hurrying her up to the loft. It was the one place he knew they could get a few moments of privacy before they were missed.

"What are you doing?" Bailey asked as he tugged her down to sit on an old loveseat he and Ben lugged up to the loft years ago.

The ragged piece of furniture had definitely seen better days, but it gave the Morgan boys somewhere to hang out and hide out when they were teens. Brice still liked to come out to the barn to think when he had a problem that needed solved or he just wanted to gather his thoughts without interruption. Usually he needed to be around people, but once in a great while he liked a little quiet.

"Collecting on our bet," Brice said, staring at Bailey. His heated gaze made her self-conscience and fidgety. She folded her hands in her lap, smoothed down her skirt, toyed with the collar of her dress then returned her hands to her lap. Finally, she grasped the stone of the necklace around her neck and rubbed it between her thumb and forefinger.

"What's that?" Brice asked, gently moving her fingers aside so he could see what she wore. Not surprisingly, it was a fossil that had been sealed and polished before being set in a silver bracket and placed on a sturdy silver chain. In the fading light, Brice could barely make out what looked like the impression of a tiny wing. "Is that a butterfly?"

"Yes, as best as can be detected," Bailey said, sitting perfectly still while Brice held the fossil carefully in his fingers. She found the fossil when she was only eleven and her parents took her to a fossil bed in Colorado.

It was a life-changing trip for Bailey because from the moment she held that fossil in her hand, she knew what she wanted to do with her life. Her dad had the fossil preserved and turned into a necklace for her which she always wore. It served as a constant reminder of what set her feet down the path of paleontology. Although the imprint of the butterfly wing was light and small, it had been enough to spark her interest.

"I've seen you rubbing this when you're nervous," Brice said, laying the piece back against her chest. Bailey felt singed when his fingers brushed her skin. "It must be important to you."

"It is," Bailey said, then told Brice about how she came to have it. Her mom thought it was silly and Sierra was too young to care, but Bailey's father had understood. He'd always understood her better than her fun-loving mother. "So instead of ballet and piano lessons or slumber parties with girls, I spent my time researching, learning, studying and planning. My summer camps were to fossil digs instead of sports or artistic excursions."

"That explains a lot," Brice said, smiling at Bailey.

"Explains what?"

"Why you're so interesting, smart and intense," Brice said, scooting closer to Bailey on the loveseat. For every inch he advanced, she slid back until she felt the arm of the chair pressing into her back.

"Thanks," she finally managed to whisper. Brice should know about intense because the look he was giving her at that moment definitely fit the description. Her stomach fluttered and she felt light-headed. Hot. She hadn't noticed before how exceedingly warm it was in the barn.

"Bailey," Brice said, sliding his hands around her back and drawing her closer to him. When she continued to stare at his chest, he tipped her chin up with his finger and raised an eyebrow at her. "Time to pay up, sugar."

Bailey took a deep breath and quickly placed a kiss to each of Brice's cheeks and then a chaste one to his lips. Sitting back she grinned. "Three kisses."

"That was pathetic," Brice said, holding her so she pressed against him. "You forfeit because you didn't do it right so now it's three kisses on my terms."

"Wait just a minute," Bailey said, trying to lean back so she could look Brice in the eye. That was a mistake because the heat radiating from his deep brown eyes, made her forget what she was going to say. "You... um..."

"You were saying," Brice said, placing a hot kiss on her neck.

Bailey managed to keep from moaning out loud.

"Something you wanted to discuss, Ms. Bishop?" Brice asked, his voice husky as he kissed her ear and nibbled on the lobe until Bailey was certain she was going to be incapable of walking again. Her legs felt languid, her knees weakened and she wasn't sure her feet were still attached or if they'd melted off at the ankle.

"No," Bailey managed to whisper before Brice placed his lips to hers.

The touch was light and soft, gentle and restrained. When she slid her arms up around his neck and leaned into his chest, Brice deepened the kiss and pulled her even closer. Until she met Brice, Bailey had no idea that kisses could be so driven, demanding, and exciting.

Finally coming up for air, they sat staring at each other, entangled in the passion and attraction that passed between them.

"That's what I meant by three kisses," Brice said between ragged breaths.

"I'll remember that," Bailey whispered, getting to her feet. She could hear Cady asking where she was and by the darkness that had settled outside, she knew it was time to leave.

Brice walked her down the stairs and out to the pickup where everyone was gathered. Thank goodness it was dark so no one could see the blush on her face or the fact that she had just been thoroughly kissed.

Helping Bailey into the back seat of Trey's pickup next to Cass, Brice kissed her cheek. She clasped his hand in hers for a moment, slipping something into his before he shut the door.

Travis gave Tess one more kiss, then turned to slide onto the front seat. Wiggling an eyebrow at Brice, he smiled. "Won your bet, didn't you?"

"Darn right, I did," Brice said, grinning like an idiot. He couldn't help it. Being around Bailey seemed to do that to him.

"What bet?" Tess asked, as Travis shut the pickup door and waved.

"One I made with Bailey," Brice said, looping his arm around Tess' shoulders as they walked back to the house. He opened his other hand to see the lip balm he'd given Bailey earlier. His grin widened. She definitely tasted like berries and some sort of nectar. Her kisses were the most delicious, sweetest thing he'd ever tasted and left him wanting more.

"And I take it by that look on your face, you won and she had to pay with kisses?" Tess teased.

"How'd you know that?" Brice asked, surprised his sister could deduce what had happened so easily.

"You've got lipstick on your cheek, BB. Shame on you for cornering her in the barn," Tess said as she sauntered up the porch steps, turning to grin over her shoulder. "You better wipe that off before Ben sees it or you'll be sorry, mister kissy-face. "

"You're the one who's going to be sorry, Tessie," Brice said, chasing her into the house.

Chapter Six

*"You don't sit down and write a wish list about
the person you are going to fall violently in love with.
It just doesn't work like that."*

Stephen Fry

"Bailey, do you want to go with us?" Cady asked as Bailey sat at the dining room table.

Papers were strewn about her and she had her laptop open, jotting down notes for a blog post she was planning to write about her new location.

"Where are you going?" Bailey asked, only half taking her eye off the computer screen.

"Over to the Drexel house. Tess wants us to come look through some things she found. Travis isn't particularly interested in boxes of old stuff, so he's working on some projects outside, but she thought it might be fun if we joined her."

"Sure," Bailey said, not really wanting to go, but trying to be a bit more social than she was normally inclined. After all, her cousins were offering her room and board for as long as she wanted and had welcomed her with genuine warmth and kindness. The least she could do was spend some time helping sort through boxes of someone else's memories.

"Great," Cady said, looping her arm through Bailey's as they walked out the door. Cady drove her car to the end of Trent and Lindsay's driveway where Lindsay was waiting. She jumped in and the three of them went on to Tess and Travis' house.

"Where's Cass?" Lindsay asked as they parked in front of the big farmhouse.

"With her dad," Cady said with a relieved sigh. "She's been wound up all day so Trey decided to work off some of her energy having her help in the barn this afternoon. She's supposed to be cleaning out stalls, but with those two, she's no doubt playing a lot more than she's working."

"Probably," Lindsay agreed, knowing Trey was a complete pushover when it came to Cass, not that Trent or Travis were any better. All three men were firmly wrapped around the child's finger.

Tess waved from the porch as the three of them walked across the yard and up the steps.

"You won't believe all the stuff I found," Tess said, pulling Cady into the house with Lindsay and Bailey trailing along behind.

"I will if you tell me," Cady said with a teasing grin.

"Come upstairs and see," Tess said, hurrying up the staircase to the second floor and down the hall to one of the bedrooms. The room had the most beautiful rose patterned wallpaper and the girls wondered if it was original. A white cast-iron bed frame sat against one wall and a walnut dresser looked to be in excellent shape.

"When I found this old trunk, I immediately thought of Denni," Tess said, opening the lid to reveal it was packed full of vintage fabrics.

"Oh, gracious, Tess," Cady said, carefully touching the old fabric. "What a treasure. Denni will definitely want to see these."

Denni Thompson was an accomplished seamstress who managed a quilt store in The Dalles. Her daughters-in-law knew she'd love all the fabric pieces. Cady also liked to sew, but not to the extent that Denni did.

"What else did you find?" Lindsay asked, seeing newspaper clippings on top of the dresser.

Tess carefully picked up a handful of the yellowed printed pages. She found an entire drawer full of old advertisements and thought some of them were hysterical.

"Did you see this one?" Lindsay asked, giggling as she held out the old paper.

"What's it say?" Bailey asked, leaning over trying to read the Ivory Soap ad.

"I've got a He-Man Husband…He's husky as an ox, but has to be babied when's he's tired or catches a cold…" Lindsay read the rest of ad, which made all four of the girls erupt in laughter.

"I think that applies to all three of you," Bailey said, wiping the tears from her eyes. It felt good to laugh with these women and she was glad she agreed to come with Cady. If she was willing to admit it, this was a lot more fun than typing a blog about her latest fossil site. "Those cousins of mine are all pretty He-Man."

"I was thinking it would be fun to frame some of these and hang them in a grouping. What do you girls think?" Tess asked, sorting through the pile and picking out five that she especially liked.

"That's a great idea," Cady said, looking at Tess' choices and nodding her approval. You could mat them with some of the vintage fabric and then use matching frames to pull it all together."

"I love that idea," Tess said, looking at the ads again, confirming her choices. "Would you help me?"

"Sure, bring the stuff to the house. I've got all the supplies we'll need. You'll just need to pick out some frames."

The girls looked through more drawers, closets, and cupboards, finding a variety of old treasures. They cleaned as they went, throwing away what was truly garbage and setting aside anything they thought might be redeemable or of keepsake quality.

Bailey found a wedding photo at the back of a high shelf in a hall cupboard. Still in a frame, the photo appeared to be in good shape. Judging from the attire of the couple, the photo must have been taken in the late forties.

"Is this Mr. Drexel?" Bailey asked, handing the photo to Lindsay, who had rented her house from the man for three years.

"Yes, I believe it is," Lindsay said, studying the photo. "I wonder why he left it behind. I'm sure this is something he'd want to have."

"It was in the back of the hall cupboard. He probably missed it when he was packing," Bailey said, fascinated by the story behind this couple and the man who left so many memories behind when he moved to The Dalles and sold his ranch to the Thompsons.

"I'll take it to him," Tess said, setting the photo with a pile of things she was going to take with her when they finished up for the afternoon. "I want to thank him in person for all the wonderful things he left behind. I wonder why he didn't take more with him?"

"I think, like Denni, he wanted to leave the reminders of his wife behind," Cady said with an insight gained only from being married and deeply in love with her husband. If something happened to Trey, she didn't think she could bear to be at the ranch. She understood why Denni packed up and left when her husband died so suddenly. It hurt her too much to be surrounded by the constant reminders of their life together.

"I don't understand how someone could just walk away from everything they spent their life building. It seems so frivolous," Bailey said, voicing her thoughts as she sorted through a drawer of old gloves.

"Maybe you'll feel differently someday," Lindsay said with a knowing smile. "Love tends to change the way we think and act."

"It most certainly does," Cady said, nodding her head. "And the Thompson men seem to be particularly talented at getting under the skin of the women they love."

"I've never seen such stubborn, mule-headed, over-protective, cocky men as those three. They could try the patience of a saint," Lindsay said, waiting for Tess or Cady to argue. When they grinned in agreement, she continued her assessment. "They are also the most generous, caring, loving, honest, and loyal men I've ever met."

"Until I moved to Grass Valley, I'd never seen three men, let alone three brothers, with such broad shoulders, strong arms, devilish smiles, and enticing charm," Cady said, fanning her face with an old magazine they'd found.

Tess and Lindsay laughed.

"You forgot the Wranglers, Cady. Don't forget how good they make the Wranglers look," Tess added, placing her hand to her forehead, acting as though she might swoon. "I'd do just about anything Travis wants when he's wearing his Wranglers, boots and Stetson, but don't tell him that."

Bailey rolled her lips together and shook her head, thinking the other girls were completely daft. "How can you let them change your lives like they have?"

"It's all changes for the better," Tess said, her face softening as she thought of Travis. "They haven't changed who we are. They make us feel complete."

"But if they infuriate you so, how did you ever fall in love with them?" Bailey wondered, realizing that Brice both infuriated and fascinated her.

"You don't choose who your heart's going to love," Lindsay said, wiping out a drawer as they talked. "It's not like we made a wish list and decided we'd fall in love with whoever met the criteria. As a matter of fact, I wasn't even sure I liked Trent until he romanced his way into my good graces."

"He did do a good job of it," Cady said, recalling all of Trent's efforts at wooing Lindsay. His hard work paid off since she was now his bride.

"Yes, he did," Lindsay said, smiling wistfully as she thought of their romantic courtship. "But my point, Bailey, is that you don't go looking for the perfect person to love. The perfect love for you will just fall into your life one day when you aren't expecting it."

Bailey thought about what Lindsay said as they continued sorting and cleaning. When Tess found a box full of rocks, she asked Bailey if she wanted to go through them. Some of them looked interesting, so Bailey took the box out to Cady's car. On her way back to the house, Travis walked over from where he was doing some work on the back side of the house putting new weather stripping around the outside doors.

"I could hear you girls laughing in there. I can only assume they are telling tales about the men in this family," Travis said as he joined Bailey at the door.

"I'm not at liberty to laugh and say," Bailey said with a grin.

"You know, you're fitting in with the rest of the females here just fine Miss Bailey," Travis said, patting her on the back as they walked in the house.

Bailey smiled at him, suddenly liking the thought of fitting in with the fun-loving group.

"Isn't it time for this hen party to break up?" Travis asked as he walked into the kitchen where the women were gathering up their things.

"Who are you calling hens, Tee?" Tess asked, kissing Travis' cheek.

"The loveliest birds any man has ever seen," Travis said, with a teasing smile.

"Flattery will get you everywhere," Tess said as she followed the other three women out the door. Bailey turned back to see Travis kiss Tess before walking her to her car.

"Thanks for coming over," Tess called as Cady, Lindsay and Bailey got in Cady's car. "I'd love for you to help me sort through the rest of the stuff."

"We'd be happy to, Tess," Cady said, "I'll ask Denni next time." Turning to her brother-in-law, Cady grinned, "See you later, Trav. Behave yourself."

"Don't I always?" Travis asked, trying to sound wounded.

"No," chorused four female voices, making them all laugh.

Dropping Lindsay off at her house, Cady and Bailey chatted on the short drive back to the ranch.

"I hope we didn't lead you to believe we aren't madly in love with our husbands," Cady said, looking over at Bailey as she parked her car.

"Not at all," Bailey said, knowing anyone who spent even five minutes in the company of the couples could see their love and devotion to each other. "I think it's a very wise thing for you to see them clearly but love them anyway."

"I think that's what true love is all about," Cady said, retrieving a stack of fabric from the back seat of her car. "It's loving someone without the rose-colored glasses on, wanting them faults and all."

Faults and all.

That was something for Bailey to consider, should she ever decide a relationship was more important than her career.

Chapter Seven

*"The hardest tumble a man can make
is to fall over his own bluff."*
Ambrose Bierce

Feeling like he'd been given a rare gift of time, Brice fueled up his pickup at the gas station in Grass Valley and grabbed a bottle of cold pop, another package of breath strips and a bag of corn nuts.

When a load of supplies supposed to be delivered at the construction site that morning failed to appear, the boss told everyone to take the afternoon off and plan to be at work bright and early the next morning.

Seizing the opportunity to spend time with Bailey, Brice turned up the radio as he headed south to Antelope. Passing through the small town, he drove southeast in the direction he thought Bailey was working this week.

She'd been on the job for a couple of weeks and Brice had hardly seen her. By the time she got home at night, it was too late for him to be hanging around. Leaving extremely early in the mornings, there wasn't time to catch her before work and his sister seemed to monopolize what little free time she had between wedding plans and getting the house ready.

Grateful Tess and Bailey were developing a friendship through their shared love of all things vintage and retro, Brice hoped Tess' sweet and sassy personality would allow Bailey to relax a little.

If he really wanted to see Bailey, one of the few places he could track her down was at the Drexel house as she helped Tess sort through boxes and trunks. Inevitably, Travis would put him to work outside far from the girl who had him completely beguiled.

At first, Brice thought Bailey was playing hard to get. After getting to know her a little better, he realized she really was lacking in relationship skills and just didn't know how to be part of a couple. He was pretty sure she enjoyed his company, despite her cool demeanor and half-hearted protests.

Brice smiled when he thought about the last few texts Bailey sent him. They were much more casual and friendly in tone than her previous messages. She also was replying in a timelier manner. If he sent her a text, he could expect a reply within an hour or two, rather than waiting for what seemed like days on end.

Trying to remember where, exactly, she said she was working this week, Brice took a dirt road and hoped for the best. He could have called and asked her, but Brice didn't want her to tell him he shouldn't come. Imagining her protests when he showed up unannounced, he grinned. It did her good to have her cage rattled once in a while, which is what he was sure his presence would do to her this afternoon.

Bouncing down the trail that passed as a road, Brice felt pretty pleased when he saw Bailey's Jeep and a pickup parked ahead. Pulling over to the side of the road, he parked behind Bailey's rig and got out. He didn't see her anywhere, so he stood listening for a moment.

Not hearing any voices, he looked around and followed footprints along a dusty path between sage brush, scraggly juniper, and clumps of dry grass.

He walked over the rise of a small hill and saw two figures working in the distance. Brice advanced toward the one wearing an ugly canvas hat. He recognized it well from the photo he spent a month studying of Bailey online. He was going to have to charm her into giving him a real photo one of these days.

Walking softly behind her, Brice watched her carefully digging away at a large rock. Beside Bailey was a length of canvas holding a variety of interesting tools like picks, chisels, brushes and something that looked like a miniature pickax.

"What's that?" he finally asked, unable to keep his curiosity from getting the best of him.

Bailey gasped and dropped the tool in her hand. Standing, she spun around and glared at Brice.

"What do you think you are doing?" she demanded, angry sparks shooting from her eyes.

"I just…" Brice started to say, taking a step back as Bailey advanced on him, fury evident in every move she made.

"You just what?" Bailey asked, poking him in the chest with a dusty finger. "Thought you'd show up and convince me to run off with you for the afternoon? Maybe give you time to charm the fossils right out of the rock? Do you have any idea how wrong it is for you to be here? Are you trying to get me fired?"

Reeling from her anger and rejection, Brice took a few more steps back only to have Bailey grab his arm and pull him forward.

"Be careful where you walk," she said, looking behind him. "You could unknowingly damage something very important."

Acknowledging for the first time that Bailey's work was more than her playing in the dirt with old bugs and plants, Brice realized he should have called and asked if he could visit.

"I'm sorry, Bailey, I didn't think…" Brice tried to apologize but Bailey cut him off.

"That is part of the problem, Mr. Morgan. You never think. You just do and fail to consider the consequences. I'll walk you back to your truck."

"That won't be necessary, Bailey," a male voice said, causing both Bailey and Brice to turn their heads toward the speaker.

"Hi, I'm Anthony, the operational manager of the paleontology center here at the fossil beds," a smaller man in his mid-forties said, holding out his hand to Brice. "You must be a friend of Bailey's."

"I'd like to think so," Brice said with a grin. He liked this Anthony, who seemed friendly and approachable. "My name's Brice. Brice Morgan."

"Nice to meet you, Brice. Did you come to see what Bailey is working on?"

"Actually, I did," Brice said, following Anthony to where Bailey had been digging.

"We're working on extracting some plant fossils in this area," Anthony said, sweeping his hand around the barren landscape, interrupted only by the occasional juniper and craggy rock formations. "We generally don't allow anyone out at the site, but based on Bailey's work ethics, I think it's safe for you to observe her this afternoon. Just follow her direction and you should be fine."

Anthony started over to where he was working but turned around and smiled at Bailey. "Make sure you leave a little early today, Bailey. You've been putting in way too many hours as it is."

Brice hid his grin when Bailey let out such a long and deep sigh, he was certain it must have started at her toes.

"If I'm going to be hindered by your presence the rest of the day, you may as well provide some measure of assistance," she said, resigned to suffering through Brice's company for the next several hours. There was a part of her so pleased to see him she wanted to throw her arms around his neck and kiss his inviting lips repeatedly. But that would go against her dislike of public displays of affection as well as the part of her that was furious with him for just strolling into a dig site like he belonged there. He had no idea what she did or how careful he needed to be. "If you are truly going to plague me the rest of the afternoon, you will do exactly as I tell you. This is completely unacceptable and I don't expect you to repeat this unfortunate blunder. Understood?"

"Yes, sugar," Brice said, trying to look properly scolded. It was hard to do when his lips kept tipping up into a smile and his eyes sparkled with mischief. "I'll be a very good boy and do exactly what you say and then you'll give me a reward for my stellar behavior."

"I didn't say anything about a reward, and stop calling me sugar," Bailey said, narrowing her gaze and rolling her lips together, annoyed not so much with Brice as her own traitorous heart, which was pounding outrageously at his nearness. Every time he called her sugar, it caused wild, hot flames to burst to life in her stomach.

"Have it your way, sugar. I know you didn't say anything about a reward, but I did. You can't expect me to act properly without some incentive," Brice said, leaning close to her ear, his minty breath tingling along her neck. "I've got a great reward in mind. Want to take me up on it?"

"Don't be ridiculous," Bailey said, forcing the shiver that was working up from her toes back down into submission. She found it difficult to turn her thoughts to her work and not Brice when he wasn't around. With him leaning over her shoulder, smelling so good, it was going to make the task of staying focused impossible. Having the handsome charmer just inches away from her was taking her beyond distracted right into disturbed.

"I'm never ridiculous," Brice said, placing a kiss on her cheek, just to further ruffle her feathers. He wasn't surprised by her scathing glare or the way she straightened her spine and rolled back her shoulders. "Don't you have work to do instead of staring daggers at me?"

"Yes, you insufferable man," Bailey said, bending down and picking up a small brush, handing it to Brice.

She went back to what she was doing and explained the work to Brice. He was given the task of brushing away debris as she worked and he soon wondered how Bailey could do this day in and day out. He was tired of bending, his back was killing him and he wanted nothing more than to get up and stretch his legs. After her warning of stepping somewhere he shouldn't, he stayed put.

"Don't you need to get up and move to keep your circulation going?" Brice finally asked, an hour into the task.

"I take a break every two hours and stretch. Keep brushing," Bailey said, returning her focus to her work. Brice, who couldn't sit still any better than her three Thompson cousins, was about to explode from inactivity. Bailey took pity on him after another thirty minutes and told Anthony she was taking a water break. He gave her a wave of agreement as she walked with Brice back to her Jeep.

"Bailey, I'm really sorry," Brice said, as she pulled two water bottles out of a cooler in her Jeep and gave him one. He played with the cap before looking Bailey in the eye. "I didn't realize how detailed and involved your work is. I apologize for thinking I could troop out here for a visit and surprise you. My intentions were good, even if it doesn't seem that way."

Bailey nodded her head and continued drinking her water. "Most people don't understand what we do or the importance of our work."

"I promise to never take you or your work for granted again," Brice said, holding up his hand as he made the vow, looking very serious. And very handsome.

Bailey grinned despite her attempts at keeping her pleasure contained.

"Apology accepted," she said, trying to ignore how attractive she found Brice, even in his carpenter jeans, steel-toed work boots and T-shirt. A bit of sawdust clung to the front of his pants and she leaned over to brush it off without thinking. Her hand connected with his hard, muscled thigh and nearly made her knees collapse beneath her.

"What are you doing?" Brice asked, his eyes darkening as he caught her hand and held it to his chest. Bailey could feel his heart galloping, keeping time to her own.

"Sawdust," she managed to say while her gaze was lost in the look Brice was giving her.

Scrambling for any safe topic of discussion, Bailey took a step back and looked around. "Have you been out to the Clarno Unit of the fossil beds before?"

"Not to actually see it. Travis and I blew through there one night back in high school when we were trying to outrun the deputy after we… never mind," Brice said, looking slightly chagrined.

"I don't want to know," Bailey said, hiding her smile. She knew Travis was the family's rebel child. It made sense that his best friend would also be a troublemaker. "How about I tell you why this particular area is important?"

"Cool," Brice said, leaning against the side of the Jeep, drinking his water. "I'm all ears."

"Not quite," Bailey said under her breath as she tried to ignore the way the T-shirt molded to every muscle in Brice's arms and chest when he leaned with his elbows braced on the hood of the Jeep, one boot propped on a tire. "The Clarno Unit is home to the cliffs of the Palisades, formed about forty-four million years ago by a series of volcanic mudflows. They preserved a wide range of fossils in an environment quite different from that of today. When the mud flows occurred, volcanoes towered over a landscape covered by a tropical-like forest that received around one hundred inches of rain a year. Can you imagine that, looking around the landscape today?"

"Not really," Brice said, scrubbing the toe of his boot in the powdered dirt that only seemed to be found in very dry, arid areas. "It's a little hard to picture."

"Well, think of a tropical place with leafy green trees and lush plants, beautiful vegetation, lots of water and interesting animals."

"What kind of animals?" Brice asked, liking animals much more than plants.

"There were crocodilians, the ancestors of today's crocodile, meat-eating creodonts who roamed the jungles and huge animals that looked kind of like a rhino. There were also tiny little four-toed horses," Bailey said, obviously passionate about her subject matter.

Brice smiled as he watched her eyes light from within and her hands flutter excitedly as she talked about ancient jungles and prehistoric animals. Her work was, without a doubt, the most important thing to her. That knowledge made Brice's heart hurt a little. He wondered if he could ever compete with her career for first place and win. Not one to easily give up, Brice was determined to give it a try.

"So when all these horrible meat-eating beasties were roaming around, where were the humans?" Brice asked.

"We've found no record of their existence here at that time," Bailey said, walking back toward the area where she was working. Brice followed carefully along behind. He didn't realize khaki cargo pants could look so good on anyone, but Bailey certainly filled them out well especially with her long legs. She wore a pale peach tank with a white shirt unbuttoned over the top and that hideous canvas hat.

Pulling a bottle from her pants pocket, she squirted out sun screen and slathered it on her hands, arms and neck. She held it out for him and he shook his head, a little off kilter from watching her work the lotion into her skin, particularly when she tipped back her head and smoothed it onto her creamy throat. He wanted to grab the lotion bottle from her and rub it down the column of her neck and along that expanse of chest exposed above the edge of her tank top.

"Well, when did humans enter the picture?" Brice finally asked, kneeling by Bailey as she returned to her work.

"An archaeologist right here in Oregon discovered evidence a few years ago that suggested humans were here in North America as early as fourteen thousand years ago."

"Really? They found a body? Where?" Brice asked, trying to remember if he'd heard anything about an ancient corpse turning up somewhere in the state.

"It was in a cave outside of Paisley," Bailey said, intently working with a pick. "That's a bit to the south of here isn't it?"

"More than a bit, sugar," Brice said, "You'd be looking at a good day trip to go there and back again."

"Oh," Bailey said, filing that information for later use. She might drive down there some weekend just for fun.

"So they found the body in a cave in Paisley?"

"Not a body," Bailey said, carefully digging rock from around the fossil she was extracting.

"If they didn't find a body, how do they know a human was there?" Brice asked, his mind trying to figure out how the existence of something could be recorded if there was no physical evidence to prove it had actually been there.

"There was other evidence."

"What kind of evidence?" Brice asked, trying to study Bailey's face, which was impossible with that horrible hat on her head.

"They excavated some coprolite containing human DNA which provided the radio carbon dating taking the human presence back to that time frame," Bailey said, bending over the fossil and gently picking around it.

"Say it in English, sugar. I don't know what coprolite means."

"Fossilized feces," Bailey said as she carefully continued her work, although her cheeks were turning a light shade of pink.

"They found petrified poo and used that to decide it was an ancient cavedweller?" Brice asked, trying not to laugh. For some reason the conversation he was having with Bailey struck him as quite funny.

"When you say it like that it completely detracts from the fact it was a significant scientific discovery that helps us better learn about our North American ancestry."

"I'm sorry, Bailey," Brice said, no longer able to contain his laughter as he sat back and chuckled. "It is kind of funny."

"Not at all," Bailey said, biting the inside of her cheek to keep from grinning. Only Brice would call one of the most vital discoveries of human evidence in the West by something so undignified.

"Then why are you trying so hard not to laugh?" Brice teased, pushing her chin up with his finger, putting her face just inches from his. Her Caribbean blue eyes danced with warmth and amusement and Brice fell into them without any thought to what would happen.

"Brice," Bailey whispered, leaning toward him before remembering where she was and what they were doing. Looking down, she resumed her efforts with the fossil.

"What's with that hat?" Brice asked, gently tapping her head trying to distract himself from his desire to kiss her.

"My hat?" Bailey asked, glancing up at the brim of the canvas hat. "What about my hat?"

"No offense, but it's about the ugliest thing I've ever seen," Brice said, with a teasing grin.

"None taken," Bailey said, as she worked intently. "I am fully aware that it is lacking in fashionable qualities, however, it serves me well."

"What's so special about it?"

"I'll have you know this hat has built-in UPF protection, the headband is moisture wicking, it floats in water, has an odorless insect shield that repels flies, ants, ticks and mosquitoes, and is completely machine washable so I can clean it whenever I want," Bailey said, casting Brice a smug smile.

"Oh," Brice said, acceding the ugly hat did have some redeeming qualities. "You seem pretty concerned about sun screen."

"Anyone with a lick of sense ought to be," Bailey said, giving Brice a look that told him he should have taken advantage of the sunscreen when she offered it.

"And why is that, sugar?" Brice liked listening to her voice and knew as long as he kept asking questions, she'd keep talking.

"Because you'll end up with wrinkled skin that looks like dried out leather not to mention the very high possibility of skin cancer," Bailey said emphatically, stopping her work to glance pointedly at Brice. "You don't want skin cancer, believe me. My grandfather died from it."

"I'm sorry, Bailey," Brice said, with sincere sympathy. "Were you close to him?"

"Yes, I was. Poppy died when I was only nine, but I have some wonderful memories of time spent with him and my grandmother. He was my father's dad."

"What did he do for a living?" Brice asked as he carefully brushed away more debris at Bailey's prompting.

"He worked for the forest service and was outside year-round. Poppy had that job for more than thirty years."

"What about your grandmother?" Brice asked, wondering if Bailey had been close to her as well.

"She lives in Denver, not far from our house," Bailey said, a soft smile riding her lips. "Grammy likes her independence, rather like Nana."

"Have you seen Nana much since you've been back?"

"A few times. She and Aunt Denni are coming to the ranch this weekend to work on wedding plans."

"That seems to be all anyone talks about these days are wedding plans. First it was Trey and Cady, although their plans only took a week, then Trent and Lindsay, now Trav and Tess. I'm convinced someone poured a love potion into the well at the Triple T," Brice said, watching as Bailey carefully extracted the fossil they'd spent all afternoon digging out.

"Perhaps," Bailey said, focused completely on the fossil. She held it up to the catch the sunlight and Brice could see the imprint of a lacy leaf against the rock.

"That is so cool," Brice said, leaning close to better study the design.

"Yes, it is," Bailey said, excited to have another fossil to study. She called to Anthony who examined the specimen, placed the fossil in a labeled bag, and encouraged Bailey to take the rest of the day off.

Picking up her tools and cleaning her work area, Bailey walked back to her Jeep and stowed the tools in a box before climbing behind the wheel. Brice stood looking at her expectantly.

"So, do you have plans for the rest of the day," Brice asked, feeling like he was fourteen again, trying to work up the courage to ask Cindy Bartlett to the harvest dance.

"No," Bailey answered honestly. She hadn't planned to have the extra time off but liked the idea of spending it with Brice.

"Would you like to go out to dinner with me?" Brice thought his T-shirt collar was about to strangle him and wondered if he'd had too much sun as overheated as he felt.

Bailey didn't answer him right away. Instead she tilted her head to one side and studied him, like he was one of her fossils. He felt like squirming but managed to maintain his relaxed stance against the side of her Jeep.

"You like to make bets of questionable nature, don't you?" Bailey asked, quirking an eyebrow at him.

Brice grinned. "You know it."

"If I beat you back to the Triple T, you can stay for dinner there, do all the dishes and then spend the rest of the evening doing whatever any of us girls tell you," Bailey said, knowing Brice would plan to win. "If you beat me back to the ranch, I'll go out to dinner with you anywhere you want and, as an added bonus, I'll even throw in a good night kiss."

"My, you are feeling generous aren't you?" Brice said, kissing her cheek and stepping away from the Jeep. "Prepare to pucker up, sugar, and eat my dust."

"I don't think so," Bailey said, jumping into the Jeep and throwing it into gear. While Brice stepped back in surprise, she turned around and headed down the bumpy road.

Brice ran to his pickup and trailed after her. When they reached the highway, he assumed Bailey would drive carefully, precisely, and cautiously.

Unfortunately, he assumed incorrectly. She took off zooming down the road and he was hard pressed to keep up with her. They made it through Antelope and Shaniko with him right on her tail when they got stuck behind an RV going really slow.

Bailey saw a short window of opportunity to pass and took it, leaving Brice plodding along behind the RV, smacking at his steering wheel. As soon as he could, he passed the slow moving vehicle and roared after Bailey, but she was long gone.

Nearing the Triple T Ranch, Brice took a shortcut that would bring him to the ranch along the old canal road. Forgetting about a fence Trent recently put in, it cost him precious moments to open the gate, drive through and close it, but he hustled as fast as he could, roaring up from the ditch bank road behind the machine shed into the ranch yard to see Bailey coming up the driveway.

Sliding to a stop, he jumped out of the pickup and ran to the porch where he sat down on the steps. Buddy trotted over to see him and the dog was sitting there grinning every bit as much as Brice when Bailey got out of her Jeep and sauntered down the walk.

"I don't know how you beat me here, but I bet you somehow cheated," Bailey said, shaking her head as she looked at Brice.

"No cheating involved. You never said I had to drive on the road, just beat you here which I did, fair and square."

"Fine," Bailey said, rolling her lips together, glad Brice won the bet. When she lost him behind the RV, she was worried she was going to win, but it didn't make her drive any slower. She was glad he knew a shortcut, although by the looks of his truck, it involved going through a lot of dust and some mud.

"What sounds good for dinner?" Brice asked, absently petting the dog that was practically flopped on Brice's lap in his bliss at receiving a good belly scratching.

"How about greasy spoon?" Bailey said with a teasing grin. "I've heard all about Viv's place but never eaten there. Cady said the food is pretty good if you don't mind your arteries clogging while you eat."

Brice chuckled. He hadn't eaten at Viv's for a while either. Between spending a lot of time at the Triple T where Cady served plenty of delicious food on a daily basis and home where his Mom would stuff him if he let her, he didn't need to eat out much. He and Travis used to grab a burger on occasion and sometimes Tess would join him for a bite to eat before driving home from The Dalles when they carpooled, but he was looking forward to eating with Bailey. The location didn't really matter to him.

"Are you sure that's where you want to go?" Brice asked, looking up at her with a gaze that made heat explode in her stomach and her heartbeat surge into a fast tempo.

"I'm quite certain," Bailey said, walking up the steps. "If you give me an hour to make myself presentable, I'll be ready to go then."

"Fair enough," Brice said, getting to his feet and tipping his ball cap to her. "I'll be back in an hour and you better be ready to pay up on both parts of that bet, sugar. Need to borrow my ChapStick?"

"That won't be necessary," Bailey said as heat climbed her neck at her rash promise to deliver a good night kiss. Shaking her head as she hurried inside the mud room door, she was annoyed at herself for looking forward to dinner with Brice as much as she did.

Chapter Eight

*"It's so easy to fall in love,
but hard to find someone willing to catch you."*
Unknown

Bailey sat at the kitchen counter slicing apples into a bowl with nervous fingers while Cady made dinner. When she heard Cass yell "Hi, Brice!" from her seat outside where she was brushing the dog, Bailey's hands trembled.

"Hey kiddo," she heard Brice say through the open kitchen window as he walked up the steps. "You're doing a good job."

"Thanks," Cass said. Bailey couldn't hear the rest of the conversation. She glanced at Cady who gave her a grin and a nod of her head toward the door. Bailey quickly washed her hands at the sink and dried them, adding a squirt of the lotion Cady kept there. She might abuse her hands by digging in rock and dirt, but she was fanatical about keeping them as soft as possible.

She straightened her skirt and picked up a sweater as Brice knocked and stuck his head in the back door.

"Hey, lovely ladies," Brice said with a charming grin, his eyes seeking out Bailey's.

"Brice, I hear you're taking Bailey to Aunt Viv's for dinner. Be sure and give her a hug for me," Cady said, motioning Brice to come in the house as he lingered at the door.

"Are you sure I can walk on the floor?" Brice asked, knowing Cady upheld the rule originally put in place by Denni when her boys were small that no boots were allowed on her clean kitchen floors.

"I'm sure your boots are clean since you're heading out to dinner," Cady said as she deftly shaped bread dough into a dinner rolls while she talked.

Brice stepped in and looked appreciatively at Bailey, who wore a straight skirt with a soft blouse and heels. She was way too dressed up for dinner at Viv's Café, but he wasn't going to tell her that. Cady obviously hadn't mentioned the fact either, since she knew as well as anyone that jeans and a clean shirt without too many holes was considered dressed up for many of the patrons at the cafe.

When she first moved to Grass Valley, Cady spent a few weeks working for her Aunt Viv at the diner which is how she met Trey. According to what Brice heard, it was love at first sight for them both. He used to think it was crazy to hear them say that, but now that he met Bailey and fell hard and fast the first time he saw her, Brice knew just what they meant.

"Did you and Trey have a good time in Portland?" Brice asked Cady, remembering they snuck off for a few days the previous week.

"We did, Brice. It was wonderful," Cady said, her face softening at thoughts of spending time alone with Trey, a luxury they rarely enjoyed. "He decided we needed to celebrate the anniversary of when we met and the day I started working here at the ranch, since they are only a day apart, so we stayed in a nice hotel, ate at some great restaurants, and he tagged along while I did some shopping. We even had a chance to see Peter and his family. Do you remember meeting him at our wedding? He was the attorney who helped us with both the custody hearing and Cass' adoption."

SHANNA HATFIELD

"Yeah, I do remember. Nice guy," Brice said, stealing a piece of apple out of the bowl on the counter. "That's great you two got away for a few days. I expect Trey treated you like a princess."

"More like a queen," Cady said, a slight blush coloring her cheeks pink.

"Did Lindsay and Trent keep Cass?"

"They did. I love that little sweetie-pie to pieces, but it was nice to get a break from the nonstop chattering," Cady said with a big grin. "And have my hunky husband all to myself for a change."

"I'll be sure and tell him you said that," Brice teased. Turning to Bailey he made a grand sweep of his Stetson toward the door. "Your dusty chariot awaits."

"I'd hurry right out before it turns into a pumpkin," Cady warned Bailey with a wink.

"Maybe that wouldn't be a bad thing," Bailey said, picking up her purse with a saucy grin. "I love anything with pumpkin."

"I'll have her back before her bedtime," Brice said to Cady, feeling like he was going to be punished if they stayed out a minute past curfew. He didn't even know what was considered curfew these days. It's not like he ever followed one when he was younger, either. Leaning closer to Bailey as they walked down the steps, he put his lips close to her ear. "If I smear on some pumpkin pie, does that mean I'm guaranteed some of your affection?"

Bailey tripped at his outrageous question and was saved from a fall by Brice's hand on her arm. "Careful, sugar."

As he helped Bailey into his truck, wishing he had time to wash it before he picked her up, he breathed in her wonderful scent. "You look amazing, Ms. Bishop."

"Thank you. You don't look too bad, for a hammer slinging hooligan." Bailey tried to keep from smiling at Brice but it was impossible when his grin was so

114

infectious. In fact, Bailey thought Brice looked extraordinarily handsome in his pressed Wranglers, polished boots, green plaid cotton shirt and cowboy hat.

Of all the men she could possibly fall for, why did she have to let this one, this rowdy cowboy in the middle of nowhere, turn her head? Maybe what Lindsay said was true about love choosing you, not the other way around.

Bailey decided to give it more thought later when she wasn't around Brice. Right now, it was all she could do to function with any degree of normalcy when Brice smelled so good and looked so appealing.

"Last chance, Bailey. Are you sure you wouldn't rather drive to The Dalles for dinner. You look too pretty to take to Viv's."

"Thank you for the compliment. To clarify your statement, Cady's aunt only lets ugly dressed people in the door?" Bailey said, attempting a joke, which made Brice look at her in surprise before smiling.

"No, smarty pants. It's just that I'd love to take you somewhere to show you off," Brice said, remembering that with Bailey all the relationship and dating information most people understood was new to her.

"Why would you want to show me off? I'm not a prized vegetable or one of the animals dragged to the county fair," Bailey said, trying to analyze what Brice was saying.

"No, sugar, you aren't," Brice said, eyeing the way the blouse fell around Bailey's nice curves. There was no mistaking her for anything except a very pretty and completely enticing woman. "What I'm trying to say is that I enjoy being with you and most guys like other people to see how proud they are of their girl."

"Oh," Bailey said, processing the fact that Brice said he enjoyed being with her and called her his girl. She liked the thought of being his girl, but the fact of it frightened her. Thinking about what he was explaining, she finally grasped the concept.

"You think by showing others that we are together as a couple it will elevate their perception of you because you, assumably, have chosen well. Some of the males may experience feelings of jealousy or anger based on that perception, indicating their selection in a female companion would not adequately measure up to the predetermined standard," Bailey said, working through the hypothetical response in her head. "In theory, if you found my appearance to be lacking of that standard you would not be seen socially with me as a companion because it would reflect poorly on your ability to choose wisely."

Brice looked at Bailey and raised his eyebrows.

"Do you really think I'm that shallow?" Brice asked, a little hurt by what she implied with all her jargon.

"Not at all," Bailey said, glancing out the window as they parked at Viv's Café. "But isn't that the reason you would want to show off a female to your male counterparts? To rub their noses in it, so to speak."

Brice laughed. When she put it like that, it did sound stupid and childish. Coming around the pickup to open the door and help her out, he squeezed her hand. Leaning toward her, Bailey could feel his warm breath by her ear.

"I was thinking more along the lines of saying, 'Look at this beautiful woman. Everyone should be so lucky to be spending time with her.'"

Bailey was left speechless when Brice pressed a wet kiss to her neck before taking her hand and leading her through the door to the café.

"Has the sky fallen? The earth stopped spinning? There must be some disaster of major proportion for the almighty Brice Morgan to grace my establishment," Viv teased as she gave Brice a big hug. She was a tall, thin woman with a head of gray hair and a very soft heart.

"Hello, Bailey. How are you, honey?" Viv said, patting Bailey on the arm as she motioned them to a booth in a corner. "How did this rascal talk you into dinner? He balking at driving you into town, cause ya sure look too pretty to be eating here."

Brice gave Bailey a look that said "I told you so," before picking up the menus and handing one to her.

"No, he offered, but I wanted to eat here," Bailey said, looking around the café with interest. "Cady said you're a great cook, so I wanted to see for myself."

"Did she tell you my cooking will make your arteries clog? She convinced Trey and Trent eating my food every day would kill them graveyard dead faster than water runs downhill."

Bailey laughed, but refrained from saying Cady had told her that exact thing.

"What's the special tonight, Viv?" Brice asked, knowing that the special hadn't changed since he was old enough to come in and order a meal by himself.

"You know darn good and well what it is, young man," Viv said, pinching Brice's cheek like he was twelve instead of twenty-five. "Now, quit giving me sass and I'll go get you both some water while you decide what you want."

Watching Viv hustle off to the kitchen, Bailey smiled. "She's lively, isn't she?"

"Very," Brice said, closing the menu. It hadn't changed in the last fifteen or so years and he knew every item on it by heart.

"You've already decided on your selection?" Bailey asked Brice as she looked over the laminated menu. Brice wedged his back between the bottles of ketchup and Tabasco sauce at the far end of their table.

"I have," Brice said anticipating a great, greasy meal. "See anything you like?"

"A few things caught my eye," Bailey said, trying to decide if she wanted to spike her cholesterol with chicken fried steak or a big juicy hamburger.

When Viv came back, both Brice and Bailey ordered the chicken fried steak. Brice gave Bailey a surprised look but didn't say anything about her choice.

Bailey worked hard and tried to do some form of physical exercise every day, whether it was walking, running, or just a series of moves to get her blood flowing, so she didn't feel any guilt about eating what she wanted.

Waiting for their meal, Bailey asked Brice about the area, some of the people who appeared to be regulars in the café, and about his family. She liked hearing him talk and enjoyed watching the animation in his face when he spoke about something he particularly enjoyed, like woodworking.

"Why don't you do that as a career, Brice?"

"Do what?"

"Woodworking," Bailey said, feeling the needle case through the fabric of her purse. Brice was an exceptional artist when it came to wood and she thought he was wasting his talents in construction work.

"Just quit my job and carve wood full-time? That doesn't seem very responsible," Brice said, shaking his head.

"But when you talk about working with wood is when you are the most passionate. I think you'd rather be doing that than just about anything else, wouldn't you?" Bailey asked, wanting Brice to think about the options open to him instead of letting himself get into the rut of working a job just to pay the bills.

"There are a few things I enjoy more than working with wood and one or two that even make me quite passionate," Brice said, his voice dropping to a husky rumble as he gave her a look filled with heat.

"Like what?" Bailey asked, leaning across the table toward Brice. She had no idea why he was talking low, but the raspy tone in his voice made her stomach flutter and her heart start pounding.

"You," Brice said, with a smile that was pure flirtation.

Bailey's heart went from pounding to racing and the tingling that had danced around her toes was quickly working its way up to her head.

Leaning back, away from Brice and his scent that always made her befuddled, she traced an imaginary pattern on the table. "That is clearly the problem. If you allow yourself to become wrapped up in the folly of relationships, you lose your focus on the important and pertinent details of your career."

"Maybe the things that I think are most important and pertinent don't have anything to do with a career. Maybe they aren't things, Bailey, but people," Brice said, wondering how anyone, let alone such a sweet-faced woman, could have such an analytical way of viewing life and be so entirely focused on her work that she would willingly forsake everything else. "Did you ever stop to think that people are more important than anything else. That relationships are what keeps us all going?"

Bailey could hear the disappointment and exasperation in Brice's voice. She looked up to find him observing her with his jaw clamped shut. It wasn't her intention to disagree with him or say things he found unsettling. Brice had only wanted to take her out for dinner tonight and have a fun evening and now she'd obviously upset him. He fished in his pocket and popped something in his mouth. The action was something she'd seen him do any number of times since they'd been around each other. Finally, her curiosity got the better of her and she had to know what he was eating.

"What is that?" she asked, pointing to his pocket.

"Pardon?" Brice said, looking down at his shirt.

"What is in your mouth? You're always putting something in your mouth, especially when I've said something you find disturbing or upsetting, which seems to be rather frequently," Bailey said, realizing the truth to her words as she spoke them.

"Breath strips," Brice said, looking like a little boy caught doing something naughty. "I guess you could say I'm an addict. I tend to put them in my mouth without thinking."

"Is that why you always have minty breath and taste so good?" Bailey asked, not thinking how her words sounded.

"Been tasting him, have you?" Viv asked with a wink as she delivered two steaming plates of food to their table. "I wouldn't let that get out to those cousins of yours. They are likely to be as overprotective of you as they are with the rest of their women."

"Oh, I…" Bailey said, feeling heat climbing up her neck.

"It's okay, honey, my lips are sealed," Viv said, patting Bailey on the shoulder before hurrying back to the kitchen.

Brice was nearly choking into his napkin with laughter. His face was red when he finally took a deep drink of water and straightened in his seat.

"So you think I taste good, do you? Are you prepared to do some more tasting later?" Brice teased, enjoying the way his words made Bailey squirm in her seat. So much for the unflappable scientist guise.

"Don't be ridiculous," Bailey said, cutting into her steak and taking a bite, hoping to calm her nerves and give her hot cheeks time to cool.

They finished dinner without further incident and when they were ready to leave Brice gave Viv a big hug, telling her it was from Cady. Viv wrapped Bailey in a friendly hug and whispered in her ear that Brice was a fine young man any girl would be happy to catch.

Bailey swallowed down her inclination to tell Viv she would never catch Brice because she wasn't chasing him, or anyone for that matter. The only thing she was chasing was her dream for her career.

Leaving the café, Brice took her for a scenic drive and ended up parking the pickup on a remote hill above rolling fields and pastures. It was the perfect place to watch the sun make its descent. The colors filling the autumn sky were spectacular.

One of Bailey's favorite things in the world was to watch the sun set, reflect on her day, and allow peace to seep into her soul. Today, she felt something extra, something new and wonderful, as she sat next to Brice and they watched a giant fireball of orange sink into the western horizon.

"That's gorgeous," Bailey whispered from her vantage point that felt like it was on top of the world. Brice slid his hand across the seat and captured hers, pressing a warm kiss to her wrist before stroking his thumb back and forth across her palm.

Bailey's initial impulse was to snatch her hand back, but she ignored it. Hushing the voice in her head telling her it was a bad idea to get any more involved with Brice, she allowed herself to enjoy the sensation.

"Describe the sunset, sugar," Brice said quietly, watching the look of pleasure on her face, hoping the gentle touch of his fingers on her hand was contributing to it.

"Are you colorblind?" Bailey asked, suddenly concerned that Brice was missing out on the beautiful colors visible through the windshield of his truck.

"No," Brice said with a chuckle. "Although Tess might tell you she thinks I dress that way sometimes. I just wanted to hear you describe what you see."

"Very well, then," Bailey said, looking at the colors streaking across the sky. "There are oranges, pinks, purples and a hint of gold."

"Nope," Brice said, taking off his hat and setting it on the truck's dash. "That won't do at all. Try again, but this time, don't look at the colors with your head, look at the colors with your heart. They are so much more than just orange and purple, Bailey. Look again. Try to really see."

Bailey considered what Brice said. Was she missing out on something by looking at the black and white facts of life instead of the colorful rainbow painted by emotions?

Studying the brilliant shades slowly fading into evening's darkness, Bailey smiled. "Tangerine orange is rising up to meet impulsive purple while decadent melon is playing in the fringes with shimmering goldenrod."

Eyes sparkling with happiness, Bailey turned to Brice, looking so young and carefree, seeking his approval for the first time since they'd met. "Is that what you meant, Brice?"

"That is exactly what I meant, sugar," Brice said with a pleased grin, about to fall into the ocean of her intense blue eyes. "I was beginning to wonder if you could see with your heart, but obviously you've got a great vision when you want to use it."

"Thank you," Bailey said, still excited about her heart vision, as Brice called it. She looked at him and thought up a few words to describe him beyond the basic terms of handsome like powerfully robust, eagerly energetic, and vibrantly virile. As searing heat filled her cheeks at the direction of those thoughts, she needed a distraction. "You try. I want to hear your descriptions."

"Are you sure?" Brice asked, stroking his fingers up her arm to the bend at her elbow. He tried not to grin when he could see goose bumps break out on her skin.

"Yes, please," Bailey said, unaware that the inside of an elbow was capable of transmitting such a storm of positively wonderful sensations.

"I'd say that the honey-gold tones are almost as lovely as the curls on your head," Brice said, sliding a little closer to Bailey. "The swath of color over there that looks like rich red wine is almost as luscious as your ruby red lips. The ardent orange sinking into the horizon is almost as brilliant as your quick and fascinating mind while the passionate purple makes me think of what lies in here."

Brice put a calloused hand to her chest, just above her heart, making Bailey's eyes go wide and dark.

"Then there's the fiery shade of attraction that ignites every time we're together," Brice said, in a voice that was deep and husky with emotion. He rubbed his thumb across her cheekbone, down her jaw and across her lips.

Noticing the look of longing he felt reflected in her magnificent eyes, he gave in to the temptation and kissed Bailey with all the love he held for her in his heart.

Lost from the moment Brice started stroking her palm, Bailey wrapped her arms around his neck and surrendered to the kiss, surrendered to the man who was making her feel things she never imagined.

When she whispered his name, he deepened the kiss, pulling her closer against him. He was half sprawled on top of her as each kiss became more urgent and demanding than the last. Brice pressed hot kisses down her neck, setting her on fire everywhere his lips touched. She ran her fingers through his hair, then let her hands slide down to the bunched muscles in his arms, somewhat in awe of the strength and power she felt there as she turned her head to give him better access to her throat.

Through the fabric of her skirt, Bailey felt searing heat from Brice's hand on her thigh, convinced his handprint would be branded on her skin permanently.

Pressing herself even closer against Brice, his muscles tensed before he buried his face against her chest.

Bailey heard him groan as her hands dug into his shoulders pulling him closer. Brice went completely still before raising his head and releasing a ragged breath.

"Sugar, I need to take you home. Right now," Brice said, sitting up and running his hand through his hair. Sliding back against the driver's side door and slapping his hat on his head, he waited for Bailey to stop blinking at him with a look of bewilderment before starting the truck. "Buckle up, Bailey."

Functioning without thinking, Bailey sat up, straightened her rumpled blouse and buckled her seat belt. She fluffed her curls and sat quietly, wondering on the drive back to the ranch what she'd done to displease Brice.

More interested in her work than dating, Bailey didn't have a lot of experience with men. She rarely went out with any guy more than twice because that encouraged them to have crazy ideas like wanting to spend time with her and thinking she'd be interested in a relationship when she wasn't. She merely wanted to enjoy an evening out. If the man had other ideas, that was his problem.

Thinking back on every single date she'd ever had, Bailey couldn't think of one she'd enjoyed more than this evening with Brice. She'd certainly never been as attracted to a man before as she was to this small-town cowboy. Apparently, he wasn't feeling the same.

Brice parked the truck by the mud room door of the Triple T Ranch house and got out without saying a word. Bailey would have hopped out and hurried inside before Brice could open the door for her, but between her heels and slim skirt, she needed his assistance getting out of the truck.

When he opened the truck door, though, instead of helping her out, he gave her a look that nearly melted her in the seat and pulled her close to his chest.

"Bailey, I'm sorry I got a little carried away, but you are so beautiful and sweet, I just couldn't help myself," Brice said, his cheek against hers and his lips near her ear. She absorbed his warmth and breathed in his rich, autumn scent, trying to analyze where the evening veered off track.

"I don't understand," Bailey said, pulling back from his embrace so she could look him in the eye. "I assumed I was doing something wrong and you weren't enjoying it. Isn't that why you stopped? Because you were disappointed?"

"Oh, sugar," Brice said, fighting down the desire that was making his legs nearly as weak as his resolve. "You were doing everything just right and I enjoyed it more than you can know. That's why I stopped and why we came home. You doing everything so wonderfully right was going to take us somewhere that would definitely be wrong."

"I see," Bailey said, feeling heat flame up her neck as she digested what Brice was saying. She would no longer harbor disdainful thoughts of anyone who mentioned getting caught up in the moment. She used to think people who said that were weak-willed and emotional. Now, she thought there was much more to it than controlling emotions. A lot more. Shamed by both her inexperience and her inability to keep her distance from Brice, she blushed.

Brice, who watched Bailey's face turn red with embarrassment, kissed her cheek and held his hand at the back of her head, buried in her silky curls. "Sugar, don't be embarrassed. It's all fine. We just can't let things get quite so far out of hand."

"No, we certainly can't or won't," Bailey said, leaning into Brice despite her better judgment. He was so strong and warm and it felt so right to be with him. Wanting to slap herself to snap out of the trance she seemed to be in, she slid forward on the seat. "I guess I better say good night."

"Okay," Brice said, not making any effort to move or let her out of the truck. Taking her chin in his hand, he forced her to look at him. "Bailey, I really didn't plan on anything happening and I'll do my best to behave, but it's hard when you're so darn pretty, and smell so nice. You make me forget everything but how much I love you."

Bailey stared at Brice like he had suddenly lost his mind. Love? Who said anything about love? Was that what this indescribable feeling was that twisted her insides, made her feel incapable of rational choices, and kept her thoughts constantly on Brice?

"Brice, I don't know what to say," Bailey said, at a loss for words. She couldn't say she loved him too when she wasn't sure she did. She certainly didn't want to be in love with him or anyone. It would wreak all sorts of havoc with her carefully laid career plans.

"Don't say anything right now, sugar," Brice said, watching Bailey's inner struggle to come to terms with what she was feeling and thinking. It was because of that struggle that he was encouraged the battle was not yet lost. "When you're ready to admit you're falling in love, I'll be right here to catch you."

Bailey smiled through the tears that were suddenly prickling her eyes and gave Brice a soft, gentle kiss on his cheek. "Thank you."

"You're welcome," Brice said, pulling her off the seat and into his arms. "It's time for you to go to bed, my sweet sugar. I hope you'll dream one or two dreams of me."

"The likelihood of that happening is quite high in light of this evening's events," Bailey said, wishing the distance from the pickup to the back door was at least twice as far. Being carried in Brice's strong arms was one of the most amazing things she'd ever experienced. She remembered being carried to her room the night she was drunk at Trent's wedding and again the next day down at the pond.

Brice chuckled as he set her down on the step outside the mud room door. The outside light was on as well as the kitchen light and he could only guess that some of the Thompsons were probably awake and watching. If not, he was sure someone from the bunkhouse was probably keeping an eye on them.

"Thank you for having dinner with me, Bailey. It's been a very interesting and educational day."

"It has been, hasn't it?" Bailey smiled as she looked up at Brice in the twilight, thinking how much she enjoyed having him with her at the fossil site that afternoon, despite her many protests.

"If you don't already have plans Friday night, would you go with me to the football game?" Brice asked, looking over Bailey's shoulder and seeing Travis peering out the kitchen window with an obnoxious grin. Brice waved his hand at his friend, making a mental note to do something to get back at Trav.

"That sounds fun," Bailey said, turning to go in the door.

Brice put his hand on her arm, making her stop and look back at him. He gave her one quick peck on the cheek then hurried back to his truck. "Sweet dreams, sugar."

Going into the house, Bailey thought volatile, unsettling and disturbing were probably better words to describe the feelings her dreams would evoke. Why had she agreed to another date with Brice when she needed to stay entirely away from the man?

If she didn't, it was going to be impossible to stop herself from doing exactly what she said she'd never do…fall in love.

Chapter Nine

*"If one devalues rationality,
the world tends to fall apart."*

Lars von Trier

"Hey, Sugar," Brice's rich voice resonated into Bailey's heart as she answered her phone. The rational part of her brain told her it was ridiculous for her toes to tingle and her thoughts spin off in a dozen directions she didn't wish them to go at the sound of his voice. The other part of her brain, the part that was speaking louder and annoying her more and more these days, loved the gravelly depths of Brice's voice. Hearing it never failed to bring to mind his enticing scent or the enveloping warmth of his calloused hand on hers.

"Hello, Brice."

"I'm running a little behind, got off work late," Brice said, sounding cheerful and a little tired. "Would you mind riding with Trey and Cady and meeting me at the game?"

"It wouldn't bother me to miss the game. If you're just leaving work, you'll need dinner and you sound tired," Bailey said, not wanting Brice to feel like he had to escort her to the football game at the high school. She really had little interest in watching the game and was, in truth, much more interested in watching Brice.

"I'm not letting you off that easy," Brice said with a chuckle, assuming Bailey wasn't all that excited about watching a bunch of teenagers run all over the field with a football. "You go on and I'll be there as quick as I can."

"Very well, then," Bailey said holding back a sigh. Her week at work had been long and exhausting. The thought of sitting quietly reading a book or, goodness forbid, watching a movie held more appeal than sitting on hard bleachers on a chilly evening to witness kids run up and down a field. However, the book or the movie didn't involve Brice and the football game did. "I'll meet you there."

"Don't sound so enthusiastic, sugar," Brice teased. "Someone might get the idea you really don't want to see me and I know that can't be the problem. You've been waiting all week just to feast your eyes on this sorry cowboy, haven't you?"

"You're insufferable and terribly conceited. I just saw you Wednesday, so I haven't been waiting all week," Bailey said, smiling at Brice's teasing. "However, I shall anxiously await your arrival at the game."

"I miss you, too, sugar. See you soon."

Bailey got out of her Jeep, where she had been sitting when Brice called, and walked into the house. Smiling faces looked up at her from the dining table where the hands joined the family for dinner.

"You're just in time to eat," Cady said, pointing to an empty seat with a plate next to Tess.

Washing her hands at the kitchen sink, Bailey sank down on the chair, wanting a hot shower and a nap more than anything else at the moment. Knowing the family would want her to join them for dinner, she'd eat then get ready to go to the football game.

Helping clear the table after dinner, Bailey escaped to her room where she jumped into the shower and let herself relax in the spray of hot water. Contemplating what one wore to a football game as she dried her hair and put on a little makeup, she decided on jeans, a soft sweater and a pair of brown boots. Grabbing a jacket, she stuffed her driver's license, some cash and a package of gum in her pocket before hustling back to the kitchen where Cass was excitedly chattering about the game and seeing her friend Ashley.

"Bailey! Are you coming with us?" Cass asked, grabbing her hand and towing her out the door.

"Apparently she is whether she wanted to or not," Trey said. The twinkle in his eyes, the same shade as Bailey's, gave away his amusement at his precocious child.

Trey held the door to his pickup while Bailey slid in next to Cass. Looking back toward the house, Trey sighed and walked to the back door, holding it open as he called for his wife. "Cady-girl, are you coming?"

Unable to hear Cady's response, Bailey wasn't surprised when Trey disappeared inside only to emerge a minute later carrying a large box in one hand and a pile of blankets in the other. Cady hurried behind him carrying a platter heaped with cookies covered in plastic wrap.

Trey handed Bailey the blankets with an appreciative nod when she reached out for the coverings, placing them on the seat between her and Cass's booster seat. With his free hand, Trey opened Cady's door, helped her into the pickup then handed her the box, which she sat between them on the front seat while balancing a plate of molasses cookies on her lap. As soon as Trey climbed behind the wheel and shut his door, the delicious scent of fall filled the pickup. Spice and something yeasty tickled Bailey's nose and she leaned over the seat, breathing deeply.

"What smells so delicious?"

"Mama made doughnuts for the bake sale," Cass said, wiggling her feet as she looked out the window. "I helped make the cookies."

"You did?" Bailey asked, smiling at the little girl. Cady had tried to subdue the little spitfire's flaming curls into two pigtails, but the springy coils were already escaping. Cass' hair would be flying every direction before the game even started.

"Yep. I got to help stir the butter and sugar together and I beated the eggs," Cass said, proud of her efforts.

"I'll have to be sure to try one," Bailey said, making Cass grin.

"Those doughnuts sure do smell good, darlin'," Trey said, giving Cady a charming smile. "Maybe I better do a little quality control before we get there. You know Brice will hog them since raised doughnuts are his favorite."

"You'll have to stand in line at the concession booth just like everyone else, boss-man," Cady said, offering Trey a flirty grin and a toss of her wavy, dark hair.

"Please, darlin', just one little doughnut," Trey begged, turning his intense blue gaze along with his most charming smile on his wife. "Please, Cady-girl?"

"Please, Mama? Daddy wants one awful bad," Cass chimed in from the back seat, always ready to champion her father's cause.

Cady released a sigh, took a doughnut out of the box, and handed it to Trey before looking back at Bailey. "Do you see what I'm up against? A handsome charmer and his adorable sidekick. How do you say no to that?"

Bailey laughed. "It is challenging, I'm sure."

"You've no idea," Cady said, turning her gaze to Trey and shaking her head with a disapproving look. "Mr. Thompson, you are the worst hooligan of the bunch."

"Nope, I'm not. Travis and Brice hold that title jointly," Trey said as he turned into the high school parking lot.

Cady brushed a bit of sugar glaze from his lip and Trey caught her hand, kissing her fingers. When they shared a private smile, Bailey averted her gaze out the window. She didn't think she would ever grow accustomed to her Thompson cousins and their demonstrative way of living. They didn't do anything inappropriate, but any display of affection had always made her uncomfortable. Bailey's mother and sister were both openly affectionate although Bailey's dad shared her dislike of public displays so they tried to respect his wishes.

Picking up the stack of blankets, Bailey watched as Cass prepared to jump down from the pickup and run off when Trey grabbed her around the waist and picked her up.

"I don't want you running all over creation tonight. You stay with us until we get settled then we'll see about finding Ashley," Trey said, holding his daughter up so she could look in his eyes.

"Okay, Daddy," Cass said, giving his cheek a slobbery kiss as he set her back down. Although she didn't run off, she hopped from one foot to the other, anxious to join the crowd of fans already filling the bleachers at the football field.

Trey and Cady carried the treats to the concession booth while Bailey and Cass waited for them at the entrance to the stands. By then, Tess, Travis, Trent and Lindsay joined them and they found seats as a group. Rather than spreading out along one row of seats, they sat together on three rows with Trent and Lindsay in the front, Trey, Cady and Cass in the middle while Travis, Tess and Bailey sat in the back. Bailey left a folded blanket beside her to save a seat for Brice.

The whistle blew to signal the beginning of the game and Bailey looked on with interest, despite her earlier trepidation at attending. Growing up in Denver and attending a big high school, she completely ignored the sports activities, focusing on her science classes and extra-curricular studies. In her twenty-seven years, she had never once been to a football game. As odd as it seemed, she'd never even watched one on television. Her dad didn't care for sports and the only reason Sierra would show any interest in anything remotely athletic was because a boy she liked was playing, not because she was particularly interested in the activity.

Looking at the lines drawn across the grass, the goal posts and score boards, Bailey tried to recall what she knew about the game. She assumed the goal posts were important, the lines would designate something and, with the padding the boys were wearing, physical contact was most likely a given. Watching the kick-off, she jumped when a warm arm settled around her shoulders.

Brice's seductive scent teased her nose as he pressed a kiss to her cheek. "Hey, sugar. I'm glad you came."

"I think I may be as well," Bailey said, unaware that she was squeezing the hand Brice gently placed on her leg. "This is most interesting. What is the object of the game?"

Studying her to see if she was kidding or serious, Brice quickly decided she was not pulling his leg.

"You've never been to a football game?"

"No, I haven't," Bailey said, watching the Sherman County boys run with the ball down the field before the player with the ball was abruptly slammed to the ground by a member of the opposing team. "Can they do that?"

"What?" Brice asked, distracted by the fact Bailey had never watched football before as well as the light shining in her bright eyes. She was never content just to watch something. Bailey wanted to know everything about how it worked, why it was done that way, how it came to be. Her inquisitive mind often left Brice reeling as he tried to keep up.

"Throw that poor boy down like that."

"That's called a tackle, sugar, and that's all part of the game."

"Oh," Bailey said, lost in the action taking place on the field.

Brice discovered Cady made his favorite doughnuts and sent Cass to the concession stand to get some. He was blissfully eating his third one when Bailey grabbed his arm, tugging his attention back to the field. "Are you sure this game is fair. The other team has more players than our boys."

Brice hid a grin behind a napkin at her calling the local kids "our boys" in a proprietary tone. "The other team is from a bigger school and they have more kids, which means they also have more players. That's all. The game's fair because they only allow the same number of players out on the field."

"It's still not fair. Based on the number of boys on each team, they have more players to rotate into the game meaning their team has the opportunity to be..." Bailey quickly counted the number of players for both teams, did rapid calculations in her head and finished her statement, "about 18 percent less exhausted than our players if they rotate in all the boys."

Mind boggling. How could the woman figure percentages that fast in her head? Not that he cared, but if he let it bother him, Brice could feel like a real dunce around Bailey.

"They don't rotate all the kids in. Some of them won't ever leave the bench," Brice said, finishing his doughnut.

"What fun is that for the kids who don't get to play? Isn't the point of athletic endeavors to teach the students skills like teamwork and sportsmanship?" Bailey asked, looking at Brice like he should be able to fix what she perceived as a problem.

"In theory, yes, those would be the reasons for kids to play. The reality of sports is that it boils down to competing, being the best, and winning," Brice said, looking around for Cass. He spied her sitting a few rows over with her little friend Ashley. With his food runner otherwise occupied, Brice poked the arm of his next victim.

"Tessie, since Cass is all tangled up with Ashley, would you be a good sister and get me something to drink?" Brice asked Tess, leaning behind Bailey.

Leaning forward, Tess poked his leg several times, causing Brice to slap playfully at her hand. She shook her head.

"Gosh, BB, for a minute, there, I thought maybe your legs were broken. Glad to see you're just fine and perfectly capable of going to get your own drink. While you're at it, Bailey and I would like some hot chocolate. It's starting to cool down."

Bailey turned toward Tess and started to say she was fine when she realized it was getting chilly and she really would like a cup of hot chocolate.

"Come on, bro," Brice said, getting to his feet and pointing to Travis. "Your woman is getting awfully sassy these days. You gonna let her treat you like that when you're married? She'll be wearing the pants and giving you marching orders if you're not careful."

Travis kissed Tess and gave her a rakish wink before stepping around the girls and down the aisle behind Brice. "She can wear the pants, the skirts, and whatever she pleases as long as I'm the one she lets…"

Bailey couldn't hear the rest of the conversation as the two men walked off toward the concession stand. Turning to look at Tess, a pink blush rode her cheeks as she gazed affectionately after Travis.

Sucking down another sigh, Bailey shook her head. It was just pathetic the way some women fell completely head over heels for a man. They lost all ability to think rationally and any historian could point to the loss of rationality as the downfall of many civilizations.

Ignoring the chill that permeated her without Brice's warmth at her side, Bailey turned her attention back to the game. When their team scored a touchdown, the crowd surged to its feet cheering. Bailey watched in annoyance as Trent kissed Lindsay and Trey grabbed Cady around the waist, wrapping her in a tight hug.

It was positively distasteful to watch. Rolling her lips together, she sank down to her cold seat on the bench, wondering why her cousins, rough and rowdy men, had to be so carefree in displaying their fondness for their mates. They were…huggy.

"Who kissed or hugged whom?" Brice asked, handing her a cup of hot chocolate as he sat beside her with a cup of hot coffee.

"Why would you ask that?" Bailey asked, wondering how Brice could possibly know what she was thinking.

"Because you get that sour lemon look on your face any time one of these Thompson boys feels inspired to show a little affection," Brice said, mischief dancing in his brown eyes.

"I most certainly do not," Bailey said in her most disdainful tone. She sat straighter on the bleacher and slid a little to the left, away from Brice's arm where it rested around her back.

"You most certainly do," Brice said, mimicking her voice and facial expression, which made Travis snort soda out his nose.

"Sorry," Travis said, swiping at the back of Trey's jacket, now covered with a fine mist of Dr. Pepper.

"If you're going to be detestable, I'll go home," Bailey said to Brice, starting to rise from the bleacher seat.

Brice set his coffee down beside him, took Bailey's chocolate out of her hand and passed it to Tess before grabbing Bailey and pulling her onto his lap. Much to her joint dismay and pleasure, he proceeded to plant a kiss on her lips that made everyone around them gape in surprise. Some spectators whistled, a few hollered comments, and Cady turned around to half-heartedly slap his leg. In shock over his outrageous actions, Bailey couldn't do anything but participate in the amazing kiss.

"I think you were just wanting a little attention of your own," Brice whispered in Bailey's ear before he let her go, setting her on the bleacher seat beside him. Picking up his coffee, he turned back to watch the game.

If his plan was to subdue Bailey and get her to stay, it worked well. Brice's kiss made her feel unsettled, fearful, wanted and wonderful. Mulling over the conflicting feelings and emotions, she refrained from making any further comments and focused her gaze on the game.

Watching a few more plays, she leaned closer to Brice and pointed to the field. "Why do they do that?"

"Do what?" Brice asked, trying to figure out what play she was questioning.

"Bend over and put their hands so close to the other player's... you know..." Bailey whispered.

Swallowing back a laugh, Brice grinned and pointed to each player. "That is the center with the ball. When he bends over like that he is getting ready to hike it to the quarterback. The quarterback can then run with the ball or pass it. That's why they get so close. They want to make sure the pass is successful."

"I see," Bailey said, finishing the last of her chocolate and cheering when the home team won the game.

Trey picked up a sleeping Cass and started out to the pickup while Cady gathered blankets.

"You'll bring Bailey home, right?" Cady asked Brice as she walked down the bleacher steps.

"Yes, ma'am," Brice said, tipping his hat to Cady as she grinned at him. Turning toward Tess and Travis, Brice watched them share a quick kiss and hold hands as they waited for their turn to walk out of the stands. "And just what do you two have planned?"

"Not that it is any of your business, BB, but I'm going back to the Running M and Trav is heading to the

Triple T. We want to get an early start on work at our house and it's been a long week," Tess said, turning to look at her fiancé with a grin. "We sound like a couple of old married people. It's Friday night and we will both be at our respective homes in bed by eleven."

"You look ancient, honeybee," Travis teased, nuzzling her neck and making her giggle.

Bailey started to roll her lips together but refrained, remembering Brice's comment from earlier in the evening.

"How about you, sugar? Want to go find something to do or are you ready to call it a night?" Brice asked, grasping Bailey's hand in his as they walked out of the bleachers toward the parking lot. Brice stopped at the concession booth to see if any doughnuts remained and purchased the last three.

"How many of those can you possibly eat?" Bailey asked as Brice carried his doughnuts to the pickup wrapped in a napkin.

"As many as I can get my hands on," Brice said with a teasing grin. "Actually, I'm full, but these will be great for breakfast. I'll just have to hide them so no one beats me to them."

"You are..."

"Insufferable," Brice supplied before Bailey could finish her statement. "I believe you may have mentioned that before, along with the fact you find me arrogant, conceited, obnoxious and annoying. Oh, and detestable. Let's not forget that one."

As Brice held her hand and helped her into his pickup, Bailey wondered if he realized how many of his good qualities she admired. She knew she was quick to point out the negative, but those attributes were minimal compared to all the good things about Brice.

Casting him a sideways glance as he climbed behind the wheel, Bailey appreciated the view of the handsome cowboy. He remained quiet as he guided the truck into the line of vehicles leaving the school.

Heading back toward the Triple T, Brice was almost to the turn-off when Bailey reached across the seat and placed a soft hand on his hard thigh.

"Brice, I just wanted you to know, I don't only think you are insufferable and annoying," Bailey said giving him a look that begged for his understanding.

"I know, sugar, you also think I'm disgusting, irritating, and a wild delinquent," Brice said, flashing his white teeth as he grinned.

"Even so, I also think you are fun and exciting, kind and handsome, and quite wonderful," Bailey said, never having spoken in such a manner before. It was hard to imagine she was doing so now, but she didn't seem to be able to keep the words from spilling out.

Brice studied Bailey thoughtfully. When their eyes connected he missed the turn to the Triple T and kept driving. He turned onto a dirt lane a few miles down the road and wandered down a trail until they were parked in a grove of trees near a creek. The evening was chilly and clear with a big moon providing all the light Brice needed to see Bailey's eyes change into liquid fire when he ran his thumb along her throat and kissed her neck.

"Brice, I thought you recommended not positioning ourselves in a secluded area where our good intentions could be easily cast aside," Bailey said, struggling to keep her composure with Brice trailing scorching kisses from her ear to her jaw.

"Stop talking and kiss me," Brice growled, capturing her lips with his. Bailey willingly surrendered before melting against Brice.

Their kisses grew more passionate, their lips more demanding, until Brice broke away and tried to remember all the reasons, any reason, he should keep from kissing Bailey all night. Rational thought had long ago fled and the only thing that came to mind was how good Bailey felt in his arms.

Struggling against what he knew he should do and what he wanted to do, he released a sigh. "Sugar, I should have taken you straight home. I'm sorry. Let's…"

Bailey silenced Brice with a finger to his lips.

"Stop talking and kiss me," she said, repeating his words. Brice groaned and dropped his dark head to her golden one.

"I want you so much, baby," Brice whispered, running his hands across her back, over her shoulders and down her arms.

"You've got me right now," Bailey whispered, kissing Brice's jaw and inhaling his scent that made her think all sorts of thoughts she shouldn't. Her hand slid down his chest and rested on his tight abs while she continued kissing him slowly, tempting him more with each touch of her lips.

"No, sugar. No," Brice said grasping at his last bit of restraint, carefully pushing her back and sliding away from her. Holding her hand in his, he kissed the back of it, his eyes still dark and molten. "I don't have you, but I will, someday. And before either of us loses what little sense we've got left, I'm taking you home."

Bailey wanted to argue, but couldn't. Instead she sat with her gaze out the window for the time it took them to get back to the Triple T.

"Thank you," Bailey finally said, looking at Brice with big, moist eyes as he helped her out of the truck.

"You're welcome, sugar."

Kissing her cheek, he left her at the door to the mud room. Brice hurried back to his truck and waved as he pulled out of the yard.

Brice's heart was still pounding while heat radiated through him. His gut was clenched in a tight knot and his head was starting to ache. It was getting more and more difficult to keep any distance from Bailey, let alone one that was respectable.

He was surprised by her words earlier. Not the ones pointing out his faults, but the words letting him know she did care.

If he was a less persistent person, he might abandon his efforts at winning Bailey's heart. Despite her protests, despite her cool demeanor, when they kissed the world exploded into showers of sparks around them. Brice could tell Bailey felt it every bit as much as he did.

That's how he knew someday the beautiful, intelligent, exasperating woman would be his.

Chapter Ten

*"Trip over love, you can get up.
Fall in love and you fall forever."*

Unknown

Bailey stood staring at Cady like she'd lost her mind, sure she misheard her request.

Cady patted Bailey on the arm and smiled at her encouragingly while somehow maneuvering her toward the door.

"You'll be fine," Cady said, gathering up a stack of blankets and handing them to Bailey. "Travis and Tess will be there and so will Brice."

At the mention of Brice's name, Bailey felt her neck warm. The church was sponsoring a hayride that night for the youth group and the Morgan family always provided the wagon and horses along with the straw bales. Cady and Trey volunteered to chaperone and provide treats while Tess and Travis agreed to help out.

Unfortunately, Lindsay called at noon to let Cady know Cass wasn't feeling well. The little girl was running a fever and sniffling, so Cady planned to stay home with Cass and decided Bailey could go as her substitute. Trey somehow managed to bow out of the obligation as well, letting Brice take his place as a chaperone.

Thermos jugs full of spiced cider and hot chocolate were already in Travis' pickup along with plates of cookies and brownies.

Cady walked with Bailey out to the truck and stacked the blankets on the floor while Travis gave Bailey a hand into the back seat.

"Are you certain my presence is required?" Bailey asked, realizing she didn't even have her purse with her. She was still wearing her work clothes and knew she had any number of things in her pants pockets like her cell phone, breath mints and hand lotion, but nothing that helped prepare her to deal with a wagon load of rowdy kids. "My past experience does not encompass being a chaperone."

"It's easy," Travis said, closing her door and sliding behind the wheel.

"You'll be great," Tess said, turning around to smile at Bailey. "Just give them that authoritative look you turn to my brother all the time and they'll be properly subdued."

Travis grinned and squeezed Tess' hand when Bailey appeared to consider what she said.

"Just relax and you'll have fun, Bailey," Travis said, trying to sound reassuring.

As they pulled up at the church parking lot, Mike and Brice had the wagon out front ready to go. It was still early enough that it wasn't too dark or cold out yet, though the air promised to turn chilly before long.

Tess and Bailey carried the treats into the church while Travis tossed the blankets into the wagon. The teens stood in groups of two or three, talking and laughing.

Travis remembered going on the hayride multiple times. He and Brice somehow managed to get Tess cornered one year when it was absolutely freezing. She sat between the two of them trying to stay warm as the three of them shared a blanket. Having loved her even then, Travis relished the close contact, although he helped Brice tie her sneaker laces together and dump a handful of straw down the neck of her sweater.

"Remembering how awful you and Brice were to me when we went on these hayrides?" Tess asked as she wrapped her arms around his waist from behind.

"You know it, honeybee," Travis said, turning around and giving her a quick kiss.

"None of that, you two," Mike teased, thumping Travis on the back. "You're here to keep the kids from doing that sort of thing, not setting a bad example."

"Dad," Tess said, rolling her eyes while her cheeks flushed pink. "Please."

"He's right, Tessie," Brice said, grabbing Bailey's hand and pulling her up into the wagon whether she wanted to go or not. "We'll be keeping an eye on you two."

"I'll be watching you right back," Tess said, giving Brice a look that let him know he better be on his best behavior, at least until the end of the hayride.

As the kids clamored into the wagon and took seats on straw bales, Bailey found herself sitting next to Brice on one end while Tess and Travis sat on the other.

Searching through her memories, she couldn't remember ever going on a hayride before and decided she would make the most of the experience.

It wouldn't be difficult to let herself enjoy it on a beautiful fall evening with the crisp scent of autumn in the air and the gentle clop-clop of the horses' hooves blending with the creak of the wagon. Most of the trees were already adorned with the colors of the season, boasting leaves in brilliant shades of crimson, orange and gold.

"How are you, sugar?" Brice whispered in her ear.

The combination of his minty breath, heady leathery scent and the proximity of his strong body close to hers made Bailey involuntarily shiver.

"Fine," Bailey whispered back, annoyed by the way her body reacted to Brice despite her intentions to remain aloof.

"Are you cold?" Brice asked, rubbing his hands up and down her arms, sending her already swirling senses into a tailspin.

"No, I'm fine," Bailey said, scooting away from Brice. When they hit a bump, his hand around her waist was the only thing that kept her from tipping off the end of the wagon.

"Careful, there. Don't want any precious cargo falling out," Brice said, looking at her with sparkling brown eyes as he pulled her closer against his side.

"Perhaps I should move," Bailey said, desperate to get away from Brice as the desire to throw her arms around his neck and kiss him nearly overtook her. Spying an empty space in the middle of the wagon, Bailey got to her feet and moved before Brice could stop her. She pretended not to see the raised eyebrow he shot her direction or the shake of his head as she took a deep breath and tried to regain her ability to think straight.

Looking around, she found she was sitting near a group of giggling girls, one of whom wasted no time in taking Bailey's place next to Brice. When he glared at Bailey, she offered him a saucy grin. Trying to deal with the obviously infatuated teen would keep him busy for a while.

Hearing a sigh, Bailey turned her attention from Brice and the girl to the boy sitting beside her. He was tall and gangly, although he was starting to fill out his frame. Glasses perched on a nose buried in a thick book. Bailey had no idea about kids, boys especially, but she would guess this one to be around sixteen.

The way he sat by himself, lost in his reading, made Bailey think of her high school years, stirring a soft response to the boy. Maybe if she'd spent a little time learning social skills then, she wouldn't be floundering so badly with Brice now.

Looking at the book the boy was reading, Bailey smiled. The history of the native people prior to Columbus arriving was pretty heavy reading for a hay ride.

"Have you gotten to the part about the Aztec capital of Tenochtitlan having running water and clean streets?" Bailey asked the boy, nudging him gently with her elbow as she spoke.

He looked up from his book, confused, before focusing his attention on Bailey. She could almost see him trying to rationalize why she was talking to him before he processed her question.

"Yes," he answered, giving her a guarded look.

"What part are you reading now?" Bailey asked, pointing to the book with interest.

"About their genetic engineering experiments with corn," the boy said, studying Bailey curiously, not certain if she was genuinely interested or just teasing him. From his past experiences, pretty girls only talked to him if they wanted help with their homework or someone to torment.

"Don't you find it fascinating how their culture was so advanced? Much more so than most historians lead you to believe. When I visited the Aztec ruins, it was absolutely amazing to envision the day to day activities that took place there, " Bailey said, looking at the boy with an open expression that was slowly gaining his trust. For some reason, she felt a need to help the kid out of his shell. Maybe because she still pulled the edges of her own around her from time to time even though she knew she shouldn't. Like now. With Brice.

"Who are you?" the boy blurted out.

"I'm Bailey Bishop, cousin to the Thompson family from the Triple T Ranch," Bailey said, holding out her hand to the boy.

"I'm Liam Anderson." Everyone in Grass Valley knew the Thompson family. Although Liam didn't have any interest in cowboying or ranching, he was familiar enough with the three brothers to know they were good people.

"It's very nice to meet you, Liam," Bailey said, continuing their conversation about the book Liam was reading.

"How do you know so much about ancient civilizations?" Liam asked as the other youth on the wagon broke into a series of campfire songs around them.

"It's part of my work," Bailey said, smiling at the boy. "I'm a paleontologist."

"Are you kidding me?" Liam said, staring at Bailey with hero-worship. "I want to be an anthropologist but my dad wants me to study agri-business and take over the farm someday. I hate farming."

"Every endeavor has its purpose," Bailey said, trying to think of the right words to encourage Liam without discouraging him from his father's wishes. "To that end, though, you have to decide where your passion lies and be willing to give your all to pursue it."

Liam considered her words and nodded his head. Bailey had already figured out he was not a big talker.

"Only you know what your dreams are, but maybe you can find a way to share them with your father so that he can see the same vision you do," Bailey said. Moved by compassion for the boy, she reached out and patted Liam on the back.

Fighting tooth and nail against what her mother wanted for her as a career choice, Bailey knew how important it was to be able to pursue dreams. Due to sheer determination and a stubborn will, Bailey finally won her mother over, but it took time and a lot of effort. "It helps to have some common ground for a starting point."

"Common ground?" Liam asked, closing his book as he looked at Bailey.

"Yes. Are there any activities or interests you and your father enjoy doing together?"

"We both like to camp," Liam said, as the light bulb went off in his head. "I get it. You're saying find something that we both like to do and then build my case from there."

"I knew you were a very intelligent young man and you've proven my assumption correct," Bailey said with a warm smile.

Had she been watching Brice, Bailey would have seen warring emotions cross his expressive features. He was amused that Bailey would choose to sit next to Liam, the perpetual loner of the young crowd.

The boy was a constant trial to his father who wanted Liam to take over the reins of the farm when he was hold enough. Liam, on the other hand, was more interested in scholarly pursuits and participated in the farm work as little as possible. He wasn't lazy, just interested in a career much different than what his father had planned.

Brice was surprised by the way Bailey reached out to the young boy, making him feel comfortable. It was nice to see her draw Liam out as they talked. Now, though, the kid was looking at her with big puppy-dog eyes and, as irrational as it was, Brice felt a twist of jealousy tighten his insides.

Trying to block out to the non-stop chatter in his ear from one of the high school girls while simultaneously looking like he was paying attention, Brice was dissecting Bailey's actions of the evening.

From past experience, he knew she wasn't the most social person on the planet. It wasn't exactly like her to seek someone out and start a conversation, but watching her with the shy Anderson boy, her face gave her away as she talked to him animatedly about the book he was reading. Brice had a feeling Bailey could relate with Liam, perhaps better than anyone else.

Watching Liam relax and talk freely with Bailey, Brice could only guess she had made a friend for life. Too bad she didn't feel as comfortable with him as she did with the kid.

As though sensing his gaze, Bailey looked up at him and smiled with such warmth and tenderness, Brice could feel pieces of his heart melting.

"Brice, don't you think that's a great idea?" the girl jabbering in his ear asked as she placed her hand on his arm. He glanced down at the bright blue painted fingernails and held back a sigh.

"I'm sorry, Miranda, I didn't hear what you said," Brice said, inching away from her.

"I said you should come chaperone the harvest dance at school. That would be so cool. You could come with me and that way you wouldn't be there by yourself," Miranda gushed, tossing her pink-streaked blond hair.

"Sorry, but that won't be happening," Brice said bluntly, softening his words with a grin. "If you're looking for someone to take you to the dance, why not ask Liam over there. He's a nice kid and tall for his age."

"Eww," Miranda said, looking at Liam. "He's always got his nose in some book about dead people or ancient stuff. He's so not my type."

"How do you know he isn't? Ever gone out with him? Done anything with him outside of school?" Brice asked, hoping to divert the young girl's attention somewhere besides himself.

"Well, duh, like I'd want the guys to get the wrong idea," Miranda said, rolling her eyes at Brice.

"What idea would that be? That you have the intelligence to see beyond the exterior and get to know someone before you judge them?" Brice asked, hoping Miranda would someday grow out of her shallow way of thinking. Then again, he wasn't much better at her age. Shoot. He wasn't much better now.

Miranda glared at him.

Brice pointed to Bailey and Liam. "He must have something going on to get a pretty woman like Miss Bishop to sit and talk to him. It looks to me like she's enjoying his company. A woman like that doesn't spend her time with just anyone," Brice said, knowing the truth to that statement. After all, she'd left him to sit with the kid.

"You really think she's, well…you know?" Miranda said, studying Bailey with narrowed eyes.

Goodness only knew what the girl was thinking.

"She's what?" Brice asked, finding his attention drawn to the way the last of the sun's golden autumn rays were settling on Bailey's honey-colored hair and her long legs tucked up neatly against the straw bale. Her hands, larger than most women's, moved animatedly as she spoke with Liam. If the kids weren't singing so loudly, he might be able to hear what she was saying, although he doubted he would understand or care about half of it.

"All that," Miranda said, making finger quotes in the air with her hands.

Brice chuckled.

"Oh, yeah. She's definitely all that and then some," Brice said, looking at Bailey with his heart in his eyes. "She's smart, clever, hard-working and beautiful."

"Hmph," Miranda said, giving her hair another flounce for good measure, although she did appear to be looking thoughtfully at both Liam and Bailey. She moved back to sit with her friends, leaving Brice on his own at the back of the wagon. Despite the chill in the air, he had no interest in snuggling under one of the blankets without Bailey there to share it with him.

At the front of the wagon, Tess and Travis were cuddled together, trying to pay attention to the youth group

THE COWBOY'S AUTUMN FALL

instead of each other. Brice shook his head and hid his smile.

Up until he met Bailey, he would have said anyone beleaguered with notions of romance needed their head examined. He would have chalked it up to a lack of sense and an overdose of sentimental claptrap.

After spending the last several weeks trying to woo Bailey, he had an entirely different perspective on the matter. Loving someone was a lot of hard work. Especially when you weren't entirely certain the person you loved was ever going to fully return those feelings.

As though sensing his gaze on her, Bailey looked at him across the wagon and Brice felt himself tumbling into the bright depths of her ocean blue eyes. Holding her gaze, he watched her cheeks turn pink.

He could almost see her thoughts churning in her head. Part of her wanted to come sit close to him, wanted him to kiss her in the worst way. The other part of her, that darn rational, analytical part of her brain, was telling her to stay far away from Brice before he managed to derail her career plans.

Grinning, he watched her lips tip up in a smile before she returned her attention to Liam.

Arriving back at the church, Brice jumped off the end of the wagon and gave a hand to the girls while the boys tumbled off, pushing and shoving in a show of how tough they were.

Tess and Bailey went inside to help serve the treats while Travis and Brice gathered blankets and loaded them in Travis' pickup.

"So, man, how are things going with Bailey?" Travis asked, slapping Brice on the back as they walked into the church. Mike already took the horses and wagon and headed for home.

"As good as they can be, I guess," Brice said, a little discouraged to see Liam following Bailey around as she poured cider and chocolate.

"I noticed she took up with the Anderson boy. Maybe if you'd start reading up on dead people and petrified relics, she'd sit by you next time," Travis teased, snatching a cookie off a platter.

Brice picked up two brownies, munching on them while ignoring Travis' teasing. He watched while Tess said something that made Bailey laugh and shake her head. Her curls danced at the motion and he suddenly wanted to bury his fingers in the silky strands.

"Does that work for you?" Travis asked, catching Brice lost in his thoughts of Bailey.

"What?" Brice asked, looking at Travis who smirked at him. "I didn't hear what you said."

"Of course you didn't. How could you when you're watching Bailey like she might disappear at any moment?" Travis said, elbowing Brice. "I asked if you could run into The Dalles with me tomorrow for the final fitting on our tuxes."

"Sure. I'll be off work at four. Is that too late?" Brice asked, trying not to glance at Bailey out of the corner of his eye.

"Nope. That works for me," Travis said, his smile widening as he spied Tess bent over refilling the cookie platter.

"Dude, she is my sister. Could you not ogle her while I'm standing right here," Brice said, rolling his eyes at Travis.

"Sorry, man, but that's part of the price you pay for being my best friend and Tess' brother," Travis said, intently watching his bride-to-be. "Cut me some slack, would you? We'll be married in less than two weeks."

"Don't remind me. Every spare moment, Mom and Tess have been bossing me around like nobody's business," Brice said, leaning against a table and taking a drink of the hot cider. It tasted like the essence of autumn with a sweet apple flavor highlighted by rich spices. "They actually expect me to clean out the loft in the barn this weekend."

"No way," Travis said, knowing the barn loft had long ago been declared sacred ground for Brice and Ben at the ranch. Growing up, it was their play area. As teens, it was their place to escape and Travis knew for a fact many girls had been wooed and pursued in the loft by the brothers. "Do you even have to move ol' Bessie?"

"More than move her. Mom's making me haul her, along with about a hundred other things to the dump or the Goodwill store when I get done cleaning out the barn. She has promised me to find a replacement for Bessie, but that ol' girl is full of memories," Brice said, finishing his cup of cider.

"Full of memories, and mice nests, and who knows what else," Travis said with a grin. "That loveseat, which happened to be so aptly named for the use you and Ben put it to, is long past its prime, dude. I'm surprised Michele let you hang onto it this long."

"She forgot it was up there until she and Tess did a complete inspection of the barn a few weeks ago. They decided it had to go," Brice put his hands on his hips and mimicked Tess in a falsetto voice as he listed all the things in the barn that needed carted off.

Travis was trying not to roll on the floor with laughter and several of the boys standing near them were also laughing.

"Find that amusing, do you?" Tess asked, smacking both Brice and Travis as she walked by.

Travis grabbed her hand and pulled her into a hug, kissing the top of her head. "I do, honeybee. Your brother's ability to portray you is spot-on."

"Hmph!" Tess said, putting just enough effort in trying to pull away from Travis that he would tighten his hold.

"No need to get riled up, Tessa," Travis said softly in her ear. "Play your cards right and we might even be able to wrangle some help for your cleaning project."

"It really is too bad about Bessie, BB," Tess said, knowing how attached her brother was to the ratty piece of furniture. "But you've got to admit, she has served you well despite her decrepit state."

"Rather like another female on the Morgan Ranch," Brice said, giving his sister a cocky smile. He wasn't surprised when Tess reached over and smacked his arm again.

"Are you sure you want to marry her, Trav? She's given to fits of violence, as you well know," Brice said, rubbing his arm and trying to look abused. The playful glint of mischief dancing in his brown eyes let everyone know the siblings were only teasing.

"I'm sure," Travis said, bending down to whisper something in Tess' ear that made her blush and duck her head against his chest.

"Hey, enough of that. We are in the church after all," Brice said, thumping Travis on the back. He turned to the captive audience around them and asked if anyone wanted to help him Saturday and got a show of hands. "Be at the ranch by nine and we'll feed you lunch."

Brice was surprised to see Liam volunteer to come help. Maybe he thought Bailey would be there, which Brice hoped she would.

If she was, Brice might have to give Bessie one more opportunity at being the loved-on seat before he hauled her off.

Chapter Eleven

"The fall of dropping water wears away the stone."
Lucretius

"Are you going to join us, Cady?" Bailey asked Saturday morning as she helped Cady wash the breakfast dishes. She and Lindsay were planning to go over to the Running M Ranch to see what they could do to help with preparations for Tess and Travis' wedding reception the following Saturday.

As a surprise for Tess, the Thompson family already cleaned the inside of the fort until it was spotless, added a moveable arbor out front and brought in pots of fall flowers to set around the building. When Tess and Travis exchange their vows in front of the fort where they first kissed as kids, the setting would be beautiful.

Trey, Trent and Travis planned to finish up work at the Drexel house and move in furniture Tess and Travis ordered to go with the antiques Mr. Drexel left behind. The Morgan family, and anyone else who could lend a hand, would work on getting the barn ready for the reception.

"I'll join you a little later this morning," Cady said as she hung the dishtowel up to dry while Bailey rinsed out the cloth she used to wipe down the counters. "I promised Michele I'd help her with food for lunch, so I'll get some things ready and then come over with Cass. Why don't you have Lindsay come pick you up and then you can ride home with one of us later."

"That would be satisfactory," Bailey said as she opened her cell and dialed Lindsay's number. After a brief conversation, Lindsay agreed to pick up Bailey in about half an hour.

Not one to sit and do nothing, Bailey went to her room and retrieved a set of pillowcases she was finishing for Travis and Tess as a wedding gift. She knew Tess would love a gift that spoke to the era of the house, so Bailey had already crocheted a table runner and six doilies of various sizes. The pillowcases had pink roses along the border with green ivy and a small white heart with Tess and Travis' name in the corner. She was crocheting a border along the edge of each case, then her gift would be complete.

Cady washed her hands even though they were clean and sat down on the barstool next to Bailey, taking the edge of one fine linen case in her fingers and admiring the handiwork.

"Bailey, I had no idea you could do work like this. It's beautiful," Cady said, admiring the even, precise stitches and the crocheted trim that looked like a froth of lace.

"It helps me relax when my mind wants to keep going," Bailey said, her silver crochet hook catching the light from the kitchen window as she whipped it in and out of the white thread. "My grandmother taught me, dad's mom."

"You must be her prize pupil," Cady said with a smile, knowing how much Tess would love the gift. Travis could care less about pillowcases, but he would appreciate the effort Bailey put into the hand-made treasure. "You and Brice should put your gifts together."

"Oh?" Bailey said, feeling the familiar flutter in her stomach at the mere mention of Brice. "What's he giving them?"

"You mean he hasn't shown you?" Cady asked, surprised Brice hadn't shared that information with Bailey. She supposed he had other things on his mind when the two of them were together.

"No, he hasn't and now I'm intrigued," Bailey said, wondering what Brice was giving the couple that her gift would complement.

"Come on, I'll give you a hint," Cady said, taking Bailey's hand and pulling her around the corner and down the hall in the north wing to the master suite she shared with Trey.

Bailey had been in the room only once before, but admired how spacious and lovely it looked.

"He's making them one of those," Cady said, pointing to a beautifully carved cedar chest. The outside was polished to a high shine and in the middle of the front panel two intertwined hearts caught Bailey's attention. Walking closer, she could see Trey and Cady's names carved into the wood, along with their wedding date.

"Brice made this for your wedding?" Bailey asked, not surprised at the fine craftsmanship of the piece, knowing Brice was very talented in woodworking.

"Yes, he did. Technically we got it when we returned from the honeymoon in February since we only gave everyone a week's notice on our wedding, but it was our gift from him. He made one for Trent and Lindsay and he's finishing up one for Travis and Tess. Ask him to show it to you," Cady said, running her hand over the smooth top of the chest. "I just thought your gift would go perfect in the chest."

"Yes, it would," Bailey said, liking the idea of giving her gift with Brice's.

Bailey heard Lindsay talking to Cass in the kitchen so she and Cady went back down the hall.

"Ask him about it, Bailey," Cady urged as Bailey gathered up her things. "Brice gets almost as excited talking about his woodworking as he does talking about you."

Flustered by Cady's teasing, Bailey could only nod her head as she followed Lindsay out the door.

Arriving at the Running M Ranch, Lindsay and Bailey stopped by the barn where a number of vehicles were already parked. They started toward the door only to step aside as Brice and Ben came out carrying an ugly, dilapidated love seat. Bailey vaguely recalled seeing it the night she and Brice were in the barn loft, although her attention was definitely not on the décor, but the man with a charming smile and muscled arms.

Those same arms were now lifting the worn-out piece of furniture into the back of a pickup, straining against his shirt and causing Bailey's heart to pound.

Turning her attention away from the all too appealing vision of Brice, Bailey watched several teens running around, recognizing most of them from the hayride the other evening.

She waved at Liam, who was helping Miranda take down posters tacked to the far wall of the barn.

Glad to see the boy enjoying the company of someone his own age, Bailey followed Lindsay into the fray.

When a bell clanged at noon letting them know lunch was ready, the barn had been cleaned from top to bottom and the guys had begun the process of stringing electrical strips across the ceiling and installing anchor hooks heavy enough to hold chandeliers.

Bailey was walking toward the back yard where lunch was being served when she felt her waist encircled by strong hands as she was swung around the corner of the barn.

"Hey, sugar," Brice said, his face mere inches from Bailey's. Her senses swam delightedly in his alluring scent while her blood warmed at his touch. "I've missed you."

"How could you possibly miss me?" Bailey asked, trying to gather her wayward thoughts. She should push Brice away and hurry to the yard where there was enough activity to distract her from thoughts of the mischievous cowboy. Instead, she wanted him to hold her closer or kiss her until she was completely senseless.

At the rate she was going, it would only take a matter of seconds for that to happen. "You saw me last night at the football game, you texted me before breakfast and I've been here at the barn all morning."

"Yeah, but not just us together. Not so I could do this," Brice said, rubbing his thumb over the curve of her cheek and along her jaw line. "Or this," he said, burying his hands into the hair she had left down, curling to her shoulders. "And definitely not this," he whispered as he bent his head and claimed her lips for his own.

Bailey forgot all about lunch, the wedding and everything else except Brice. When he held her so close, kissed her so passionately, she felt like she had finally found a place where she belonged. He accepted her for who she was and for that she was truly grateful. Brice made her feel beautiful, exciting, and very wanted.

"Brice," Bailey whispered when they came up for air. "We… we better go see about lunch or…"

"Someone will come looking for us," Brice said, finishing her sentence for her. "I know, but you just look so dang cute today, I can hardly think straight."

"Oh," Bailey said, surprised by his honest statement, looking down at her dusty jeans, denim jacket and cotton shirt. "Thank you."

"Anytime, sugar," Brice said, taking her hand in his as he pulled her back around the front of the barn. "Let's go get some food. I'm half-starved."

The hour they took for lunch was filled with lively conversation as the younger set teased and joked while some of the adults joined in. The girls begged Tess to show them her dress, so she took them inside the house while the boys continued trading jokes and jabs in the yard.

"Cady said I should ask you about your gift for Travis and Tess," Bailey said as she and Brice watched the boys teasing each other.

"Would you like to see it?" Brice asked, getting to his feet and holding his hand out to Bailey.

"Yes, I'd like that very much," Bailey said as she stood, placing her hand in Brice's and following him out to a building behind the machine shed. It looked like it may have been a shop or some sort of work area in the past. It wasn't huge, by any means, but looked solid with two windows across the front of the building and one on each side along with a big garage-style door on the front.

Brice dug a ring of keys from his pocket and used one to unlock the small side door. Stepping inside he turned on the light switch and smiled at Bailey to enter.

Speechless, she looked around at an array of finely crafted furniture, stacks of wood and an assortment of tools she didn't recognize.

Running her hand across the smooth finish of an old-fashioned rocking chair, she admired the detailed carvings along the back. She noticed a dining room set, some end tables and what appeared to be a headboard and dresser set.

The piece that got her attention, though, was the one Brice was obviously making for Tess and Travis.

A large cedar chest had a curved bottom edge as it stood on four solid, square feet. With an exterior made of cherry wood, it would perfectly match the bedroom set in the master bedroom at the Drexel house. Looking closer, Bailey smiled to see roses, vines and honey bees carved into the lid of the chest. Bailey ran her fingers across Tess and Travis' names, their wedding date and a small B and M to designate Brice was the craftsman.

Brice lifted the lid and the scent of cedar filled the room. A tray sat on a built-in ledge to hold smaller items. Lifting it out, the chest still offered plenty of room for blankets or other treasures.

Placing her hand on Brice's arm, Bailey squeezed it gently and looked at him impressed.

"It's perfect, Brice. Tess is going to love it."

"I hope so. She and Trav didn't give me much time to work on it with their one-month engagement. Although, truth be known, I started working on this right after Trent and Lindsay got married."

"I think everyone was under the assumption that Travis and Tess would be next to exchange vows," Bailey said. She sniffed, appreciating both the smell of cedar and Brice's warm, tantalizing scent that she was convinced should be labeled something like "sensuous autumn."

"It was a pretty safe bet," Brice said, setting the tray back in the chest and closing the lid. "I've got a few more coats of varnish to apply and then I'll be done."

Looking around the shop, Bailey held Brice's hand as she examined each piece.

"I knew you were very talented, Brice, but nothing I imagined came close to this," Bailey said, waving her free hand around his work space. "Why are you wasting time doing construction? You could make a small fortune selling handcrafted furniture. I'm certain there are places in Portland that would be ecstatic to offer pieces of this quality."

Brice shrugged, pleased by her words, but also a little embarrassed. Making things out of wood was something he had always enjoyed. His grandpa taught him how to whittle and carve, then to make the furniture. Brice was devastated, at the young age of fifteen, when his grandfather passed away.

Although he inherited his grandfather's woodworking tools, his old saddle, and the pocket knife his grandfather carried with him everywhere, Brice would much rather have his grandpa alive, working beside him.

"I'm not offering superfluous accolades, Brice. You have a real and rare talent," Bailey said, turning the heat of her gaze Brice's direction. "It is amazing what you can do."

"Thanks, sugar," Brice said, feeling humbled by her praise. "It's something I enjoy doing when I have time."

"But Brice, you could…" Bailey started to say and was cut off when Brice suddenly wrapped his arms around her and kissed her soundly.

"Why did Cady tell you to ask about my present?" Brice asked, trying to distract Bailey from further discussion about pursuing furniture building as a career.

He'd love to do it, but he was afraid he wouldn't be able to make enough money consistently to have it as his sole source of income. If he thought his pieces would really sell, he might pursue it, but it was better to be employed with a hobby he loved than to be destitute with a talent he no longer enjoyed.

"She saw the gift I was making and thought our two gifts might be combined into one," Bailey said, thinking how much she'd like Brice to kiss her again.

"And what is your gift? Some of your wicked stitchery?" Brice asked, his eyes twinkling with mischief.

"It is stitchery and there is nothing wicked about it, you ridiculous man," Bailey said, trying to hide her smile at Brice's teasing. "I made some doilies and a set of pillowcases. Cady thought it might be fun to put them in the cedar chest."

"I think that's a fine idea," Brice said, leading Bailey to the door and back out into the afternoon sunshine. "We can write on the card from 'Brice and Bailey.' How does that sound?"

Bailey nodded her head, although the sound of what Brice was saying nearly brought her up short. What was she doing, becoming part of a couple?

She had no business, none at all, getting this involved with Brice. She really needed to put a stop to things before either of them got any more lost in this relationship. Distracted, pensive, frustrated and flustered didn't even begin to describe the array of feelings and emotions she'd experienced since she met Brice. Bailey grudgingly acknowledged Brice also made her feel challenged, accepted, amused, cherished, protected, and loved.

Brice made her feel things she'd never felt before. She wasn't used to thinking of anything or anyone beyond what she wanted and Brice had somehow brought out a tender, softer part of her heart she didn't even know existed.

If she kept going down this road, there would soon be no turning back.

"Ready for more fun?" Brice asked as they returned to the barn where the kids were untangling dozens of strands of white lights left from Trent and Lindsay's wedding. Tess was pointing out where she wanted the lights strung and Michele was shooing the group away from the area where Brice and Ben were going to soon construct a temporary stage at the back of the barn. Mike was up in the loft making sure all the power strips were working and securely anchored.

"Certainly," Bailey said, walking over to where a couple of the girls were untangling one particularly bunched up string of lights and lent a hand.

While Brice and Ben cut and pounded wood into a stage, the rest of the group got all the lights strung around the barn following Tess' direction. As the last string was plugged in, they all stood back and looked around, admiring the way the lights lit up the interior and made it seem not so much like a barn and more like a fun place for a celebration.

Bailey was quiet most of the afternoon, her thoughts continuing to mull over her relationship with Brice. Unlike most girls, Bailey had never dreamed of her own wedding. Caught up in the romantic, festive atmosphere, Bailey found herself planning an outdoor wedding in spring when everything was blooming and fresh. As much as she enjoyed the autumn season, she would definitely want a spring wedding with soft pastel colors and apple blossoms, baskets of tulips and fluffy white bows. Someone would play a harp and Brice would wear a tux and…

Giving herself a mental scolding at letting her thoughts turn so fanciful, Bailey felt the beginnings of a headache and realized she didn't bring her purse along with her migraine medication.

Deciding to ignore the dull pounding in her head, Bailey was helping sweep the barn floor when she smelled Brice's scent about the same time his hand settled on her waist.

"Close your eyes and open your mouth," Brice said, his breath tickling her ear, making a shiver work its way from her head to her toes.

Bailey stood completely still and followed Brice's orders, opening her mouth. She felt something cool on her tongue and tasted something sweet, like white chocolate. Biting down, the flavors of pumpkin and spices filled her mouth and she popped her eyes open in delighted surprise.

Kissing her cheek, Brice watched her face fill with pleasure.

"Like it?" he asked, holding her hand in his as she finished eating the candy.

"That was one of the best things I've ever eaten," Bailey said, pleased that Brice remembered she liked pumpkin. "Where did you get it?"

"There's a shop in The Dalles that sells truffles. When Trav and I went into town the other night we ran by and I picked up a few pumpkin flavored ones," Brice said, handing her a small box. Bailey opened the lid to see five more truffles nestled inside. Two looked to be milk chocolate, two dark chocolate, and another white chocolate.

"That is so very thoughtful, Brice. Thank you," Bailey said, stretching up to give him a kiss on the cheek. He turned his head at the last minute so the kiss instead landed on his lips.

Bailey gave him an exasperated look. "You are completely in…" Brice cut her off with a finger to her lips, causing her to wonder if they might explode from the tingling sensation his touch produced.

"Need of more of your kisses, I know. But we've got more work to finish up before we can think about that. If you're a good little girl, I might even take you out for dinner later," Brice said, giving Bailey a wink as he walked back to where he and Ben were cleaning up the stage construction project.

The next thing Bailey knew, Brice and Ben had music blaring and the kids were making sure there was plenty of room for dancing in front of the stage. Bailey found herself swept into Brice's arms before she realized what was happening.

Grateful for Sierra's insistence she learn how to dance, Bailey could hold her own on the dance floor. Staying on the outer fringe of the teens, Brice put her through the paces of a fast two-step.

As he spun her around for the third time, she felt dizzy as the pain of her headache hit with full force. Bursts of pain blazed behind her eyes, skewing her vision, and she suddenly felt clammy and hot.

Fighting to keep upright, Bailey stopped in mid-step and reached out blindly as her face lost all color.

"Sugar, you okay?" Brice asked, alarmed at how fast she'd gone from dancing to staring unseeing at him with pain-glazed eyes.

"I'm not..." Bailey said before her legs gave out and she started to sink to the floor. Brice caught her before she hit the concrete on the barn floor and swept her into his arms.

Carrying her out of the barn into the fresh air, Brice sat down on a bale of straw and held Bailey. No one had noticed them leave the barn so Brice sat quietly, waiting for her to tell him what was wrong.

Opening her eyes, the bright afternoon sunshine sent a wave of nausea crashing over Bailey. Squeezing her eyes closed, she blocked out the light. Swallowing hard, she tried not to move, not to blink, and just focus on taking one breath then another.

Her head felt like someone was trying to split it in two by driving a stake behind her right eye. It had been years since she'd had a migraine this bad and, of course, she wasn't anywhere close to her prescription. Once the nausea set in, she was going to have to ride it out.

"Home, please," Bailey managed to whisper as Brice leaned over her, fanning her face with his hand. She was cold and clammy, yet beads of perspiration dotted her forehead and upper lip.

"Ben!" Brice bellowed back into the barn. "Get my truck!" Some of the kids near the open door, ran outside to see what was wrong, concerned to see Bailey looking so pale.

Ben ran by them, grabbing the keys Brice tossed and quickly returned with Brice's pickup.

"You want me to drive?" Ben asked as Brice nodded, still holding Bailey in his arms. Ben opened the passenger door and Brice somehow managed to climb in without letting her go. Ben floored the pickup and they headed toward the Triple T.

"Is she diabetic or something?" Ben asked, watching Bailey turn an even more startling shade of white.

"No, I don't think so," Brice said, trying to remember if Bailey had mentioned having any ailments. As far as he knew she was about as healthy as a girl could be. Digging his phone out of his pocket, he called Sierra.

She answered on the second ring and started to chat, but Brice cut her off, asking if Bailey had any medical issues they needed to know about.

When Sierra told him no, he described what happened.

"That's a migraine," Sierra said, concerned for Bailey. The headaches didn't come with any regularity and Bailey had even gone a year and a half once without having one. "She has some medication she takes for it. If it's a really bad one, she'll be a little out of it for a day or two. Keep the room dark and quiet. Sometimes it makes her throw up, so be warned. And they always make her grumpy."

"Thanks, Sierra. I'll call later and let you know how she's doing," Brice said, glad that he and Sierra had struck up a friendship in their mutual desire to see him together with Bailey.

Looking down at Bailey, he could see her pain in the way she held her lips rolled together and squeezed her eyes tightly shut. Brushing the hair off her damp forehead, he bent down and kissed her nose.

Opening one eye, Bailey glanced up at Brice. She wanted to smile at him, wanted to thank him for his caring touch and tender care. But she couldn't. If she moved at all, she was going to start throwing up and that was something she could not even contemplate as Ben turned off the highway and started up the Triple T Ranch's long driveway. When he hit a bump in the road that jostled them, Bailey whimpered and held onto her head with both hands.

"Careful, bro," Brice cautioned Ben, casting a warning look at his brother. As much as he loved Bailey he really didn't want to think about what would happen if she threw up right then. Instead, he lightly rubbed her jean-clad leg and offered words of encouragement. "We're almost there, sugar. Hang on for just a few more minutes."

Ben pulled up at the door to the mud room and ran around the pickup, opening the door for Brice then hurried to hold open the door to the house. Brice carefully slid off the seat cradling Bailey to his chest then hustled up the steps, through the mud room, and into the kitchen.

Calling for Cady, Ben remembered her saying she was going over to the Drexel house to see how the guys were doing before coming home. She probably hadn't gotten back yet.

Brice walked down the hall to the room where Bailey had been staying since she returned to the ranch. Gently placing her on the bed, she sank back and lay perfectly still.

"What do you need, sugar?" Brice asked, watching Bailey swallow a couple of times.

"Water," she managed to say between clenched teeth.

Brice left the room and went to the kitchen where Ben was waiting.

"Why don't you go back home?" Brice said as he got Bailey a glass of cold water. "I'll stay with her until Cady comes back."

"Are you sure?" Ben asked, knowing Brice had never once in his life taken care of a sick human. He ran away from anyone with the sniffles and Ben knew if someone threw up in front of Brice, he was likely to repeat the action himself. Sick animals he dealt with just fine. Sick people were a whole different story.

"We'll be fine. Go on," Brice said, turning back toward the hallway. "Thanks for driving."

"Anytime, bro. Good luck," Ben said as he went out the back door, hoping for Brice's sake that Bailey wouldn't get any sicker than she was now.

Unfortunately by the time Brice returned to the bedroom, Bailey was in the bathroom with the door closed. The sounds Brice could hear let him know that Bailey was feeling much worse instead of better. It made his own stomach flutter and he took a deep breath to steady himself.

"Sugar, you need some help?" Brice asked, hoping she'd say no.

Bailey held back the need to throw up until she could send Brice from the room. Knowing him, he had some gallant idea about taking care of her in her hour of need. The last thing she was going to let happen was to have Brice sit there and watch her throw up. She might not know a lot about guys and relationships, but she was quite certain that was probably a deal-breaker right there.

Hurrying into the bathroom and emptying her stomach, Bailey now felt so dizzy and sick she was convinced there was no way she could make it back to the bed short of crawling there.

Sinking down to the floor, she leaned against the wall, holding her head in her hands and crying at the sheer pain that washed over her in excruciating waves.

Maybe if she sat still long enough, her headache would go away, Brice would go away, and she could go to sleep.

When Brice tapped on the door and asked if she needed help, it took every ounce of strength she had to raise her voice enough to respond with a "no."

All was quiet for a few minutes until she felt the nausea hit her again. Leaning against the sink after rinsing out her mouth, she stood clutching the counter to remain upright when the bathroom door opened and Brice walked in. He took one look at her, picked her up and carried her to the bed. Tears leaked from her closed eyes and she hid her face against his chest, embarrassed.

"Bailey," Brice said, laying her on the bed as carefully as he could. She was hot and flushed and looked even worse than she had when he went to get her a drink. He held the glass of water to her lips and she took a few sips before turning her head away. "How can I help you, sugar?"

"Go home," she whispered, mortified Brice was seeing her weak and sick as she was. She would die, absolutely die, if she threw up in front of him, which was a strong possibility.

"Not happening," Brice said, walking across the room and drawing the drapes closed on the windows, cloaking the room in a muted darkness.

Going back to the kitchen then out to the mud room, Brice found an old dish pan that would serve the purpose for which he intended and returned to Bailey's room.

Despite the fact he knew she would protest, he took off her shoes, removed the denim jacket and cotton shirt she was wearing, leaving her in a tank top and her jeans. He knew the jeans couldn't be comfortable feeling as awful as she did and informed her either she was taking them off or he would.

She opened one eye long enough to shoot him a scathing glare then pointed toward a drawer. It took him three tries to find the one she meant and pull out a pair of soft knit pajama bottoms. Handing them to her, he turned his back. The sound of a zipper sliding down had never resonated so loud. He could picture her easing the jeans down her hips and along those long legs.

Calling himself ten kinds of a fool, he tried to focus on the matter at hand, which was making Bailey more comfortable. He waited another minute before turning around to see her perfectly still on the bed, the jeans in a wad at her feet, the pajamas in place.

"Better?" he asked, not really expecting a response.

To his surprise she fluttered one eye at him in what could have been interpreted as a wink.

Picking up the jeans, he tossed them in the corner with her jacket and shirt before going into the bathroom and running a washcloth under a stream of warm water. He wiped her forehead, then her cheeks and along her lip. He could visibly see her relax so he rinsed out the cloth and repeated the process.

Bailey's breathing finally evened out and deepened so Brice knew she was asleep.

He pulled up a side chair next to the bed and sat watching her.

Smiling to himself, he thought about what he discovered in the second dresser drawer he'd opened.

Not even in his wildest dreams would he have imagined Bailey Lorinda Bishop, uptight paleontologist, would own a collection of beautiful lacy lingerie that could put a Victoria's Secret model to shame.

Dreaming about seeing her wear some of what he glimpsed made the room seem unbearably warm. Brice was just getting ready to go find something cold to drink when he felt a soft touch on his shoulder and looked up to see Cady.

She nodded her head toward the door and he followed her back to the kitchen.

"Tess called," Cady said as she handed Brice a cold pop from the fridge along with a glass of ice. "How's she doing?"

"Better. For a while there, I wasn't sure what to do but once she quit throwing up she seemed to improve."

Cady raised both eyebrows and stared at him. "You mean to tell me you took care of a sick woman? All by yourself?"

"Well, she wouldn't let me in the bathroom, but I put her to bed, shut the drapes, got a barf bucket, found her pjs and behaved like a gentleman while she changed, then sponged off her face. That's about the time she fell asleep, so I've just been sitting with her."

"Brice, I'm so proud of you," Cady beamed at him, patting him on the back like she would Cass when she accomplished something new. "After the way you lit out of here a few months ago when Cass threw up all over the kitchen floor, and the way you tend to stay far away from sobbing, hysterical, or upset women, I'm thoroughly impressed. Good for you."

Nodding his head, Brice grinned as he and Cady walked back toward Bailey's room.

"I guess being crazy in love with someone makes all the difference, doesn't it?" Cady asked with a sassy grin.

"Maybe," Brice said, knowing she was teasing. "If it's okay with you, I'd like to sit with her."

"Go ahead. You're pretty much stranded for a while anyway, so you might as well stay for dinner. Someone can run you home later if Tess doesn't show up before you're ready to leave."

"Sounds good," Brice said, walking down the hall to Bailey's room. Brice, who was hardly ever still, sat quietly in the chair next to the bed, watching Bailey. He loved the way her lips curled up in a smile while she slept, the way her eyelashes fluttered against her cheeks, the way her honey-colored curls swept around her face in disarray. Her fresh scent filled his nose and he breathed deeply.

How he loved this strong, independent, frustrating, alluring woman. If someone had asked him a few months ago about love, he would have pointed to the Thompson brothers and laughed. Brice would have said it was crazy and silly and the stuff of fairy tales. Now, he would proclaim it from the rooftops that love was a wondrous, magical, painfully exciting experience. It made you care so deeply for another that it felt like part of your soul had been ripped out and given into that person's care.

Bailey, always so strong, confident and precise, appeared so young and sweet as she slept, Brice wondered if she looked like that as a child. Laughing to himself, he thought she most likely only looked like that when she was sleeping since her inquisitive mind seemed to run on overdrive.

Wanting to touch her, to feel the soft smoothness of her skin against his, he gingerly picked up her hand and kissed the back of it before carefully cradling it in his own.

"I love you, Bailey," Brice said, feeling his heart soften at the sight of the sick girl on the bed.

"I love you, Brice," Bailey whispered, so quietly, the sound barely made it past her lips but it was loud enough for Brice to hear. He straightened in his chair, waiting for her to open her eyes, to substantiate that most welcome declaration with something more.

Instead she didn't rouse from her slumber, snuggling deeper against the pillows of the bed.

Sighing, Brice swiped his hand over his face and sat back in the chair, wondering if Bailey meant what she said, even though she was asleep. He knew Bailey cared for him, more than she was willing to admit even to herself, but he was starting to wonder if that would be enough. Would she ever allow herself to fall in love with him completely, to be part of an amazing relationship, to share in the passion that he felt for her.

Knowing he needed to be patient, Brice resigned himself to waiting for however long it took Bailey to return his love and affection. Given enough time, he would wear down her resistance and she'd finally fall in love.

One hug, one kiss, one moment at a time.

Chapter Twelve

*"If you're gonna fall apart,
do it in your own bedroom."*

Margot Kidder

"I love you, Brice," Bailey heard herself say. How had the words escaped her lips? Then she realized she was dreaming, and in her dreams she could say and do all the things she was afraid of facing in reality.

In her dreams, she could share her heart with Brice, tell him how much she had come to love him, even if it seemed crazy. Bailey had never been in love before. Never wanted to be in love. Despite the short time she had known Brice, she knew what they felt for each other was something very special.

That's why it frightened her beyond reason.

The more time she spent with Brice, the easier it was to brush aside her all-consuming focus on work and let her thoughts float over things like love, marriage, a future with Brice, and starting their own family.

Thinking her work made her happy and fulfilled, in the past month she had come to realize her work was just that - work. Oh, she loved it, enjoyed it, thrived on it. But not as much as she loved being with Brice. Not as much as she enjoyed the banter they shared. Not as much as she thrived on his touch, his laugh, his teasing smile meant just for her.

Being with Brice made her deliriously happy and was the one place she felt at home, at peace, like she belonged. Which is why she had to fight it.

When the day came she had to choose between Brice and her career, and Bailey knew it would come, she didn't want to see the look of hurt on Brice's face when she chose her work over him.

It was the way things had to be. There just wasn't room in her life for both love and work. She couldn't be consumed with one and leave the other dangling. It was all or nothing for Bailey and the longer she spent getting to know Brice, the more she realized he would get her all and her work would end up with nothing.

Thinking about losing Brice made her heart hurt more than her pounding head. Remembering her headache and Brice's sweet and attentive care made Bailey even more distraught. How was she ever going to be able to tell that handsome, teasing cowboy goodbye? Especially when he was always going to hold a very big piece of her heart in his strong, calloused hands.

Tears escaped around her closed eyes and Bailey didn't even try to stifle the sob that rose in her throat.

She gasped in surprise, though, when she felt rough thumbs brushing away her tears and a soft, deep voice speak near her ear.

"What's wrong, sugar?" Brice asked, wondering if Bailey's headache was worse. Her color was better and the brackets of pain around her eyes and mouth had gone away. She'd been peacefully sleeping until a few minutes ago when she started acting agitated then he saw the tears on her cheeks. Crying in her sleep couldn't be a good sign. "Can I get you something? What can I do to help you?"

"Brice," she whispered, opening her eyes to convince herself he was real and not just a dream. She took a deep breath and inhaled his scent, the scent that would forever be imbedded in her mind and heart, reminding her of the first and only man she was ever going to love. More tears rolled down her cheeks and she found herself needing to be close to him. "Hold me."

Scooping her into his arms, Brice sat down on the bed with his back against the headboard and cradled Bailey to his chest. Her hands trembled as they clutched at his shirt front and her tears grew in frequency until she was sobbing, great wracking sobs that shook her frame.

"Bailey, what's wrong? Does it hurt that bad?" Brice asked, tenderly brushing the hair from her face with one hand while he held her close with the other. He rubbed her back, kissed her temple and murmured softly to her. "It's okay, sugar. Everything is just fine. Take a deep breath, baby. Just take a nice deep breath."

Everything wasn't fine. Nothing would ever be fine again. Why couldn't Brice understand that? Why couldn't he walk away before they lost any more of their hearts to each other?

Struggling to control her emotions and tears, Bailey felt embarrassed at having lost control. It wasn't like her to fall apart, especially not in front of anyone, particularly not in front of a man she cared more about than anything or anyone else.

Taking a deep breath, then another, she swallowed back the rest of her tears, swiped at her cheeks and leaned back in his arms. Staring into Brice's face, she drank in the love she could see in his warm brown eyes.

"Thank you," she whispered when she found her voice.

"Anytime, sugar," Brice said, continuing to rub her back comfortingly.

"I didn't mean to fly into pieces all over you," Bailey said, sounding remorseful as she wiped away the last traces of tears from her cheeks with the sheet, observing the soaked front of Brice's shirt.

"Seems to me your own room is as good a place as any to fall apart," Brice said, giving Bailey a jaunty smile. "I'll always be here to catch you and help put the pieces back together, so you fall apart any time you want."

"I don't plan on ever doing that again. And I don't want you to say things you can't promise," Bailey said, shaking her head, which still hurt, although not with the overwhelming pain she'd felt earlier.

"I never make promises I don't intend to keep, Bailey," Brice said, growing serious, taking her chin in his hand and forcing her to look in his eyes. "You remember that. If I promise you something, you can bank on it."

She refused to let him make promises she had no intention of letting him keep. Not willing to discuss her thoughts with Brice, she glanced at the clock and feigned a yawn.

"I think I'll go back to sleep, now. You don't have to keep babysitting me. It's about time for dinner. Why don't you go eat?" Bailey said, needing some distance from Brice. If he kept holding her so gently and lovingly, she didn't know how much longer she could keep herself together. She could dream about him holding her this way for a lifetime. But that's all it could ever be. A dream.

"I don't want to leave you," Brice said, kissing her damp cheek.

"Please go eat. I'll be fine for a while on my own," Bailey said, scooting away from Brice and sliding down on the bed, her back to the door.

Brice pulled the sheet and a light blanket over her, kissing her on the temple. "Sleep well, sugar." Leaving the room, Brice closed the door behind him.

Bailey rolled onto her back and once again let the tears flow down her cheeks. Maybe this was a new symptom of her headaches, the feeling of panic and hysteria that was building in her was not something she'd experienced before. She was the one who was always calm, cool, and collected. The sobbing mess of raw emotion that had taken over her body was not like her at all.

In addition to her headache, her chest hurt, burned, along with her stomach. Maybe she was sicker than she thought from her migraine. Or maybe she was heartsick from thoughts of breaking things off with Brice.

Bailey was enjoying her work at the John Day Fossil Beds as much, if not more, than she'd enjoyed working anywhere. The director hinted that a permanent position might open up in the spring if Bailey was interested.

Could she actually be contemplating setting down roots and staying in one place?

Mulling over all the positive reasons to stay in the area, she would have work she found fascinating. She would still be close to her Thompson cousins, whom she was learning to love like brothers and sisters. The open sky and craggy country never failed to amaze and inspire her. Then there was Brice.

If she stayed, Brice would be nearby. Even though she knew she had to let him go, she would at least be able to see him on occasion. He would eventually forget about her, move on and marry some sweet girl, like Sierra, who was bubbly and fun.

The idea of seeing Brice in love with someone else brought another round of tears that soaked the sheet Bailey clutched in her hand. Exhausted, she finally cried herself to sleep.

When Brice returned to the room after dinner Bailey had tear tracks on her cheeks and the damp sheet held tightly in her hand. Shaking his head, he once again brushed the curls back from her face, kissed her forehead and quietly left the room.

Cady and Tess were finishing the last of the dishes when Brice walked back into the kitchen and sank down on a barstool at the counter.

"What's up, BB?" Tess asked, concerned by the look on Brice's face. He wasn't one generally given to worry, but the way his forehead crinkled and a frown rode his normally smirking lips, she knew something serious was bothering him.

"I'm worried about Bailey," he said, swiping his hand over his face before pulling his grandpa's old pocket knife out of his pocket and digging at his fingernails with the sharp blade.

Tess had seen that move thousands of times over the years. Brice did it whenever he was bored, anxious, upset, or trying to think. It was one reason his nails were always so clean and neat.

"What about Bailey?" Cady asked, putting away the last dish while Tess wiped off the counter.

"She woke up crying before dinner. Hysterically," Brice said, glancing up to see Cady and Tess both looking at him in surprise. It wasn't like Brice to handle a crying woman without reinforcements. "I held her and let her cry and she seemed better. She said she wanted to sleep and told me to come eat dinner. When I went back in to check on her, I could tell she'd been crying again. Do you think it's the migraine?"

"I don't know?" Cady said, looking at Tess, since she was the one with a medical background.

"It could be from the migraine, Brice, but I can't really say. They affect everyone differently and having never experienced one myself, I don't know what to tell you. Why don't you try calling Sierra again?" Tess said, drying her hands before giving Brice a hug around his shoulders.

Brice called Sierra who assured him Bailey never cried and she didn't think the sobbing had anything to do with her headache. She told Brice to let Bailey rest and she would call later to check on her. Sierra also planned to call Cady and see what her take on the situation was. Sierra knew her sister well enough to know Bailey was falling hard and fast for Brice and it no doubt scared her witless.

"I guess I'll let her be then, for now," Brice said as he and Tess went down the mud room steps outside, followed by Cady.

Walking out to Tess' car, Travis waved from where he worked with Trey out by the barn. Cass ran over with her dog Buddy following close behind.

"Brice!" The little girl called as she ran up to him and patted his legs with her grubby little hands.

"What, kiddo?" Brice asked, picking her up and tossing her in the air.

"Will you dance with me at Uncle Travis' wedding?" Cass asked between giggles as Brice set her down and tickled her sides.

"I don't know. I've seen your moves on the dance floor and I'm not sure I could keep up," Brice teased the precocious redhead.

"Please? Just one dance? I promise to let you keep up," Cass begged, looking up at him with the big baby blue eyes that somehow coerced most of the men in her life to do her bidding. The kid was going to be lethal to the male population when she grew up. With that wild red hair, rosebud mouth and big blue eyes, it would take a stronger man than him to tell her no.

"Okay, just one. But only if you promise not to leave me in your dust," Brice said, squatting down so he was on eye level with Cass.

"Yippee!" Cass said, throwing her arms around his neck and squeezing before running back to Trey. "I get to dance with Brice at the wedding, Daddy!"

"You just made her day, Brice. Thank you," Cady said, smiling at him gratefully.

"No problem," Brice said with a grin. "Just remember not to laugh at me when I'm keeping my promise of dancing with her. I've watched her flailing moves before, you know."

Everyone laughed as Travis walked Tess to the car and held her door for her. He gave her a quick kiss and whispered in her ear before waving at Brice and heading back to the barn.

"Well, Tessie, one more week and you'll be Mrs. Travis Thompson and move into your own home. What do you think about that?" Brice asked as she drove back to the Running M, thinking about how glad he was for his sister and best friend, but also how much he would miss having her at home.

"I think it's about the most wonderful thing ever and I can't wait for the week to fly by," Tess said with flushed cheeks, although she was grinning broadly.

"In case I haven't mentioned it before, I'm really happy you and Trav finally got together. You two were always meant to be," Brice said, squeezing Tess' hand. "And if he doesn't treat you like the queen bee you are, you let me know and I'll set him straight in a hurry."

"I don't think you'll have to worry about that," Tess said, her hand going to the topaz bee necklace she wore, a gift from Travis that served as a loving reminder that she was his honeybee. "Thank you, BB, for all you did to bring us together. Once we get back from our honeymoon, maybe we can work on getting you and one lovely, albeit distracted paleontologist together."

"As much as I want that to happen, I just don't get the idea she's ready or willing," Brice said, shaking his head as he looked out the window.

"She's crazy about you whether she's willing to admit it or not. Don't give up hope. You can ride bulls, race cars and skydive without blinking. Surely you can figure out how to make one woman laser-focused on her career fall in love with you."

"When you put it that way, it sounds like a piece of cake."

"Pumpkin cake, from what I understand," Tess said with a laugh. "Maybe this is one princess who prefers the pumpkin to the fancy carriage."

"Maybe," Brice agreed.

><><

Stretching lazily, Bailey opened one eye then the other and realized her headache was gone. She still felt fuzzy-headed and tired, but the fact she could sit up and move her head without wincing was enough to spur her out of bed and into the shower.

Recalling the previous evening when she'd fallen to pieces all over Brice, Bailey resolved herself to breaking things off with him right after the wedding. She didn't want to cause any trouble this coming week and her telling Brice they couldn't see each other again would definitely throw everyone off kilter.

Towel drying her hair, wrapped in a big soft robe, she walked back into the bedroom and noticed a little box on the nightstand next to her bed. She recognized it as the box of candy Brice gave her yesterday afternoon. A note was on top of the box, written in his bold scrawl.

Sugar,
Didn't want you to miss out on your pumpkin sweets.
Feel better soon!
Enjoy and think of me,
Brice

Bailey wondered when Brice brought them in. She knew he didn't have them when he brought her home yesterday and after that things got a little hazy.

Recalling his help after she'd been ill, she remembered Brice assisting her out of her clothes and tucking her into bed. His hands had been so gentle as he sponged off her face and brushed her hair back from her cheeks. Brice never acted like anything was off when she cried all over him, pulling up the sheet and tenderly smoothing back her hair before leaving her to sleep.

Most men would have left her to her own defenses. Her father certainly wouldn't have sat by her mother's bedside ready to provide care if needed.

Brice was someone special and Bailey wondered again how she was going to force herself to let him go.

She had to, though, before things became any more complicated. Before her heart finally spoke what it was whispering in her dreams - that she was undeniably and completely in love with Brice Morgan.

SHANNA HATFIELD

Chapter Thirteen

"I can't help falling in love with you."
Elvis Presley

"I've never seen the old fort look so good," Trey said, smiling as he stood with Travis, Trent and the two Morgan brothers outside their boyhood fort, waiting for the wedding to begin.

Constructed by their father, Drew, for his three boys when Travis was barely old enough to walk, the fort had been made to last for generations.

"Dad would be proud today, don't you think?" Travis said, grinning at Trey and Trent.

"He surely would be, Trav. I know we all are," Trey said, his bright blue eyes glowing with pride and love. Travis had a hard time when he arrived home in December from his last tour of duty in Iraq, but thanks to Tess' loving care and Travis' willingness to get some help for his PTSD, he was well on the road to recovery. Trey and Trent were both so proud of the strides he had made in the last few months.

Travis stood next to the pastor from their church beneath the arbor that had been temporarily placed in front of the old fort. Green vines were twined throughout the arbor while baskets full of fall flowers and bronze ribbon sat on each side. Brice stood next to Travis as the best man while Trey, Trent and Ben rounded out the groom's bridal party.

Seated in chairs placed in a half-circle around the fort was a group of about fifty people that included family and ranch hands, as well as a few very close friends.

Tess and Travis wanted a small, intimate wedding followed by a bigger reception. Envisioning just a few people watching them exchange vows, the wedding guest list kept growing until there was now a sizable group gathered for their noon nuptials.

Travis didn't care if two people or two thousand people watched him declare his love for Tess today. He was much more interested in what would happen after they landed in Las Vegas for their honeymoon. Keeping his hands off his all-too enticing fiancé the past month had stretched both his patience and his resolve, but after today he was free to let loose of the reins and fully enjoy his beautiful bride.

Thinking about Tess made the wing tip collar of Travis' crisp white shirt feel like it was about to choke him on this warm, sunny day. The air was sharp and fresh with the hint of ripening apples, settling earth, and spicy autumn riding the breeze.

"Dude, I so don't want to know what completely inappropriate thoughts you're having about my sister, but pull it together. This thing's gonna start in a minute and you need your head on straight," Brice whispered to Travis, trying not to smirk too broadly.

Travis shot him a glare that turned into a grin as they heard the recorded music begin to play.

Since the fort was most easily accessible by foot, horseback or four-wheeler, most of the guests walked to it from the ranch house. Mike Morgan brought over his wagon and team of draft horses to give those who didn't want to walk a ride on straw bales covered with blankets. Tess and the bridal party rode the wagon out to the fort and she stayed hidden just behind a little rise in the hill where her dad would escort her down to her anxious groom.

The groomsmen all beamed when they saw the bridesmaids approach on a path made of bronze tulle, strewn with fall leaves. The girls wore gowns in a simple yet elegant style reminiscent of the 1950s era. Although the styles matched, they were each attired in a color of autumn, carrying bouquets of burgundy, coral and gold roses. Bailey, dressed in burgundy, was first to take her place opposite the groomsmen, followed by Lindsay wearing gold, Cady dressed in dark green and Tess' best friend Jenny attired in coral. They looked like a lovely bouquet of autumn beauties.

Cass skipped along the pathway, beaming a huge grin in her peach colored dress. Although her title was flower girl, instead of tossing petals, she carried a sign that sent the attendees into bursts of laughter.

Uncle Travis!
Here comes your girl!

While the guests chuckled and smiled, Cass took her place next to Bailey, waving to her daddy and leaning around Bailey and Lindsay to smile at her mother.

As the processional began, the guests stood and all eyes turned to see Tess escorted down the aisle on the arm of her father, who was having a hard time keeping the moisture in his eyes from escaping.

Travis thought Tess couldn't have looked more beautiful if she'd tried. Her rich, dark hair spiraled into curls on top of her head where a short half-veil was held in place with a crown of cream roses. The white satin wedding gown featuring a sweetheart neckline, short sleeves, ruched waist, and full skirt looked like something out of one of the vintage ads Tess was so fond of with its accents of antique lace. She carried a bouquet of white and cream roses and wore a string of pearls around her neck.

Tess, trying to remember how to walk normally as her dad helped her along the pathway, was enthralled with how handsome her husband-to-be looked in his black cutaway jacket, shiny black boots and black Stetson. The groomsmen all appeared quite dashing, but none looked nearly as handsome or heart-stopping to her as Travis.

Walking up to Travis, he held his hand out to Tess and kissed her cheek. "You're gorgeous, honeybee," he whispered in her ear before stepping back and giving her a dazzling smile.

Tess' dad kissed her other cheek then gave Travis a long look. "Be good to my little girl, son."

"Always," Travis whispered, smiling at Mike, who gave him a pat on the back before taking his place next to Michele.

The ceremony went quickly and smoothly and at the end, Travis lifted Tess' veil and stared at her beloved face for a moment before meeting her lips in a kiss that left everyone clapping and cheering.

"Let her come up for air," Brice said, nudging Travis in the side. Travis straightened, smiling at his bride while Tess tried to ignore her flushed cheeks. They looked so happy and young, so in love.

Strolling hand in hand down the aisle and back to the wagon, they visited for a few minutes with the guests. The wagon would take everyone back to the ranch house and from there the celebration would move to the Running M.

Travis hired a vintage stretch limo, circa 1930, to take the bridal party to the reception in style. The photographer spent the next hour taking posed photographs at the fort, in the car, by the barn and anywhere else that looked interesting before the bridal party needed to join the rest of the guests for the reception.

Trent and Trey left their pickups at the Running M earlier that morning so they could get back home after the celebration. Brice and Ben caught rides with their folks to the Triple T and Tess' car was waiting to take the honeymooners to Portland to catch their flight later that afternoon while Travis' pickup was parked at their new-to-them home.

Brice somehow managed to finagle his way next to Bailey in several of the poses and it didn't take the photographer long to figure out there was more than one couple in love in the bridal party. She took photos of the Thompson brothers with their brides, of each couple individually, of the Morgans all together and several of the entire bridal party as well as what seemed like hundreds of photos of just the bride and groom.

Finally, they piled into the limo amid the girls' full skirts and headed to the Running M.

A bottle of chilled sparkling cider was opened and poured into flutes then a toast was made by Brice, as best man. "To happily ever after and a lifetime of romance and love."

"To love!" the group echoed.

In high spirits as they arrived at the reception, Tess held Travis' hand tightly in hers as they stepped into the barn and stared in wonder at the transformation.

Crystal chandeliers, rented from a bridal shop in Portland, hung throughout the barn. The white lights they'd installed the previous weekend glittered along the edges of the walls and across the ceiling like fairy lights. Round tables, covered in cream linen with pools of bronze chiffon in the centers, held towering topiaries of fall flowers on clear glass pedestals. A table next to the barn door held a guest book, an arrangement of fall colored roses in an old cowboy boot, and a basket made of rope for collecting cards. An old buggy parked near the door held the gifts.

More tables were set up in the yard around the barn as well as in the barn loft. With more than three hundred expected guests, and most of them already there, the sounds of a joyous celebration filled the air.

"You make a beautiful bride, Tessie," Brice said, walking up behind Tess and giving her a hug.

"Well, you don't look half bad yourself, BB. I had no idea you could clean up so well," Tess teased, as she attempted to straighten his already straight collar.

"Who woulda thunk it?" Brice teased, reverting to the improper grammar that would make Tess laugh.

"Bailey looks stunning in that gown, don't you think, BB?" Tess said, smiling at Bailey as she stood off to the side behind Brice.

"Stunning is a good description," Brice said, reaching a hand out to Bailey which she hesitantly accepted.

When he first watched her walk down the aisle in the burgundy gown, his mouth began to water at the thought of spending the rest of the day with her. He nearly got distracted watching the sunbeams highlight her honey-gold curls during the ceremony and had to snap to attention when it was time to hand Travis the ring.

Burgundy was most definitely her color. It made her lips look like ripe cherries, sweet and ready for the picking, while her cheeks glowed pink and her eyes glittered with aquamarine brilliance.

Bailey offered him a shy smile, seeming lost in what she should do as a member of the bridal party. Brice decided action was needed to put everyone at ease.

"I don't know about the rest of you, but I'm starving. If the bride and groom would shake a leg and go through the buffet, the rest of the bridal party can fall in line behind them," Brice said, putting his hands on Tess and Travis' shoulders and turning them toward the tables bearing the food. "Put me out of my misery here, guys. Someone, who shall remain nameless although she is currently wearing a beautiful white gown, had the house in such a state of upheaval this morning, I didn't even get to finish my bowl of cold cereal."

"I'm ready to eat, too, honeybee," Travis said, walking Tess on the shortest path he could find through the crowd to the food. "Let's get something to eat. I'm pretty sure I'm going to need all my strength later."

Tess blushed and squeezed his arm as they reached the food table. Mike clanged a metal triangle and the crowd quieted while the pastor asked a blessing on the food, on those gathered, and the newly married couple.

When the bridal party was seated at the head table, Brice made sure Bailey was sitting next to him.

"Are you feeling better, sugar?" Brice asked, watching Bailey pick at her food. He liked that she normally ate with a healthy appetite and worried she still wasn't feeling well. With all the wedding hoopla the last week, he'd hardly had time to see her. The few times he did, she still looked pale and tired.

"I'm quite well, thank you," she said, keeping her eyes on her plate. It was torture to be here with Brice today. Walking down the aisle, seeing him standing in a tux looking so handsome, all she could think about was how badly she wanted to be the bride, to have him be the groom, to be embarking on a new life together.

Sitting next to him, picking at the meal she couldn't get past the huge lump of regret in her throat, she didn't know how she would endure hours of being close to Brice. Between his delectable scent, tender glances, teasing smiles, and the warmth of his hand searing through her dress right to her skin, she wasn't convinced she had the inner fortitude to keep him an arms-length away. The worst part was, she didn't really want to try.

What she really wanted was to turn around, grab his face between her hands and kiss him with all the passion she dreamed of sharing with him each and every night.

Instead, she rolled her lips together and stared down at her untouched food.

"Try a bite of this," Brice said, holding a fork to her lips. Rather than fuss at him or turn her head away, she obediently opened her mouth and accepted the bite. If her mouth hadn't been as dry as sawdust she might have appreciated the way the beef practically melted on her tongue with a rich, buttery flavor.

Smiling, she nodded at Brice. "That's good."

"Want some more?" he asked, holding his fork out to her again.

"No, thank you. You enjoy it," Bailey said, picking up her fork and pushing food around on her plate, taking small bites so Brice would think she was eating.

Bailey turned to talk to Lindsay, who was sitting on her other side. Surprised when Brice stood, he leaned down by Bailey and whispered in her ear.

"Don't run off and I'll bring you back a little something special." He didn't wait for her response but wandered off in the direction of the dessert table where an assortment of cookies and cupcakes sat around the impressive wedding cake.

Brice filled two plates and returned, setting one down in front of Bailey, pushing aside her untouched lunch.

"I think you'll like this," Brice said, pointing his fork at the dessert on her plate.

Bailey could smell the pumpkin and spice and forced herself to take a bite. It was a pumpkin cheesecake bar and was so delicious, she managed to put aside her self-torment long enough to enjoy every bite.

"That was really good," Bailey said, leaning toward Brice as she set her fork on the edge of the empty plate.

"Knew you'd like it," Brice said smugly, finishing his own plate of sweets, including a big chocolate cupcake.

Bailey looked around, wondering what was now expected of her. She was quite surprised and pleased when

Tess asked her to be a bridesmaid. Although they didn't know each other well, she did enjoy Tess' company and felt a kinship with the younger girl. Not having been in a wedding before, she wasn't certain what to expect. It was simple enough to participate in the silly girl talk as they got ready, to walk down the aisle and smile for the photographer afterward, but now that the wedding was over she didn't know what to do.

"Just relax, sugar. You're doing fine," Brice said, as though reading her thoughts. "As soon as everyone gets done eating, Jenny and I will toast the happy couple and then the dancing will begin. You did promise to dance every one with me."

"I did no such thing," Bailey said, snapping to attention. She'd been watching the way Brice's lips moved all too invitingly as he talked instead of really paying attention to what he said, until that last part about dancing. "You, Brice Morgan, have completely lost what little sense you've had."

"Nope," Brice said, leaning toward her. "Whether you know it or not, sugar, you're my dance partner for this party and I'm not planning to share. I want you and that cute little swing thang you've got all to myself."

Brice winked at her, got up from the table and joined a group of guys talking to Travis.

Lindsay leaned over and patted Bailey's arm as she sat stunned, watching Brice walk away.

"He's a little outrageous sometimes, but completely loveable," Lindsay said quietly. "He reminds me a lot of Travis. That's probably why they get along so well."

"Yes, he is," Bailey agreed without thinking what she was saying. "I meant… I wasn't implying…"

Lindsay laughed.

"I know what you mean, Bailey. It's okay," Lindsay said with a knowing smile. "I actually despised Trent before he romanced his way into my good graces. Once I decided to give him a chance, I just couldn't stop myself from falling in love with him."

Bailey mulled over what Lindsay said as the crowd broke into groups, chatting and visiting until Brice and Jenny toasted the couple. After several dances, Bailey found herself standing with Tess, her aunt Denni and Sierra, admiring Tess' ring, when Ben Morgan came up and put a hand on Denni's shoulder.

"I don't know who this foxy lady is, but will someone please introduce us?" Ben asked, his eyes twinkling with mischief, so much like his younger brother's often did.

Denni turned and smacked at Ben's arm. "Benjamin Michael Morgan, you know good and well who I am so you just stop with your teasing, although I wouldn't mind a little more flattery."

As a surprise to everyone, Denni arrived at the wedding looking completely different than she had the night before at the rehearsal with a sassy new haircut. It made her look ten years younger, which she said she needed since her baby was married.

"Yes, ma'am," Ben said, tugging on Denni's hand until she followed him to the dance floor. "You can even box my ears if you want to, but how about you dance this one with me. It'll make all the girls jealous."

"You've always been a sweet talker," Denni said, letting Ben lead her in a moderately paced dance.

Watching them, Bailey realized she didn't even know Brice's full name. Or how tall he was. What his favorite foods were. Whenever they were together he managed to ask one or two questions until he had a trove of details about Bailey. She knew practically nothing about Brice except that he was very talented at working with wood, he had a bit of a wild streak, loved to tease, was devoted to his family and friends, and was a genuinely good man.

"Are you ready for me to dance the shoes right off your feet?" Brice asked, his minty breath brushing like a caress across her face. Bailey knew he was beside her before he said a word. She could smell his spicy scent, feel his warmth, sense his presence.

Spinning around, she put her hands on his arms and looked up into his sparkling brown eyes. "What's your middle name?"

"Nathaniel, after my grandpa. Why?" Brice asked, caught off guard by both Bailey's question and the intense look on her face.

"I wanted to know. I want to know any number of things about you," she said, as Brice tipped his head at Sierra and led Bailey out to the dance floor.

"Like what?" Brice asked as they started a slow dance. He settled one hand on her waist and pulled her respectably close as his other hand held hers in a traditional pose.

"How tall are you? When is your birthday? What's your favorite meal? What's your favorite dessert? Why are your nails always so clean? How do you always smell so good?" Bailey said rattling off the questions as they popped into her head.

"Whoa, sugar, slow down," Brice said with a grin, tipping his head to look at her and finding himself lost in her turquoise eyes. This was the first show of real interest Bailey had exhibited in getting to know him on a more personal, intimate level. Brice took it as a very good sign. "I'm six feet tall barefooted, my birthday is the eighth of January, I love Mexican food especially carne asada, and I like chocolate cake and banana cream pie better than about anything. My nails are usually clean because I have a habit of constantly scraping them with my grandpa's old pocket knife."

Brice twirled her around on the floor, then bent to whisper in her ear. "And I'm glad to hear you think I smell good. I wouldn't want you to think I was just another stinky ol' boy."

The smile Bailey tried to suppress found its way free and lit up her face. "I'd never think you were just another malodorous member of the male species."

"I'm happy to hear that, sugar," Brice said, letting go of her hand so he could put both of his around her waist and draw her a little closer. "What else do you want to know?"

"What's your favorite color? Who's your favorite author? What type of music do you like best? What's your favorite song? What brings you the most satisfaction?" Bailey asked, oblivious to the fact that a fast song was playing and they were still dancing slow.

"My favorite color is black. I like Zane Grey books if I have to read something besides the sports page or the funnies. You've probably already figured out I like country music best and right now my favorite song is *Angel Eyes* by Love and Theft because there's this beautiful girl I know with eyes such an unusual shade of blue, they make me feel like I'm looking into a little bit of heaven. As to what brings me the most satisfaction, I'd have to say making her smile," Brice said, giving Bailey a devilish grin, which did, indeed, make her smile.

"Do you really think this girl you know has angel eyes?" Bailey asked, extremely flattered by Brice's words.

"Absolutely," Brice said, pulling her even closer now that another slow song began. "Eyes of an angel and the body of a little devil that tempts and torments me."

"Oh," Bailey said, not certain how to respond. No one had ever said anything like that to her before. She didn't know whether to be flattered or insulted, inspired or frightened. She was saved from any further comment to Brice when Cass ran up to them and begged Brice for her promised dance.

"Okay, kiddo," Brice said, bending down to pick Cass up in one strong arm while still keeping his hand on Bailey's waist. He walked her off the dance floor and back to the table where Sierra was visiting with Denni, tipping his head to her before making a grand show of sweeping Cass out on the dance floor.

At the little girl's pleading he danced the slow dance as well as the fast dance that followed with her before pointing out some little boys who needed a dance partner. She scampered off in their direction and Brice turned to reclaim Bailey only to find the table empty. He saw Denni dancing with Trey, but couldn't spot Sierra either. He decided the girls must have gone to powder their noses and went over to the refreshment table to get himself something cold to drink. Although the Bradshaw boys had been banned from the reception by their parents, Travis and Tess made sure the table was well guarded to prevent tampering with any of the beverages.

Brice dug around in a galvanized tub filled with ice and pulled out a Dr. Pepper. Opening the bottle he drank half of it before turning around to study the crowd.

Although skeptical of Tess' vision for the reception, he had to admit her plans came together in such a way the inside of the barn looked like a very fancy reception hall. Everything about the decorations said class, elegance, and romance.

The romance part was especially getting to him this evening.

Looking around, he still didn't see Bailey anywhere, so he decided to ask his mom for a dance, wondering what inspired all of Bailey's questions. Hoping she was finally ready to admit her interest in him put a smile on his face he couldn't wipe off, even if he wanted to.

><><

Sierra and Bailey watched Brice twirl little Cass across the dance floor. The child's face was so full of joy, they both laughed at the sight of it. Denni went to find her camera to take a photo and Sierra took the opportunity to grab Bailey's hand and tug her outside where the noise level was considerably less. Walking across the yard near the house, Sierra asked Bailey about her job and mundane, everyday questions, then talked about school and a boy she'd met that she was sure could be in the running for a future steady boyfriend.

Sitting down on the front porch swing, where it was quiet, Sierra pumped Bailey for information about her relationship with Brice.

"Do you care about him, Bailey? Even a little?" Sierra asked, wishing Bailey would act like a normal woman. Anyone with eyes in their head or a heart in their chest would be head over heels in love with a man like Brice.

"Of course I care about him," Bailey said, sounding agitated.

Hiding her grin, Sierra knew agitated was good. It meant Bailey was feeling things she didn't want to feel, thinking thoughts she didn't want to have. "Not like a brother or a neighbor or a coworker. Like a man, Bailey. Do you like him? Love him? Want to spend forever with him? Do you dream about him holding you? Kissing you?"

"Good grief, Sierra. Did you injure your head on the plane? Are you suffering from a lack of oxygen? What sort of ludicrous question are you asking?" Bailey asked, getting to her feet and pacing the length of the porch.

"There's not a ludicrous thing about the questions and you know it," Sierra said, shaking her finger at her sister. "I think you like Brice. Honestly, I think you're in love with him but you're too big of a coward to admit it."

"I'm not a coward!" Bailey said, her voice rising in volume. Realizing they weren't exactly having a private conversation since anyone walking by could hear them, Bailey dropped her voice. "I'll tell you the truth if you promise to keep it to yourself."

"I promise," Sierra said, holding her right hand in the air. "I won't speak of it to anyone."

"Fine," Bailey said, plopping back down on the swing next to Sierra. "I've … I've never been in love before, so I'm not sure if what I'm experiencing fits the description. According to your theatrical declarations, you've been in love approximately fourteen times since your junior year of high school, so I assume you have some idea of the symptoms."

"I do," Sierra said, nodding solemnly, waiting for Bailey to confirm what she already knew. "And what are your symptoms?"

"For one thing, he's completely riddled my ability to concentrate and focus full of holes. I even miscategorized a fossil last week. Can you believe it? That is the first time it has ever happened. Thankfully, I caught the error when I was filling out the report," Bailey said, still distraught over her mistake at work. She never made mistakes. Ever.

"Okay, what else?" Sierra said, caring not at all about the wrongly dated rock or bug or whatever it was Bailey found.

"My palms get all clammy and my stomach feels like there are butterflies flitting around inside whenever I think of him. I can feel his presence near me before he ever says a word, his scent is now firmly entrenched into my senses and I find it hard to process rational thoughts when I look in those brown eyes full of mischief," Bailey admitted, feeling silly and inexperienced.

"I see," Sierra said, forcing herself to remain calm and not jump up to do a happy dance. "Anything else? Any other symptoms?"

"His touch feels like fire on my skin. I love to watch him move or just listen to him talk and when he kisses me I feel all tingly and lightheaded. More than all that, though, I worry about him, wonder about him, want him to be happy," Bailey said, looking over at her sister. "Is that love?"

"That, dear sister, is most definitely love. You do realize some people go their entire life without the opportunity to experience what you've found with Brice. You're not going to throw that away are you?"

"I'm not throwing it away, I'm going to let it go," Bailey said, lifting her chin and stubbornly setting her jaw. "I can't do both, Sierra. I can't love Brice like I want to, like he deserves to be loved, and have my career."

"Why can't you have both? There is no rule or law that says it has to be one or the other. All you have to do is decide you want both and make it work," Sierra said, exasperated with her sister. She had never seen such a dense woman when it came to relationships, men or love.

"It can't be both. It won't work," Bailey said, getting to her feet and wrapping her arms around the porch rail. She pressed her cheek to the warm wood and wished, not for the first time, that she could have everything she wanted, because Brice would be part of that very attractive package. But she couldn't.

"Why won't it work, Bailey? I don't understand," Sierra said, walking over to Bailey and placing her hand on her sister's shoulder. "Why?"

"Because..." Bailey said, looking heavenward, hoping Sierra kept her promise as she bared her soul to her sister. "We all know I have a very focused and intense personality. It's just who I am and how I operate. I'm already losing my focus on work, Sierra. I'm becoming lost in Brice. The passion I feel for him, in just this short time, is more than I've ever felt about my career. What will it be like in a year or five years from now. I won't be me anymore. I won't have a career. I would be completely consumed with Brice. What if I woke up one day, full of resentment for letting go of everything I've worked so hard to achieve in my career just to be a cowboy's wife? I can't do that to Brice. I love him too much to hurt him like that. I can't do that to my career. Don't you see? I have to choose."

"But Bailey, you don't have to choose. You really don't. Talk to Brice. Tell him what you just told me. You can figure this out. If anyone can, it's you," Sierra said, hugging Bailey. "You're the smartest person I know, but how can you be so dumb and blind when it comes to Brice. He loves you Bailey, with his whole heart. If you walk away from him, that is the one thing you'll regret all your life. Don't do anything right now. Give it some time. Give it some thought."

"I don't know, Sierra," Bailey said, feeling swayed by her sister's words, but still uncertain.

"Just let yourself be young and in love and see what happens. You can always change your mind later. It's not like you're engaged or anything. Let yourself experience the wonder of falling in love," Sierra said, taking Bailey's hand and leading her back toward the barn. They both failed to notice Brice leaning against the corner of the house.

"Young and in love," Bailey said, musing over the thought of it. "I'll give it due consideration."

"I'm sure you will," Sierra teased as they walked back in the barn.

><><

Tired of waiting for Bailey to reappear, Brice went searching for her. Walking through the yard, he thought he heard her voice out front. He was ready to step around the corner of the house when he heard Bailey talking about losing her focus and being consumed with him.

Not intending to eavesdrop, he couldn't make his feet move away, eager to hear what she had to say. The way she held herself back from him now made perfect sense.

She was afraid she'd lose her identity if she let herself become part of a couple. Knowing her tendency to become consumed with whatever was driving her passion, Brice could well imagine how it would frighten her to give herself over to loving him.

Discovering where the road block was on the journey to his happily ever after with Bailey, Brice had to start working on his game plan to go over, under or around it. Failure to get to the other side was not an option.

Waiting a minute to return to the barn, Brice grinned when he heard the band launch into the song *Honey Bee*. The dance floor cleared and Travis led Tess out for their last dance. Watching his sister and best friend through the barn door, Brice didn't know how Travis could dance at all with the way he was kissing Tess and holding her close.

Amid cheers and whistles, the newlyweds finished the dance then Tess' bridesmaids whisked her back to the house to change while Travis traded his tux for jeans, boots and a cotton shirt in the bunkhouse.

Ben drove Tess' car, adorned with streamers on the bumper and a big "just married" sign taped in the back window, up near the front of the house.

Travis stood at the bottom of the porch steps, flanked by their many guests, waiting for Tess to come out and toss her bouquet. Cady, Lindsay and Bailey finally made their way out of the house laughing, followed by Jenny and finally Tess. Michele ran up the steps to hug Tess one more time then Tess stepped forward and held her hand out to Travis.

Kissing her palm, he walked up the porch steps and joined her while her bridesmaids walked down to stand in the crowd. Brice tucked Bailey against his side while they waited.

Travis looked around and gave Brice a nod of his head, shooting the garter straight at him. Brice laughed as he caught it and everyone cheered.

Not even bothering to turn around and toss her bouquet, Tess leaned off the porch and dropped it into Bailey's arms, laughing at the shocked look in her face.

"You never know," Tess said to Bailey with a wink before turning back to her new husband.

The two of them ran down the porch steps to her car amid hundreds of bubbles being blown by the crowd from the wedding favors passed out earlier. Travis held Tess' door, gave her a kiss, then hurried back to the driver's side.

"Thanks everyone!" he called before shutting the door and waving to the wedding guests.

In the two hours it took them to drive to Portland, Travis voiced his opinion on cancelling the plans to go to Las Vegas and stopping at the first hotel they could find.

Tess assured him he needed to keep driving.

Travis was convinced the trip was going to last half of forever, especially since Tess looked so alluring in one of her signature bombshell dresses in a rich shade of purple. Her dark hair was still piled on her head and her eyes seemed to glow a rich brown, lit by an inner flame. One Travis hoped to spark into a full-fledged fire in just a few hours.

With a quick flight to Las Vegas, Tess stood looking around the lobby of a swanky hotel in wonder, especially when she found out Travis reserved a honeymoon suite for them.

"Tee, you didn't need to go to so much bother," Tess said, squeezing his firm bicep in her hand, gazing at him with love and warmth. It was hard for her to believe the handsome daredevil cowboy was finally hers.

"It's no trouble, honeybee. I want our honeymoon to be extra special, so don't you worry about a thing. Just enjoy."

"But, Trav," Tess started to say but was cut off when Travis kissed her right there in the lobby. She tried to gather her composure as she and Travis followed the bellman to their room and waited while he opened the door and set their luggage inside. Travis gave him a tip, scooped Tess into his arms and carried her into the room that would be theirs for the next five days.

The suite was nearly as big as the entire first floor of their new home and Tess looked around in awe, trailing her fingers over a marble table top before Travis slowly set her down. She took in the bouquet of flowers filling the room with a tropical fragrance, a bottle nestled in a chiller with two glasses waiting nearby on a low table, and a basket filled with fruit, cheeses, bread and chocolates.

"You are so beautiful, Tessa. Perfectly gorgeous," Travis said, leaning against the back of the couch, watching her. "Every inch of you looked stunning and lovely at the wedding."

"Thank you," she said, blushing a little under his intense perusal that started at the top of her head and ended at the toes of her high heeled shoes. "I can't wait to see the photos, since you looked quite handsome and dashing yourself."

"Thanks," Travis said, pushing away from the couch. "Are you hungry?" he asked, taking off his watch, emptying his pockets and kicking off his boots.

Tess's eyes widened as she watched him, feeling both excited and frightened. He appeared to be a man settling in for the evening, which seemed odd since it was only half past six.

"If I say yes, are you going to put your boots back on and take me out to eat?" Tess asked, finding a little sassiness in between her bouts of fear.

"No, I'm not, honeybee. We'll order room service, you can eat everything in that basket, but I don't plan on leaving this room for a good long while," Travis said, unsnapping his cuffs and pulling the tail of his shirt out of a pair of Wranglers that fit him like a smooth glove.

Tess took a moment to drink in the sight of him. With sandy hair in the short military cut he favored, blue eyes the color of a summer sky, strong jaw, devil-may-care smile, and his tall, fit physique, Travis was handsome enough to set any red-blooded girl's heart to pounding. Hers was beating so fast, Tess could feel the frenzied thumping in her chest.

Closing the distance between them, Travis wrapped his arms around his bride and kissed her neck. "If you're hungry, I'll order something."

"I'm fine," Tess whispered as a shiver raced up her spine at Travis' moist, hot kiss on the pulse pounding wildly in her neck.

"You're sure?" Travis asked, kissing his way along her jaw to her chin.

"I'm sure," Tess said, raising her hands to rest on Travis' strong arms, needing to steady herself as her limbs went languid. "Are you hungry?"

"Yes, ma'am. I am," Travis said, pulling the pins from Tess' hair, one at a time, before burying his hands in the mass of her dark curls, shaking them down over his arms. He breathed in her scent, got lost in her sweet softness, and knew the time had come for his long held dreams to become reality.

Bending down so his lips were against her ear, she trembled from both his words and the deep timbre of his voice. "I've never been so hungry for anything in my life as I am for you, Tessa. I've been starving for you for more years than I want to think about and finally you're mine. All mine."

"Travis," she whispered, raising her lips to meet his in a passionate kiss. Without breaking the seal of their lips, Travis maneuvered her into the bedroom where he slowly slid down the zipper of her dress, pushed it off her arms and watched it fall to the floor.

Holding her hand as she stepped out of it and kicked off her heels, Travis knew he'd never seen anything as lovely as his curvaceous bride in her lacy lingerie. As he ran his hands up her arms, across her shoulders and down her sides, Tess felt heat flood through her.

Watching his blue eyes turn to liquid heat, Tess unsnapped Travis' shirt in one fluid movement and tugged it off his powerful shoulders. She bent down and kissed the shrapnel scar on his side and was working her way up to his lips when she heard Travis groan and felt a frission of anticipation pass over him as he moved beneath her hands.

"Oh, honeybee," Travis said in a husky voice, wrapping her in his arms and carrying her to the big, soft bed.

><><

"Where did you tell Trav they should stay?" Brice asked, trying to remember what hotel Bailey recommended to Travis for the honeymoon.

"The Venetian," Bailey said. Just because she didn't have any romantic prospects when she was in Vegas didn't mean she didn't hear what others said. "From my understanding, some of their suites are quite spectacular and they have any number of interesting activities."

"I'm guessing there's only one activity Trav is going to find of any interest," Brice said, wiggling his eyebrows at Bailey while giving her an absolutely wicked grin. "Suppose they've arrived?"

Bailey ignored his comment and turned to glance at her watch then remembered she wasn't wearing one. Judging by the way the night was nearly upon them, she'd have to guess that Travis and Tess had long ago landed and found their way to their room.

After the newlyweds left, the guests continued on with the party for a couple of hours before they began leaving.

A few lingering family members and close friends helped restore order to the chaos, picking up trash, putting away food, folding chairs and loading them into a trailer along with the tables, and helping take down the lights and decorations. By the time dusk fell, it would have been difficult to tell a wedding reception had taken place at the ranch earlier in the day.

Exhausted, but not quite ready to call it a night, Brice and Bailey sat on the edge of the barn loft watching darkness settle over the ranch.

"That was quite a celebration, wasn't it?" Brice asked, swinging his feet as he sat as close to Bailey as she'd allow, which seemed like a mile away.

"It was wonderful," Bailey said, gazing out into the night. "Tess was so beautiful and Travis looked quite handsome, but then again those cousins of mine always do. Ben looked exceptionally handsome as well. Too bad you two don't look more alike."

Brice's head whipped around to look at Bailey in surprise. Everyone said he and Ben looked enough alike they could be twins, so he wondered what, exactly, she was implying. Then he noticed the way her lips were twitching at the corners.

"If I didn't know better, Miss Bailey Bishop, I'd say you were teasing me," Brice said, grabbing her hand and pulling her a little closer.

"Perhaps," Bailey said, holding the gaze of longing that was passing between them. Brice's hand on her waist was hot enough to sear through the fabric of her gown and she felt her toes begin to tingle at his touch. His minty breath caressed her face and she felt her mouth go dry. "May I please have one of your breath strips?"

"Sure," Brice said, digging the packet out of his pocket and handing it to her. She took one and returned the rest to him, staring at the darkness. The air was quickly cooling and unless they did something different soon, she was going to be chilled and ready to go home.

Thinking about Brice so close and smelling so tempting combined with the cool night air made her shiver. Brice tightened his arm around her and looked at her concerned.

"Are you cold, sugar?"

"A little," she said, realizing it was probably past time to tell Brice good night anyway.

"Don't move," he said, getting to his feet and disappearing down the stairs of the barn loft. He wasn't gone long when she heard the clomp of his boots running back up the steps.

Dropping back beside her, Brice draped a soft, fleece blanket around her shoulders and pulled her closer against his chest.

"Better?" he asked quietly, his chin resting on her head as his arms wrapped securely around her.

"Perfect," Bailey whispered. She had never, in fact, felt so wrapped up in warmth, love and security before. Held close to Brice was one of the best things she had ever experienced.

Cautiously sliding her arms around his chest, she nestled closer against him, breathing in his scent, soaking up his presence and strength.

They sat without saying anything for a while, enjoying the quiet of the evening as well as the opportunity to be together.

When a huge harvest moon shone down on them, Bailey turned her inquisitive gaze to it and smiled.

"It's so lovely, Brice," Bailey said, trying to remember if she'd ever taken the time to sit and study a harvest moon. Unable to recall doing so, she realized if she had, it was not one so bright and glowing. Not one where she felt so loved and wanted.

"Lovely," Brice echoed, his gaze not on the moon, but the luminescent beams highlighting the curve of Bailey's cheek. Her skin looked radiant in the moonlight, her scent tormented him and the feel of her body next to his was an intoxicating invitation he was finding hard to refuse.

"Don't you think…" Bailey started to say, but when she turned to look at Brice, her words were forgotten. Everything fell away except for the electricity zinging between the two of them, the intense attraction that pulsed with a fervored beat.

"Yeah, sugar, I do," Brice said, tracing his thumb across her smooth cheek, getting lost in her eyes. In the moonlight, they glowed and burned, igniting an answering blaze in his own. Not caring about anything but being as close to Bailey as possible, Brice scooped her into his arms and swung his legs around so he could scoot over and lean against the inside barn wall. He didn't want them to fall out of the loft if they got too carried away with the kisses he planned to lavish on her in the next few minutes.

Making good on his intentions, Brice kissed her ripe lips, savoring the sweetness he found there. Leaning back, he bent his knees, tipping her into his chest.

Fumbling to free her hands from the blanket clutched around her shoulders, Bailey wrapped her arms around Brice's neck, toying with the hair above his shirt collar.

Several moments, several kisses later, they were both struggling to hang on to their common sense, fighting to catch their breath.

"Brice," Bailey said, her head resting on his shoulder while his hands branded her where he pushed up the sleeves of her dress so he could touch her silky skin.

"Hmm?" Brice asked, looking dazed and distracted.

"Brice, I think you better take me home now," Bailey whispered. While her words suggested they stop what they were doing, she made no effort to move. She was way too content in Brice's arms.

"I probably should," Brice said, bending down to kiss her again, lost in the feel of their lips, their bodies, their hearts connecting.

"I meant now," Bailey said, a small smile teasing up the corners of her mouth.

"Right now?" Brice asked, lifting his head as her words finally penetrated the Bailey-induced fog in his mind.

"I think so," Bailey said, pushing at Brice's chest as she struggled to her feet, which was no small task since she was tangled in a blanket, the full skirt of her dress wrapped around her legs, and wearing high heels. Brice smirked as he watched her tug the dress in place and attempt to smooth her hair.

"You're a regular party pooper. You know that?" Brice said, grabbing her hand and leading the way down the loft stairs and out to his pickup.

"You aren't the first to make that declaration and I'm sure you won't be the last," Bailey said, sounding miffed.

"Aw, sugar, now don't be mad at me. I'm only teasing," Brice said, trapping Bailey as he pressed her back against the pickup, his arms on either side of her holding the bed of the truck. He dropped a series of scorching kissing along her neck before she grabbed his shoulders and squeezed.

"Please, Brice," she said, beginning to sound frightened. "Please stop."

Brice let out his breath, dropped his arms and took a step back. "I'm sorry, Bailey. I didn't mean to come on so strong. You're just so dang pretty and smell so nice and feel so good in my arms."

"Brice," Bailey said, flinging her arms around his neck and hugging him. "That's one of the nicest things anyone's ever said to me. I'm not afraid of you. I'm afraid if you don't stop, I won't be able to either. That's why I think you better get me home while I'm still willing to go."

"Oh, sugar, I really wish you hadn't told me that," Brice said, grappling with what he wanted to do versus what he knew he needed to do. Holding her close, he took a deep breath and willed himself to calm down.

Kissing Bailey's temple, he opened the pickup door and helped her inside then drove her home. The only noise in the pickup cab was the radio. It was playing one too many songs about love, so Brice finally changed it over to a station that played jazz music. Acoustical songs were safe.

Pulling up at the Triple T's mud room door, Brice noted lights on in the kitchen, so he held Bailey's hand and walked her to the door, pecking her cheek as he said good night.

When she stood staring at him instead of going inside, he winked and told her to have sweet dreams before driving home to a restless night of little sleep.

The next morning, she checked her messages to find Brice had sent her a song. As she listened to Hunter Hayes sing *Wanted*, Bailey knew she was in way too deep with Brice. That was exactly how he made her feel – wanted, cherished, beloved.

Chapter Fourteen

"Into each life some rain must fall."
Henry Wadsworth Longfellow

"You're certain we have enough time to get there and back today? It seems like a very long drive to only spend a few minutes there and turn right around," Bailey said as Brice held the door of her Jeep while she climbed in.

"Are you saying you want to take me on a long weekend getaway and keep me overnight?" Brice asked with a teasing glint in his eye, although Bailey couldn't see it in the pre-dawn light. It was barely five in the morning and they were embarking on a seven hour drive to the see some fossilized rock in the southeast corner of Oregon. "Why, Miss Bishop, what kind of guy do you take me for? Why didn't you tell me you wanted me all for yourself? I didn't even think to pack a bag."

"Oh, hush, you insolent man," Bailey said, enjoying Brice's teasing. When Brice suggested they make this trip, she was excited at the prospect. She heard about the Pillars of Rome from any number of colleagues and wanted to see them for herself. Spending the entire day with Brice was an added bonus.

During the last week since Tess and Travis' wedding, Bailey had not allowed herself to dwell on the what-ifs of her relationship with Brice and was instead trying to enjoy the time she spent with him.

It had been wonderful.

Although they both were busy with work during the week, Brice managed to come to the Triple T for dinner twice and they went to the high school football game the night before. For someone who had never attended any sporting event prior to moving to Grass Valley, Bailey found she immensely enjoyed cheering on the local boys and watching them play ball. She researched the game and no longer pelted Brice with questions. He seemed impressed last night when she understood the calls the refs made.

After the game, Brice brought her straight home, knowing they would both be dragging this morning if they didn't get some sleep.

As they made their way down the long Triple T drive, Bailey sat behind the wheel of her Jeep, insisting they take it instead of Brice's pickup, since he usually drove. Arriving in John Day several hours later, Brice talked Bailey into stopping for a break before getting back on the road. Their journey took them through Burns before veering toward the far reaches of the southeastern corner of the state.

Pulling up at the small café in Rome at noon, they enjoyed a simple lunch of soup and sandwiches before driving a few miles further to see the fossilized rock formation.

Turning onto a dirt road, it was easy to spot the behemoth mass, rising in an odd white color from the high desert country.

Getting out of the Jeep, Brice and Bailey stood looking at the formations, stark against the leaden gray sky.

Keeping an eye on the weather, Brice grabbed Bailey's hand and they walked as close to the formations as they could. Bailey took out her camera and snapped several photos.

"So, sugar, why don't you tell me all about the famous Pillars of Rome," Brice said, watching her take photos from a variety of angles.

"Made primarily of volcanic tuff, the pillars were created between twelve to fifteen million years ago when volcanoes erupted and river waters created the impressive bluffs from volcanic detritus. The formations tower a hundred feet over the desert floor and measure about five miles long and two miles wide. The chalk and clay in their composition not only creates the distinguishable white coloration, but also makes them very brittle," Bailey said, putting her camera back in the Jeep. When she returned to where Brice stood, she leaned against him and he wrapped an arm around her shoulders.

"So they're big and tall and made of volcanic rock," Brice said, somewhat concerned by the way the sky was getting darker and filling with ominous looking clouds. "What else makes them unique?"

"Pioneers traveling through the area likened the pillars to the Roman ruins, and that's how the community received the name of Rome," Bailey said, giving Brice a sideways glance. "How's that for a history lesson?"

"Very good, professor Bishop."

"I would bet my doctorate degree there are some amazing fossils just waiting to be discovered in there. Too bad it isn't accessible," Bailey said, looking wistfully toward the large formations that sat on private property.

"I'm not going to argue with you there, sugar, but if you're done admiring these hulking rocks, we better get a move on. I'd be willing to bet my hat and boots that we'll see some rain on the windshield before we get too far down the road," Brice said, pointing to the south where they could see a storm rolling in. The temperature was already dropping although it was early afternoon.

"I suppose we better go, then," Bailey said, giving the pillars one last look before she ran to the Jeep and got behind the wheel.

"You want me to drive?" Brice asked as she started down the road back toward the highway.

"Of course not," Bailey snapped, annoyed Brice would even ask. She wasn't some sissy girl driver who couldn't handle bad roads. She grew up in Denver, after all, and the fact she drove a manual transmission should say a little about her ability to handle a vehicle.

Brice threw his hands in the air and shrugged. "Just thought I'd offer."

"Thank you, but I respectfully decline," Bailey said, focusing her attention on the road as rain drops began to fall.

Sixty miles later when the rain was pouring down in torrential sheets and she could barely see the center line on the highway, she began to rethink her hasty refusal. Her hands hurt from gripping the steering wheel and if her neck got any more tense, she was certain it would be permanently cramped in a position by her ears.

"You doing okay?" Brice asked, rubbing a gentle hand on her leg, which only served to distract her from driving.

"I would be if you keep your hands to yourself," she said tersely, not taking her eyes off the road.

Brice jerked his hand away with narrowed eyes. Driving in bad weather must make Bailey grumpy. According to Sierra, anything out of her daily routine made her grumpy. Brice laughed to himself, thinking how much his presence in her life was far outside of her normal routine. No wonder she was quite often disgruntled or snippy. Determining it wasn't something she did to be mean; rather, it seemed like her way of coping with the new and unknown.

Glancing at her, Brice noticed Bailey was staring at the specks of white now mixing with the rain.

"That can't be..." she said, pointing to a snowflake sticking to the windshield.

"But it is," Brice said, looking up at the sky and shaking his head. "Snow. In the middle of October. Just great."

Wanting to force Bailey to pull over so he could drive, Brice was sitting on his hands and biting his tongue to keep from saying or doing anything. She was a good driver, but it bothered him to see her so tense and obviously upset trying to maneuver safely down the road in the bad weather. He had a strong feeling it would get a lot worse before it got better.

If it was cold enough to snow, he worried about the moisture on the roads turning to ice.

"Do you have chains?" Brice asked, keeping his eyes straight ahead.

"Chains? Tire chains?" Bailey asked, trying to remember if she'd taken them out of her Jeep when she unpacked it or left them in. "I do. I'm just uncertain as to their exact location at the moment."

"That's really helpful and quite informative," Brice said, knowing he should have brought his pickup. He had tire chains, a shovel, probably enough lost candy bars and stray bottles of water behind and underneath the seat to last them for a couple days if they somehow ended up stranded.

"No need to spew sarcasm," Bailey said, sending him a glare. When the Jeep slid on a slick spot in the road, Bailey pulled over and they dug around, finally finding her chains. Brice attempted to make her sit in the Jeep while he put the chains on, but she insisted on helping. Clearing the frozen slush from the windshield wipers, they climbed back inside, half-frozen. What was now falling from the sky appeared to be slushy ice. It froze to the windshield wipers and the road upon contact.

An hour later, they were crawling along, trying to see through the ice-streaked windshield and hoping to make it back to Burns alive. Bailey was mad, annoyed and exhausted. She finally pulled over in someone's driveway and slid to a stop.

"You want to drive for a while?" Bailey asked, looking at Brice with a raised brow that dared him to make any smart-aleck comment.

"Sure," Brice said, noting her frown and the stubborn set of her chin. He got out and cleaned the windshield wipers again on his way around the Jeep, climbing into the driver's seat while Bailey slid across to the passenger side. She soaked in the warmth of where Brice had been sitting and took several deep breaths, inhaling deeply of his scent. That, more than anything else, gave her a sense of calm.

"We'll be fine, don't worry," Brice said as he cautiously pulled out on the road. After another hour, they made it to Burns. A drive that should have taken less than two hours had taken more than four.

"I'm going to find us a place to spend the night. There is no way we're driving the rest of the way home in this," Brice said, maneuvering the Jeep into town.

"I don't know if that's a good idea," Bailey said, looking at Brice disapprovingly. It was hard enough for them to keep their hands off each other when they knew people were waiting at home for them. How would they manage when they had an entire night to themselves?

"You've got a better one? You're exhausted, I'm tired, and the roads are going to get worse instead of better. It would be stupid to even think we could make the rest of the trip home in this. We're staying here," Brice said, pulling into the parking lot of a hotel. He hurried inside only to discover they were full due to the storm. Rather than drive around town trying to find a room, Brice smiled charmingly at the young desk clerk and asked if she could call around to find him a room. She placed several calls and finally located a room at a hotel down the street. Brice asked her to have them hold the room for him and thanked the desk clerk for her assistance.

Hurrying back outside, Brice climbed into the Jeep and drove to the hotel. Fortunately, a restaurant sat in the parking lot so they could get a hot meal and some rest before heading out in the morning.

"Let's go see about a room," Brice said, opening Bailey's door and walking her inside. The warmth that hit them at the door felt wonderful. Bailey fought the urge to let her teeth chatter as she stood waiting for the desk clerk to assist them. When they put on the tire chains, she was soaked to the skin and her clothes still felt cold and damp.

"My name's Brice Morgan. Someone phoned in a reservation for me a few minutes ago," Brice said, leaning against the front desk counter and offering the girl behind the desk an engaging smile.

"You're quite lucky, Mr. Morgan. You got our last available room," the girl said, giving him a flirty grin until she saw Bailey. "We only have the one room."

"Oh," Bailey said, and started to say something to Brice, but he shook his head and squeezed her hand.

"That's right. One room," he said, tipping his head toward Bailey with a devilish grin. He grabbed her around the waist and pulled her against his side, kissing her noisily on the cheek. "The little woman and I just need the one. We're feeling fortunate to have a room tonight."

"Yes, sir. That storm is a boon for our business, but not so pleasant for travelers," the girl said, swiping Brice's credit card and handing him two room keys. "Your room is at the end of the hall on the second floor. Breakfast is served from six to nine through those doors over there and the restaurant across the way is open until ten tonight."

"Thank you," Brice said, taking the keys in his hand and guiding Bailey back out the door in the direction of the restaurant.

"What are you doing?" Bailey asked, irritated by the high-handed way Brice had taken over. She was perfectly capable of managing for herself. There was no way she was spending the night alone with him in a hotel room. No way. "I don't know how you arrived at the incorrect conclusion that I'm incapable of taking care of myself or making my own decisions, but I would most appreciate an immediate ceasing of your overbearing leadership post haste. I am not, have never been, nor will I ever be anyone's 'little woman.' If you will kindly hand me the keys to the Jeep, I'll go secure my own room."

"No you won't," Brice said, grabbing her hand and continuing across the parking lot toward the restaurant. "I had the clerk at the last hotel call all over town. This is the last room. The last. There aren't any more available and you aren't going anywhere. Let's eat a hot meal then worry about the technicalities later," Brice said, holding the restaurant door for her to enter. "And you can quit glaring daggers at me because I already know you're ticked at my bossy man-ways and peeved that we're going to have to share a room. It's either share or sleep in your Jeep and one of us would be frozen before morning. It's been a long day and will no doubt be an even longer night and I'm not up to coddling you into a better mood, so deal with it."

Chapter Fifteen

"A man falls in love through his eyes,
a woman through her ears."

Woodrow Wyatt

Brice had never spoken to her in such a gruff tone and Bailey didn't like it. Not one bit. Ready to offer a retort, she stopped and considered the fact that he had to be as tired, cold and hungry as she was.

She also admitted to herself that she had been snappish and fractious with him any number of occasions, including multiple times that afternoon. It wasn't news to Bailey that she could be difficult to deal with when things didn't go her way. She generally didn't care about her reaction. People could accept her or leave her alone.

Only, she didn't want Brice to leave her alone or have to deal with her bad attitude. Always teasing and charming, right now Bailey was missing Brice's lighthearted banter and gentle tone.

Seated at a booth by a window, they quickly glanced at the menu and placed their orders. As they sat waiting for the waitress to return with hot tea for Bailey and hot cider for Brice, they both called their families to let them know they were fine, although stuck in Burns for the night.

Talking to Trey, Bailey was surprised when he asked her to put Brice on the phone. Handing her cell to Brice, she gave him a bewildered look as he took it from her.

"Brice, only you could find an ice storm in October," Trey said, sounding both amused and concerned.

"I know," Brice said, the smile on his face carrying through in his voice. "What are the odds of that happening?"

"Slim to none," Trey said, chuckling. "We had rain here today and it was cooler, but nothing like what Bailey was describing. I'm glad you two are fine and smart enough to stay in Burns tonight. I expect you to behave yourself where my cousin is concerned."

"You don't need to worry," Brice said, still out of sorts with Bailey. He knew the cold outside was probably nothing compared to the arctic blast headed his way from being so blunt with her earlier, not to mention the way he'd annoyed her in front of the hotel clerk. "The weather here isn't the only thing that's chilly."

Brice heard Trey's chuckle. "Just be sure you don't completely melt through that wall of ice before you get her home tomorrow."

"There's no chance of that happening, man," Brice said, nodding at the waitress as she set a steaming mug of spicy cider down on the table. "I promise."

"Since you're as good as your word, I'll trust you. Sleep well and be careful driving back," Trey said, disconnecting the call.

"What do you promise?" Bailey asked, letting a tea bag steep in the hot water filling her mug.

"To get you home safe and sound tomorrow," Brice said, knowing that would further annoy the independent self-sufficient woman sitting across from him.

"I'm perfectly capable of..." Bailey said, cut off by Brice waving a dismissive hand her direction.

"Doing anything I can do, only faster, better, and smarter. I get it," Brice said, taking off his Stetson and denim jacket, hanging them on a hook at the end of the booth.

Bailey looked taken aback by his words, but didn't say anything further while she stirred sugar into her tea, taking a sip. Cradling the mug to warm up her hands, she held it close to her face, breathing in the fragrant steam.

Absently staring out the window, Bailey felt hurt by Brice's curt dismissal of what she was going to say. She didn't really think she could do anything he could do. There were any number of things she couldn't even begin to try to do that Brice did so effortlessly. Realizing her words and actions had given him a false perception of what she believed, she knew at some point she would need to correct it.

Casting a furtive glance at his clenched jaw and tense shoulders, she knew now was not the time for a discussion.

Seeming to relax a little when plates of hot, savory food arrived, they ate in silence. When the waitress left the bill, Brice picked it up, shrugged into his jacket, put his hat on his head and waited for Bailey to get to her feet. She would have argued about paying the bill, but the look in Brice's eyes warned her to keep quiet.

Although she wasn't in any hurry to be locked in a tiny hotel room with Brice, she did like the idea of taking a hot shower and climbing into a warm bed.

Brice and Bailey stepped outside into air that seemed even more frigid than it had earlier. Keeping their distance as they slid across the parking lot, Bailey almost fell and Brice quickly caught her arms, holding her upright. After that, he walked with her tucked against his side, one arm around her waist, the other holding her hand.

"I'd like to get a few things out of the Jeep, please," Bailey said quietly as they crossed the parking lot.

Nodding, Brice veered that direction and waited while she dug out a small duffle bag. Deciding not to push his luck, he let Bailey carry the bag, taking her hand in his as they walked across the slick surface of the parking lot to the hotel lobby.

Once inside, the warmth felt wonderful against their cold cheeks and damp clothes. Neither of them was dressed for freezing temperatures and both were chilled to the bone.

Bailey was starting to worry about Brice by the time they found their room. He hadn't spoken a word since his comments after hanging up with Trey back at the restaurant. Usually full of lively conversation, it didn't seem like him at all to be so quiet and subdued.

Swiping the card in their door lock, Brice took a deep breath and prayed for strength as he held the door open for Bailey to enter. He was sorry he snapped at her earlier, but had no intention of apologizing. If they were going to make it through the night without doing something they shouldn't, it was best if neither of them were feeling romantically inclined. In fact, if she was miffed at him, all the better.

Every ounce of patience he possessed was probably going to be tested and he planned on keeping his word to Trey.

Walking in the room and locking the door, Brice turned and cringed. The room was even smaller than he thought it would be. A king-sized bed, two night stands with lamps, a small desk and a straight-backed chair made up the room's furnishings. Surprisingly, a flat-screen TV was mounted on the wall across from the bed.

Crossing the room, Brice turned the thermostat up and then removed his hat and damp jacket. Finding hangers in the closet, he hung up his jacket then reached for Bailey's as she slid it off her shoulders. If they got the room warm enough, maybe their clothes would dry out before morning. Taking off his boots, he set them by the heat register and motioned for Bailey to leave her hiking boots there as well.

She did, then snatched up her duffle bag, going into the bathroom and quietly shutting the door.

Realizing he didn't even have a comb, Brice reluctantly pulled his boots back on and went in search of a vending machine. He found one that had toothbrushes, toothpaste, deodorant, combs and razors. He'd skip a shave, but brushing his teeth was pretty high on the list of things he'd like to be able to do.

Going to the front desk, he asked the friendly desk clerk to break a twenty dollar bill into something he could feed the machine. Handing him change, Brice thanked the clerk before returning to the vending area where he purchased two toothbrushes, toothpaste, deodorant and a comb.

Returning to the room, he could hear water running in the shower. Envisioning Bailey in the steamy water made his temperature start to climb. Brice distracted himself by taking off his damp boots, turning on the television, and sitting in the straight back chair with his feet up on the desk. He leaned the chair back to balance on two legs and tried to relax.

Staring at the TV without actually watching, Brice's mind wandered back to Bailey. He had no idea how they were going to get through the next awkward hours, but get through them they would.

Swiping his hand down his face, he tried to chase away visions of Bailey along with thoughts of being alone with her all night.

Grabbing the remote, he started flipping through the channels until he found a station playing old reruns. Nothing like a little Mayberry to calm him down.

By the time Bailey came out of the bathroom, Brice was laughing at an episode of *The Beverly Hillbillies*. As steam from the bathroom rolled around him, his laughter died on his lips. Dropping his feet off the desk, he sat forward so fast the front legs of the chair thudded on the floor.

Bailey wore a bright pink T-shirt that hit her mid-thigh and nothing else, at least from what Brice could see. He felt his heart-rate pick up speed so fast, he thought it might explode.

Her hair was damp and curling wildly around her face, her lips were pink and soft, and her legs looked a mile long before disappearing into the hem of her shirt. On closer examination, he decided it was probably a night shirt, since he'd never seen her wear any T-shirts that big and loose-fitting. She smelled fresh and clean, making his blood start to boil.

"There appears to be an ample supply of hot water should it interest you in taking a shower," Bailey said, quickly walking to the far side of the bed, putting it between her and Brice. "It was most satisfactory in chasing away the chills I experienced earlier."

"Good to know," Brice said, getting to his feet and continuing to stare at her. He wanted more than anything to go to her, to lay her down on that bed and kiss her until they both forgot about fossils, freak storms or responsibilities. If Bailey thought the hot shower chased her chills away, Brice had a few ideas that would certainly keep her warm and toasty.

Instead, he retreated to the bathroom with his vending machine toiletries.

Bailey let out the breath she'd been holding and looked at the bathroom door. Carrying an overnight bag in her Jeep, she had everything she needed for an unexpected night away from home from the nightshirt she was wearing to the change of clothes she'd put on in the morning. After brushing her teeth and flossing, she was feeling much more like a human again. Clean and warm, she felt a sense of confidence that she and Brice could share a room without losing their ability to think rationally.

A quick pep talk soothed her tumultuous thoughts until she opened the bathroom door and saw the look of desire in Brice's sparkling brown eyes. The sparkle intensified as his eyes grew dark and a strong current of longing arced between them.

Inexperienced as she might be, Bailey recognized the magnetic draw to Brice and needed space from him. Putting the bed between them seemed like the only logical thing to do. When Brice got to his feet she half expected him to dive across the bed and grab her. She half wanted him to.

Still staring at the bathroom door, she could hear the shower water running. Shaking her head to clear her thoughts, she dug through her purse finding what she was seeking, then climbed into bed, piling the pillows behind her back and putting on her reading glasses. Deciding she wouldn't think about what would happen when it was time to turn out the lights, Bailey was going to pretend she was alone with nothing better to do than pass a quiet evening. Wishing she had some stitching to work on, Bailey contented herself to read a book instead.

Once the shower water stopped running, Bailey heard the whir of the blow dryer and smiled to herself, picturing Brice styling his hair. Was he really that vain? He didn't seem like the blow dryer type. He seemed more like the barely take time to comb his hair type.

When he opened the bathroom door a few minutes later with his hair damp and falling into tempting waves around his forehead, Bailey knew for a fact he was not a blow dryer kind of guy.

He was the kind of guy who could instantly make her pulse rate double and inspire any number of thoughts she shouldn't be having as he stood wrapped in nothing but a white towel around his waist.

Although she knew Brice had muscles to spare, seeing them still tan from the summer and on display made her mouth flood with moisture. The sight before her was the kind of physique she could find described in one of

Lindsay's romance novels. She'd been reading one, frivolous as it was, when Brice came out of the bathroom and distracted her so thoroughly she thought perhaps the hero of the story had come to life.

But the flesh and blood male standing a few feet away, looking like a poster boy for a gym membership, was about to make her overheat.

Glancing over her glasses at the handsome cowboy, Bailey tried to remember something, anything, other than Brice.

><><

Trying to kill as much time as possible, Brice hand-washed his underwear and socks then took a long shower. After drying off, he blow dried his briefs then slipped them on before wrapping a dry towel around his waist. Brushing his teeth, he ran a comb through his hair and took a cleansing breath.

Coming out of the bathroom, he hung his damp, dirty jeans and shirt with their jackets, hoping they would dry by morning. He walked across the room and placed his socks near the heat register so they would dry quickly.

He could have left his cold, damp clothes on, but that thought didn't appeal to him any more than prancing around the hotel room in his underwear. Without any extra clothes, he really didn't have a lot of options, so he figured the towel gave him a faint degree of modesty where Bailey was concerned.

Glancing her direction, she looked entirely too appealing. He wondered if she had any idea that she was giving the sexy professor look a whole new meaning as she sat propped in bed against the pillows with her glasses sliding down her nose and something she had obviously been reading open on her lap.

Trying to divert their attention from the electrical storm passing between them, he studied what she was holding from his spot across the room.

"What's that?" he finally asked unable to decide what was in her hands.

"An electronic device that allows me to download books and read them," Bailey said, still ogling him over her glasses.

Brice felt both flattered and uncomfortable under her close scrutiny. Stepping next to the bed, he looked down and could see text on the screen.

"So it's like a Nook or a Kindle?" he asked, knowing Tess and Lindsay both had ereaders.

"Yes," Bailey said, surprised Brice would know what she was talking about, but then again, he seemed to keep up on the latest electronics.

"Would you mind reading aloud?" Brice asked, pulling the chair over by the bed. Settling into it, he lifted his feet onto the bed, tugged the towel around his legs in an effort at propriety and grinned at the wide-eyed look Bailey gave him. Her eyes were huge and luminous and he wanted more than anything right then to fall into the Caribbean blue depths.

"I…um…I…" Bailey stuttered at a loss for words with Brice so close and so… so…nearly naked.

"I'll read," Brice said, grabbing the device out of Bailey's hand and starting at the top of the page.

His calloused fingers sent spiraling tendrils of desire coursing down the silky expanse of her back as her moan of pleasure echoed in his ears. Tightening the corded strength of his arms around her, Felicity's ample bosom heaved against Damon's thickly muscled chest and he knew the moment was ripe to…

"Sugar, what are you reading?" Brice asked, half-teasing, half-tempted to keep reading. Bright pink splotches highlighted Bailey's cheeks as she snatched back her ereader and closed the cover with a snap.

"An entirely ridiculous fictional tale of love and romance suggested by Lindsay. Apparently she is quite taken with this particular genre," Bailey said, unable to meet Brice's eyes as she focused her attention on smoothing the sheet over her lap.

"Does Trent know about it?" Brice asked, trying to sound serious. Trent, with his romantic tendencies, probably had Lindsay reading him a bedtime story every night. Brice knew if he continued reading the book Bailey had started there was no telling what might happen this evening.

"That is information I am not privy to," Bailey said, her cheeks still flushed with embarrassment. Thinking about the books she had available at her fingertips, she opened the cover and quickly scrolled through her options, finding what she was looking for.

"If you'd like me to read, listen to this one," Bailey said, sharing a collection of humorous short stories by Mark Twain.

After one particularly funny story, Brice was laughing so hard, he had to wipe the tears from his eyes. Bailey, having forgotten the awkwardness between them earlier, was laughing as well. She was a strong, animated reader and they both enjoyed the engaging tales.

Glancing at the bedside clock, Bailey turned off the ereader and set it on the nightstand, followed by her glasses. "I guess we should probably turn in," she said, wondering how they would decide who got the bed.

One of them was either going to have to sleep on the floor, which made her shudder in revulsion, or sleep in the chair, which was nearly unthinkable in the discomfort that would bring.

The sensible thing to do would be to share the bed, but Bailey didn't know if she could trust Brice to behave and she was afraid her own willpower wasn't strong enough to refuse him if he didn't.

Before Brice could say anything, Bailey hurried into the bathroom to buy herself some time. Brushing her teeth again, she stared into the mirror, giving herself another mental pep talk before putting a generous amount of lotion in her palm and opening the bathroom door. Walking to the bed, she stood staring at it while Brice disappeared into the bathroom. When he came back out, he still had the towel around his waist and seemed to be studying her.

Attracted to Bailey for a multitude of reasons and in any number of ways, Brice thought she was going to be his undoing as she stood by the bed, the light filtering through her nightshirt, rubbing lotion up her arms and into her hands. He didn't know why, but that particular movement seemed so intimate and sensual, he clenched his hands into fists at his sides to keep from lunging across the bed and sweeping her into a passionate embrace.

"Look, Bailey, we both need to sleep, there's only one bed, so let's be adult about this and agree to stay on our own sides. Will that work for you?" Brice said, trying to gauge her reaction. He expected the fiery blush that filled her cheeks. He wasn't prepared for her vehement refusal, though.

"Absolutely not," Bailey said, crossing her arms across her chest. "It's completely inappropriate, highly improper, and not a good idea. Not at all."

"Do you have any better ideas?" Brice asked, trying to remain calm. Why did she always have to be so pig-headed, argumentative and cute?

"Well, I could…you could…" Bailey sighed in frustration. "No. I don't."

"Come on. We can do this," Brice said, motioning for Bailey to climb in bed. She did and turned off the lamp beside her. Brice turned off the lamp next to him, dropped his towel, and climbed between the blankets and the sheet, giving Bailey some small degree of separation from him.

Feeling a dip in the bed from Brice's weight, Bailey held her breath, waiting for Brice to scoot over and pull her against him. When he didn't, she felt a little disappointment along with her relief.

"Sleep tight, sugar, and have sweet dreams," Brice said, rolling toward her and kissing her cheek. Bailey knew then he'd left the sheet between them.

"Thank you, Brice," she whispered, reaching out to squeeze his hand before rolling away from him to face the wall.

They both waited quietly in the dark, listening for the other to breathe deeply in slumber. Instead, the air crackled with tension and pent-up longing.

Finally, Bailey couldn't take it any longer. Rolling onto her back, she lifted her arm from beneath the covers and slid her hand across the bed until it connected with Brice. She rested her hand on his shoulder, content just to touch him, when she felt the warmth of his hand on her cheek.

"What's wrong, sugar? Why aren't you sleeping?" Brice asked, his voice subdued by fatigue and longing.

"I don't know. I feel quite unsettled," Bailey said, annoyed with herself. She knew she'd never get to sleep unless Brice at least kissed her. Just once. Then she could relax and close her eyes. Having envisioned a day spent with him kissing and teasing her, and at least one sizzling good night kiss, all her hopes had been blown off course when the storm rolled in. Instead, they'd both been short-tempered and grumpy with one another and now Brice was acting like she was a buddy rather than his current love interest. Bailey felt frustrated and snubbed.

"What would settle you?" Brice asked, hoping her answer wouldn't require him to get dressed and go find somewhere to order hot tea or warm milk.

"Perhaps if you'd hold me, just for a minute or two, it would help," Bailey whispered, fearful of voicing her longing too loudly. There was something magical about being in Brice's arms. Something that made her feel warm and safe and loved. She needed that right now. Needed it so badly, she could think of nothing else no matter how hard she tried.

"I'll hold you as long as you want, Bailey," Brice said in a husky voice, reaching out and gently tugging Bailey closer to him. When her head settled against his chest, he pulled up the blankets and felt her relax. Although it made every nerve ending in his body stand at attention, he did feel more restful with her nestled in his arms. If only that blasted sheet wasn't between them, he could fully enjoy the experience.

Rather than dwell on that, Brice took a deep breath, then another as he lightly stroked his fingers along Bailey's back and shoulders through the thin cotton of the sheet. Her breathing deepened and Brice knew she was asleep. Smiling to himself, he allowed his thoughts to still and was soon lost in his dreams.

Bailey couldn't remember ever sleeping so peacefully before. She snuggled into the warmth beneath her cheek and smiled. She didn't recall her pillow being so firm before. Maybe Cady bought new ones and didn't mention it.

When the pillow beneath her moved, Bailey swallowed back a scream and popped open her eyes, only to find herself staring into Brice's sparkling brown ones.

"Brice Morgan! What do you think you're doing?" Bailey asked in a demanding tone before she remembered being stuck in Burns for the night. She was curled up around Brice like he was her own personal body pillow. He looked at her like she'd lost what little bit was left of her mind.

"I was enjoying a little cuddle time with you before you started yelling at me," Brice said, the mischievous glint back in his eyes. "I let you use me all night for your pleasure and that's the thanks I get?"

Spluttering, Bailey thumped Brice on the chest before he caught her hand in his and kissed her cheek.

"I think I kind of like waking up with you. You're feisty and full of sass bright and early, just like you are the rest of the day," Brice said, wearing a wicked grin. "You want to make this a permanent arrangement?"

It was on the tip of Bailey's tongue to say yes. She'd like nothing better than waking up each morning in Brice's arms, but that was not meant to be.

"Don't be impertinent," Bailey said, knowing she sounded like a school teacher scolding a student.

"Never," Brice said, running a hand over her tousled curls while the other was warm and comforting on her back. Brice awoke and watched Bailey sleeping until she began to rouse. Apparently, they both had either been so tired, or so content to be held in each other's arms, they hadn't moved all night. Completely entranced with watching Bailey sleep, completely enthralled with her sleeping on his bare chest, Brice didn't want to ever let her go.

This feeling of love and belonging was what he'd been waiting for his entire life. Being with Bailey was like finding a part of him he hadn't even known was missing. Despite her quirks, every day she became more important to him, more a part of him, as he fell deeper in love.

She fit against him like she was the lone person in the world created just for that purpose.

Pressing a kiss to her temple, he watched her slowly awaken and couldn't help smiling when she cuddled closer against him.

"Now you're lying," Bailey said, trying to sound stern, but unable to hide a smile. "You are always impertinent and quite often behave like a hooligan."

"Gee, and here I thought you were starting to like me," Brice said, looking crestfallen.

Bailey's head jerked up and she saw a grin tugging at the corners of Brice's mouth.

"Not at all," she said, stretching up and pressing a kiss to the mole at the edge of his bottom lip.

"You best not start something we can't finish, sugar," Brice said, acutely aware that the only thing between him and Bailey was a measly little sheet, and his promise to himself and Trey to behave like a gentleman.

Bailey nodded her head in understanding and started to push away from Brice.

"No need to get in a hurry," Brice said, glancing at the bedside clock. Even if the weather had drastically improved, he figured there was no need to get on the road before eight. It was just a little after six. He pulled her against him and continued stroking his hand across her back.

"Well, we certainly can't stay here like this all day," Bailey said, wanting to do exactly that. Brice's enticing scent, even without his cologne, has a heady fragrance. The warmth of his bare skin against her palm, the beating of his heart, strong and steady, beneath her cheek was reassuring and pleasant.

For the first time in her life, Bailey felt completely cherished and secure, loved for who she was without exception. Brice put up with her waspish tongue, ignored

233

her spurts of temper, overlooked her occasionally snobbish attitude, and loved her. Truly loved her.

Sierra told her to allow herself to enjoy being young and in love, but it was so much more than that. She wasn't just in love with Brice, she loved him to the very depths of her soul and didn't want to think about how she would ever live without him.

Her mind circled back around to her decision that marriage and career would never work together for her and Bailey dreaded the day when she'd have to tell Brice goodbye. The more time she spent with him, the harder it was going to be and yet, she couldn't seem to stay away from him.

Blocking out thoughts of what might come tomorrow, Bailey decided to enjoy the moment, to soak up every second of this quiet morning spent in Brice's capable arms.

Looking up at him, some of what she was feeling was conveyed in her bright eyes, drawing Brice into their ocean-blue depths.

"Bailey," he whispered, shifting slightly so he could cup her face in his hands before pressing his lips to hers.

Bailey smiled against his lips when she tasted his minty breath strip on her tongue. It was so like him and the familiarity of it melted her heart.

She ran her hands up his chest, over his shoulders and twined them behind his neck, toying with the back of his short hair.

He moaned and pulled her closer, finding her entangled in the sheet. Bailey moved away from Brice, kicking the sheet down before he rolled her on top of him. The sensations produced from that made Bailey feel light headed while her limbs began to tingle and go weak. Their kisses grew in urgency as Bailey pressed herself against Brice, relishing the contact.

A shiver started at her toes and worked its way to her head when Brice ran his hands along the backs of her thighs, up to the hem of the nightshirt. He suddenly stopped and she felt his forehead pressed against hers.

"Sugar, we can't do this. Not here. Not like this. It's not right," Brice said, breathing heavily as he tried to get control of himself.

"I know, but why does it have to feel so wonderfully good?" Bailey asked, resting her head on Brice's shoulder. Deciding to end the torment, she slid off Brice and the bed, getting to her feet. "I'm sorry," she said, escaping to the bathroom.

By the time she emerged, Brice was dressed and waiting for her.

After eating breakfast, they started the drive home, grateful the temperature had risen and the roads were clear. Lost in their own thoughts, it was a quiet trip back to Grass Valley.

When Brice parked the Jeep at the Triple T later that morning, Trey sauntered over from the barn and gave them both a look, trying to surmise if any damage had been done. Grinning, he thumped Brice on the back and thanked him for getting Bailey home safely.

Brice nodded, not willing to admit, even to himself, how close he came to breaking his promise.

Chapter Sixteen

"So go ahead. Fall down.
The world looks different from the ground."
Oprah Winfrey

"Who needs gas in their car?" Tess asked as she barreled into the kitchen at the Triple T.

Back for more than a week from their honeymoon, Tess and Travis were settling into the routine of daily work while enjoying life as newlyweds in their new home.

Since Tess was often late in the evenings and Lindsay didn't cook, Cady continued to feed everyone dinner at the big ranch house. Brice often joined them so he could spend time with Bailey as well as torment Tess and Travis.

Tonight was no exception as Brice teased Travis relentlessly. Trey and Trent, along with the ranch hands joined in while Bailey and Cady visited. Lindsay picked at her food, still suffering from flu-like symptoms that had plagued her for the last week and Cass carried on her own conversation in her seat next to Trey.

At Tess' abrupt arrival and unexpected question, all eyes turned her direction in surprise.

When no one answered, Tess looked at the female occupants of the table. "Cady, do you need gas?"

"No. Trey filled my car yesterday," Cady said, wondering what had spurred Tess' sudden interest in the level of their gas tanks.

"Bailey?" Tess asked hopefully.

Shaking her head in response, Tess turned her gaze to Lindsay.

"I was going to fill the tank after school tomorrow," Lindsay said, staring at Tess. The girl was acting odd.

"Great!" Tess said, grabbing Lindsay and Bailey by the hands, since they were sitting side by side, and tugging them out of their chairs. "Grab your keys and let's go."

"Go where?" Lindsay asked, looking confused as Tess motioned for Cady to join them.

"To the gas station. Pronto," Tess said, kissing Travis on the cheek. He grabbed her arm and held on.

"Honeybee, why are you in such an all-fired hurry to get to the gas station? What's going on?" Travis asked, noting the mischief dancing in his bride's eyes.

"The new owner of the gas station is out pumping gas himself," Tess said, grinning broadly. "You girls have got to go see him. He looks exactly, and I mean exactly, like Jon Bon Jovi."

"You're kidding?" Lindsay said, snatching her purse off the floor by the kitchen counter as she and Cady hurried toward the door, dragging Bailey with them.

"Hey, where are you girls going?" Trey asked, half-rising from his chair at the far end of the table.

"Didn't you hear the woman? Lindsay's car needs gas," Cady said with a grin and a wink as the four women hustled out the door.

"Well, boys, I think we've just been abandoned for greener pastures," Trey said, looking around the table, noting the frowns on the faces of his brothers as well as Brice.

"I got bandonized, too, Daddy. Mama didn't take me either," Cass said, standing up in her chair and stepping over to Trey's lap.

"She sure didn't, honey," Trey said, running his big hand over the top of his daughter's curly head.

"What's a Jovi?" Cass asked, looking at Trey as she jiggled her foot from her seat on his lap.

"Bon Jovi was a very popular singer and actor a few years ago. Some women think he's quite handsome," Trey explained to the little girl as she looked from her father to her uncles.

"Even handsomer than you, Daddy?" Cass asked, staring adoringly at her father.

"Apparently," Trey grumbled, wishing the girls had at least taken Cass so he wouldn't have to answer her million questions.

"Even handsomer than Uncle Trent and Uncle Travis and Brice and all the guys?" Cass asked looking around the big dining room table filled with men.

"Absolutely not," Brice said with a wicked grin. "Nobody's that handsome."

The hands started laughing as they all pitched in to do the dishes and set the kitchen to rights. When the girls failed to return nearly an hour later, their husbands began to worry.

"It shouldn't take more than fifteen minutes to go fill the car with gas. What do you suppose they are doing?" Travis said, staring at his watch for the sixth time in the last ten minutes.

"Who knows?" Brice said, leaning against the counter. "If it makes you feel better, I met the man. He bought the gas station and owns the new house and barn we've been building. We're just finishing up with the project and he came by yesterday to check it out."

"And?" Trey and Travis both asked, wanting more information.

"He seems pretty nice. Must have some money because that house and barn are really something," Brice said taking out his knife and picking at his already clean fingernails.

"But what does he look like?" Trent asked, joining the questioning.

"About like Tess said. I thought at first it was Bon Jovi, but then realized there was no way he'd be hanging out in Grass Valley," Brice said, noticing the hard looks that settled on the faces of the Thompson brothers.

"You guys haven't got a thing to worry about," Brice said reassuringly, trying to act calm, knowing Bailey was along for the ride with the other three women. He was as tied in knots as his friends, but he sure wasn't going to admit it.

"Who is this guy?" Trey finally asked, sending Cass outside to play with her dog so they could have a few minutes of quiet.

"He owns the Renegade gas stations and convenience stores. From what I heard him tell my boss, he started out with one station, then two, and his enterprise grew from there," Brice said, still striving to keep a sense of nonchalance.

Trent whistled. "Then he does have an extra penny or two to spare. Those stations are all over the northwest. There's got to be about thirty or so of them."

"The one here in Grass Valley, once he changes the name and puts up the signs, will be number fifty-two, same as his age," Brice said, doling out the details a little at a time. "His name is Hart Hammond. Said he spent his childhood summers somewhere around Prineville with his grandparents and used to drive through here on his way to and from his home in Spokane. He liked the area and that's why he decided to finally settle here. I got the idea he's lived all over the place, from Seattle to LA and everywhere in between."

"Did you say Hart Hammond?" Travis asked, suddenly sitting up at attention.

"Yeah. Why?" Brice asked, studying his friend, wondering what Travis knew that he didn't.

"I wonder if he's *the* Hart Hammond," Travis said, drumming his fingers on the countertop, looking thoughtful as he stared at Brice.

"Who the heck is Hart Hammond?" Trey asked, running a hand through his thick honey-colored hair.

"Hart Hammond was one of the best bull riders of his time. He was on his way to being the world champion when he went off the grid. He quit competing and seemingly fell off the face of the earth," Travis said, warming to the subject. He and Brice both had ridden bulls. For Brice it was a way to have fun and hang out with his friends but Travis was much more competitive and driven about the whole thing. "Hart was gored by bulls twice in the same year and still managed to place third in the ranking. The next year he came back and took second place. All indicators pointed to him claiming the title the following year. He disappeared just a few weeks before the finals."

"Have you seen photos of him?" Trent asked Travis.

"Sure. Even thirty years ago, he looked like Bon Jovi," Travis said, realizing one of his bull-riding heroes was most likely the same man who purchased the gas station. He might have to go fuel up his truck in the next few days to see if was true.

"Fantastic," Trey muttered. "Just what we need to keep our women all stirred up. A good-looking, former bull riding, rich guy with a fancy new house."

"I doubt he was still at the station by the time the girls got there," Brice said, trying to sound positive.

No one had a chance to reply as the door burst open and the girls came in chatting excitedly. They each held a to-go cup of coffee and were all smiling.

"Well?" Trey asked, trying his best to look authoritative and cross.

"Well, what, boss-man?" Cady asked, kissing his cheek and giving him a flirty grin.

"Where were you for the last hour?" Trent asked, giving Lindsay a narrowed glare. "Surely it didn't take that long just to fill your car with gas, did it, princess?"

"Nope," Lindsay said, grinning at her husband, taking a sip of the coffee in her hand.

"Mr. Hammond was so nice. He invited us to come in and see the changes he made in the convenience store. You won't believe this, but he's got coffee. Really good coffee. As in, I have a caramel macchiato in my hand kind of good coffee," Cady said, taking a quick sip of her drink before Trey pulled it out of her hand and tasted it, nodding his approval.

"Does he really look like Bon Jovi?" Trent asked. All four girls nodded their heads and smiled dreamily.

"Exactly," Tess said, glancing at Travis and batting her eyelashes at him.

"You girls should be ashamed of yourselves setting such a bad example for cousin Bailey," Travis said, pointing to the three sisters-in-law. "You're supposed to be loving and responsible married women. What kind of behavior are you exhibiting? Certainly not the actions of a devoted wife."

"Oh, pipe down, Tee," Tess said, throwing her arms around his neck and kissing his cheek. "We're just having some fun. No harm in that. Besides, it's not every day someone new buys the gas station and it certainly isn't every day we get celebrity look-alikes pumping gas."

"Be that as it may, you ladies should..." Trey started to say but was cut off when Cady put a hand over his mouth.

"Get out and have fun more often, I know," Cady said, nodding her head at Trey. "Thanks for suggesting it."

"That is not what I was going to say, darlin', and you know it. You are officially in big trouble," Trey said, scowling at her.

"I'm not too worried about it," Cady said turning away from Trey. She grinned over her shoulder when he popped her bottom before getting to his feet and following his brothers out the door.

"If you girls set out with the intention of making your men jealous and driving them crazy, job well done," Brice teased as he grabbed Bailey's hand and hurried them both out the back door.

Giving her a kiss she thought might melt the insulated coffee cup she still held in her hand, Brice took a long drink from it and handed it back to her.

"Should have known it would be pumpkin-flavored coffee, sugar. You have a serious pumpkin problem," Brice said, climbing into his pickup while Bailey stood by the door.

"My biggest problem is that I don't get nearly enough of it," Bailey said, taking a sip of the coffee.

"One of these days I'll come to find you and you'll have turned into a big ol' orange blob, won't you?" Brice said, starting his truck.

"Maybe," Bailey said, feeling unusually flirty. "Would you kiss me until I turned back into a girl?"

"I'd kiss you until I used my whole tube of ChapStick, blistered my lips and wore out my ability to pucker, if that's what it took to turn you back," Brice teased, waving at Bailey as he headed down the driveway, leaving her smiling.

><><

"I'm sorry, Mr. Atticus," Brice said, looking at his employer with a somewhat dazed expression at the news the man had just delivered. "I thought you liked my work."

"I do, Brice, and you've been a great employee. Even when you worked for me part-time when you were in school you always did a good job, but I have to lay some people off," Brice's employer said, not quite looking Brice in the eye.

Today was the last day on the job at Hart Hammond's place. Brice assumed he'd drive to The Dalles on Monday and report for work at a new location. Only Mr. Atticus was now walking through the crew, letting some of them know they no longer had jobs to report to, effective immediately.

"I hoped to make it through a few more months before it came to this, but even with this big job," Atticus said, waving his hand around the impressive Hammond home, "I've got to cut some expenses. I'd like nothing better than to keep you on, Brice, but some of these guys have families to support. I know you understand where I'm coming from."

"Sure, Mr. Atticus," Brice said quietly, shocked at this news. If he'd seen it coming, had time to prepare for it, it might not have been so bad. He got up this morning, expecting to have a great last day on the project, looking forward to whatever new job they'd be starting next week.

Only for him, there would be no next project with Atticus Construction.

"Look, Brice, I'm really sorry about this and if I could, I'd keep you on," Atticus said, putting a hand on Brice's shoulder and squeezing. "I'm happy to write you letters of recommendation, whatever I can do to help."

"Thanks," Brice said, trying not to rail at the man who had just pulled the rug out from under him. It wasn't Brice's style.

Giving him another pat on the shoulder, Atticus walked off, squaring his shoulders to deliver the unwelcome news to another of his employees.

Brice's mind spun in a hundred directions while he finished his work. Atticus was letting those he was laying off leave at noon rather than working a full day. Quite generous of the man, Brice thought with a thick dose of sarcasm.

At noon, Atticus walked around handing those he'd given their walking papers their final paychecks.

Brice packed up his personal tools and made the rounds, wishing his coworkers and friends well. Sitting in his pickup, it didn't surprise him when he opened the paycheck to see the amount was for his exact wages owed, not a penny more. He should have listened to his dad years ago when he told him not to trust Atticus.

Not used to feeling depressed or down, Brice drove home and went out to his woodworking shop. Turning on some music, he lost himself in a carved side chair he was making for his mom's friend.

There wasn't a rush on getting it done, but he'd have plenty of time to complete it much sooner than he expected. As the smell of wood shavings and the motions of carving a design into the smooth grain soothed him, Brice wondered again if he could really pursue his dream of woodworking and be successful at it.

Several people had encouraged him to make furniture for a living, he just wasn't sure he'd be able to support himself, let alone a wife and family.

Thinking about a wife made his thoughts turn to Bailey. How could he hope to have any sort of committed relationship with her when he didn't even have a job? She would see this is a failure on his part. He knew she would.

Wondering how he could feel any lower, he ignored his mother's request to come in for dinner, refusing to tell her, or his dad when he came out later, what was bothering him.

A soft knock at the door an hour later caused him to frown and ignore it. When the knock came again, he still wasn't ready to deal with anyone.

"I already told you, I'm not hungry, I don't want to come in, and I'm fine," Brice yelled, hoping his parents would leave him alone. This is what he got for still living at home.

"You don't sound fine," a decidedly feminine voice said as a honey-colored head poked around the door. "You sound mad and upset to me."

"Bailey," Brice said, releasing a little of his anger. Just seeing her seemed to have a calming effect on him. "Sorry, sugar, I thought it was Mom or Dad coming out to annoy me again."

"They care about you, Brice, that's all," Bailey said, walking into his workshop and closing the door. Instead of immediately going over to Brice, she wandered around, running her hand over some of his projects, savoring the smell of wood and Brice that filled the room, taking her thoughts to a spicy autumn afternoon spent in golden sunshine.

"I know, but they still are annoying sometimes," Brice said, with a half-hearted smile.

Bailey might not be good at reading people or understanding relationships, but it didn't take an expert to see something was bothering Brice. Something big. According to his parents, he'd been locked in his workshop all afternoon. Normally, he didn't get off work until four, so that in itself gave her reason for concern.

"Why don't you tell me what stole the sparkle from your eye and the smile from your face?" Bailey said, placing a gentle hand on Brice's arm. They both felt the tingle at the contact and Brice tried not to jerk away. He wasn't in the mood to have his anger softened. Feeling like he'd earned the right to be mad and brooding, he planned to nurse it for as long as possible.

"Nothing. I'm fine," Brice said, ignoring Bailey's touch and the hint of compassion in her voice. "And if Mom sent you out here to try to get me to come eat dinner, tell her to feed it to the dogs. I'm not hungry."

"Yes, I gathered that much from the yelling when I knocked on the door," Bailey said, deciding it was her turn to tease Brice out of a funk. Goodness only knew he'd done it for her more times than she wanted to think about. Plopping down on the stool at the workbench, Bailey placed her elbows on the counter, leaned back and crossed her legs, watching Brice.

She knew something was wrong when he didn't reply to the text message she sent earlier confirming their date tonight for the football game. When he didn't show up for dinner, as he usually did on Friday night, everyone wondered what was going on. Travis and Tess both tried calling him and got his voice mail, then a call to his folks confirmed he was hiding out in the workshop, not talking.

Tired from a long day at work, Bailey drove over to the Running M with the intention of finding out what was wrong. Now that she was here, she wasn't certain how to go about getting Brice to open up or even how to cheer him up.

"Why don't you tell me what has you acting like me and we'll decide an appropriate course of action?" Bailey asked, hoping that would at least make Brice smile. He didn't even pretend to hear her as he kept his focus on the wood he was smoothing.

Bailey suddenly wondered if this is what other people felt like when they were dealing with her in one of her snits. If so, she would have to be more mindful of not repeating similar behavior. It was unpleasant and quite distressing.

Thinking about what would get Brice's attention or inspire him to talk, Bailey studied him for a while. The heat was turned on in the workshop, making the room toasty and inviting. Brice had peeled off his outer layers until he was down to a T-shirt that molded to every muscle in his arms, back and chest.

Bent over, smoothing a piece of wood, Bailey enjoyed watching him work, watching those muscles bunch, move and flex. Brice was beautifully formed and the very fact of that often left Bailey a little off-kilter. Guys that attractive were usually self-centered jerks.

Like her good-looking Thompson cousins, though, Brice seemed to take it in stride. He was a genuinely kind, big-hearted man who didn't seem to dwell too much on his looks. Bailey, however, spent enough time for three people dwelling on how good he looked.

"Brice," she said, sliding off the stool and walking over to him. "I'm fairly certain if you tell me what's bothering you, it will not only make you feel better, and it will also allay the concerns of those who care about you."

"No," Brice said gruffly, rubbing his hand over the wood and giving it a close perusal. Finding a rough spot, he went back to sanding and smoothing the piece.

"No, it won't make you feel better or no, it won't help give everyone else some peace of mind?" Bailey asked, stepping behind Brice and placing her hands on his tense shoulders. She slowly began rubbing away the tight spots, massaging his muscles. Brice tried to hold onto his anger, but with Bailey slowly incinerating his skin through his T-shirt, he finally let it go and enjoyed the feel of her capable hands smoothing out the tension.

Smiling to herself, Bailey was quite pleased to see Brice's shoulders drop down where they should be as he stopped his work and stood quiet and still. She wasn't experienced in giving anyone a back rub, purely following instinct. "Are you ready to converse now?"

"Not really," Brice said, tipping his head forward to give her better access to his neck. He felt her fingers on his skin and it made waves of heat wash through him.

"Why don't you try it anyway?" Bailey asked, standing on tiptoe so she could press a moist kiss to his neck.

Brice spun around and pulled her to him, crushing her lips against his with a brutal force that caught Bailey off guard. Always sweet and gentle, if somewhat mischievous with his kisses, this demanding, possessive kiss was unlike anything she'd ever experienced.

"Brice!" she gasped when he let her up for air.

"I'm sorry, sugar," Brice said, dropping his arms and taking a step back. "I shouldn't have done that. I just…"

"You what?" Bailey asked, grabbing Brice's hands and holding them in her own. He was behaving so unlike himself, Bailey was really beginning to worry. "You just what?"

"I needed you," Brice whispered, staring at his boots. "I needed to feel you close."

"And that's a bad thing because why?" Bailey asked, thrilled at Brice's admission since she so often felt like the needy one in their relationship. She was coming to need Brice like she needed air to breath, water to drink, and food to eat.

"Because I had no right to kiss you like that. I've got no right to want you like I do," Brice said, trying to turn away from her, but Bailey kept a firm grip on his hands.

"What's going on Brice? You aren't acting like the teasing flirt I've come to know and…" Bailey caught herself before she admitted she loved Brice. Somehow she knew once she said the words aloud to him, there would be no going back, no changing her mind, no telling him goodbye.

"And what?" Brice said, perking up a little as he stared at her intently.

"Care about greatly," Bailey said, hoping he would be satisfied with her answer. He studied her face, his eyes meeting hers and he seemed to find what he needed in the depths there because he nodded and let out a sigh. "Brice, it isn't like you to bottle things up. Tell me what's wrong and I know you'll feel better."

"I highly doubt it, sugar, but since I won't get any peace until I tell someone, I'll tell you. I lost my job today," Brice said, staring at the floor, somehow wishing it would open up and suck him inside.

"What happened?" Bailey asked, trying to think of all the reasons Brice would find himself unemployed. Other than lunacy on the part of his employer, she couldn't come up with anything. Brice was a hard worker with a unique talent. No one with any intelligence would willingly let him go. She knew he was well-liked by his peers and had a good reputation.

"Atticus went around this morning letting about half of us know he was laying us off. Said he had to make some cuts and those of us without families were the ones to get the ax. He sent us home at noon and that was that," Brice said, pulling his hand from Bailey's and walking over to lean against the workbench, staring out the window into the darkness.

"Brice, that's terrible. That's no way to run a business or treat employees," Bailey said, indignant and outraged on Brice's behalf. "Why, that is positively idiotic on his part."

Glancing at Bailey, Brice noted the splotches of anger filling her cheeks and the sparks shooting from her eyes. He had definitely read her wrong on this count, convinced she'd think he was at fault. Instead, she was jumping to his defense. Maybe she liked him a little more than he gave her credit for.

"As ridiculous as it might be, it still leaves me unemployed," Brice said, drumming his fingers on the work table, causing a pile of wood shavings to bounce to the tune his restlessness created.

"This is a good thing, Brice. A very good thing. Sometimes the best way to get a fresh perspective is get down to ground level and look up," Bailey said, smiling at him with a knowing look. "Now you have both the time and opportunity to apply yourself to your woodworking talent and see where it takes you, if that's what you want to do."

"What if takes me right to the poor house?" Brice said, swiping his hand over his face. "I've got a few jobs lined up, but not enough to replace my income with any degree of security."

"Then we'll figure this out," Bailey said, spying some sheets of paper and a pen on a corner of the workbench. She grilled Brice about how fast he could work, how long it took to do certain types of projects, if he had a filing or billing system and places he could promote his work.

By the time they finished putting some plans on paper an hour later, Brice was feeling a little better and a lot more hopeful.

"Thanks, sugar," Brice said, wrapping his arms around Bailey from behind as she finished writing down some notes. "I'm glad you braved the lion's den and came in tonight."

"Me, too, although I'd say it was more like a grumpy bear's cave," Bailey said, not even glancing up from the paper so Brice could see the teasing gleam in her eyes.

"Grumpy bear?" Brice said, nuzzling her neck and making her squirm. "I'll show you grumpy bear."

Bailey jumped up from the stool and started for the door but Brice caught her, swinging her into his arms before she was even half-way there.

"I love you, sugar," Brice said, kissing Bailey so gently, with such tenderness, it was all she could do to keep from saying the words her heart begged her to share with Brice.

Chapter Seventeen

*"Our greatest glory is not in never falling,
but in rising every time we fall."*

Confucius

On his way home from The Dalles where he made inquiries with a few shops about selling his furniture on consignment, Brice pulled into the gas station in Grass Valley to fill his truck. Hart Hammond was running the pump and smiled at Brice when he got out of the pickup.

"Hey, Brice Morgan, right?" Hart said, shaking Brice's hand. "Didn't you work on my house?"

"That's right," Brice said, smiling at the man who did, in fact, look a lot like the celebrity that had the girls in the little community all dressing a little nicer and taking more care with their appearances than usual.

"If I've got my facts straight, you're the man who did the finish work in the office and the kitchen, is that correct?" Hart asked, as he pumped the gas.

"That was me," Brice said, hoping Hart liked the work he'd done.

"You're quite a craftsman for someone so young," Hart said, turning off the pump when the tank was full and screwing the gas cap back in place. "If you ever want to do some work for me on the side, let me know."

"Is that a solid offer, Mr. Hammond?" Brice asked, hoping his luck was about to take a turn for the better.

251

"As solid as the ground you're standing on," Hart said with a big grin. "And call me Hart."

"Well, Hart, it just so happens Mr. Atticus gave some of us our walking papers the day we finished your house and I've got plenty of time if you've got some work you'd like done."

"Did he now?" Hart said, not liking the way Atticus waited until the job was done to let some of the boys go. He'd heard plenty of rumors about what the man had done and none of it sat well with him. It wasn't any way to run a business and Hart certainly wouldn't hire him again, although the crew working for him did an excellent job. "How long have you been working in construction?"

"Since I was seventeen, for Mr. Atticus," Brice said, leaning against the side of his truck. "I took two years of construction management before I started working for him full-time five years ago."

"You don't say," Hart said, motioning for the clerk in the convenience store to come outside to watch the pumps.

"Yes, sir," Brice said, nodding his head. "I like woodworking and have a shop at home where I make furniture in my spare time."

"What kind of furniture?" Hart asked, interested in the types of projects Brice was capable of handling.

"All kinds," Brice said, sticking his thumbs in his back pockets and looking Hart in the eye. He liked the man. From what he could see, he was upright, honest and friendly. "Bedroom sets, chairs, dining tables, rocking chairs, bread boxes. I can do just about anything made out of wood."

"Since you, as you say, will have a lot of time on your hands, how about I commission you to make a few pieces for my new house. If I like them, we'll talk about you doing several more for me. How does that sound?"

"Like a great idea," Brice said, his smile going from his mouth up to his eyes. "I can get started right away."

"Good," Hart said, shaking Brice's hand. Brice liked that the hand he was shaking was calloused and scarred. It meant Hart, despite his wealth, was willing to work hard and get his hands dirty. "If you've got some time now, let's go into my office and I'll throw a few ideas at you."

"Thanks, Hart," Brice said, still grinning. "I appreciate this opportunity."

"I know you do or I wouldn't have offered it," Hart said, leading the way to his office at the back of the store.

If Travis wanted confirmation of Hart's involvement in the rodeo, it was hanging in full-color all over the office. Photos of him riding bulls, trophies, belt buckles, and framed newspaper and magazine articles lined the walls.

Hart noticed Brice's interest in his bull-riding days and grinned.

"Used to ride bulls a little," he said, sitting down at a big desk and pointing Brice to the chair across from it.

"I'd say more than a little. One of my friends mentioned that he thought you were quite good at it. We've ridden a few bulls, but he was much more into it than me," Brice said, studying a photo of Hart riding a bull with a big grin on his face. It really reminded him of Travis.

"And what's your friend's name? Does he live around here?" Hart asked, pulling out a notebook and pen and sliding them toward Brice.

"Travis Thompson. He and his brothers, Trey and Trent, own the Triple T Ranch just down the road. Their wives met you the other night and raved about the great service you offer along with the coffee," Brice said, grinning. "The coffee really got to them,"

"Ah, I know who you're talking about," Hart said, liking the good-looking young man sitting across from him. He seemed like an honest, happy-go-lucky sort. He'd heard about the Thompson family, as well as the Morgans, and knew both names were respected in the community. "Let's see if I remember correctly - there was a super tall blond, two gorgeous brunettes, and a serious one with golden curls and eyes unlike any shade of blue I've seen. Those Thompson men are pretty lucky if you ask me. Now, which girl is married to whom?"

Brice laughed. "Cady, she's the petite brunette, is married to Trey. Trent's wife Lindsay is the tall blond and Travis is married to the curvy brunette who happens to be my sister, Tess."

"And Travis is the bull rider?" Hart asked, leaning back in his chair.

"Not anymore. He pulled both hamstrings this summer saving a kid while he was windsurfing and is just now regaining most of his mobility. He and Tess got married a few weeks ago. Actually, all three of them have been married less than a year."

"Something in the water out there on the ranch?" Hart asked with a broad smile, liking this Morgan kid more by the minute. "What about the other girl? The one with the beautiful eyes."

"That's Bailey. She's their cousin and my girlfriend," Brice said, feeling a little defensive about someone twice his age commenting on Bailey's beautiful eyes or beautiful anything. "When you meet Trey you'll know who he is by the eye and hair color. He and Bailey share those traits in common."

"Good to know," Hart said, pointing to the pad of paper. "How about I describe what I want, you take some notes and we'll see what you come up with."

Thirty minutes later, Brice had sketches along with rough measurements of what Hart wanted and decided that maybe losing his construction job would turn out to be a blessing. He always wanted to have a woodworking business, but never had any reason to quit his day job to pursue it. Now he had every reason in the world to do his best to try to turn his part-time hobby into a successful career.

"Let me know if you need anything to get going on this project," Hart said as he walked Brice outside and shook his hand. "I look forward to seeing what you can do."

"Me, too," Brice said with a grin before jumping in his pickup. He felt like celebrating, wanting to share his excitement with Bailey, so he drove to the Triple T Ranch. Glancing at his watch, he was right on time for dinner.

Parking, he got out of his pickup and watched the Thompson men along with the ranch hands on their nightly pilgrimage to the mud room door, ready to sit down to one of Cady's delicious meals.

"How is it you always seem to show up just in time to eat?" Trey teased Brice, thumping him on the back as they walked inside. While the hands washed up before coming to the house, the Thompson brothers took turns washing at the kitchen sink followed by Brice.

"By the grin on your face and the spring in your step, I'm guessing you had some good news today, Brice," Cady said, passing everyone a platter or bowl to carry to the table.

"Yes, ma'am," Brice said, his eyes twinkling. He looked around, hoping to sit by Bailey only to see she wasn't home. "Where's Bailey?"

"Guess she's running a little late tonight," Cady said, glancing at the clock on the wall as she sat down at the table.

Trey asked the blessing on the meal before everyone dug in. Brice didn't want to share his good news until Bailey arrived, so he asked the hands a few questions which turned into a lively conversation.

Cady was just cutting a sheet cake into squares when Bailey came in the back door. She washed her hands then took a seat next to Brice, smiling at him wearily. Filling her plate, she ate quietly, letting the conversation flow around her.

When Travis asked Brice about his good news, Bailey perked up and looked his direction. He slid a hand to her thigh and squeezed before giving her a wink.

"I went to The Dalles today and found a couple of stores willing to carry some of my pieces on consignment," Brice said, wanting to drag out the excitement of the moment. "But the really great news is when I stopped to get fuel Hart asked me to make several pieces for his new house. I'm going to start on the project tomorrow. Just with his work alone, it will keep me busy well into the new year.

"Brice, that's awesome," Tess said, beaming at her brother with pride.

Congratulations and words of encouragement came from all around the table.

"I'm hoping you'll be able to pencil in some time for a construction project in the spring," Trent said, looking at Lindsay, who nodded her head at him and blushed.

"What kind of project, bro?" Brice asked, finishing the last bite of his chocolate cake.

"It seems we need to add on to our house and then see about filling a room with some baby furniture," Trent said, already grinning like a proud father.

The squeals from the females around the table nearly shattered the men's eardrums, but they all were grinning as Cady and Tess jumped up to hug Lindsay.

Trey and Travis both slapped Trent on the back and Cass was bouncing in her seat, although she didn't understand what the excitement was about.

"Nothing like working fast. That didn't take you long, man," Travis said to Trent, wiggling his eyebrows.

Lindsay's cheeks went from pink to a deep shade of red. "It wasn't… we didn't plan…" she gave up trying to explain as the men chuckled.

"It's okay, princess. You don't have to say anything. They get the idea," Trent teased, squeezing her hand under the table.

"So when does this addition need to be finished?" Brice asked, pleased for his friends at their happy news.

"The end of May," Trent said, still grinning at Lindsay's flushed cheeks.

"So that means you got her..." Trey noticed Cady tipping her head toward Cass and altered what he was going to say. "You had a really great honeymoon."

"Something like that," Trent said, not the least bit embarrassed by the direction the conversation had turned.

"To the newest Thompson," Brice said, holding up his glass of apple cider.

"To the newest Thompson," everyone echoed as they held their glasses up in a toast.

"Mama, is someone else coming to live with us?" Cass asked, looking down the table at her mother.

"No, sweetie-pie," Cady said, motioning Cass to come to her. Cass slid out of her chair, running to Cady and climbing on her lap. "What it means is that Aunt Lindsay and Uncle Trent are going to have a brand new baby come live with him just about the time school gets out in the spring. Isn't that exciting?"

"Yippee! A baby!" Cass said, with her trademark enthusiasm. "Do I get to play with him and hold him? My friend Ashley gets to hold her baby brother. Can I have a baby, too? Huh, Mama? When can I have a baby? Will you and Daddy give me one for Christmas?"

Trey's choking on his cider at the other end of the table caused another round of laughter.

"Well, um... it's not..." Cady stuttered, trying to think of an appropriate reply to her daughter's questions.

"You know, Cass," Bailey said, placing her fork on her plate and looking intently at the little girl. "No matter how much you want or wish for it, you can't request a baby like you can a present or a piece of candy. Remember when your friend Ashley's dog had puppies a few weeks ago?"

"Yep," Cass said, bouncing both feet as she leaned against her mother.

"Your dogs didn't have puppies, did they?" Bailey asked.

"Nope."

"Even though you wanted your dogs to have puppies, they didn't. And puppies, like babies, arrive in God's own time," Bailey said with a soft smile. "Your Uncle Trent and Aunt Lindsay must be pretty special to be getting a baby next spring. I'm sure they'll need you to help them take care of it when it comes."

"Absolutely, goofball," Trent said, winking at Cass.

"Yippee!" Cass said again, jumping down from Cady's lap. "Can I go tell Buddy?"

"Sure, sweetie-pie," Cady said, grinning as Cass ran out the door to find her dog. When the door shut behind her, Cady smiled at Bailey. "Thank you for that wonderful explanation, Bailey."

"You're welcome," Bailey said, picking up her fork and taking a bite of her cake. Her face was still soft and filled with a special light as she thought about the miracle of babies and how much she recently realized she wanted to have her own someday.

Glancing at Bailey, Brice thought she'd never looked so much like an angel as she did right at that moment with her face soft and her eyes glowing. If just the mention of a baby did that to her, he wondered what she'd look like if the day ever came when they could announce they were expecting.

That thought made him feel overheated, so he sat back and took a deep drink of his cold cider.

"Brice, I was just thinking," Lindsay said, leaning over to get his attention. "My brother's fiancé said she was shopping in Silverton a few weeks ago and found this fabulous home interior store that offers custom furniture orders. You should contact the store and see if they would be interested in placing orders with you."

"That's a great idea, Lindsay. Thanks," Brice said. He was beginning to believe his dream of owning his own woodworking business could in fact become a reality. "Do you know the name of the store or the owner?"

"No, but I'll find out from Maren. She said it's a woman and her two daughters. They've got a flower shop upstairs and a bistro in the front of the store," Lindsay said. "Since it's so close to Portland, it sounds like the store attracts a lot of customers. I'll get the contact info and send it to you."

"Thanks," Brice said, ready to turn the attention back to the big news of the evening. "So let's talk about this expansion to your house and the family."

><><

Bailey arrived home to find pumpkins blazing a trail to both the front and back doors of the Triple T Ranch house.

Halloween.

A ridiculous celebration filled with candy, ghouls and pranks. Growing up, the only redeeming thing she could find in the whole day of senseless shenanigans was the haul of candy she would have at the end of the night.

Once trick-or-treating was out of the question, the day lost what little charm it held for her.

Knowing her Thompson family, though, there would be a feast, frivolity and fun in store for the evening.

Going up the front walk, she grinned at the life-sized scarecrow sitting by the door and rang the bell.

Staring at the ornately carved pumpkins illuminated with battery-operated candles, Bailey swallowed the gum she was chewing when a gloved hand gripped her arm from out of nowhere. Spinning around, she found herself looking into the face of the scarecrow, which seemed menacing and demented as his white teeth glowed against the paint of his face.

Sucking in a gulp of air, Bailey was prepared to scream, when the scarecrow started laughing and pointing at her.

"Got you, sugar," Brice teased, nearly doubled over with laughter. "I got you good."

"Oh!" Bailey said, giving in to the urge to stomp her foot. "This is why I hate Halloween!" Bailey said, slapping Brice on the arm with enough force to make him wince. "I hate being scared. I hate being surprised and in case you didn't hear it clearly the first time, I hate Halloween!"

"I'm starting to get the idea you aren't fond of Halloween," Brice said, trying to look somber but it was impossible with the cheery scarecrow cheeks and lopsided grin painted on his face. "What have you got against a holiday that involves candy, treats, costumes and lots of fun?"

"Stupid people who dress up in idiotic costumes and scare the living daylights out of others who have sense enough not to participate in such... such... foolishness," Bailey said, trying the front door and finding it open.

Marching inside, she was tempted to slam the door in Brice's face, but refrained as he strolled in right behind her.

Travis, Trent and Trey all stood in the foyer, trying to subdue their chuckles.

"I suppose you three troublemakers enjoyed the show," Bailey said, disgusted with her cousins. They, along with Brice, didn't act any older than Lindsay's first grade students sometimes. It appeared today was one of those occasions.

"Actually, we did," Travis said, trying not to laugh outright. "You didn't jump nearly as high as Cady when Brice grabbed her arm. We decided due to Lindsay's delicate condition she gets a free pass, but as soon as my honeybee gets home, she's in for it."

"Not if I tell her first," Bailey said, pulling her phone from her pocket. It was promptly grabbed by Trent and held over his head. Huffing, Bailey scowled at the four men. Even at her generous height, she'd need a step stool to reach that high since Trent towered over everyone at six-five without his boots on.

"If you boys don't behave yourselves, you're going to be sent to your rooms without supper, and that includes you, Brice," Denni Thompson called to her boys from the kitchen where she helped Cady finish dinner preparations.

Right after school, Cady hosted a Halloween party for Cass' friends. The last of the youngsters left more than an hour ago and Cass went home with Ashley for dinner. Trey and Cady would pick her up later to take her trick-or-treating and Denni wanted to go along. She and Nana drove out for dinner and would head back to The Dalles after Cass finished making the rounds of candy-gathering.

"Mama, you wouldn't do that to us," Travis said, giving his mother a sideways hug as they all walked into the kitchen. "I know for a fact Cady has made all kinds of treats and it would be cruel and unusual punishment to deny us."

"Maybe you should have worried about that before you boys decided to scare the stuffin' out of the female population here on the ranch," Denni said, patting Travis on the cheek. "I'm not sure Nana's heart could take a repeat. You boys should know better."

"We didn't know you were bringing Nana and by the time we realized she was out there, Brice was already making his move," Trey said, sounding only slightly repentant of frightening his grandmother half to death.

"Don't you guys have work you should be doing? Something productive and less life-threatening?" Cady asked as she began dishing up their meal. Lindsay, who was suffering from morning sickness all day instead of just the mornings, was resting on the couch in the great room with Nana.

"I can think of something productive," Trey growled in Cady's ear, pulling her back against his chest as he kissed her neck. "But that will have to wait until later."

Cady blushed, making Trent and Travis laugh at the way Trey teased his wife.

Bailey rolled her lips together, making Brice squeeze her hand. "You know, every time you roll your lips together, it just makes me want to kiss you, so you won't be jealous of the attention the other girls are getting," he whispered low enough only she could hear. She smelled his warm, leathery scent and felt the scratchy straw around the neck of his costume brush against her head.

Searching for a safe topic, she turned to look at Brice. "Where did you get that costume?" Bailey asked, looking him over from the top of his battered straw hat and ratty bib overalls to the scruffy boots threatening to spill out straw. It really was a great costume.

"A friend of mine wore it to a costume party last year, so he let me borrow it," Brice said, looking down at his gloved hands. "It's pretty good, isn't it?"

"Very," Bailey said, tilting her head and offering Brice a jaunty grin. "If you go for that sort of thing."

"And what sort of thing do you go for, little girl," Brice said in a creepy voice that made the hair on the back of Bailey's neck prickle as he put his arms around her, trying to tickle her sides.

"Brice, stop! Could you behave?" Bailey gasped, trying to get away from him, but not really wanting to.

"I could, but what fun would that be?" Brice asked, attempting to steal a kiss. Bailey twisted away from him and ran over to hide behind Denni.

Bailey was saved from further torment when they heard a car pull up.

"It's Tess," Travis said, looking out the kitchen window. Grabbing Brice by the arm, Travis propelled him out of the kitchen into the mud room. "Quick, dude, sit on the bench."

Everyone was quiet as Tess came in the back door. When the sound of her scream, followed by a shout and slap reached into the kitchen, the group erupted into laughter.

"BB, you are in so much trouble," Tess said as she stomped into the kitchen. Turning her fury toward her husband, she shook her finger at Travis. "If I know you, Tee, you put him up to it. Are you sure you want to make me mad? Having me on the warpath could greatly alter some of your current enjoyment of life."

"Simmer down, honeybee," Travis said, taking Tess into his arms and kissing her cheek. "So far the only female we haven't terrified is Lindsay, so don't feel like you're extra special."

"And that's supposed to make me feel better?" Tess asked as she glared at her husband and then her brother. "Are you two ever going to grow up?"

"I certainly hope not," Denni said, wrapping her arms around each of their waists, sandwiched between the two men. "How dull would things be around here without these two rabble-rousers?"

Bailey agreed with Denni, but tried to hide her smile. Brice and Travis were lively and fun, especially when they were feeding off each other's energy. Throw Trent and Trey into the mix and all kinds of antics were possible.

Since it was nearly dark by the time the hands ambled to the house for dinner, Brice parked himself by the mud room door on a straw bale, looking like part of Cady's festive decorations. He waited until two of the five guys started up the steps to the door before reaching out and grabbing Danny by the leg.

The cowboy kicked, cussed and shouted, as they rest of the guys broke into fits of laughter, especially when they figured out it was Brice.

"You smart-aleck. You'll get yours," Danny said, shaking his head at Brice. In spite of his embarrassment, Danny was able to join in the good-natured laughter.

"I'm sure I will," Brice agreed, following the guys inside for dinner. After removing his hat, gloves and the straw collar around his neck, Brice sat down by Bailey, giving her an exaggerated wink.

"Are you sure you're fit company for the dinner table?" Bailey whispered, leaning toward Brice.

"As fit as I usually am, and you haven't complained before," Brice said, reaching beneath the table to squeeze her knee.

Bailey gave him a reproachful glare that caught the attention of Nana across the table.

"Brice Morgan, if you can't keep your hands to yourself any better than that, I just might need to box your ears," Nana said. Her eyes, the same shade as Bailey's, sparkled with humor.

"Yes, ma'am," Brice said, trying to act properly chastened although he winked at Bailey's grandmother. He'd been in plenty of trouble with her over the years and knew she viewed him as one more of her rowdy grandsons.

Bailey looked around the table and took in the extensive efforts Cady put into preparing a Halloween themed meal. Everything from mashed potato ghosts to bread sticks shaped like fingers complete with an almond fingernail made even the toughest of the hands grin as the food was passed around the table.

Dessert consisted of an array of sugar cookies in fall shapes left over from Cass's party as well as cupcakes bearing spooky decorations like edible eyeballs and spiders made from gum drops and licorice whips. Cady also served pumpkin ice cream, which got Bailey's full attention.

Tasting like frozen pumpkin pie, the delicious treat was creamy, laced with cinnamon, and utterly wonderful. Closing her eyes as she savored a bite, she opened them to find Brice grinning at her, wiggling one of his painted eyebrows at her.

"Miss pumpkin girl gets her fix," Brice teased, waving a sugar cookie her direction.

"That's right and I'm not sharing," Bailey said, hovering over her bowl possessively as Brice tried to dip his cookie into her ice cream. "Get your own, buster."

After dinner, Cady, Trey and Denni left to take Cass trick-or-treating. Once the dishes were done, Lindsay and Trent went home in case any kids stopped by. Tess and Travis departed soon after, and Brice reluctantly decided he'd better get home as well. His mom wanted him to sit outside and scare the little ghosts and goblins coming to their house for treats.

Walking Brice out to his pickup, the thought of kissing him good night made Bailey's mouth water and toes tingle.

Leaves falling from the surrounding trees, particularly the big oak in the front yard, crunched beneath their feet and Bailey relished the sound. The air was cold, sharp and crisp with the spicy bite found only on cool autumn evenings.

Opening the pickup door, Brice tossed in the costume accessories he removed at dinner. Leaning against the side of his truck, he pulled Bailey to his chest and wrapped his arms around her.

"Do you want a trick or a treat, sugar?" Brice asked, nuzzling her neck.

"Since you've already tricked me, I believe a treat is in order," Bailey said, pulling back from Brice. She watched a smile fill his face as he dug something out of his pocket and held it out to her.

Holding it up to the yard light, Bailey thought it looked like a tiny pumpkin made of wood.

"A pumpkin?" she asked, anxious to take it inside to get a better look.

"You guessed it," Brice said, kissing her cheek. "Happy Halloween, sugar."

"Happy Halloween, Brice. This is the nicest one I've had since Mom made me stop trick-or-treating with Sierra," Bailey said, throwing her arms around Brice's neck and giving him a hug. "Thank you."

"You're welcome," Brice said, giving her a quick kiss on the lips.

"Since your Nana is here, I'll spare you the embarrassment of explaining how you got my scarecrow paint all over your face," Brice said, waggling his eyebrows at Bailey. "Have fun the rest of the evening."

"You, too, Brice. And thank you, again for the pumpkin," Bailey said, backing toward the door.

"Anytime, my pumpkin girl," Brice said, getting into his pickup and waving before he started down the drive.

Bailey shook her head at him, carefully holding the pumpkin in her hand. She wished she could tell Brice how much she cared for him. How much she was coming to love him. That day could never happen, no matter how badly she wanted it to. Giving herself over to loving Brice was a chance she wasn't willing to take.

Chapter Eighteen

*"You only fall in love once, the rest is merely practice
to make sure your heart can take it."*

Unknown

"What's in your hand, honey?" Nana asked as Bailey sat beside her on the couch in the great room. Ester Norden, known by most everyone simply as Nana, was busy crocheting a baby blanket in a soft shade of yellow. She was eagerly anticipating the arrival of her next great-grandchild in the spring and was quite excited when Trent and Lindsay shared the news with her a few days earlier.

Holding out her hand, Bailey admired the intricately carved wooden pumpkin Brice made. Every little detail seemed real, from the bumpy texture of the pumpkin to the stubby stem and twirling vine on top. She absolutely loved it. Turning it over, she noticed in the lamp light a tiny heart with a BM carved in the bottom.

"That from Brice?" Nana asked, smiling at Bailey.

"Yes," Bailey said, absently, her thoughts miles down the road with the fun-loving cowboy, thinking of how he'd frightened her earlier.

"Such a nice young man. Kind-hearted, fun and good manners, at least most of the time," Nana observed, still miffed about the boys scaring her with their antics.

"I suppose so," Bailey said, moving the pumpkin back and forth in the light to study every interesting detail.

"He's quite a handsome boy, isn't he?"

"Yes."

"And you're quite in love with him, aren't you?" Nana asked, a knowing gleam lighting her bright blue eyes.

"Yes," Bailey said, realizing too late what she'd admitted. "Well, I... but it's not... I, um..."

Nana smiled and patted Bailey's knee.

"What's so bad about falling in love with Brice? You couldn't find a better young man, Bailey," Nana said, setting aside her crochet work to study her granddaughter. "He's talented, loyal, hard-working, caring, and it seems to me he is more than a little sweet on you."

"I know, Nana, but it's just..." Bailey said, hesitant to share her thoughts.

"It's what, honey? You can tell me," Nana said, grasping Bailey's strong hand in hers.

Bailey stared down at her Nana's hand, worn by time, yet still elegant and small. "Nana, I can't let myself love him. I just can't."

"Why on earth not?" Nana asked, squeezing Bailey's fingers lightly.

"I'm fully committed to my job. There's no room in my life for a husband or a family," Bailey said, sighing as she refused to look into her grandmother's face, where she knew she'd see disappointment. "I have to make a choice and I've worked too long and too hard to toss aside my career because I'm in love with the most wonderful man on the planet."

"I knew you were in love with him," Nana said, beaming. "That's wonderful news, Bailey."

"Aren't you listening to me, Nana. It's the most disastrous news ever. I've tried to stay away from him, but I can't. I think I'm going to have to leave because the more time we spend together and the more I see him, the more I want to forget about my career and make everything about Brice. I can't let that happen. I should never have let things get this involved but every time I try to tell him goodbye, I find…"

"Yourself kissing him? Held in his strong arms? Wishing for things you shouldn't be thinking about?" Nana asked, catching Bailey off guard.

"Nana!" Bailey said, shaking her head at her grandmother. "When Sierra was here for Travis and Tess' wedding she told me to enjoy being young and in love. So I did and I enjoyed it entirely too much. I promised myself I'd never fall in love and now that it's happened, I don't know if my heart will ever recover. Every time I think about never seeing Brice again, it hurts so badly, I think it might break into a million pieces."

"Oh, honey," Nana said, wrapping her frail arms around Bailey and pulling her head to rest on her shoulder. "Did it ever occur to you that you can have both? That you don't have to choose."

"No. You know how I am, Nana. I'm focused, intense, driven. It's how I succeed at what I do. Brice is too much of a distraction. He makes me want to focus on him instead of my work," Bailey admitted. "When I'm with him, I want to forget I even have a job. He makes my stomach all fluttery, my hands and feet tingle, and my head fuzzy. He makes me care, makes me feel, makes me want so much."

Nana chuckled, stroking Bailey's hair back from her face. "That's called love, Bailey. Honest to goodness love."

"Well, why did I have to be afflicted with it? I was minding my own business, everything was going along fine, then I turned around at Trent's wedding and knew nothing would be the same the minute I saw Brice."

"Did you ever hear the story about how I met your grandfather?" Nana asked, changing the subject, hoping Bailey would both calm down and glean a nugget of wisdom from what she was about to share.

"If I did, I don't remember," Bailey said, snuggling against her grandmother and appreciating the moment together.

"Honey, you don't realize it, but you and I are a lot alike," Nana said, with a smile that was very much like Bailey's. "In fact, if I was six inches taller and sixty years younger, we could be twins."

"Nana," Bailey said, not quite sure if her grandmother was teasing or serious. Looking into eyes the same ocean blue shade as her own, Bailey wondered if maybe it was true. Even though Nana's hair was now white, Bailey knew she and Trey got their hair and eye color from Nana. Bailey suddenly wondered what other traits she'd received from her enigmatic grandmother.

"When I was a sweet young thing back in the day, I lived in Los Angeles and worked for a talented photographer. He was gaining notoriety in all the right circles and was sometimes called upon to do portraits of celebrities. As his assistant, I often tagged along, helping set up equipment, handling the paperwork and any other details as needed. To keep a steady income, he took photos for businesses. You wouldn't believe how many corporate offices wanted portraits of their executives back then. In a pinch one day, he handed me a spare camera and asked me to take some photos for him. We both discovered I had quite a knack for it, so I became more of his apprentice than his assistant."

"I had no idea, Nana," Bailey said, surprised to hear of her grandmother's adventures before she wed. "Mom never mentioned it."

"I don't suppose she would, since none of my kids really knew about my life before they came into existence," Nana said with a grin. "Anyway, I loved being a photographer. It was something that drove me out of bed in the mornings. It spurred my passion and I was entirely focused on learning to be the best. One day my boss sent me to take photos of a bunch of stuffy bank executives. Expecting a room full of stodgy cigar-smoking geezers, I was surprised to find one very handsome young man in the group. He was a go-getter, could charm the bees right out of their honey and my gracious, but one look from him turned my knees to butter and my head to mush. I managed to get the portraits taken without incident, but he helped me carry the equipment back to my car and asked me out for dinner. One thing led to another and the next thing I knew we were married. While your grandfather excelled with his business, I did equally well with mine. So well, in fact, that my employer asked me to join him as he traveled around the country on an assignment taking photos for a national magazine. It was about that time that your grandfather was asked to transfer to a bank in Portland. So I hung up my camera and never looked back."

Bailey stared at her grandmother, knowing how the story ended but wondering if Nana ever regretted giving up her career aspirations.

"I can see what you're thinking, Bailey, and no, I never regretted my decision. Not for a minute," Nana said, patting Bailey's leg. "I loved being a photographer. I loved every single thing about it. It made me feel alive, and I could spend hours in the darkroom not even knowing the time had passed. But as much as I loved my career, it was a drop in the bucket compared to how much I loved your grandfather. When we moved to Portland, I gave up my career and started a family. I've never been sorry for that choice. In today's world, though, Bailey, I could have had both. Back then, once you married, you stayed home and raised a family. We didn't juggle all the things today's modern women do. Don't limit yourself with one or the other, honey. Think in terms of both."

"Don't you sometimes wish and wonder, Nana?" Bailey asked, curious how her grandmother could just give up everything for love. "Don't you think about what could have been?"

"No, honey, I don't. Maybe I would have been good enough to be a famous photographer some day. Maybe I wouldn't have. It doesn't matter to me because I've got a beautiful, wonderful family I love very much. Much, much more than I ever did photography."

"But, Nana…" Bailey was interrupted by her grandmother squeezing her hand again.

"No, buts, Bailey. Jobs, careers, aspirations to greatness don't mean anything unless you have someone to come home to, someone to love like Brice loves you," Nana said, picking up her crocheting and returning her attention to the baby blanket. "Don't let your ideas about your career rob you of something you won't ever find anywhere else, honey. True love doesn't happen every day, you know."

Grateful to hear the kitchen door open, Bailey made the appropriate comments over Cass' fairy costume, accepted a piece of candy the little girl was willing to share, then retreated to her room to think.

><><

"You're out and at 'em early today, Bailey," Anthony said as he walked into the paleontology center fossil lab a few days later to find Bailey already busy at work despite the early hour. "Is there some point when you are going to feel comfortable enough in your position to not put in quite so many hours?"

"No," Bailey said, not looking up from the fossil she was analyzing. "I like working."

"Something wrong?" Anthony asked, wondering what had Bailey even more close-mouthed than usual. He'd never seen anyone so fervently focused on their work as this young woman. She was driven, almost obsessed, with her efforts. He liked the young man who had ruffled Bailey's feathers on more than one occasion. Recently, he thought Bailey may have shown more than a passing interest in the guy, but the past few days, she had been withdrawn and sullen.

"I'm fine," Bailey said, then suddenly turned her gaze to her boss. "Do you know of any places for rent nearby?"

"Funny you should ask," Anthony said, smiling at Bailey. "I ran into one of the local ranchers the other day. He's got a small house he was hoping to rent out. Seems his mother-in-law lived in it for the last several years but they had to move her to a care home so the house is empty."

"Perfect," Bailey said, looking expectantly at Anthony.

"Would you like me to give him a call?" Anthony asked, wondering why Bailey suddenly was interested in finding a house nearby. She'd been commuting for almost two months from Grass Valley and didn't seem to mind the drive. He wondered if she was concerned about bad roads and winter weather.

"I can call him if you have his name and number," Bailey said, hoping this would be an answer to one of her problems.

"Here you go," Anthony said, handing her a slip of paper with the information she needed scrawled on it.

Later that morning, Bailey called the rancher, drove out to see the house and paid him a deposit along with the first month's rent. It was only a few miles from where she'd spend the winter working and made much more sense than driving a couple of hours on bad roads every day back and forth to Grass Valley.

The house was small but tidy and snug and came fully furnished, which made things even easier on Bailey.

She told the rancher she would move in that weekend, which would give her time to pack her few belongings at the Triple T, let her cousins know she was leaving, and tell Brice goodbye once and for all.

That last part was going to be the challenge Bailey was certain would break her heart, as well as Brice's.

After talking to her grandmother the other evening, Bailey was even more convinced of her need to block out everything but her work. Understanding what Nana was trying to tell her, Bailey didn't think the advice applied to her. She had to get over Brice and move forward with her life. Maybe some women could balance love and career obligations, but Bailey was convinced she wasn't one of them.

Even now, she wondered what kind of career her grandmother could have had if she'd pursued it. Nana could have been famous, had her photographs grace the covers of national magazines, but instead she married a banker, moved to Portland and then The Dalles, and raised five kids.

Yet, Nana seemed happy with her decision. Would she have been happier with a career? If she hadn't married Papa and followed him to Oregon, would Nana have spent her life wishing she hadn't passed up true love? Somehow, Bailey knew the answer to that question would be yes.

Bailey was too scared of the unknown to admit how very much Brice meant to her, how much she was coming to need him in her life. She wasn't willing, wasn't ready, to take a chance that she could have both a career and marriage. Knowing herself as well as she did, she just couldn't see a way to make it work.

"Not that he's proposed," Bailey mumbled as she finished her work and began the long drive home. Brice had never once mentioned marriage or even hinted at a long-term commitment, other than his teasing comment when they woke up together in Burns about making it a permanent arrangement.

Maybe he acted this way with every girlfriend he had until one or both of them decided to move on.

Arriving at the Triple T just in time for dinner, Bailey was both excited and sad to see Brice at the table, saving the chair next to him for her.

After washing at the kitchen sink, she sat beside him and tried not to think about what she needed to do.

Brice touched her leg, brushed her hand, bumped her arm throughout the meal, as he always did, and each contact made Bailey more withdrawn, more depressed, more resolved that she had to make a clean break and soon.

"What's wrong, sugar," Brice finally leaned over and asked in a whisper. His breath was warm on her neck and she could almost feel the touch of his lips by her ear.

"Nothing," Bailey said, shoving down her desire to grab his hand in hers and hold on to it for a lifetime.

"Nothing sure makes you look like you've been sucking lemons," Brice teased, jostling her shoulder with his, hoping to bring out a smile. "What's got you down in the mouth today?"

"I already told you I'm fine," Bailey said quietly, her tone brusque.

Brice raised an eyebrow at her, but left her alone through the rest of the meal.

Holding back until dessert was finished and the hands shuffled out the door for the evening, Bailey looked around at her cousins, her family, and sighed. Waiting wouldn't make what she had to say any easier, so she cleared her throat.

"There is a piece of pertinent information I need to impart to all of you," Bailey said, reverting to her formal mode of speech.

"What's that, Bailey?" Tess asked from her seat next to Travis. At the look in Bailey's eye, Tess felt the need to reach out and squeeze Bailey's hand in reassurance.

"As of today, I have secured adequate lodging arrangements closer to my place of employment and will take up residence there this weekend," Bailey said, looking around the table at all the startled faces, avoiding Brice's.

"What?" Brice said, sitting up straight in his chair so fast, he knocked over what was left of his glass of apple cider. Cady jumped up and grabbed a towel to mop at the liquid while Trent, who was sitting next to Brice's other side, put a hand on his shoulder. Brice shrugged it off and turned to glare at Bailey. "Are you telling us you're leaving? Moving to where?"

"I've located a furnished home to rent from a rancher just a few miles from the center. It will save me a lot of driving on bad roads this winter," Bailey said, trying to take the practical approach. If nothing else, her cousins wouldn't argue with common sense reasons for doing things. "The house is clean and the rent is reasonable."

"But Bailey, we'll miss having you here," Tess said. She and Bailey had struck up a friendship during the weeks leading up to the wedding and she'd miss their chats about everything from vintage home décor to fashion.

"Really?" Bailey asked, not sure she had been anything to her family but a bother since her arrival.

"Of course we'll miss you," Cady said, giving Bailey a hug around her shoulders. "It's been a pleasure to have you here with us."

"You'll come home on the weekends, won't you?" Travis asked, trying not to let the look of fear and loss on Brice's face get to him.

"Not every weekend, but once in a while, if the roads are good," Bailey said, toying with her silverware, no longer able to make eye contact with anyone at the table, knowing they were all wondering why she was distancing herself from them, especially Brice.

"Have we done something to make you not feel welcome, Bailey? If so, I'm truly sorry. We enjoy having you here and really don't want you to go," Trey said, giving Bailey a long look that made her squirm in her chair. She didn't seem to be fooling her cousins with her excuses for leaving.

"Not at all, Trey. Everyone has been wonderful," Bailey said, wanting to escape to her room away from their questions and hurt looks. "At this point in time, I believe it is the best decision for me to make."

"Best for whom?" Brice asked getting up from his chair and pulling Bailey to her feet. Propelling her toward the mud room before she could utter a protest, Brice turned to the group as he opened the kitchen door. "Excuse us a moment." He closed the door behind him and grabbed Bailey's coat from a peg on the wall.

"Put on your coat," Brice said, holding it for her. Bailey crossed her arms over her chest and glared at him. Brice dropped her coat back on the peg, put on his own and snatched a fleece blanket from a shelf above the coats, wrapping it around Bailey as he pushed her out the door into the cold evening.

"What do you think you're doing?" Bailey asked, turning to go back into the warmth of the house.

"Getting to the bottom of things," Brice said, keeping his hand on Bailey's back, refusing to allow her to return to the safety of the house and her family. "You and I apparently need to have a talk so start talking or walking, sugar."

Yanking the blanket more firmly around her shoulders, Bailey set off at a brisk pace down the hill toward the pond. Realizing where they were at, Bailey immediately decided coming to the spot where she first kissed Brice was a bad choice for trying to break up with him. Memories of his arms around her, his lips melding with hers, flooded over her and she wanted nothing more than to lean into him and relish his kisses.

She felt his hands on her shoulders as she stood staring at the moonlight reflected on the surface of the pond. It was lovely. Perfect and lovely and romantic. Too bad it was wasted on her tonight.

"Sugar? What's going on?" Brice asked, turning her around to face him. He looked into her face and saw her fear, the uncertainties, in her eyes.

Rather than answer Brice, Bailey buried her head against his chest and tried to gain control of her emotions. Tears were burning the backs of her eyes and her throat felt like it was squeezing shut.

"What is it, baby?" Brice asked, gently rubbing her back. "You can tell me."

Drawing on every ounce of strength she possessed, Bailey pushed away from Brice and took a step back.

"I'm sorry, Brice. I didn't mean for things to get so complicated, but it's over," Bailey said, biting the inside of her cheek to keep from crying. "I enjoyed our time together and getting to know you, but this has to be goodbye."

Stunned, Brice didn't know what to say. How could Bailey be telling him goodbye, mumbling some rubbish about things being complicated? The only thing that was complicated was the idiotic way she kept pushing aside her feelings for him.

"I realize this may come as a shock to you, and I'm sorry, but I think it's best for us both to end things now before we…" Bailey's voice caught and she couldn't go on.

"Before we what? Fall in love? Lose our hearts? Decide we've finally met the one person who makes us complete? Is that what you were going to say, Bailey?" Brice asked, his anger mounting as he stood looking at her. "Because if you were going to say something about before we get hurt, it's too late for that. You've been holding my heart in your hands since the day I met you. Why don't you throw it on the ground and stomp all over it? Oh, wait. You just did."

"Brice, I didn't mean for you to fall in love with me. I didn't mean to…" Bailey stopped herself before she said something that would make this even harder.

"You didn't mean to what?" Brice asked, taking her arms in his hands and pulling her close. His eyes were dark and his jaw was clenched as he looked at her face, bathed in the moonlight. Any other night, he wouldn't have been able to resist the way she looked with the moonbeams softening her porcelain skin to perfection. Tonight, he was angry and hurt and somehow felt betrayed.

"I didn't mean to let you think we had a future together," Bailey said, looking down, unable to meet Brice's gaze.

"A future?" Brice laughed derisively. "Now that's funny. How could any man have a future with a woman who loves digging up bugs dead thousands of years more than she loves this?"

Brice took Bailey's lips in a savage kiss, stealing the breath from her lungs. Unable to stop herself, Bailey felt the blanket drop from her shoulders as she ran her hands up Brice's arms and twined them at the back of his neck, toying with the short hair above the collar of his coat.

Bailey's knees trembled, her stomach quivered and heat exploded through her as Brice deepened the kiss, holding her so close, his belt buckle dug into her stomach and the buttons on his shirt pressed against her soft skin through the fabric of her blouse. Suddenly, he let her go and she took a stumbling step back.

"When you're sitting all alone surrounded by your fossils, remember that, sugar," Brice said, swiping a hand over his face and releasing a sigh. He gave her one long, final look. "My offer still stands, Bailey. When you're ready to fall, I'll be waiting to catch you."

Bailey watched Brice's form disappear into the darkness as he walked back to the house. She heard the sound of an engine and knew he'd gone.

Letting the tears fall, she sobbed into her hands, ignoring the cold, ignoring the fact that her legs had given way and she sat on the frigid, damp grass.

When she felt the blanket drape back around her shoulders, she looked up to see Trey hunkered down beside her.

"Bailey, let's get you back to the house. It's freezing out here," Trey said, standing and offering her his hand. Bailey took it, along with the handkerchief he held out to her. She mopped at her tears and didn't pull away when Trey put a strong arm around her shoulders and let her lean against his side as they walked up the hill.

Grateful for her cousin, who now seemed more like a caring older brother, Bailey tried to stem the flow of tears.

"I'm sorry," Bailey whispered as they neared the back door.

"No need to apologize, Bailey," Trey said, holding the door open for her. "You have to do what you think is best, and we're here to support you no matter what you decide."

"Thanks, Trey. I appreciate it," Bailey said, squeezing his arm before she disappeared down the hall toward her bedroom.

It was one very long night as Bailey cried out her tears and realized a heart really could be completely broken in two.

Chapter Nineteen

"Love is like quicksand:
The deeper you fall in it the harder it is to get out."

Unknown

"What do you think, old man?" Brice asked his horse, Xavier, as they rode out to survey the damage done from a big storm the night before. Wind and torrential rain had taken down trees, a few power lines and blown around anything that wasn't securely fastened.

The horse snorted and shook his head.

"That's what I think, too," Brice said, realizing his horse was the one living thing he felt like talking to the last few weeks since Bailey packed up and left.

Burying himself in his furniture projects for Hart Hammond, Brice was either working in his shop, riding Xavier or trying to avoid all human contact. After the first few days of his terse replies, his parents had left him alone. Ben, Tess and Travis took a while longer to convince to let him lick his wounds in peace, but they'd finally given up a week ago.

With Thanksgiving days away, Brice was finding it difficult to find much to be thankful for this year.

He had been so sure he could win Bailey's heart, change her mind, and make her fall in love with him.

How wrong he had been.

You couldn't win what didn't exist and right now he was convinced Bailey was a heartless shell, albeit a lovely one, who cared only about furthering her career.

"Guess I should have listened to Trav in the first place, huh, Xavier?" Brice said, rubbing the horse's neck.

The horse bobbed his head again, nickering at the sight of another horse and rider. Brice waved to one of the Running M ranch hands. Stopping a few feet away, they discussed what they'd both found, where some fence needed repairs, and continued on their way.

Brice ignored his phone when it rang, tugging the collar of his coat up higher, trying to block out the chilly air. He should have remembered to put on a scarf or at least wrap a wild rag around his neck before he saddled up Xavier and headed out an hour ago. These days he was lucky to remember to put on his jeans and socks before pulling on his boots, since his thoughts seemed to be lost somewhere else.

So far, the storm damage to the Running M was minimal and Brice was glad the repair work needed could be completed quickly. Since he was no longer working construction, he'd been spending more time helping his dad with the ranch when he needed a break from his woodworking.

When his phone rang again, Brice dug it out of his pocket and looked at the number belonging to one of the neighbors.

"Hey, Chris, what's up?" Brice asked, trying to force a somewhat civil tone into his voice.

"Hey, man, we've got some trees down over here from the storm I thought you might want for your woodworking business," Chris said.

"Sure," Brice said, mustering a little enthusiasm. "What've you got?"

"There's a huge walnut tree and two maples that bit the dust. My wife's been after me for two years to take those trees out because they were old and she was afraid they'd kill someone if they ever fell over. Lucky me, the storm took care of all that work of cutting them down."

"Sometimes nature can be really helpful," Brice said with a trace of humor in his voice. He knew the wood from those trees would be worth a pretty penny. "What can I pay you for the wood?"

"Shoot, Brice, I don't want anything for them. You'll be doing me a favor if you come haul them off. Maybe you could make something for the missus and we'll call it even," Chris said.

"That's a deal. I'm tied up today cleaning up over here and tomorrow I've got to run into Portland, but I could come the following day," Brice said, thinking about the best way to move the trees without cutting them into pieces. He wanted the trunks in one solid piece if possible. "I'll borrow the Triple T's flat bed and haul the trees that way."

"I'll be gone that morning, but you could come and start taking off the limbs and by the time I'm back in the afternoon, we can use my loader tractor to lift them onto the trailer.

"Sounds great," Brice said, excited about the gift of wood. "Thanks a lot, Chris, I really appreciate this."

"Anytime, man. I appreciate you taking them off my hands."

Brice disconnected the call, feeling better than he had for a while. Riding the rest of his section of fence, Brice was thoroughly chilled by the time he got back to the barn and brushed down Xavier. He took time to wipe down the saddle and carefully store it in the tack room. Although it had seen better days, Brice liked to ride with his grandfather's old saddle. The leather was smooth and worn and it always made him think of his grandpa.

Going into the house, he made himself a cup of hot chocolate and a sandwich then hurried out to his workshop to finish up some samples he was making to take to Portland with him the next day.

Calling several exclusive furniture stores and home décor galleries, Brice had six appointments the following day to show off his wares and hopefully contract to sell some pieces.

He knew the work for Hart would take him a while to finish, but he wanted to make sure he had business lined up for future projects.

Travis, with his computer design skills, created business cards and a simple brochure for Brice. Deciding to call his business BM Wood Crafts, Travis created a logo using an image of a piece of wood, rich with grain, highlighted by a BM branded on it. Under the brand were the words wood crafts followed by Brice's name.

Thankful for Travis' help, Brice now had a website with photos of some of his creations, a list of the types of wood he used and information about the types of orders he accepted. He'd already received a few phone inquiries about some custom pieces in the last week.

Although his business seemed like it was on the verge of taking off, Brice had a hard time balancing his excitement about it with the residual pain from Bailey's rejection.

Trying to give her time and space to come to her senses and realize she loved him every bit as much as he loved her, Brice hadn't called or texted her once. Talking to Sierra every few days, she kept him updated on what was happening with Bailey.

According to her, Bailey was miserable, depressed and Sierra claimed she'd never heard her sister sound so unhappy before. Sierra was concerned, as was Brice, but Bailey was an adult and had to deal with the consequences of her choices.

The last time he spoke with Sierra, she encouraged him to reach out to Bailey, convinced she would talk to him if he called.

Fairly certain she wouldn't, Brice just wasn't ready to put himself through more pain and rejection where Bailey was concerned. He had to talk himself out of driving to Dayville to see her more than once and almost daily he started to send her a text message before he realized what he was doing.

He hoped at some point either his heart would start to mend or Bailey would open the door she had so firmly closed behind him. If something didn't change soon, though, Brice thought he might either break down the door or bust out a window.

><><

"Are you sure you should go over there by yourself?" Travis asked for the second time as Brice climbed into the Triple T semi and started it. He was borrowing their truck with the long flat-bed trailer to haul his trees from the neighbor's ranch. The Running M didn't have a flat-bed trailer, although all three of the Morgan men were licensed to drive a semi.

"It's fine, Trav," Brice said, stepping out of the truck and looking to make sure the tie down straps he'd brought along were securely stored until he needing them on the trees. "I can't believe everyone decided to be gone the same day."

"Yeah, what are the odds of that?" Travis asked with a laugh. Trent went with Lindsay to a doctor's appointment in The Dalles, Tess was at work and Cady accompanied Trey to Madras to pick up a load of supplies at the feed store. Travis was on his way to Condon to check out a couple of horses for sale. Mike Morgan was at a farm sale in Prineville, Michele was at her job in Moro at the bank and all the hands from both ranches were still busy cleaning up from the storm or involved with their regular duties.

"By the time I get the trees ready to load, Chris said he'd be home then Dad should be back at the ranch when I get the trees over there," Brice said, climbing back in the truck. "Piece of cake."

"Yeah, well just be careful with that chainsaw," Travis cautioned, uncomfortable with the idea of Brice not having any help.

"Yes, mother hen," Brice laughed as he shut the door and started the truck down the Triple T's long driveway.

Pulling up at the neighbor's place, Brice drove out in an empty field to turn around then got to work on the walnut tree.

Using the chainsaw to strip off all the branches, he realized his safety goggles would have been helpful to remember as chips flew around his head. Donning his sunglasses, he was grateful the day was only cool and not rainy. Working up a sweat, Brice stripped off his coat. Warm in his shirtsleeves as he finished the walnut tree, he was grateful he at least remembered to put on his chaps to keep his legs from being hit by all the flying wood debris.

Walking a few hundred yards closer to the house, the maples had fallen together and were harder to access. It was almost noon when he stopped to get a drink of water from the jug he brought with him. Taking out his phone, he checked his messages, responded to his texts and started to send Bailey a message before he caught himself.

Old habits died so hard.

Running a hand over his face, he pocketed his phone, put his sunglasses back on and tugged his gloves into place. Picking up the chainsaw, he returned to his work.

Cutting into one of the last limbs on the second maple tree, Brice was hoping Chris would get back soon so they could load the trees.

Flashes of orange visible through the tree limbs gave Brice a glimpse of pumpkins piled next to the house's back step. Seeing the orange orbs immediately sent his thoughts chasing after visions of Bailey.

He thought of the day he took her to the local pumpkin patch and they snapped photos sitting together on one monstrous pumpkin. There was the day they drove to Portland with Travis and Tess to go to the corn maze, the afternoon they'd all gone apple picking, and the night he'd talked her into going horseback riding beneath a harvest moon.

Even though it had been three weeks since he'd seen her, Brice could feel the silky smoothness of her skin, taste the sweetness of her kisses, hear the sultry sound of her voice when she whispered in his ear. He'd thrown out his mother's green tea because the scent of it pained him beyond reason, bringing to mind all too clearly the unique fragrance that was Bailey.

Lost in his thoughts of Bailey, Brice wasn't prepared when the chainsaw was pinched in the cut he was making. In a lightning-fast reverse reaction, the guide bar kicked back, slicing into his leg.

Brice killed the motor and looked to see blood flowing down just above his knee from a gaping cut through his chaps and jeans. Lowering himself to the tree trunk, Brice dug out his phone and started to call for help, remembering no one was around. Leaving messages with his dad and Travis, who would most likely be home soon, he pulled off his belt and wrapped it around his leg, while trying to call his mom. Realizing too late he pushed the wrong number, Brice managed to say "help me, please," before he blacked out.

><><

In her twenty-seven years, Bailey had never known the true definition of several words until she told Brice goodbye.

During the past few weeks, she had become intimately acquainted with what misery, desolation and heartsick really meant.

With every breath she took, she missed Brice. Instead of the pain lessening as the weeks went on, it grew more intense, consuming her thoughts. She felt like she was sinking in quicksand. The more she struggled to get over Brice and move on, the further she sank into her feelings for him. To make matters even worse, she couldn't stop herself from listening to the song *Wanted* several times each evening, resulting in many tears and self-loathing.

If she thought she was distracted when she was dating Brice, it was nothing compared to what she was now. She could barely function, forgot to eat, and had made more errors in her work than she'd made in her entire career.

"Bailey, I need you to quit for the day," Anthony said, walking behind her and shaking his head. Since Halloween, Bailey had been like a different person. He didn't know what was going on with her, but something needed to change. She was miserable at best and she was too good of an employee to lose.

He was afraid she'd move on somewhere else if she couldn't resolve what was bothering her here. With plans in the spring to offer Bailey a permanent position, Anthony was almost certain she'd take it.

"What? Why?" Bailey asked, turning around to look at her boss, confused by his words.

"It's Friday. Pack a bag, go back to Grass Valley for the weekend and take care of whatever it is that has made you so upset these last few weeks. You can't go on like this," Anthony said, giving Bailey a pointed look.

"I'm sorry," Bailey said, forcing herself to maintain eye contact with Anthony. "I realize I've been a little distracted lately. I'll do better, I promise."

"If your definition of a little distracted is categorizing that last *Patriofelis* bone as a magnolia, then I agree, you've been a little distracted," Anthony teased.

Blushing, Bailey was still mad about that embarrassing error. The large cat-like predator was anything but plant-like. It was humiliating to make stupid mistakes even a green intern would be smart enough to catch.

"My apologies, Anthony. I realize my work has been subpar and I'll do my best going forward to perform at a much higher level," Bailey said, her throat tight with the range of emotions she was experiencing.

"Bailey, you've worked circles around me, and everyone else, since you arrived. Something is obviously bothering you. Go home. Get it taken care of. Since next week is Thanksgiving, take the week off and plan to come back the following Monday. That gives you ten days to get whatever is bugging you fixed. I'd much rather you rectify that situation than worry about a simple mistake or two here," Anthony said, looking at his watch. He took Bailey by the shoulders and turned her toward the door. "Go home. Now. I insist. I'll see you the Monday after Thanksgiving."

"But, Anthony, I can't just…" Bailey spluttered as Anthony pointed toward the employee access door where they kept their personal belongings.

"Yes, you can and you will. Have a great Thanksgiving, Bailey, and do whatever you need to do to mend things with that young man of yours," Anthony said with a raised eyebrow and knowing smile.

"How could you possibly…" Bailey asked, then cut herself off. "Thank you. Happy Thanksgiving."

Making herself eat some lunch, Bailey was packing a bag to take to Grass Valley when her cell phone rang. Seeing Brice's face pop up on the screen, she was surprised he would call. He hadn't sent one text or email, or left her any messages since she told him goodbye. Why today, of all days, would he call?

Unable to stop herself, she answered on the third ring.

"Help me, please," Brice said before the line went dead.

Bailey listened and heard only silence. Brice sounded odd, in pain, maybe. Frightened, she tried calling him back only to have his phone ring then go to voice mail. She left him a message to call her back, then tried calling Tess and Travis, getting only their voice mail as well.

Grabbing a last few things and stuffing them in a suitcase, Bailey set the thermostat in the house, called and left a message with her landlord that she was going to be gone for ten days in case there were any problems at the house, then hustled out the door.

Hurrying to her Jeep, she was grateful the weather was clear today, even if the temperature was cool.

Speeding as fast as she dared, Bailey felt like she'd swallowed a rock as her stomach tightened at the thought of something happening to Brice. He'd never called and left her a message like that and the only time she'd heard such pain in his voice was the night she watched him walk away from her.

An hour away from Grass Valley, Bailey decided to try Brice's phone again. When an unfamiliar woman's voice came on the line at the fourth ring, Bailey nearly dropped her phone.

"Brice Morgan's phone, may I help you?" the woman said.

"I'd like to speak to Brice, please," Bailey said crisply, annoyed beyond belief that Brice let some woman answer his phone. What was he doing? It didn't seem like it took him long to get over his broken heart and move on.

"I'm sorry, Brice is unable to speak. My name is Sandy, I'm a nurse at the hospital here in The Dalles."

"The hospital! Is Tess or Travis there?" Bailey asked, in shock.

"No. Brice was just brought in and we've been unable to contact any of his family. I personally know Tess and she's out doing home visits today. We've not been able to get through on her phone."

"Oh," Bailey said, feeling panic settle over her. "What happened? Will he be okay?"

"I'm not at liberty to discuss that, miss, but if your name is Bailey, Brice was asking for you when he came to a few minutes ago."

"That's me. I'll be there as quick as I can. I'm a couple of hours away right now," Bailey said, relaying information to the nurse about how to reach Michele Morgan. Bailey called her Aunt Denni and asked her to go to the hospital as soon as she could leave the quilt shop where she worked.

Hitting the accelerator, Bailey no longer cared if she got a ticket as she hurried to the hospital. She tried calling Tess and just happened to catch her between appointments. Bailey agreed to swing by and pick her up on her way through Grass Valley. Tess was waiting at the diner owned by Cady's Aunt Viv. Bailey barely stopped when Tess jumped in and they were back on the road.

"Mom is on her way, dad's still not answering and neither is Trav," Tess said, wiping tears from her cheeks. It wasn't that many months ago the family had rushed to the hospital when Travis was injured in a freak windsurfing accident.

"Where is everyone today? I tried calling the ranch house and no one answered," Bailey said, wondering how no one could be home at the Triple T.

"Cady and Trey went to Madras and I just remembered Lindsay said something about Trent going with her to a doctor's appointment. Trav went to look at a couple horses in Condon, and dad's at a farm sale in Prineville," Tess said, surprised at the how fast Bailey was driving. "I called the hospital and they said one of the neighbors hauled Brice in with a bad leg wound."

"What was he doing?" Bailey asked, afraid of what they'd find at the hospital when Tess said he was cutting up trees.

"I'm guessing the chainsaw went through his leg," Tess said, anxious as they sped toward The Dalles.

"Chainsaw?" Bailey managed to say around the pounding in her heart.

"That big storm we had a few days ago felled a lot of trees. The neighbor asked Brice if he wanted some so he was over there getting them ready for transport. I knew he should have listened to Travis and waited until someone was around to help him," Tess said, twisting a strand of loose hair around her finger nervously.

"But a chainsaw through his leg could be... could mean..." Bailey said, faltering when tears closed off her throat.

She felt Tess' hand squeeze hers. "Let's think positive. Brice will be fine. He's too ornery to be anything else," Tess said, as much to convince herself as Bailey.

"I certainly hope that is the case," Bailey said, taking the exit and following Tess' directions to the hospital.

"How did you know he was hurt?" Tess asked as Bailey pulled into the parking lot.

"He called and asked for help then the line went dead. I was heading home for the weekend anyway, so I hurried out the door and kept trying to call him back. When I finally got through a nurse named Sandy answered the phone."

Tess managed a smile at her friend's name.

"If he's with Sandy, she'll take good care of him," Tess said, grabbing Bailey's hand as they hurried into the hospital.

They arrived to find Michele pacing in the waiting room with Denni while their neighbor, Chris, sat nearby wringing his ball cap in his hands.

"Mom, how is he?" Tess asked as she hugged her mother.

"Oh, Tess, he's lost so much blood," Michele said, reaching out to hug Bailey as well. "When Chris found him, he rushed him to the hospital, but they think he may have been out there for a while before Chris got to him. They said if he hadn't been wearing his chaps, it might have severed his leg before he turned it off."

Tess stepped over to their neighbor and offered him a hug when he stood. "Thank you for bringing him in."

"I feel like this is my fault," Chris said, running his hand through his hair. "I knew he was coming over this morning and should have stayed there. My wife told me he shouldn't be out there cutting up those trees alone, but Brice said he wasn't worried about it. I got home about one and saw the truck there but not Brice so I started looking for him. He was between the two maple trees that fell down with blood all around him. I figured I could bring him in faster than the ambulance could get out there and back, but it sure scared me to find him like that."

"I'm sure it did," Tess said, squeezing their neighbor's hand. "We appreciate everything you did for him."

"I finally gathered enough sense to call your mom when I brought him in. Brice has been asking for Bailey since he came to a bit ago," Chris said, turning to look at the girl he met a few times at various functions.

While they waited for someone to give them any news of Brice's condition, Travis showed up followed by Ben. Bailey felt like an outsider as she sat with the family waiting for news. When Mike Morgan finally arrived, Michele fell against him and burst into tears all over again.

Sitting next to her aunt, Denni rubbed Bailey's back soothingly while they waited. "I'm glad you're here, honey. Brice will be so happy to wake up and see you."

"Not after what I've done," Bailey said, trying to hold back her tears. From the moment she heard Brice ask for help, Bailey realized with utter clarity what she wanted. It wasn't a career filled with accolades, it wasn't her name on brilliant dissertations, or a record of her great finds in the world of paleontology. It was Brice. She wanted more than anything to have a future with Brice. "I've been so stupid."

"Yes, you have, but you'll have plenty of time to fix that," Denni said, smiling at Bailey when she stared at her. "If Brice will take you back, and I'm certain that he will, I'd say the smartest thing you could do would be to hang on to him for a lifetime."

"What if he isn't going to be okay, Aunt Denni? What if I never get the chance to tell him how I really feel?" Bailey asked, swiping at the tears that trickled down her cheeks.

"You'll have your chance, honey," Denni said, rubbing Bailey's shoulder comfortingly. "Just make sure you take it when it comes. Our Brice is too stubborn to be down for long. You mark my words, he'll be fine."

Waiting for what seemed like hours, finally a doctor came to speak with them. Everyone got to their feet as he looked around the room. Hearing the news, Trey, Cady, Trent and Lindsay had joined the group, leaving Cass with Aunt Viv.

"We've had Brice in surgery and he should be just fine. He might not walk quite the same when he's healed, but he'll have full use of both legs for a good while to come as long as he doesn't have any more encounters with a chainsaw," the doctor said, smiling at the group and their collective sigh of relief. "One of our biggest concerns was the amount of blood loss. He tried to use his belt as a tourniquet but must have passed out before he got it tightened enough to do any good."

"What happened?" Mike asked, taking a step closer to the doctor.

"From what we can gather, the chainsaw kicked back and sliced into his leg just above his knee. He managed to pull it away before it reached the bone. The trouble with chainsaw accidents is that it not only cuts the skin but chews up tissue. So instead of a nice clean cut we can stitch, the wound is ragged, dirty and hard to mend. We flushed the wound, removed debris and bits of tissue and stretched the muscle to reattach it. These types of wounds don't hold stitches well, but Brice can boast one hundred and thirteen stitches in that leg of his since we managed to get three layers in to hold the tissue together," the doctor said, watching the impressed look on the faces of the men. "Due to the type of injury, they also tend to form a lot of scar tissue which can shorten the muscle and decrease function. I know Brice has an excellent physical therapist to help him stretch that muscle once it is healed. I would guess, with proper care, he'll probably regain ninety-nine percent mobility on his leg."

"When can we take him home and what do we need to do for him?" Tess asked, knowing she would be the one primarily giving care to her brother, although Trent could also be called on since he doctored animals and humans on both of the ranches.

"We'll keep him overnight, just to make sure there aren't any complications, and release him in the morning. He'll need to be restful for several days, walk on crutches and in general take it easy. I'll want to see him in two weeks and he needs to keep the bandage in place, not disturbing the stitches. Brice can take showers if you wrap that area well with plastic to keep the water out and I'd say a few days in bed with his leg up wouldn't hurt him at all. After that, he should start getting up and walking with his crutches a little each day."

"How long will his recovery time take?" Travis asked, remembering the painful weeks he spent in bed with his hamstring injury.

"Probably ten weeks total," the doctor said, glancing at his watch. "Brice should be in recovery by now. Once he's moved into a room, a few of you can go in to see him at a time."

"Thank you, doctor," Mike said, shaking the man's hand as he turned to walk away.

Turning to look at the group, the Thompson and Morgan family blended together by friendship and love, Mike asked them all to bow their heads as he gave a prayer of thanks for Brice's safekeeping. Knowing that his son could have lost his leg made Mike realize the depths of his gratitude for Brice's well-being.

"We might as well head home," Trey said, hugging Michele and shaking Mike's hand. "Too many visitors will just wear him out tonight."

"Probably," Michele agreed, hugging Trent and Lindsay as the two elder Thompson boys and their wives left with a wave and disappeared down the hall along with their neighbor Chris. Denni announced she would stay until Mike and Michele were ready to leave. It was agreed that Ben, Tess and Travis would visit Brice first, since Ben had to get back to Portland for work.

An hour later a nurse came and led the first group to Brice's room. Michele and Mike went next and Bailey continued to sit with Denni, wondering if she'd be allowed to see Brice.

When Michele came back, teary-eyed but smiling, she patted Bailey's arm. "He's been asking for you, Bailey. Go on in."

Bailey stood and straightened her spine before moving down the hall.

Entering Brice's room, Bailey walked quietly to the bed and stood staring down at Brice. His hair was a tousled mess, his face was stubbly like he'd forgotten to shave that morning, and he looked pale. Reaching out, she gently smoothed the wave of hair from his forehead and ran her hand down his firm jaw.

"Hi, Bailey," Brice whispered, not opening his eyes.

"How'd you know it was me?" Bailey asked, placing her palm on his cheek, absorbing the fact that Brice was alive and would be fine.

"I could smell you for one thing," Brice said, opening one eye, then the other. He looked a little dazed from the pain medication. "And no one else's hands make me feel all tingly inside like yours."

"Oh," Bailey said, smiling through the tears that were rolling down her cheeks.

"Don't cry, sugar," Brice said, weakly. "Doc says I'll be right as rain in a few months, although this is sure gonna slow down my new business."

"Yes, it will," Bailey agreed, running her hand down Brice's arm and grasping his hand in hers. "I know I can't stay long, Brice, but I want you to know, I'm…"

"Not now, sugar. Don't say anything now. Let's talk later when I'm not half-drugged," Brice said, with a lopsided grin.

"Okay. We'll talk later," Bailey agreed. When a nurse didn't immediately come chase her out, Bailey pulled a chair up next to the bed, held Brice's hand and talked to him about what had gone on at work, things she'd found or done. She even told him about mixing up the prehistoric cat with a magnolia, which made him grin.

"I can't keep my eyes open, sugar. I'm gonna sleep awhile," Brice said, finally allowing himself to close his eyes and rest.

"You go to sleep, Brice. We'll be here in the morning to take you home," Bailey said, standing up to press a kiss to Brice's forehead.

"Promise?" Brice whispered, only partially awake.

"I promise," Bailey said, watching as Brice's breathing grew deep and he appeared to be sleeping. She let go of his hand and rubbed fingers softly along his face. Kissing his lips, she whispered "I love you" before leaving the room.

Denni, Mike and Michele were waiting for her when she came back.

"He's sleeping," she said, wondering what Mike and Michele must think of her for dumping Brice the way she had, then showing up today.

"Good," Michele said, looping her arm through Bailey's as they all walked toward the door. "I'm so glad you're here, Bailey. I don't know what happened with Brice and you, I don't need to know, but he's missed you terribly. If you're here for the weekend, we'd like you to come to the house and spend some time with him."

Bailey nodded her head. "I'd like that very much."

"Good," Michele said, giving her a hug and wave as she and Mike left.

Denni and Bailey walked through the parking lot together. "Why don't you come home with me tonight, honey. It will save you the drive back to the ranch and you can come bright and early in the morning to see Brice."

"Thanks, Aunt Denni. That would be great," Bailey said, smiling at her aunt.

"I'm glad you're back, Bailey. We missed seeing you around the last several weeks," Denni said, stopping next to her car.

"I know and I'm sorry. I'm sorry for running away, for closing everyone out, for letting Brice think..." Bailey couldn't continue talking as tears filled her eyes.

"Oh, honey, it's okay," Denni said, giving her headstrong, independent niece a hug. It was about time the girl finally realized she was head over heels in love with Brice. Everyone else knew it weeks and weeks ago. "Let's go home and you can tell me all about it."

Bailey nodded and followed Denni to her house.

After a good visit, they went to bed although Bailey didn't get much sleep. She arose early the next morning, wondering what time they let visitors in to see patients at the hospital.

Knowing Bailey would wear a groove in the floor if she kept pacing, Denni shooed her out the door, telling her she might be able to get in to see Brice before the family came to take him home.

Walking to his door, Bailey was surprised when no one stopped her from going in Brice's room. He was in bed, still looking pale and weak, but not as bad as he had the night before. She took his hand in hers and held it a while before his eyelids fluttered open.

"Hey, sugar. I was dreaming you were here and now you are," Brice said, still a little buzzed on medication. "It's like magic."

"Most definitely magic," Bailey said, unable to hide her grin. "Did you sleep well?"

"Heck, no. They were in here poking and prodding me every few hours. How do they expect a body to rest that way?"

"I don't know?" Bailey said, trying to swallow back a laugh. "Maybe that's why they plan to send you home this morning."

"Yep. That's what the doctor said when he stopped by a while ago. He went to sign my release papers and as soon as my taxi service arrives, I'm out of here," Brice said, some of the spark returning to his eyes.

"How about I sit with you until then?" Bailey said, sitting down in the chair next to the bed.

"I'd like that," Brice said, grinning at her. "I'd like it even more if you'd kiss me again and tell me you love me like you did last night."

"What?" Bailey asked, surprised. How could he possibly know what she'd said? He was asleep, or so she thought.

"You heard me and I heard you last night. You said you loved me," Brice said, looking at her with eyes that pleaded for confirmation. "Did you mean it?"

No time like the present to finally tell him the truth.

"Yes, Brice, I meant it. More than you could possibly know," Bailey said, holding his hand between hers. "When I realized something was wrong with you yesterday, I couldn't think of anything except finding you. If something had happened to you, if I couldn't have… I'm sorry, Brice. I'm so sorry."

"I know, sugar. Let's talk about all that later. I just want to enjoy looking at you and seeing your smile before they shoot me full of something else that knocks me out for a while," Brice said, squeezing Bailey's hand. "We'll have all weekend to get things straightened out."

"Actually, I've got the entire week free if you'd like me to spend it with you," Bailey said, pleased by the look of surprise and happiness that flew across Brice's expressive face.

"A whole week of your playing nursemaid for me? I think I'm still dreaming," Brice said with a cocky grin. "Maybe you better pinch me."

"Maybe I will later," Bailey teased as she heard the Morgan family coming down the hall.

Chapter Twenty

*"Jump, and you will find out how to
unfold your wings as you fall."*

Ray Bradbury

"How many more chairs do we need, darlin'?" Trey asked Cady as he carried two more chairs to the dining room table. The big farmhouse table, normally able to seat fourteen comfortably, was made even longer with the addition of a few card tables.

Using tablecloths in a warm shade of brown, Cady placed miniature pumpkins, creamy candles and bowls of nuts down the center of the table on a runner made of burlap. Set with cream plates and polished silverware, the table looked both rustic and elegant.

"We need a total of twenty-three chairs, boss-man," Cady said with a grin from the stove where she was working to put the finishing touches on the Thanksgiving feast. In addition to all the Thompson and Morgan clan gathering around the dinner table in less than an hour, Cady's Aunt Viv and Uncle Joe, Cass' friend Ashley and her parents, a few of the ranch hands and Hart Hammond would be there.

Denni and Nana arrived earlier and were artfully folding cream-colored napkins at each place setting as Trey dusted off the last of the chairs, listening to the football game Trent and Travis were watching in the great room. Cass was flitting between the kitchen, great room and her bedroom, excited to have her little friend coming to join in the festivities.

Finished with the dusting, Trey stepped into the kitchen and put his arms around Cady, drawing her back against him. She relaxed in his embrace and smiled when he nuzzled her ear.

"This is a little different picture than a year ago, isn't it darlin'?" Trey asked, kissing her neck.

"It sure is. It's hard to think that just last Thanksgiving poor little Cass was living in neglect, Travis was still in Iraq, Trent and Lindsay were avoiding each other like the plague and you were planning the best way to sweep me off my feet."

"My planning paid off, didn't it?" Trey asked, sweeping Cady into his arms and swinging her around the kitchen.

Bailey walked in from the hallway and smiled. The affectionate nature of her cousins no longer bothered her in the least.

"See you're at again, Trey," Bailey commented, grinning at her cousin as she picked up salt and pepper shakers to set on the table. "Can't you control yourself at all?"

"Not with this beautiful wife of mine," Trey said, kissing Cady on the cheek before setting her down and playfully swatting her bottom. Winking at Bailey, he sauntered off to the front room to watch football with his brothers.

"It is so cold out there," Tess said, hurrying in the back door with a bag of paper plates. Cady was worried they'd run out of extra plates by the time the guys had several helpings of dessert so Tess ran home to get some paper plates. Setting the plates on a side table in the dining area, she kissed Denni and Nana's cheeks before going back to the mud room and hanging up her coat.

"Do you think it will snow tonight?" Tess asked as she washed her hands and joined Cady and Bailey in the kitchen. Cady made gravy while Bailey mashed potatoes and Tess buttered the tops of the rolls, hot from the oven.

"I don't know," Cady said, glancing outside. "Anything can happen around here with the weather."

"That's a fact," Bailey commented, remembering the ice storm that trapped her in Burns with Brice. Thoughts of that made her face fill with warmth and turned her cheeks pink.

"I don't know what you're thinking, Bailey, but I'm guessing it is something naughty about my brother," Tess teased, noting that Bailey's cheeks were nearly the same shade as the burgundy of her sweater.

"Now, sugar plum," Denni said, giving Tess a squeeze, "you quit teasing her. It wasn't that long ago you were blushing every time you thought about my baby."

"He still makes her blush," Cady said, pointing a gravy-coated spoon at Tess. "Just ask her about what they saw in Vegas other than the hotel room and her cheeks turn bright red."

Denni laughed as Tess' cheeks turned pink and she grinned at Bailey. Putting her arms around both Tess and Cady's waists, Denni gave them each a kiss on the cheek. "I'm so glad to have all you girls in the family. Who's up for a shopping trip tomorrow?"

"Count me in," Cady said, remembering all the fun she and Denni had last year hitting the day after Thanksgiving sales. "I've already warned Trey he is on his own tomorrow and he and Trent better not gorge themselves on leftovers like they did last year."

"What did they do?" Bailey asked, looking at Cady.

"I went with Denni shopping all day last year. When I got home, those two cousins of yours had eaten through a good portion of the leftovers and could barely waddle to the couch to lie down in bloated misery. They've been on tight supervision since," Cady said with a grin.

"If Trav was here, he would have been in on it, too," Tess said, placing rolls in a cloth-lined basket.

"In on what?" Travis asked as he retrieved three cans of pop from the fridge.

"The eating frenzy your brothers went on the day after Thanksgiving last year," Denni said, patting Travis on the arm. "You boys will not do that this year."

"Are all you girls going shopping tomorrow?" Travis asked, hopeful of being able to sneak whatever he wanted from the fridge unseen.

"No, we're not. Lindsay doesn't feel up to it and decided she could stay here to keep an eye on you three," Tess said, shaking her finger at her handsome husband.

"I'm offended that you girls don't trust us," Travis said, slapping a hand to his chest. "What kind of gluttons do you take us for?"

"The very worst kind, Tee," Tess teased as Travis kissed her cheek and went back to the football game.

Trey was summoned to carve the turkey while Cady sliced a ham. Bailey, Tess and Denni dished up the rest of the food while Nana sat with Lindsay in the parlor.

It seemed like all at once the company began to arrive and Cady sent Cass to be the door greeter.

Bailey wiped off her hands and went running down the steps when the Morgan family parked by the mud room door. Ben hurried around the pickup to help Brice out onto his crutches while Michele and Mike gathered up their contributions to the meal.

Giving his cheek a kiss, Bailey walked with Brice to the door, her eyes intently watching him. Ben held the door for everyone as Brice slowly made his way up the steps and inside the warmth of the kitchen.

"Happy Turkey Day," Brice called as he leaned on one crutch and Bailey helped him remove his coat.

In the past several days since his accident, she spent the majority of her time at the Running M, helping care for Brice.

Although no one would have deemed it possible, Bailey provided attentive and gentle care. She gave Brice back rubs, read books, told stories and made him laugh. When he was ready to go for his first little walk outside, Bailey was the one who helped him on with his coat and walked with him around the yard.

Even though they still hadn't gotten around to a serious talk yet, Brice seemed to know that something was different with Bailey. She was no longer holding a part of herself back from him and Brice was thrilled to see the changes in her.

"Look at you, Brice. You'll be dancing the two-step again before we know it," Denni said, giving him a careful hug. "Why don't you go ahead and sit down at the table then you won't have to get up and move again in a few minutes."

"If no one minds, I think I'll stand until we're ready for dinner. I'm already tired of sitting and lying down. It feels pretty good to be vertical," Brice said, turning to see Cass leading Hart Hammond down the hall from the front door. He was grinning at the little redhead as she chatted a mile a minute, talking about her family, horse, and dog Buddy. Travis invited the gas-station owner, saying no one should be alone on a holiday.

"Brice, I should have known you'd be here," Hart said, tipping his head Bailey's direction. "A house full of lovely ladies and from what I hear some of the best food in the county."

"You've got me pegged, Hart," Brice said with a smile.

"Hart, glad you could make it," Travis said, sticking out a hand toward their guest.

"Thanks for the invitation, Travis. I appreciate not having to warm up a microwave dinner or trying to find a restaurant open today," Hart said with an engaging grin.

"Have you met everyone?" Travis asked, sweeping his hand around the room.

"I've met all the Morgans and your family, but I see two lovely ladies I have not yet had the pleasure of making their acquaintance," Hart said, walking toward Denni where she stood with her arm around Nana's shoulders.

"This is my grandmother, Ester, but everyone calls her Nana," Travis said, as Hart took Nana's hand and kissed the back of it. "And this is my mama, Denni Thompson."

Denni's faced turned a bright shade of pink when Hart kissed the back of her hand, holding it just a minute longer than was necessary.

"A pleasure to meet you, ma'am. Thank you for having me at your home today," Hart said, his blue eyes twinkling at Denni. "I thought Travis was going to introduce you as a sister I hadn't heard about yet. You don't even remotely look old enough to be a mother to those three strapping boys of yours, let alone a grandmother, if what I hear is true about Trent and Lindsay."

"You are a charmer, aren't you Mr. Hammond?" Denni said, blushing an even brighter shade of pink. "The rumors about a new Thompson arriving in the spring are true."

"Well, congratulations to you all, then," Hart said, stepping forward to shake Trent's hand and nod his head politely at Lindsay.

Cass broke the moment with childish squeals of joy when Ashley and her parents arrived. Once they were all inside, Trey asked everyone to be seated and shared a heartfelt blessing for the meal.

Trey smiled at Cady when he finished and nodded his head.

"We thought it would be fun to start a new tradition of going around the table and having everyone say one word that symbolizes what they are most thankful for this year," Cady said, looking around the group and smiling. "Trey said since it was my bright idea I had to go first, so here is my one word - family."

As they progressed around the table, Bailey slid her hand down to capture Brice's, loving the feel of his strong, calloused fingers meshing perfectly with hers. When it was her turn, Bailey looked at the wonderful man sitting beside her, hoping he could see what she felt in her heart reflected in her eyes. "Brice," she said as she gave him a tender smile.

Brice sat staring at her a moment, lost in the depths of her turquoise eyes before he felt a nudge from Travis on his other side. "Dude, one word."

"Weddings," Brice said, kissing Bailey's cheek.

"Why weddings?" Cass asked from where she sat next to Ashley.

"Because if it wasn't for Trent and Lindsay's big shebang wedding, I'd never have met Bailey," Brice said, winking at Cass.

Travis, who said home as his one word, made most of the females teary eyed, when he leaned toward Tess and said "because home is with you and it's where my heart was all those years away, where it will always be."

Once Ben said "last" everyone laughed when he explained he was the last one to offer a word so they could start eating the feast before them.

An hour later, as waistbands felt too tight and stomachs were painfully full, the men cleaned off the table while the women did the dishes. Cass and Ashley went to her room to play fairies and Nana decided to go lie down for a quick nap.

Trey and Travis put away the extra chairs while Trent and Ben folded the card tables and stored them before joining the other men in the great room to watch football.

When the kitchen was set back to rights, the women put desserts out on the counter along with a stack of plates, made a big pot of coffee and sat down at the table to browse through the sale ads for the following day.

"Are you sure you don't want to come, Lindsay?" Denni asked, patting Lindsay's leg where she sat next to her at the table.

"I don't think I have the energy for it and I know at some point I'll be sick in the morning," Lindsay said, sipping on a cup of mint tea, hoping to make it through the afternoon without feeling nauseous. "You girls will enjoy the day more without having to worry about me tagging along. Trent has promised me some surprise tomorrow that will take my mind off feeling like a weak-stomached invalid."

"We'll miss you being with us but will somehow carry on without you there," Denni said with a teasing smile. "Bailey, you're going with us aren't you?"

"I was thinking I should probably stay home. I've got to head back to work Monday and I'll only have a few more days to spend with Brice. I'm not a great shopper and you girls know I'm only good at dealing with masses of people for very short periods of time," Bailey said, not interested in the early-morning shopping frenzy that seemed to have Cady, Tess and Denni all excited. "Thanks for the invitation, but I'll pass."

"I know Brice will be grateful to have more time to spend with you, Bailey," Michele said from across the table where she sat next to Tess. "I plan on joining these girls shopping tomorrow, so Brice will be glad to have someone to talk to besides his dad and Ben."

"Nursemaid Bailey just wants to stay home and have BB all to herself," Tess teased with a sassy grin.

"Maybe I do," Bailey admitted, making them all laugh.

"Sounds like you girls are having too much fun in here," Brice said as he slowly worked his way to the table.

"Do you want some dessert?" Bailey asked, getting out of her chair and moving toward the impressive display of sweets on the counter. Along with the pumpkin pies she made, there were cakes, gooey bar cookies and Cady even made a pumpkin trifle just for her. Too full to indulge now, she hoped there would be plenty left later.

"I sure do, but the sugar I'm craving I'll get outside," Brice said giving Bailey a sexy grin that was pure male flirtation.

"Oh," was all Bailey managed to say as she followed Brice into the mud room. She helped him with his coat and put her coat on then held the door as he maneuvered outside and down the steps.

"Where are we going?" Bailey asked, walking slowly beside him as he made his way to one of the four-wheelers.

Deciding he couldn't straddle the seat to drive, he turned to Bailey. "You know how to drive this thing?"

"Sure, but I don't think you should be riding on it," Bailey said, looking at Brice like he'd lost his mind.

"You let me worry about that. Climb on and start it up," Brice said, motioning to Bailey with his crutch. When she had the machine running, Brice sank sideways onto the seat with his side to Bailey's back. Handing her his crutches, she placed them in the gun rack on the front of four-wheeler and waited for his direction.

"To the pond, if you please," Brice said in her ear using his best imitation of a British accent.

"Yes, sir," Bailey said, feeling like giggling. She was the last girl on the planet that would giggle, finding it frivolous and ridiculous, but today it fit her lighthearted mood. The past few days with Brice had been some of the most wonderful she could remember. They spent a lot of time just getting to know each other better. The more she discovered, the deeper in love Bailey fell.

Driving slowly and carefully down the hill to the pond, doing her best not to jostle Brice, she parked the four-wheeler close to the bench beneath the willow tree. She discovered from Tess the Thompson boys had dubbed it the kissing bench. Apparently she and Brice weren't the only ones to make use of its secluded location.

Handing Brice his crutches, she waited while he got himself upright and moving forward before getting off and stepping beside him to the bench where he eased himself onto the seat. Laying the crutches on the ground, he waited for Bailey to sit beside him before putting his arm around her shoulders and drawing her close. She placed her head against his chest, listening to the rhythmic beat of his heart beneath her ear while his chin rested on top of her head.

Neither spoke for a while, just enjoying the crisp autumn day and the spectacular view of the pond with the rolling hills in the background.

"Brice?" Bailey finally said, breaking the quiet.

"Hmm?" he answered, sounding content and happy.

"I'm so sorry," Bailey said, not wanting to lift her head and expose the tears in her eyes to him.

"For what, sugar?" Brice asked, rubbing his hand lightly on her back. She could feel his warmth, even through her coat and sweater.

"For hurting you, for leaving you, for putting up walls between us," Bailey said, swiping at the tears that were making tracks down her cheeks. She felt such remorse for the time she'd spent pushing Brice away when all he'd ever offered her was love. Unconditional love and true friendship.

"I know you are," Brice said, kissing the top of her head. "What I need to know is if you're going to do it again."

"No. Never again, Brice," Bailey said, raising her head so she could look in his eyes, so he could see the sincerity and love shining in hers. "I'll never leave you again."

"I'm glad to hear that," Brice said, wiping her tears away with his thumbs. He kissed both cheeks, her forehead and the tip of her nose before gently kissing her lips. Although she'd seen him yesterday, it seemed like so long since he'd truly held and kissed her. Between the weeks they were apart, his injury and having family constantly around, this was the first time they'd been alone since a few days after Halloween.

"I need to tell you something, sugar," Brice said, pulling back and cupping her face in his hands.

Bailey looked into his warm brown eyes, feeling drawn into the sparkling depths. She looked at him, waiting for him to continue. "What is it?"

"I know how important your career is to you and I never intended to take you away from it. Dang it, Bailey, you're unbelievably brilliant. Sometimes that brain of yours runs circles around all of us and I feel like an illiterate idiot next to you. You need to use your mind, do what you love, and be everything you dream of being," Brice said, swiping a hand over his face as he sat back and looked at Bailey. "I won't hold you back and I won't be a stumbling block to you. What I would like, very much, is to walk right along beside you. I want for you to be happy, sugar, and I hope you can somehow figure out a way to allow me into the equation."

"You think I'm brilliant, Brice, but I'm truly quite ignorant," Bailey admitted, looking at Brice with the hint of a saucy grin. "I might be able to rattle off all sorts of unimportant facts and figures, but I have a hard time with the basics. Like one plus one equals something magic."

"Sugar," Brice said, starting to draw her close, but Bailey put her arm against his chest and pushed back, smiling.

"If I agree to find a solution to this equation, I think you need to agree to help me learn some very important things as well," Bailey said, tipping her head toward Brice.

"Like what?" Brice asked, fingering the fossil necklace she always wore. It was warm from her skin and made his temperature kick up a notch.

"For starters, I'm a complete dunce when it comes to relationships. You are going to have to coach me on how to be a proper girlfriend. With no prior experience, I honestly don't have a clue," Bailey said, trying to look serious. "I'm hopeless at idle chit chat, I'm terrible at parties, and I really must insist you begin a series of rigorous lessons in teaching me the fine art of kissing. I'm feeling terribly uneducated in that department."

"I'd be happy to start those lessons right away," Brice said, wrapping his arms around Bailey, holding her close to his chest. She could feel his smile against her lips. "Lesson one, always taste as sweet as you do right now."

Brice kissed her softly on her bottom lip. "Lesson two, always carry ChapStick for when our lessons require extensive practice and extra effort."

Bailey felt Brice kiss her upper lip as tingling sensations started working their way up from her toes to her head.

"Lesson three, always remember how much I love you, Bailey Bishop. Always, always remember that," Brice said, kissing her square on the mouth. "Lesson four, never forget to practice your lessons. You have to diligently devote time to it every day."

Brice nuzzled her neck, trailed kisses up her jaw, and sent goose bumps skittering over her skin when he teased her ear with his lips.

"Lesson five, and this one is very important, kisses should only be given if you really mean them."

Bailey surrendered to Brice when his lips met hers in a fiery kiss full of passion. As his arms wrapped tightly around her, she felt at home, cherished and loved, and knew here was where she wanted to spend the rest of her life.

"What's the next lesson?" Bailey whispered, her lips tantalizing Brice's as they brushed his once, twice.

"Lesson six, if you want to make me lose my mind, kisses should be long, slow and deep."

"Like this?" Bailey asked, locking her lips to Brice's every bit as much as she was locking their hearts together.

Working her hand inside his coat, Bailey rested it over his heart, loving the feel of the steady beat against her palm while Brice deepened their kiss. One strong hand cupped the back of her head while the other wrapped around her waist inside her coat. Lost in their love, in the wonderful sensations of their kisses, Bailey had never known such happiness and contentment.

Touching his forehead to hers, Brice ran his thumb along her lip and smiled.

"Why is it you think you need lessons?" Brice asked, trying to catch his breath. "You've made me nearly explode with your kisses more times than I can count."

"I have?" Bailey asked innocently, unaware of the effect she had on Brice.

Brice released a choppy laugh. "More than once, you've driven me to the point of hanging on to my self-control by a frayed thread, my beautiful pumpkin-loving, analytical-thinking, dirt-digging girl. I love you, Bailey."

"I love you, Brice," Bailey said without hesitation, kissing Brice's cheek and chin. "I love you with all my heart, and if your offer still stands to catch me, I'm more than ready to fall."

"Sugar, you've already fallen," Brice said, taking her lips captive with his as he breathed in her scent, basking in the warmth of her love. "We both fell the first time we laid eyes on each other. It's just taken you this long to figure out I've caught you."

"In that case, hold me tight and don't ever let me go," Bailey said, gazing into Brice's face, loving every single laugh line, scar, and most definitely the mole by his tempting bottom lip.

"I'm not going to hold you tight, Bailey, it would stifle you," Brice said, pulling her against his solid chest and rubbing his hand on her back as he held her close. "The next step is to learn how to fly. Together. I figure it's going to take fifty or sixty years to master."

"At least," Bailey said, thrilled at the way her hand fit perfectly in Brice's. She was very much looking forward to a lifetime spent with the man she loved. Putting her hands on either side of his face, she was guiding Brice's lips to hers when a loud shout startled them both.

"Brice! Are you guys spooning again?" Cass yelled from the top of the hill. "Uncle Travis said to tell you to come up to the house before you wear out the bench down there. What are you doing? Are you kissing? Brice? Can you hear me?"

Bailey grabbed Brice's collar and gave him a teasing grin. "I'd like very much to continue our lessons later. I'll bring the ChapStick."

"You're on, sugar," Brice said, kissing her soundly as they heard Cass and Ashley running down the hill. "We'll start with lesson seven."

"What's lesson seven?" Bailey asked as she got to her feet, handing Brice his crutches.

"The proper way for a girl to kiss her future husband."

###

For detail about the John Day Fossil Beds, go to:
http://www.nps.gov/joda/index.htm

If you are ever in the area and have time to visit even one
of the units, it is well worth your time.

If you're looking for an easy, delicious pumpkin recipe - this is it! It comes together in a hurry and tastes even better the next day when all the flavors have blended.

Pumpkin Trifle Mousse
1 box of gingerbread mix, baked
4 ounces cream cheese, softened
1 small box instant cheesecake pudding
2 cups milk
1 cup pumpkin pie filling
1 tsp. pumpkin pie spice
1 tbsp. cinnamon
1/2 cup caramel sauce
2 cups whipped cream
Toffee bits for topping (optional)

If you are making your own gingerbread, bake and let cool. You need about 2 cups of cake cubes. You can also use pound cake as a substitute.

Mix pudding with two cups of milk. Add in softened cream cheese and blend. Then mix in pumpkin and spices. Blend well and set aside for about five minutes. Whip up whipped cream, set aside. Cut cake into cubes and start layering in a trifle bowl, large glass bowl or individual glasses. You are going to do three layers, so use everything in thirds (guess-timates work just fine).

Top cake with pudding mixture then drizzle with caramel sauce. Spoon on a layer of whipped cream, then start again with a layer of cake. Finish with a layer of whipped cream. You can top with toffee bits and cinnamon or another drizzle of caramel and cake crumbs. Whatever strikes your fancy.

Find more recipes at savvyentertaining.com

Available Now!

Savvy Autumn Entertaining - Ideas for fall party themes, tips for bringing autumn into your home and yummy fall recipes are included in this quick and easy guide for savvy entertaining at home!

From Savvy Entertaining's blogger, this book includes her favorite fall tips!

Coming Spring 2013!

The Cowboy's New Heart - Years after her husband suddenly died, Denni Thompson can't bear to think of giving her heart to anyone else.

With three newly married sons, a grandchild on the way, and a busy life, Denni doesn't give a thought to romance until she meets the handsome new owner of Grass Valley's gas station.

Former bull-rider Hart Hammond spent the last twenty years building up a business empire while successfully avoiding love. He buried his heart the same day he made his last bull ride and has vowed to never make the mistake of loving a woman again. Then he meets Denni Thompson, the beautiful mother of the fun-loving Thompson tribe.

Can a broken-hearted widow and a heartless cowboy find love?

Find out in Spring 2013 …

Coming for the 2012 Holiday Season!

The Christmas Bargain - As owner and manager of the Hardman bank, Luke Granger is a man of responsibility and integrity in the small 1890s Eastern Oregon town. Calling in a long overdue loan, Luke finds himself reluctantly accepting a bargain in lieu of payment from the shiftless farmer who barters his daughter to settle his debt.

Philamena Booth is both mortified and relieved when her father sends her off with the banker as payment of his debt. Held captive on the farm by her father since the death of her mother more than a decade earlier, Philamena is grateful to leave. If only it had been someone other than the handsome and charismatic Luke Granger riding in to rescue her. Ready to hold up her end of the bargain as Luke's cook and housekeeper, Philamena is prepared for the hard work ahead.

What she isn't prepared for is being forced to marry Luke as part of this crazy Christmas bargain.

TURN THE PAGE
FOR AN EXCITING PREVIEW
OF SHANNA HATFIELD'S
NEW HOLIDAY ROMANCE...

The Christmas Bargain

Chapter One

Eastern Oregon, 1893

"I done told ya already, Luke, I ain't got the money," Alford Booth whined in a nasally tone that made Luke Granger tightly clamp his square jaw while a vein pulsed in his neck.

Slowly removing his hat and running his hand through his thick golden hair, Luke tried to keep his irritation with the man from showing. If Alford spent a little less time drinking and a lot more time working his land, they wouldn't be having this discussion. Luke rued the day Alford had ever stepped foot in his bank and asked for a loan.

"I've extended all the time I can, Alford. You know the loan is already ten months past due," Luke said.

Alford stared at him a moment through glazed eyes before spewing a stream of tobacco juice that barely missed Luke's boot.

"Well, ya know I planned to pay ya off after harvest. Weren't my fault we had a drought this year and the crop failed. Weren't my fault at all."

Releasing a sigh, Luke leveled his icy blue stare on Alford. He was somewhat gratified to see the man grow uncomfortable and uneasy. "It's never your fault, is it Alford? Always someone else's fault, but you aren't the only one who's had a hard year. I'm sorry about that but you've got to make some form of payment."

"Some form?" Alford asked with an odd glint in his eye that made Luke wary. "Ya mean ya'd take somethin' other than cash?"

Luke thought carefully about his response. Alford would weasel his way out of the loan if Luke gave him an inch of finagling room. "It would greatly depend on what that something was."

Alford smiled, revealing several missing spaces in his rotten teeth. "I'll give ya my daughter. Will that settle the debt?"

"What?" Luke's head jerked up, sure he misheard the drunken old coot. "What did you say?"

"Take my daughter. She ain't much to look at, but she can cook and clean. She's strong and can work all the day long. The girl ain't too bright, though. Sometimes ya got to show her who's boss, but a firm hand straightens her out in no time. Ya need a cook and housekeeper, don't ya?"

Seething with disgust that the man would try to barter his daughter to settle his debts, Luke clenched the brim of his hat in his hands to keep from popping Alford with his fist. "That is not an acceptable payment, Alford. Not at all."

"Then I guess I'll give her to Cecil to settle my bill. He said he'd give me some cash besides. I can haul her in this evening after she cleans up the supper dishes and get ya yer money tomorra," Alford said, scratching his rotund belly with a dirt-encrusted hand.

Luke was seeing red. He didn't care how homely the girl was or how desperate Alford might be for cash, he couldn't rationalize that a father would trade his daughter to Cecil Montague, the local saloon owner and keeper of the town's "soiled doves," to pay off his bills.

"I'll take the girl," Luke said, surprised when the words rushed out, wishing he could reel them back.

Alford smiled again and nodded his filthy head. "I'll send her over to yer place tomorrow."

"No," Luke said, not trusting Alford to keep his word. "I'll take her with me now."

"But what about my supper?" Alford whined, suddenly realizing he'd be losing his own cook and housekeeper.

Luke stood to his full height of six-foot, three-inches, and towered over the sniveling man before him. "What about it?"

"Ah... well..."Alford said, fear filling his face as he backed away from Luke and the menacing look that was turning his blue eyes hard and cold. "I reckon I can make do."

"I reckon you will," Luke said, walking toward the house with Alford following along behind. When they got to the door, Luke waited for Alford to open it and go inside. Expecting filth and foul smells, Luke was taken aback by the clean, albeit shabby interior. Everything was neat and tidy and the delicious smell of stew filled the small cabin, making his mouth water. A tall figure, clad in a dress the color of dirt, leaned over a scarred table, setting down bowls and spoons. Her hair was covered with a kerchief, and a large white apron hid the rest of her.

"Philamena, ya remember Mr. Granger. He owns the bank in town," Alford said, pointing to Luke as he ambled to the table and pulled up a chair.

The woman, who was painfully thin, cast a quick glance Luke's direction, but never raised her eyes to his. She quietly nodded her head as she stood clasping her work-reddened hands primly in front of her.

Luke tried to think of the last time he had seen Philamena Booth. He vaguely recalled her as a happy, smiling child from school days, but being a few grades behind him, he hadn't paid her any attention. She didn't come to church, shop in town or, as far as he knew, ever leave the farm.

He remembered seeing her once when he rode out trying to collect on a loan Alford made a few years ago. She was out at the barn and ran to the house while he was dismounting. If memory served him correctly, she was garbed in an ugly dirt-colored dress then, too.

Luke tipped his head her direction, trying to reconcile himself to his decision. The last thing he wanted or needed was a timid scrawny woman on his hands. But he couldn't exactly ride off and leave her, knowing her father was willing to turn her over to Cecil. No woman deserved that kind of fate.

"Ma'am," Luke said, softly. "Pleasure to see you again."

She barely nodded her head, then turned and got another chipped bowl from a cupboard and set it on the table. Alford motioned for Luke to sit down, which he did.

Pouring them both a cup of cold water, Philamena dished up heaping bowls of stew for the two men. Her bowl hardly had enough in it to feed a bird, causing Luke to study her. She ate with fine manners, her back straight as a rod while her father shoveled in his meal like it was the last one he'd have.

When his bowl was empty, Alford banged it once in Philamena's direction then burped loudly. She got up from the table and filled his bowl with the remains in the stew pot before quietly returning to her seat.

Finished eating, Alford scratched at his scraggly beard then glanced Luke's direction. Luke offered a cool glare that seemed to loosen Alford's tongue.

"Daughter, Mr. Granger has come to collect on his loan and seein' as how we can't pay, he agreed to settle for somethin' else. Get yer stuff, yer leavin' with him."

Philamena's head shot up and she stared at her father, unmoving. From his seat at the table, Luke could only see her profile, but imagined the look of shock that had settled on her face.

"Ya heard me, gal. Clean up them dishes then get yer things." Alford drained his water cup and set it on the table with a thunk.

"But, Pa…" she said. Luke was surprised by the soft, husky voice.

Leaning her direction, Alford sneered and raise his hand menacingly. "Don't ya start that sass with me. Get to it."

Philamena ducked her head, gathered up the dishes and washed them without saying a word. She disappeared behind a curtain and was soon back with a small bundle tied up in a burgundy and green quilt.

Luke stood from the table, pinning Alford in place with an irate glare. Turning toward Philamena he felt more pity for the woman than words could express. He couldn't begin to imagine how awful it would be to live with a man like Alford.

"May I help you with your coat, miss? The ride back to town might be chilly," Luke said as he stepped next to Philamena. Although she was dressed in dowdy, shabby clothes, they were pressed and clean. That told Luke a lot about her sense of personal pride. Someone at some point had taught her well.

"She ain't got a coat. No need for one since she don't go nowhere. Too homely for any man to come courtin'. She'll be fine. Wouldn't be the first time out in the cold for her," Alford said, picking his teeth with a straw he'd pulled out of his pocket.

Luke swallowed down the rage that was boiling inside him at a man who treated his animals better than his own flesh and blood.

"We best get on the road, then," Luke said, opening the door for Philamena, who hesitantly took a step through. She turned, for just a moment, to give her father one last glance, then walked out toward Luke's horse that stood tied to the one section of the yard fence not tumbling down.

Before following her out the door, Luke stared meaningfully at Alford. Although he didn't know a thing about Philamena, he'd seen enough to know she was being abused at her father's hand. "Let's make one thing perfectly clear. I'll consider your debt paid but only if you never, ever come near your daughter again. Understood?"

Alford gave him a surprised look before nodding his head. "I'm right glad to finally be rid of the troublesome snit. After twenty-seven years, she finally turned out to be worth somethin'."

Luke stalked out the door and slammed it with enough force to break the windows that weren't already cracked before he gave in to his urge to beat some sense into Alford.

Placing his hat on his head, Luke ate up the ground to his horse Drake in a few long-legged steps. Removing his coat, he draped it around Philamena's thin shoulders. Untying the reins, Luke mounted in one smooth motion. He took the sorry little bundle of belongings from Philamena and hung it from his saddle horn before leaning down and offering her his hand. She took it without looking into his face and swung up behind him. He was somewhat taken aback by her agility and ease around a horse.

Riding back toward town, Luke tried to keep a conversation going but it was difficult when all he received was "yes" or "no" responses whispered against his back. He expected Philamena to hold onto his waist and sag against him in relief at being rescued. Instead, she held herself stiffly away from him, a firm grip on the back of his saddle keeping her seat on the horse.

Giving up on talking to her, he instead thought about the mess he'd gotten himself into as he tried to keep his teeth from chattering in the frosty chill of the November evening. What was he going to do with Miss Philamena Booth?

<><><>

Philamena had been waiting thirteen years to be rescued from the prison her father called home. When her mother passed away giving birth to a stillborn boy, her father changed from a loving, caring man into a drunken, dirty tyrant.

The last time he allowed Philamena to leave the farm was when she turned sixteen. She went into town for her birthday and bought a hair ribbon the same shade of green as her holly-colored eyes. Philamena saved up her meager pennies for months and hid the money from Pa. Begging and pleading to go to town, he finally relented.

When she came home with the ribbon tied in her thick mahogany curls, followed by one of the livery owner's boys who had taken a shine to her, her father ripped it from her head and ordered her to stay away from town. He took away not only her freedom, but also any color from her life, forbidding her to wear anything but the ugly, plain brown garments.

None of it made any sense to Philamena, but then again, nothing had after her mother died. Pa started drinking heavily after that with the years between becoming a blur of hard labor interrupted by his drunken rages and random beatings.

Philamena finally learned that being quiet and meek was the only thing that kept him somewhat mollified. It was difficult to see the disgusting man Alford Booth had become and remember what a gentle father and loving husband he had once been.

Back then, their farm had been prosperous, their home happy and life joyous. Now, their land was a desolate mess.

To be bartered to the local banker to pay her father's debt somehow didn't shock Philamena like it should. She knew Luke Granger was a kind, honest man. At least she assumed he was from how she remembered him during her childhood years.

Attending the one-room school until she was fourteen, when her father imprisoned her at home, Philamena remembered Luke being a friendly, generous boy who was a few years her senior. He was the type who stood up against bullies, made sure the littlest children weren't left out of schoolyard games, and excelled in his school work.

Like most of the girls at school, she was sweet on Luke before he went back East to school. No wonder he grew up to be successful and own the town's bank.

As she sat behind him on his horse, Philamena wondered just what exactly he planned to do with her. Breathing deeply, she mentally shrugged and settled his coat more tightly around her. It smelled of leather, horses, and a warm, spicy scent she could only describe as uniquely Luke.

Of all the men in their small town of Hardman to come to her rescue, Philamena would have been less mortified but not nearly as pleased had it been anyone else. Luke was an extremely handsome man that any woman would fawn over.

Nearly lulled to sleep by the steady rhythm of the horse's gait, Philamena struggled to stay alert. She felt her eyes sliding closed and jerked herself awake, noticing they were riding down the main street of town toward the parsonage at the Christian church, rather than toward Granger House at the far end of town.

Reining his horse to a stop outside the parsonage, Luke gave Philamena his hand and helped her dismount before stepping out of the saddle and handing the quilt-wrapped bundle to her. She dared not raise her gaze to his, and instead studied the ground as Luke took her elbow and propelled her toward the door.

She heard him rapping and felt the heat from the cozy inside of the cottage-style home flow around her when the pastor opened the door. Philamena knew from her father's ramblings that the pastor was one of her former classmates, Chauncy Dodd. He and Luke had been good friends in school.

"Luke," Chauncy said with a broad smile. "What brings you by this evening?"

"I'm hoping you can help me with a…um…situation," Luke said, turning his gaze to Philamena. She clutched her little bundle tightly to her chest and studied the worn toe of her shoe.

"Who do we have here?" Chauncy asked, kindness lacing his voice. He opened the door wider and Luke escorted Philamena inside the cheery home. The yeasty smell of bread nearly made Philamena fall to her knees. It had been so long since she'd had bread, she could barely remember the delicious taste of it.

"Philamena Booth," Luke said pushing her forward a bit. She still refused to raise her gaze and make eye contact with anyone. "She needs a place to stay tonight and I was hoping you and Abby would take her in."

"Absolutely," Chauncy said as a petite woman, large with child, waddled into the front room.

"Hello, Luke," Abby said, squeezing Luke's hand when he bent down to kiss her cheek. "I thought I heard you. Have you had supper?"

"Yes, ma'am. Miss Booth made a nice bowl of stew. Would you be able to make her comfortable tonight?"

"Most definitely," Abby said, reaching out a hand and capturing Philamena's. Tugging her toward the kitchen, Abby began a friendly conversation that elicited short, quiet responses from Philamena.

When the women were out of earshot, Chauncy motioned to two chairs in front of a roaring fire. "Suppose you tell me what trouble you've gotten yourself into now?"

Luke shot his friend a warning glance and settled into the comfortable chair, enjoying the warmth of the fire. "I went out to collect from Alford Booth and he refused to pay again. When I demanded payment he said either I could take his daughter to cancel his debt or he'd sell her to Cecil. I didn't feel I had a choice. I couldn't let him take her to the Red Lantern."

"No, you couldn't, but what are you going to do with her?" Chauncy asked, studying his friend and former cohort in all sorts of boyish crimes. "You can't leave her here indefinitely and you certainly can't take her home with you. It wouldn't be proper."

"I could move her into the hotel," Luke said, thinking about his options. "I could get her a room at the boarding house. She could have the entire second floor of my monstrous house to herself."

"You know tongues will wag. They'll be flapping as it is that she is finally off the farm. You don't want to make things worse for her, do you?" Chauncy had tried many times to convince Alford to change his ways, to let Philamena leave the farm. His suggestions fell on deaf ears. He knew the minister from the Presbyterian Church tried to talk to Alford as well. Now that Philamena was off the farm, he intended to make sure she wouldn't have to go back. From what he knew, she would make someone a good, dutiful wife. And that someone would be Luke. Chauncy couldn't explain how he knew this with such certainty, but he did.

Luke raked his hands through his hair and leaned his elbows on his knees. Letting out his breath, he turned and stared into the dancing flames in the hearth. "You might as well tell me what you think I should do, instead of waiting for me to get around to your way of thinking."

Chauncy grabbed his chest and feigned a look of pain. "You wound me, Luke. When have I ever tried to talk you into anything?"

"Nearly every time I see you," Luke said, a small smile finally cracking his full lips. "I wouldn't have made nearly so many trips to the woodshed as a kid if it wasn't for your suggested ideas."

"We did have a lot of fun, didn't we?"

"That's beside the point," Luke said, leaning back and turning his ice blue gaze on his long-time friend. "Let's hear it. What do you think I should do?"

"Marry her."

Luke bolted upright in the chair and glared at Chauncy like he'd grown a second head. "I'm sure I didn't hear you correctly. Would you mind repeating that?"

Chauncy grinned and leaned forward. "I said you should marry her. You've avoided matrimony long enough. You're pushing thirty and it is long past time for you to settle down. After all, the town banker should have a wife and a family."

"Huh," Luke grunted, annoyed at his friend. Chauncy knew the last thing he wanted was to be tied down to a woman and family. Luke's father was a perfect example of what happened to a good man when a woman got under his skin.

Never content with their life back East, his father insisted on moving West. They settled into the town of Hardman when Luke and his sister were just little tykes. His father established the bank and built his mother the huge Victorian house at the edge of town everyone called the Granger House.

It wasn't good enough.

His mother hated every day she spent in Hardman and finally talked his dad into moving back to New York, where her family lived, the year Luke graduated from college. Luke's sister was all too glad to escape the "wilderness," as his mother called it. His father preferred the wide open spaces of Hardman, but he'd do anything for Dora, his wife of thirty-six years.

Luke loved the rugged landscape and the community of Hardman. After he finished up his courses at the snooty school his mother insisted he attend in the East, he returned home, took over the bank from his father and moved into the hulking house. Now, eight years later, he owned the bank and the house, having purchased both from his parents.

The house sat on a five acre lot with a huge barn and carriage shed. With six bedrooms, indoor plumbing and every modern convenience available, most people thought the Grangers were a bit extravagant when they built the house.

Luke would have to agree. He hated rattling around in the big empty place and had closed off all but a couple of rooms. Between the bank and his livestock, he tried to spend as little time inside as possible.

If he brought a woman home, that would all change. Luke didn't need a wife to complicate matters. He liked his life exactly the way it was.

Sitting back against the chair, Luke stretched out his long legs and studied Chauncy, who had fought against married bliss nearly as well as Luke. Right up until Miss Abigail Sommers moved to town and opened a dress shop down the street from the mercantile.

Chauncy was a goner the first Sunday she sat in the congregation and turned her big brown eyes his direction.

Now, three years later, Chauncy and Abby were about to embark on the adventure of parenthood.

"You need to come up with a better plan," Luke said, steepling his tapered, callused fingers in front of him. "What else have you got?"

"Nothing," Chauncy said, still grinning. "You better take this payment and make the best of it. You might find out it's a blessing in disguise."

"You've got the disguised part right. Between that ugly dress and the rag on her hair, she could be covered in warts with not a tooth in her head," Luke said, shivering at the vision his words conjured.

Chauncy laughed. "Oh, you might be surprised, my friend."

Luke gave him a doubtful look. Chauncy sat forward and slapped Luke's leg.

"Come on, Luke," he said, trying to sound encouraging. "Think this through. You don't want a wife. I seriously doubt she wants a husband, but she can cook and clean. She can make your home warm and welcoming and not quite so lonely in the evening. You, in turn, give her a comfortable, safe place to live and some sense of security. Seems like an ideal partnership to me. Just look at it as a business deal, a Christmas bargain. She is supposed to be payment for a loan. If you hired a full-time housekeeper and cook, like my lovely wife has been after you to do for more than two years, think about the wages you would pay for that position. I know you have Mrs. Kellogg do your laundry and dust, but you really do need someone to care for your home. Give this a try until Christmas. If you both despise the arrangement at the end of that time period, you could always have the marriage annulled."

"Well, it doesn't sound quite so crazy when you put it that way," Luke said, thinking about how nice it would be to go home to a hot meal instead of eating at the restaurant, mooching dinner from Chauncy and Abby, or making do with what he could rustle up. "But what makes you think she'll be willing to go along with it?"

"Gratitude."

"Gratitude?"

"Wouldn't you be grateful and feel indebted to the person who saved you from Alford Booth?"

"Possibly," Luke said, giving the idea of marriage consideration. "But those rags have got to go. Can Abby set her up with some new clothes? I'll pay for everything, of course."

"Of course," Chauncy said, trying to hide his grin. Talking Luke into getting married didn't take nearly as long as he anticipated. "Tell you what, today is Monday so why don't we plan the wedding for Saturday afternoon. Miss Booth can stay here this week and you two can get used to the idea of being married. By Saturday, if I know Abby, she'll have a new wardrobe ready for your bride-to-be and then you can move her in. It will look like a real courtship and should keep the gossips in town from having too much fodder."

Luke nodded his head. "That's a sound plan."

Standing up, Luke extended his hand to Chauncy and gave it a friendly shake before the two of them walked to the kitchen where Abby chattered away while Philamena quietly helped dry the dinner dishes.

"Miss Booth," Luke said, trying to get her attention. She turned his way, but never raised her eyes up where he could see them. He wasn't sure he could spend the next fifty years with someone boring holes into his chest because they couldn't make eye contact. "I'm heading home but you'll stay here until Saturday. Pastor Dodd will marry us then and you'll come to my house at that time. Is that acceptable to you?"

His only answer was a brief nod of her head.

Abby, on the other hand, squealed with delight and gave him a big hug, or as big as she could around her protruding tummy.

"Oh, Luke, that is wonderful news!" Abby said as she squeezed his arm. If she hadn't been expecting, Luke knew she'd be flitting around the room in excitement. "We'll have a nice little ceremony in the church, won't we Chauncy?"

"Absolutely," her husband chimed in, sending her a wink.

"Would you help Miss Booth with her clothes, Abby? She's going to need some warmer things for the winter and she might like a wedding dress," Luke said, picking his coat off the kitchen chair where Philamena had draped it earlier. Sliding it on, he buttoned the front and pulled warm gloves out of the pockets.

Turning toward his soon-to-be-bride, Luke tried to give her a once over but couldn't get past the hideous dress and equally ugly cloth covering her head. "Would you like a wedding dress, Miss Booth?"

"That would be nice," she said quietly, studying the floor. "But I don't want to be any more in debt to you."

"Don't worry about it," Luke said, leaning over and kissing Abby on the cheek. "Thanks, Abby. I'll see you all tomorrow."

Chauncy walked him to the door and waved as Luke mounted Drake and headed the horse toward the other end of town.

Whistling, Chauncy stuffed his hands in his pockets and walked back to the front room to sit by the fire and gloat. He knew Luke and Philamena being together was right. He didn't know what the future held for those two, but he was looking forward to finding out...

ABOUT THE AUTHOR

SHANNA HATFIELD spent 10 years as a newspaper journalist before moving into the field of marketing and public relations. She has a lifelong love of writing, reading and creativity. She and her husband, lovingly referred to as Captain Cavedweller, reside in the Pacific Northwest with their neurotic cat along with a menagerie of wandering wildlife and neighborhood pets.

Shanna loves to hear from readers.
Connect with her online:

Blog: shannahatfield.com

Facebook: Shanna Hatfield's Page

Pinterest: Shanna Hatfield

Twitter: ShannaHatfield

Email: shanna@shannahatfield.com